Flora Ste[...]

N. F.

TEMPESTUOUS . . .

"Let me go!" she panted, trying to arch away from him but finding it impossible, his arms tightening about her.

"Your words tell me one thing, Merewyn," he said, his breathing ragged, "but your body tells me another. You want me as much as I want you."

"N-no" she moaned, despising herself as she realized that it was true. There was searing heat wherever they touched, their bodies fitting together as though they had been made for each other . . .

PASSIONATE . . .

With a groan Ian pulled her to him, covering the length of her firm body with his. His hungry lips moved from her mouth to the smooth curve of her throat. Her hands explored the broad expanse of his back, the muscles rigid beneath his chambray shirt, her fingers entwined in his dark curls as he roved her body with growing need, determined to know every part of her before slaking his desperate thirst within her . . .

REAP THE SAVAGE WIND . . .

Merewyn and Ian, starcrossed lovers who together battle danger and death—and their own raging emotions until every battle is won—and they surrender to each other!

Reap the Savage Wind

ELLEN TANNER MARSH

ACE BOOKS, NEW YORK

TO MY BROTHER, HORST, FOR ALL
HIS INSPIRATION

Reap the Savage Wind

CHAPTER ONE

"Merewyn! Slow down!"

Merewyn MacAilis, her golden curls gleaming beneath a rakish hat with an ostrich feather curling above one smooth cheek, turned her mare into the wind and urged her into a gallop, the long-legged animal needing only the slightest tap from the bone-handled quirt to increase her stride. The brisk April wind was cool as it came down from the mountains towards the sea, bringing with it the tantalizing smell of pine and heather and the promise of spring.

The spongy turf beneath the mare's pounding hooves was still damp with the snow that had melted only a week ago, but she was a surefooted creature bred by the MacAilis laird himself, and born in the middle of the savage Highland winter not four years ago. It was her Clydesdale ancestry that gave her not only the heavy neck and thick brisket, but also the docility and hardiness needed to survive on the rocky coast where Cairnlach Castle, the MacAilis stronghold, stood.

"Merewyn, I said slow down!"

Reluctantly, she obeyed the shouted plea of her brother Malcolm, whose lumbering mount was striving in vain to catch the swift-footed mare. Dark blue eyes sparkling, her delicately molded cheeks flushed with ex-

1

citement, Merewyn waited impatiently, keeping a strong check on the mare who tossed her head and snorted in protest at having been interrupted during her run.

"You've let Drummond grow too fat this winter!" she scolded her brother as he drew alongside her stamping horse, the Clydesdale's thick neck flecked with foam.

"You know damned well Drummond's a plowhorse," Malcolm retorted good-naturedly.

Merewyn tossed her small head haughtily. "That's no excuse! You insisted on breaking him to the saddle when you could have bought a real hunter instead!"

" 'Twas a challenge," Malcolm replied unperturbed. "We've been through all this before."

"I'm just teasing you," Merewyn countered, her large blue eyes dancing as she studied him with a fond smile.

Though only three years separated them, brother and sister could not have looked less alike. Malcolm was tall and reed slender, his eyes dark brown and his thick hair chestnut in color. His features were those of his late father, rough-hewn and angular, and his temperament was similar, calm and slow to anger, careful in what he said and rarely inclined to express his innermost feelings.

Merewyn, on the other hand, was exceedingly fair. Her shining curls were the color of ripening wheat; her large, expressive eyes a deep blue, the depths flecked with gold although they could easily take on vast ranges of greens and azures as her quicksilver moods changed. Her features were delicate, her jaw slender, her chin small beneath a finely molded mouth. Hollow cheekbones, a smooth brow and a slim, aristocratic nose gave evidence to her Nordic ancestry, a trait that had shown itself in almost every MacAilis generation since the first Vikings had landed on the Scottish mainland and left their stamp upon the dark Gaelic folk.

At seventeen, Merewyn had seen little more of the world than the comforting walls of Cairnlach Castle and an occasional trip to Glasgow and Inverness with her brothers on business matters. She had been educated at home with the best of tutors, and considered Glen Cairn to be the finest place on earth. She was slender and breathtakingly beautiful, possessing a delicate Nordic beauty so rarely found in the Highlands, but was cursed, as her brother Malcolm all too often pointed out, with a highly volatile temperament and an intense passion for life that he thought utterly tiresome.

"Can't we take a simple, leisurely ride?" he demanded, straightening his cap that had been blown awry during the whirlwind gallop his sister had goaded him into.

Merewyn smiled, revealing a dimple in one soft cheek. "Oh, Malcolm, don't be such a complaining old woman! 'Tis the first truly warm day of spring! What better way to celebrate its advent than a gallop?" She lifted her small face to the welcoming warmth of the sun and spread her slender, velvet-clad arms wide. " 'Tis over, Malcolm, the long, dull winter. Aren't you glad?"

"No," her brother grumbled, thinking of the work that would soon begin. The lambin' had started several weeks ago and would eventually carry them through the shearing, and then the numerous trips to the mills in Glasgow would begin. . . .

"You're too much like Alex," Merewyn accused, tugging at the reins and urging the mare forward at a brisk trot. The ostrich feather in her little hat bobbed jauntily, brushing against her wind-reddened cheek.

"And you ain't enough like him," Malcolm growled good-naturedly.

The horses continued onward at a steady clip, their hooves caking with mud as they made their way down the bog paths where the myrtle and arnicas would soon be blooming. Above them, on a rocky protrusion facing the swiftly moving Lieagh River, stood Cairnlach Castle, its massive stone walls blackened both with age and

the remaining effects of the fire that had raged through
it when the redcoated English soldiers had razed it after
the defeat of Prince Charles Edward Stuart at Culloden
Moor in April of 1745, almost twenty years ago.

To any visitors viewing the castle for the first time its
very size was intimidating until they learned that only
half of it was in use, the other still a burned out ruin, the
MacAilis family having rebuilt only the western wing. A
crenellated roof replete with battlements and towers liberally strewn with arrow-slits ran the entire length of the
fortress, but it was a welcoming structure nonetheless.
The tree-lined allée, planted in the 1600's by the current laird to prove his clan no longer felt itself threatened by an attack—the barren knoll having been maintained for centuries to discourage surprise encounters—
softened the harsh stone walls and brought a touch of
elegance to its southern façade.

To Merewyn MacAilis the castle represented home
and permanence, for a member of the MacAilis family
had been living on the land since A.D. 896, when Nils
Ackgaarson had arrived with other Vikings out of the
mist. Rather than pillaging and retreating, as was Nordic custom, he had married Mairi MacAlieagh, a local
village lass, and built a home for her high on the cliffs.
To help gain acceptance from the suspicious villagers he
had taken Mairi's surname, which had been shortened
through the centuries to MacAilis.

Aye, Merewyn had thought to herself on many occasions, the MacAilis clan was a proud one, its history
carefully documented, no individual deleted or forgotten no matter how ignoble his past. Her favorite he-
roes were Eoberth and Gunnar MacAlieagh, the infamous twins. Eoberth had been the eldest by ten
minutes and had become clan chief and laird of
Cairnlach Castle in 1286. Gunnar—disappointed, it was
said, that Cairnlach hadn't gone to him—had built himself an identical castle, though slightly smaller in size,

right across the river that flowed into the Minch; and the twins vowed eternal devotion to one another.

So it had continued for over four hundred years, the two families, always closely tied through marriage, keeping friendship strong between them—especially during Scotland's long and bloody history, when she had tried again and again to wrest her independence from the hated English. In times of peace the MacAilises shared the grazing lands and the navigational rights to the river, which belonged to Castle Montague, named by Gunnar's self-indulgent great-grandson Montague MacAilis as a legacy, he claimed, for his descendants.

Then came 1745 and Charles Edward Stuart's attempt to regain the throne from the Hanoverian king George II in the name of his ousted father James. Ardent supporters known as Jacobites rallied immediately for the exiled King over the Water, as James was affectionately called, and eager plans were made to see Scotland's rightful king crowned at Scone. But here the alliance of the MacAilis clan was suddenly torn asunder.

Douglas MacAilis, leader of the Montague sept, swore his loyalty for the Hanoverian and marched against his own kin throughout the entire campaign. The Cairnlach MacAilises loyally raised the Standards for the Stuart King as both septs had done together during the first abortive attempt by James himself in 1715. They met the Montagues on the battlefield of Culloden, their newly forged rivalry exploding into a terrible slaughter. Alastair, Merewyn's father, fell in the battle as did his kinsman Douglas MacAilis, leaving both houses without a leader.

The victorious and vengeful English burned and looted Cairnlach Castle and the surviving family—Alastair's widow, her two sons and infant daughter—were forced to flee to relatives in the Lowlands. There followed lean years during which Alexander grew to manhood, but the MacAilis blood was strong in him and, at eighteen, he returned to Cairnlach and rebuilt. Meanwhile, the English government had done its best to see the Highland clan system abolished, the chiefs bereft of their power and prestige. Still, the old spirit lingered on and Alexander was able to draw about him his faithful followers and, with diligent work and the eventual restoration of his lands, was able to bring Cairnlach at least back to a shadow of its former glory.

Though the castle had been looted by the English, Alexander managed to recover many treasures among the rubble. Portraits of his ancestors, ancient armaments, and even the coveted jewel-studded baldric given to Eoberth MacAilieagh by Robert Bruce after the Battle of Bannockburn in 1314, were brought untouched out of their hiding places deep below the dungeons where faithful servants had buried them before fleeing for their lives.

The years that followed were peaceful ones for the MacAilis clan, but not without some trouble. Douglas MacAilis had been killed at Culloden and, because he had fought for King George, his holdings were left undisturbed during the vast sweep of revenge by the triumphant English troops. When it became clear that the great house of Montague would remain empty, King George II had invited a favored courtier to take possession of it.

Edward Villiers, a nobleman whose ancestors had come to England from France with William the Conqueror, quickly accepted the King's offer, seeing the chance to rebuild the once magnificent estate as a challenge. At the same time he accepted also the title of Marquis, which the King generously bestowed upon him as a symbol of their friendship.

The MacAilises took the news with stoic calm, though inwardly they were seething. Not only did half the wool mills in Glasgow and the water rights to the river now belong to a Sassenach, a hated Englishman, but they were forced to accept the fact that Edward Villiers had been rewarded for Douglas MacAilis's treachery by being given the King's blessing through a blood-money title.

Alexander found himself hard pressed to deal reasonably with the tightfisted and hard-bargaining English Marquis. Unfortunately, both Cairnlach Castle and Montague were too closely tied in land and business holdings to make either independent of the other, and Lord Montague, who himself held the advantage, was never loathe to exercise it. Meetings between the young MacAilis laird and the older Marquis were rare, kept deliberately at a minimum, but the situation was tenuous at best, and more often than not explosive. Lord Montague made no secret of the fact that he wanted all the land and the mills in Glasgow for his own, and Alexander was hard pressed to keep them from him.

"I wonder if Alex will come home today," Merewyn said wistfully as the horses turned down the rocky path leading to the stables. "He's never been away on business this long before!"

Malcolm nodded, his brown eyes half shut as he surveyed the rarely seen sun that reflected with glaring brightness off the mullioned windows of the castle. "I wonder if there's trouble at the mills again," he mused.

Merewyn's soft lips tightened angrily. "You think 'tis that stinking bastard Villiers again?"

Malcolm shot her a disapproving look. "God's teeth, Mother would turn in her grave if she could hear you talk like that!"

Merewyn rested a gloved hand on her slender hip, giving only a brief moment of thought to the beautiful woman she could scarcely remember. "I don't care! You know perfectly well that horrible man has been making Alex's life miserable for years! If only we had enough money to buy out of the partnership! If only that fat

German pig had given all of it to Villiers in the first place so that we'd at least have been able to start over again on our own! 'Tis terrible to have to grind our faces in the muck like this and bear the brunt of all the expense!"

"You really shouldn't be troubling your wee head with business matters," Malcolm said, shifting uneasily in the saddle because he knew his words were futile. Their mother had died when Merewyn was six and Alexander, inexperienced at raising his younger brother and sister, had made no exceptions with Merewyn. She had been trained right alongside Malcolm in the management of sheep, the business matters of the estate, the transport of wool to Glasgow and the running of the mills there, half of them owned by Villiers himself. Merewyn, who had a quick mind and a grasp for business Malcolm found astonishing, knew as much as her brothers did, but Malcolm felt inclined to believe that her unorthodox upbringing had only contributed to developing the rebellion and wildness that were an integral part of her temperament.

"Perhaps there's nothing wrong after all," he remarked encouragingly. "The war's finally over and Alex may have been detained with planning the new export markets."

The Treaty of Paris had ended the Seven Years' war less than three months before and the seas were again safe for cargo vessels. Among the ships affected by the halt in trade during the years when privateers and frigates-of-war roved the Atlantic were those belonging to Cairnlach. Alexander had departed for Glasgow shortly after the treaty had been signed, but neither Merewyn nor Malcolm had expected him to stay away this long. Merewyn firmly believed that Edward Villiers had something to do with her brother's extended absence and suspected that Malcolm believed the same.

As they turned their horses toward the barn that

stood across the uneven stone courtyard behind Cairnlach's kitchens, both of them were silent, preoccupied with their own thoughts. Merewyn dismounted, thinking to herself that she would love nothing more than to see Edward Villiers dead, but her schemes as to how to achieve this were forgotten when she was unexpectedly greeted by a welcoming nicker from one of the box stalls.

" 'Tis Greyfriar!" she cried excitedly, hurrying forward to peer over the rough boards at her brother's prized stallion. "Alex must be back!" She tossed the reins to the redheaded groom who came forward to meet them. "When did he arrive, John?" she demanded, pulling off her gloves.

"About an hour ago, Miss Merewyn," came the smiling reply.

"Come on, Malcolm." She tugged impatiently at his sleeve, her dark indigo eyes shining. "He's been gone for weeks!"

"You go on," Malcolm told her, smiling indulgently as he unbuckled the girth from Drummond's massive belly. "You never let me get in a word edgewise. I'll talk to him later."

She turned without the flippant retort he had expected and raced outside, her velvet skirts billowing about her. Running headlong through the arched door she scampered up the worn flight of stone steps and burst into the castle's west wing. She knew she would find him in his study—for he always retired there after the long ride— and promptly flew through the door without knocking.

"Alex! Welcome home!"

He was standing with his back toward her but turned and gave her a welcoming smile as she came in, his careworn face softening as it always did when he looked at her. He was tall and well-built for his thirty years, as slender as his brother and as yet unmarried. His dark mane of hair was carelessly combed, and he looked every inch the clan chieftain in his tartan coat; a glass of Scotch was in one long-fingered hand.

He wore breeches, not a kilt, the Disarming Act of 1746 having taken away the right of proud Highlanders to wear their ceremonial dress or play the bagpipes, although Alexander was known to do both on occasion in blatant defiance of the law. He had mastered the pipes as a wee lad and had taught his younger brother and sister to dance the strathspeys and flings Alastair himself had shown him. The times he loved best were the long winter evenings spent before the fire in the study with the haunting melodies echoing to the raftered ceiling, Merewyn's heart-shaped face shining as she performed for him the Ghillie Callum with ethereal grace.

"John told me you were out riding," he said now in his deep, richly resonant voice, his brown eyes surveying her approvingly, for she looked beautiful and slender in her lincoln-green habit. "I should have known this weather would lure you outside."

She flew to him, laughing, throwing her arms about his neck, and depositing kisses on his leathery cheek. "Oh, I've missed you so," she murmured, her small face pressed against the clean-smelling softness of his white muslin shirt and neatly folded stock.

"And where's Malcolm?" he asked, returning her embrace affectionately.

"In the stables. He'll be in soon." Her tilted eyes sparkled as she looked up at him. "Did all go well in Glasgow? Tell me we're the richest family in the Isles!"

He laughed, but she noticed for the first time that there was a weary look to his rugged features.

"You're tired," she said, pushing him down into the big leather chair that stood behind his desk. "Should I bring you tea? Are you hungry?"

He shook his dark head, his fingers closing about her slim wrist as she made to leave the room. "Merewyn, sit down. I've something to say to you. Both of you."

"What is it?"

" 'Twill have to wait until Malcolm comes."

"There's naught wrong with the mills, is there?" she asked anxiously, seating herself on the arm of his chair, studying his face carefully although she could read nothing of his thoughts there.

"No, not at the mills," he responded heavily. "At least not this time."

Merewyn's blue eyes reflected her bewilderment. "Does it have anything to do with the Treaty? Are there trade conditions we didn't know about before?"

Alexander smiled reassuringly. "No cause for concern there, my love. I expect a profitable year and safe seas to travel on."

"Then what is it?" Merewyn demanded impatiently, her soft lips tightening ominously. " 'Tis Lord Montague again, Alex, I know it! What's he done now?"

She herself had never laid eyes on the Marquis of Montague, although both of her brothers had dealt with him frequently. Lord Montague himself had never set foot on MacAilis soil, at least not that which lay on the south side of the river, nor had Alexander ever been to Castle Montague since Villiers had been living there. All business between the two men was conducted by messengers or in subdued meetings in faraway Glasgow or the closer town of Inverlochy.

In Merewyn's eyes Lord Montague was a monster and her imagination, fed by the fact that she had no idea what he looked like, had painted him into some hideous creature so hated that she would have liked nothing better than to find the chance to destroy him. Alexander had lost his fiancée to him two years ago, Lord Montague having lured her away with his charm, for 'twas said that he had a great deal of it despite his age. But he had grown weary of the redheaded Jeannie Sinclair soon enough and had discarded her at his whim. Merewyn knew that the disgraced girl had been sent away by her parents to live with an elderly aunt in Edinburgh, and Alexander had dismissed the entire affair with admirable grace, although she suspected that inwardly he had suffered greatly.

Alexander rose from his chair and paced moodily about upon the elegant carpet in the study. He was ruggedly handsome, a typical Highlander in build, sturdy and a man of the earth, both ruthless in business and dour in manner. But Merewyn loved him dearly, for he had taken Alastair's place in her heart as the father she had never known.

"What sort of trouble do you mean?" she asked him now, her smooth brow wrinkling.

" 'Twill have to wait until Malcolm arrives," Alexander reminded her with a preoccupied smile. "I don't want to repeat myself."

Merewyn stamped her small foot on the floor. "How like you to be so mysterious!" she protested. " 'Tis bad news, Alex, I can tell. What is it? Has German George made Villiers a duke, now? Or even heir to the throne?"

Alexander was forced to smile despite himself, his careworn features relaxing a bit as he looked down into her dark blue eyes and saw the fury within them. "I wish 'twere that simple."

"Well, then, what is it? What did that sniveling knave say to you?"

"Actually, I didn't lay eyes on the man. 'Twas curious, to tell you the truth. His solicitor hasn't been there in quite some time, or his steward either. In fact, no one has laid eyes on the Marquis for quite some time. The only person I did see was a messenger who brought me a written declaration from the castle."

"And what did it say?" Merewyn demanded breathlessly, the sudden gravity of Alexander's behavior making her suspect that something dreadful had happened.

Alexander gave her another indulgent smile. "I told you 'twould have to wait."

Merewyn was silent a moment, then said thoughtfully, "Actually Edward's absence isn't very odd at all. You told me yourself that sometimes he doesn't show up for weeks on end."

"Aye, 'tis true," Alexander conceded, "but his solicitor is always there. I talked to almost everyone in the mill and no one claims to have seen Mr. Bancroft for at least a fortnight now."

Merewyn restlessly tapped the quirt she still carried against the leg of the chair in which she had lowered herself. "What do you think they're plotting?" she asked at last.

Alexander opened his mouth to speak but was interrupted by the opening of the study door. "Ah, Malcolm," he said, his tone warm as he came forward to greet his brother.

Merewyn waited, wriggling with impatience, while they exchanged hearty backslaps and handshakes. Then she blurted, "Alex says there's trouble at the mills, Malcolm."

Malcolm's brown eyes narrowed and he dropped into another chair before the massive oak desk, stretching his long legs before him. "What is it?"

Alexander moved restlessly to the window and stared outside, oblivious to the grandeur of the surrounding mountains and the emerald beauty of the moors in the sunshine. "I was just telling Merewyn before you came in about Lord Montague's strange disappearance. For all practical purposes he seems to have dropped off the face of the earth."

Malcolm's expression grew puzzled. "I don't know what you mean, Alex. You know as well as I he takes to making these business vacations quite often."

Alexander propped himself comfortably on the windowsill, hands thrust deep in the pockets of his coat. "Aye, 'tisn't unusual behavior for him, and his solicitor always knows where he's gone, but Bancroft himself hasn't shown his face in Glasgow for over two weeks."

Malcolm ran a hand through his tousled hair and said with a halfhearted smile, "Doubtless they're both sequestered at the castle plotting our demise."

"I wouldn't be surprised," Alexander said, startling both of them with his grimness. "I received a sealed note from a Montague messenger the morning I left and I returned here posthaste after reading it."

"What did it say?" Malcolm asked, and Merewyn leaned forward in her chair, her slim fingers tightening on the handle of her leather crop.

" 'Twas a declaration, simple and direct," Alexander said abruptly. "Lord Montague has revoked our rights to the river."

There was shocked silence in the study.

"I can't believe it!" Malcolm sputtered at last.

"But how can he stop us from using it?" Merewyn asked in bewilderment.

"The sheriff can seize and impound any of our wool boats traveling down the Lieagh," Alexander informed her grimly, his brown eyes focused somewhere beyond the mullioned windowpanes. "I've no doubt he'll have it well patrolled."

"But how will we send down our wool?" Merewyn demanded. " 'Twould take three times as long by land and be much more costly!"

"Exactly." Alexander turned away from the window again and regarded his sister soberly. "He's got us where he wants us at last."

"But why?" Merewyn asked, her young face filled with worry. "What does he want from us?"

"He's been trying to increase the market price of our virgin wool this entire year," Alexander explained. "I've been against it and I imagine he's using the waterway as a lever to make me agree."

"That's blackmail!" Merewyn shouted, her indigo

eyes flashing. "Oh, Alex, he can't do this! 'Twill ruin us!"

"It may," he agreed.

"So what shall we do?" Malcolm asked, regarding his brother calmly. "Should we agree to the price boost?"

"We can't!" Merewyn cut in before Alexander could reply. "You know our competitors will undercut us if we do! We'd lose a large percentage of the market."

" 'Tis a possibility," Alexander said grimly.

" 'Twould seem to me," Malcolm put in slowly, tracing a pattern on the arm of his chair with his forefinger, "that something has to be done. Not only about the waterway but about this entire situation. It's gotten completely out of hand. Trouble will come to a head eventually. If it won't about this, then it will about something else. How can we make this a peaceful merger once and for all?"

"I think we should break with the swine completely!" Merewyn cried.

"You know we can't," Alexander pointed out reasonably. "He owns a third of our grazing land as well as half of the Glasgow property. No, Malcolm's right. If we're to succeed we have to make peace with him once and for all."

"But how?" Malcolm asked.

Alexander shook his dark head, and then lowered himself into the leather chair behind the massive oak desk. Reaching into the cabinet behind him, he took out a crystal decanter and two glasses, pouring himself a dram of whiskey and another for Malcolm. "I've been thinking about it the entire way home and I've no answers."

"Can't you see what he's doing?" Merewyn demanded, her hands clenched on the desktop, leaning forward to stare into her older brother's face. "He's undermining us little by little, and when he thinks he's weak-ened us sufficiently he'll strike just like the snake he is!"

"He won't succeed," Alexander informed her harshly. "The entire pox-ridden Sassenach army couldn't keep MacAilises from their land before. I won't let a power-hungry marquis have it now."

Merewyn's fearfully racing heartbeat slowed. When her brother spoke that way he sounded as ruthless as any chieftain preparing to gather his clan for war. At times like this she actually believed they would some day find a way to resolve their problems with Lord Montague, the hated English monster.

Alexander's strong hand covered hers and he smiled at her warmly. "You're an impetuous lass, my love, and you react too often on an emotional level. 'Tisn't the end of the world this time, so don't look so frightened."

She returned his smile tremulously, the tilted blue eyes filled with renewed optimism. "I'm sure you can handle this," she said, the set of her small chin suddenly defiant, "whatever plans that muck-eating boar has up his sleeve!"

Behind her Malcolm gave a low chuckle. "Lud, Merewyn, if you were a man I'd warrant you'd challenge Villiers to a duel."

She rounded on him, hands on her slim hips, her dark eyes flashing. "Aye, that I would, and I'd have little doubt about the outcome!"

"He's a hell of a swordsman," Malcolm warned her with a grin.

Merewyn regarded him with a flippant toss of her golden head. "Oh, go on, you great dunderhead. I'm going upstairs to change. I'm tired of talking about Monsieur le Marquis."

"Then we'll meet for tea," Alexander said, and she nodded with a cheerful smile as she exited through the door.

"Ooh, I wish that man were dead!" she groaned to herself, hurrying up to her room where she pulled off her boots in a frenzied burst of energy and tossed them into a corner. If only she were a wee bit older she really would take on the Marquis herself—not with strength, for she knew that a slender lass such as herself couldn't possibly hope to duel with the notorious Marquis, but with beauty. Malcolm had told her on many occasions that Lord Montague had an eye for a pretty face.

Aye, if she were only a few years older, she'd capture that Englishman's black heart with her charms and make him grovel in the dust at her feet! In stockinged feet she padded to the mirror that hung above her dressing table, critically looking herself over.

The dark green habit transformed her blue eyes into emeralds, the long lashes that framed them fanning her smooth cheeks. Her golden hair, pinned to her head in a haphazard fashion, was awry, and shining curls spilled about her shoulders. She pursed her small lips and turned this way and that, surveying the slender line of jaw and throat, then thrust out her chest to study the firm, rounded breasts of which her friend Ellie, who lived in the village, was so very envious.

Ellie was eighteen and flatter than a wee lad, her arms and legs as thin as matchsticks. Still, she liked the lads and they liked her and Merewyn suspected that her friend was already quite promiscuous.

"But am I bonnie enough?" she asked herself curiously. "They say I am, but surely not as bonnie as Jeannie Sinclair and Lord Montague didn't want her!"

"There ye be again, moonin' afore that mirror like a lovesick ewe!" came a sharp voice behind her and Merewyn turned, flushing self-consciously, as an iron-haired old woman in somber attire strode into the room.

Tall and gawky, her long nose perpetually reddened, her flinty hazel eyes sharp and calculating, Annie Fitzhugh had been with the family since Alexander's birth. Sharp-tongued and disinclined to show anyone the least bit of affection, she was nonetheless intensely

devoted to the MacAilises and adored her youngest
charge as though Merewyn were her own daughter.

" 'Tis high time ye were married," Annie added,
stooping down to pick up Merewyn's discarded boots
and missing the rebellious expression that passed across
the young face. "Och, an' look at these, will ye, caked
wi' mud an' God kens what else!" Her long nose
wrinkled distastefully. "Ye'd be better off sleepin' i' the
byre wi' the beasties the way ye smell. C'mon, off wi' yer
things, ye need a guid strong bath!"

"Oh, please, Annie, not now," Merewyn begged.

The old woman was unrelenting. "Get yer clothes off.
I'll see tae the bath."

Merewyn sighed, aware that it would prove futile to
argue. She stepped grudgingly out of her habit and embroidered chemise, tossing them over a chair, but by the
time her bath was ready she was shivering in the chilly
afternoon air and was eager to warm herself in the brass
tub. Barefooted, she hurried into the adjoining sitting
room where she slid gratefully into the hot water and
closed her eyes with a long, contented sigh, trying to
drive from her mind all thoughts of the present, of
Alexander's disturbing news, and especially her absurd
schemes of ensnaring the hated Marquis of Montague.

Beneath the clear water her ivory body was flawless,
her hips gently rounded, her thighs firm and sleek. Hers
was a body that could easily unleash wild desire in any
man had she but known it, but Merewyn MacAilis had
little thought at the moment of the force of her seductive
powers, concentrating instead on the soothing, fragrant
water that lapped about her and the warm glow of the
fire that crackled in the stone fireplace before her. Alexander was home and she was happy. What else could
possibly matter?

When she came downstairs a half hour later she was
demurely dressed in a gown of soft rose satin, her hair

washed and gleaming in the firelight. Alex and Malcolm, she learned from Annie, had ridden down to the paddocks to check on the lambs. Bored and disheartened she wandered restlessly about the empty rooms, pausing in the library to study the portraits there.

Originally they had been hanging in the long gallery in the east wing, but that had been burned by the English and had not yet been rebuilt. These paintings, as well as the other valuables had been hidden away in a secret compartment in the dungeons that were now sealed off, and had remained untouched by the searing heat of the flames that had gutted the once magnificent structure, and the years of harsh weather that followed.

The portrait of Eoberth, Cairnlach's oldest possession, not including Robert Bruce's baldric, hung above the mantel, a giant of a man, if one could judge from the span of his shoulders, with a thick neck and barrel chest, his straight hair closely cropped and golden in color. A high, furrowed forehead was set above piercing blue eyes and an unsmiling mouth, his burgundy tunic of heavy cloth bearing a strange and intricate pattern.

Merewyn stared curiously up at the portrait, wondering to herself what it must have been like to live in Scotland during Eoberth's time. Bloody the years had been, so history told her, what with a half dozen men laying claim to the Scottish throne at any given time—noblemen, all contenders for the Crown, betraying one another, stabbing one another, each determined to lay hands on the greatest prize of all.

Women had also played a significant role in Cairnlach's history. To the left of Eoberth's portrait hung that of Lady Agatha, who, in 1491, her husband away from home, had single-handedly withstood an attack by one of the bloodthirsty Isle clans that feuded constantly with the Scottish Crown and that had marched that spring to ransack Inverlochy and the surrounding strongholds, Cairnlach included.

Lady Agatha, small and frail and six months pregnant with the would-be MacAilis heir, had lit the burning cross herself, summoning the clan together and leading them in dispersing the attackers. Merewyn had always liked the portrait of Lady Agatha, finding the gray eyes filled with spirit and the whimsical half-smile that played on her lips bespeaking a woman with a strong, though loving nature. All of the MacAilises who hung on these walls were as much a part of her past as she would be of Cairnlach's future.

A small frown marred the smooth perfection of her brow. Could there be a future for Cairnlach's other than financial ruin? Did the treacherous Marquis of Montague plan to destroy them and then take control of Cairnlach altogether? She wouldn't let that happen! Like Lady Agatha, she was prepared to wage full-blown war against anyone who threatened her home. Bloody Sassenach, she thought contemptuously to herself, did he think his underhanded scheming could possibly defeat them? She'd think of her own schemes, she would, and she'd see to it that Edward Villiers would come to rue the day he had ever set foot in the Highlands. . . .

In contrast to the mild spring weather of the day before, the next morning dawned cold and overcast, snow flurries falling from the sky when Merewyn awoke and peered out of her window with a frown of disappointment. She shivered as she drew on her gown and plaited the thick coil of golden hair into a braid and pinned it into a chignon at the base of her slender neck. If the weather was bad 'twould mean Alexander was out with the sheep to help with the lambin' and she wouldn't have the chance to speak with him.

Yesterday, when he and Malcolm had returned,

they'd sequestered themselves in the study, doubtless discussing the Marquis of Montague's latest actions, and she'd not had the courage to interrupt them and ask what they planned to do. At dinner Alexander had told her briefly that everything was being attended to, and she left it at that, trusting as always in his judgment.

Descending the staircase she found Annie in the breakfast room with fourteen-year-old Morag, who was clearing away the older woman's dishes. Annie, her services as a nanny and governess no longer required, was still considered a member of the family and took all her meals with the MacAilises, a matriarch who ruled the servants as housekeeper, mistress, and administrator alike. Still, she was just and fair, taking most of the responsibility of running the household from Merewyn's hands. And the servants liked and respected her, so the arrangement was satisfactory for all concerned.

"Ye slept late this mornin'," Annie observed as Merewyn entered the room yawning widely. She studied the dark circles beneath the young girl's eyes and asked worriedly, "Did ye no sleep well, wean?"

"Aye," Merewyn lied. In truth she'd spent half the night worrying about the Marquis's latest act, but she'd sooner cut out her tongue than confess her fears to anyone.

"Then ye maun no be eatin' richt," Annie decided, and doled out great helpings of eggs and kippers from the sideboard onto a plate. "Sit and eat!"

Merewyn's stomach turned at the sight of so much food, but to please the older woman she did as Annie asked. "Have Malcolm and Alex gone to the hills?" she asked between mouthfuls.

"Lord, where be thy manners?" Annie demanded in exasperation, seating herself beside her young charge and shaking her gray head despairingly. "Aye, they did. At four this mornin'." She clucked sorrowfully. "Never seen them work sae hard than at lambin' time, except maybe at shearin'."

Merewyn's lower lip protruded petulantly. "I offered to help them but—"

"Ye'll do nae sich thing!" Annie admonished, wagging a warning finger. "I've enough trouble tryin' tae keep ye frae bein' sae wild! I said it yestreen an' I'll say't again, ye maun be married, wean, and soon! Lord kens Master Alex canna keep ye reined in an' Master Colm refuses tae try! What ye need, bairn—"

"Please," Merewyn choked, gazing impatiently at her old governess, her indigo eyes wide in her delicate face, "can we talk about something else?"

Annie continued to look stern. "Aye, but dinna think I've said the end o't! As soon as Master Alex returns I think I'll hae me a wee talk wi' him! Look at ye, wean, ye be burstin' at the seams! Ripe for the takin'! 'Tis time the laird found ye a proper husband."

"Annie—"

"Nae, nae, I've said enough, I ken, but I mean what I say."

Merewyn sighed deeply. "Aye. 'Tis what I'm afraid of."

Annie rose to her feet now that Merewyn's plate was nearly empty. "Finish that," she admonished, "an' nae throwin' it tae the beasties," she added, indicating the two deerhounds that belonged to Alexander, lying dutifully beneath the table, their eyes fastened on their young mistress who was not above giving them a handout every now and then.

"I won't," Merewyn promised, although it was exactly what she had in mind. As soon as the door shut behind the tall woman the deerhounds bounded to their feet and received their expected reward. Rubbing their silky fur affectionately Merewyn giggled as she fended off their swishing tongues.

Romulus and Remus were offspring of a long line of

deerhounds that had been in the MacAilis house even before the first Stuart uprising. Alexander had taken his dog with him when the English had come and had brought back to Cairnlach a bitch pup when he left the Lowlands forever. These two littermates were grandsons of his beautiful Dina, who had died on the very day Edward Villiers had taken possession of Montague Castle —an omen, some of the superstitious ghillies had whispered among themselves, that portended the troubles that were to come.

"If I ate everything on my plate Annie puts there," Merewyn told the whining dogs, "and you weren't there to eat it for me I'd be fatter than Widow MacEachin in the village!"

She got up and went to the window, sighing when she saw that the snow had turned to rain that was running in rivulets down the glass. Propping her arms on the sill she stood there deep in thought, then jerked upright as she became aware of movement on the drive far below. Peering down she saw that it was a horse coming toward the castle, its rider leaning low in the saddle, his collar turned up against the rain and biting wind. He was bareheaded, however, and his thinning hair clung damply to his head. Though she strained her eyes, Merewyn could not recognize him and her curiosity grew.

Pushing aside the dogs who were eagerly awaiting another handout, she hurried into the stone-floored hall and watched impatiently through the peephole until she saw the horse enter the cobbled courtyard. It was only then that she recognized the rider as Norman Flint, Alexander's steward. She threw open the heavy oak door and he hurried inside, shaking himself like a wet dog, dripping pools of water onto the stones beneath his booted feet.

"Lord, Miss Merewyn, 'tis a foul day!" he remarked, pulling off his soaking cloak.

"Aye," Merewyn agreed, taking it from him and

hanging it on the rack of antlers behind her to dry. Alexander had shot the hart himself on his fifteenth birthday and no amount of moaning and haranguing on his part could break his younger sister of the habit of using it as a coat rack. "Come inside, you're wet to the bone!"

Norman Flint was approaching fifty, a short, heavy man with a thick gray mustache and beady black eyes. He had served the MacAilises far longer than Merewyn could remember and, next to Alexander and Malcolm, knew more about the family's sheep than anyone else. He resided in a cottage not far down the slope towards town and had eight children of varying ages, the eldest married to the sister of Ellie Shields, Merewyn's friend from the village.

"Alexander's gone to the fields," she explained, leading Norman into the comfortable study where a warm fire glowed in the hearth. "Sit down and I'll send someone to fetch him."

"That willna be necessary," Flint replied, seating himself and stretching his numb fingers towards the fire. "I've a message for him and you can gie't to him as well as I."

"At least stay until you've warmed yourself," Merewyn protested.

His black eyes twinkled. "I'd be warmed a wee mite faster if you'd spare me some of the laird's fine whiskey, Miss Merewyn."

She dimpled. "Aye, I'm thinking you would, Norman Flint, and I'd not be parting with it without his permission except to the likes of yourself because I know he serves you a dram whenever you come."

"Ah, that's my lass," he exclaimed, speaking with the familiarity of long acquaintance, having known Merewyn since she was a child.

She took out the cut-crystal decanter Alexander kept in the cabinet behind the desk and poured the tacksman a generous helping. He sipped and smacked his lips appreciatively, then downed a larger swallow.

" 'Tis what we do best in the Hielands," he sighed approvingly.

Merewyn's gold-flecked eyes were filled with laughter. "You mean drink whiskey?"

"No, my dear, make it." He tilted his glass at her by way of a toast. "And drink it, for that matter, now that you mention it. Word's always been a Hielander can hold his Scotch far better than any other mon."

She laughed with him, then asked curiously, "What did you want to see Alexander about, Mr. Flint? Naught's amiss, is there? I can't think of any other reason why you'd come up in this terrible weather."

"I was at Castle Montague," Flint replied, growing serious and setting aside his glass. "Master Alex sent me there yesterday afternoon."

"To Montague?" Merewyn repeated, sinking into the big leather chair behind the desk, her large, tilted eyes fastened to his. "Did you see him? The Marquis?"

"Nay. I brought over the figure your brother was prepared to offer him."

"The new price for the wool?"

"Aye."

"And what did he say?" she asked breathlessly.

Flint shook his graying head. "Wouldna even look at it."

"So the waterway is still closed," Merewyn said worriedly.

"Aye, that it is."

"Did the Marquis name the price he wanted?"

"He wouldna even see me, Miss Merewyn. I couldna even get through the door. I dinna ken what the laird can do to change his mind."

"I don't understand why he's avoiding everyone," Merewyn mused with concern. "I don't care for this mysterious plotting."

Norman Flint nodded his head in agreement. "That

mon hasna ever made a secret of anything before. He
kens what he wants and goes after it, not carin' who or
what stands in his way. Has me wonderin' this time, he
does. I canna help but think he's working on summat
curious.''

"Ooh, that despicable man!" Merewyn fumed, jump-
ing from her chair and regarding the steward with
flashing eyes, her hands balled into small fists. "I'd love
to see him swinging from the gallows!"

"Aye, 'twould be the best place for the likes of him.''

"What's he like, Mr. Flint?" Merewyn asked curiously. "Do you know I've never set eyes on him before."

"Thank the Lord for that, miss!" Flint shook his head
emphatically. "I canna think of another mon I distrust
more. He's an arrogant bas—blackguard, to say the
least. Enjoys playin' cat 'n' mouse with your brother, he
does.''

"Well, that's going to stop once and for all,"
Merewyn predicted direly.

Norman drained the amber liquid in his glass and rose
to his feet, shaking his head resignedly. "I dinna see how
that be possible if the Marquis willna even see your
brother. Nae, 'tis impossible unless we have a miracle.''

" 'Twill happen," she promised.

He sighed. "I'd be the first mon to drink to an end o'
all this, Miss Merewyn, but I dinna see how it can happen unless the laird's got a plan up his sleeve I haven't
heard of yet.''

Merewyn's soft lips tightened with sudden determination. "Perhaps he has.''

Flint looked unconvinced, and as he followed the
slender girl into the hall he asked, "You'll tell the laird
I was here, lass?"

"Of course," she replied warmly, then smiled ruefully
as she handed him his damp cloak. "I'm afraid 'tis still
wet. Are you certain you don't want to wait until the
rain stops?"

"I'd be here for weeks," he laughed, his black eyes twinkling. Abruptly he sobered and slipped the cloak over his thin shoulders. "I'll be by tomorrow. Tell Master Alex that Lord Montague wouldna see me at all. Tell him I didna get past the front door."

Merewyn's blue eyes darkened with renewed anger. "I will," she promised, refraining from adding that she was growing extremely impatient with the Marquis's refusal to see anyone.

After she had shown the tacksman out she went upstairs and changed quickly into her warmest wool gown. Drawing on her riding boots and wrapping her cloak about her, she swiftly left the castle by the service entrance behind the kitchen, making sure that none of the servants, least of all Annie, saw her. The curtain of rain that continued falling steadily shielded her from any curious eyes that might be turned beyond the windows, and she made no attempt to hide herself as she hurried across the wet grounds towards the cliffs.

Taking the path that led down to the shore, and stumbling over the slick stones, she came at last to the overturned punt that John had carried down for her from the storage barn only the day before when all of them had naively thought the warm spring weather would last. The rain had increased the water table in the river but Merewyn, scanning the gray water with experienced eyes, saw that it was still easily navigable.

She had been rowing herself about on the Lieagh since she was a wee lass, first with Alexander to help her, then alone, for she was an excellent swimmer and had no fear at all of the water. Only when she went to the island that lay so far out in the Minch was she required to have an escort, and it was usually Malcolm, who loved Lieagh Dubh and its dark green hills as much as she did.

She righted the small boat with difficulty, her hands numb with the cold, and pushed it across the pebble beach down into the water. Wading in after it she soaked the hem of her gown, the icy river swirling about her boots and freezing her small feet. She was soaking wet by the time she began to row, but she gritted her teeth, determined to go through with her plan. Alexander had often labeled her rash and impetuous, acting on whims and impulses that she rarely thought through. She conceded that perhaps this idea was not the best, but she didn't know what else to do.

"I've got to see him," she whispered to herself, straining her small body and leaning with all her might into the oars. "There must be some way to get through to him!"

Her teeth were chattering by the time she beached on the opposite shore, and the trip had taken her far longer than she had anticipated. If she wanted to complete her mission and be back before Alexander and Malcolm returned from the hills she would have to hurry.

Pulling the boat out of the water she stood for a moment, hands resting on her narrow hips, her back aching from the exertion. Lifting her small face she studied the shoreline, looking for a way to get up onto the mainland. Her keen eyes spotted a small cave not far above her and from there a faint trail leading onto the cliffs. Pushing her sodden hair from her eyes she began to climb.

By the time she reached the crescent she was no longer shivering with cold, the circulation having been restored to her hands and feet. Coming to a halt at the end of the path she turned to look behind her and was surprised to see how beautiful the view of Cairnlach was from here. From her vantage point she could see it distinctly despite the misty blanket of rain. The turrets and parapets rose on the far shore high above the knoll upon which they had been built for strategic purposes, the river flanking the northern exposure, and a long, rolling moor stretching away to the mountains gave it an excellent view of the surrounding countryside from the east, west, and south.

This was Glen Cairn itself, a scenic valley nestled on three sides by the braes, the Lieagh River forming its northernmost boundary. Downstream where the river was widest, Merewyn could see the deep water dock where the wool was loaded after shearing to be taken down to Glasgow for carding, drying, and weaving. Her attention wandered back to the grassy hills behind her, wondering where Castle Montague stood. Though she'd never seen it, Merewyn knew that unlike Cairnlach, it had not been built with protection in mind.

Gunnar MacAilieagh had resorted instead to beauty, choosing a site that nestled the stone edifice between a stand of ancient larches and a flat, winding bend of the Lieagh River. If an attack did come, he had reasoned, he would row his family across the water to Cairnlach, and all of his descendants had kept a boat ready in a cave far above the waterline where it could be launched with ease on the pebbly shore even in the darkest of nights.

But the past did not hold Merewyn's thoughts for long, for it was the future that troubled her deeply, and she stared resolutely down into the pleasant glen, searching for her first glimpse of Castle Montague. Above a tall stand of barren larches she could easily make out a solitary stone turret and she set her small chin defiantly.

"Into the dragon's lair, then," she murmured to herself as she started down the path.

The Marquis of Montague stepped out of the brass hip bath that stood before the fire in his magnificent mahogany-paneled bedroom in Montague Castle. His manservant Davis was instantly at his side, extending a towel that had been warming before the fire for his master's use.

"I've laid out your things, m'lord," he informed the
Marquis politely, and retreated without waiting for a
reply.

Lord Montague, his thoughts preoccupied, dried himself, and strode naked across the room to the dressing
table where his clothes had been hung in readiness by
the fastidious valet. He was an extremely large and well-
built man, standing several inches taller than Alexander
MacAilis himself. Muscles rippled in his broad back and
shoulders, but his torso tapered into a smooth and narrow waist above a well-endowed manhood and strong,
muscular thighs. Cold gray eyes were set in his finely
chiseled face, the cynical twist to his sensual lips giving
his aristocratic visage an indolent, almost bored look.

His mane of dark hair hung carelessly long and was
rarely worn in a fashionable manner except when he
chose to tie it in a queue. Bronzed from long hours in the
sun, even during the winter months, he moved about his
room as gracefully as a cat despite his immense size,
dressing and flexing his powerful arms, feeling refreshed
after his bath. He had been out since long before dawn
with his shepherds, overseeing the lambing of the
younger ewes that had been bred to drop their offspring
later than the older, more seasoned ones. He had arrived
at the castle toward noon, covered with mud and sheep's
blood.

Adjusting his stock and drawing on his vest, he allowed a half-smile to play on his lips as he stared at the
giant in the glass who looked back at him, thinking of
the havoc he must have wreaked upon the inhabitants of
Cairnlach Castle with his announcement that they
would no longer be permitted to use the river to transport their wool south. 'Twas a cheap thing to do, he
knew, but he shrugged it off as a necessary means of
survival. Alexander MacAilis, afraid to alienate his
long-standing customers, had been reluctant to raise the
price of his wool, even after he had been shown the ex-

pense sheets, which showed plainly that rising expenditure costs were beginning to eat into their profits.

Damn the whole MacAilis clan, Lord Montague thought irritably. 'Twould be best to be rid of them, but he had been told that they would never agree to sell out their share, nor would he ever make the offer though he did have the money. He was prepared to match wits with Alexander MacAilis who, 'twas said, was a bloodthirsty and often unpredictable man possessing a shrewd mind for business. The challenge had brought him here to this remote corner of the Highlands, a challenge that should prove much more interesting than any diversion he might be able to find back home in England—not discounting, of course, the beauties of the English court whose intrigues had kept him amused since he'd been a young lad.

"M'lord, would you be caring for dinner?" Davis had reappeared in the doorway, his faded brown eyes glancing at the clock ticking on the mantel, frowning as he noticed the lateness of the hour.

Lord Montague nodded, realizing suddenly how hungry he was. There was a twinge in his left shoulder as he pulled on his coat and he massaged it impatiently, thinking to himself that he wasn't exactly cut out to play the role of farmer. If he was wise he'd leave all that to his foreman, but one could never trust these hard-necked, reticent Highlanders. "I'll be down in a moment, Davis," he replied, his deep voice curt. "Set out whatever you can find."

Later, as he sat at the table tackling with relish the cold fowl and bottle of claret Davis had provided, he found himself thinking about his next move concerning the MacAilises. Trading messages with a mere steward wasn't enough. He wanted to see Alexander personally, speak with him face to face, and he'd not relent until the MacAilis laird swallowed his damnable pride and appeared at his doorstep. He had a feeling that 'twould take more than a mere invitation to lure Alexander to Montague. Would desperation do the trick? He chuckled, thinking it might, and refilled his wine glass a fourth time.

"Will ye be wantin' summat else, yer lordship?" The quavering voice from the doorway belonged to Jock Gowerie, an incredibly tiny old man with stooped shoulders and snow white hair whose age was indeterminable. His face was deeply lined, his hands gnarled, and he confessed with an apologetic smile whenever asked that he himself didn't know his own birthdate. He was one of the very few servants remaining at the castle, most of them having, to the Marquis's infinite anger, slipped quietly away one day last week after tendering seemingly nervous resignations, although relief at being free from Villiers's rule was clearly written on their faces.

Jock Gowerie annoyed the Marquis of Montague. The little man rarely spoke, but once he started, it was usually a long reminiscent tirade on the grandeur of the castle before the death of Douglas MacAilis and the heartbreaking defeat of the proud Highlanders at Culloden.

"Och, an' I'll never forget thot black day when the laird called us all intae the great hall," Jock had told the Marquis on more than one occasion in the past fortnight alone. "We was all i' a fash, I can tell 'ee, whot wi' expectin' tae hear him say he be raisin' the Standards for our bonnie Prince an' then tae hear him tell us he maun march wi' Billy the Butcher!" The black little eyes in the ancient visage were filled with sudden tears.

" 'Twas vurra near the end o' me days, yer lordship, I can tell 'ee thot! Me puir heart! I couldna take it, thinkin' how our laird'd be marchin' agin Sir Alastair, sich a braw mon an' sae well liked here!" He shook his grizzled head and inhaled sorrowfully, his thin chest expanding with the weight of a deep, aching sigh.

"But what could we do? He was the laird, we couldna

do naught else but stand by him! An' after Culloden, when they told us he be dead, nae bairns left tae take his place, they all left, they did, them beastie ghillies, just like them did last week, yer lordship, but I didna leave then and I willna leave the noo."

"Your loyalty is most commendable," the Marquis growled impatiently, wishing the tiny man had taken himself off with the rest of them.

The black eyes blazed with long-worshipped memories. "Och, 'tis for the MacAilises I maun stay, sir, i' the hope thot some day they be back in their richtful hame."

"Are you expecting them to displace me?" Lord Montague asked with a warning glint in his steely gray eyes.

Jock's thin shoulders jerked fearfully. "Och, nay, yer lordship, nay! 'Twas—"

"That will be all, thank you," the Marquis had replied ruthlessly, the underlying hardness to his handsome face making his expression extremely forbidding.

" 'Ee be wantin' summat else?"

The towering Englishman's gray eyes narrowed as he pulled his thoughts back to the present. "Another bottle of claret," he commanded and the wizened man scurried away with the empty bottle in his gnarled hands.

Lord Montague expelled air with an ill-tempered exclamation and helped himself to more meat. He had no idea why the servants had all quit on him unless they'd finally found the courage to do so now that—

"There be nae more claret, yer lordship," came Jock's timorous voice from behind him.

Lord Montague's huge fist struck the table, making the chime rattle. "Then get me port or something else, you stupid fool!"

With a frightened squeak Jock withdrew and Lord Montague massaged his aching temples with strong fingers. God's blood, he'd have to get some decent help soon or he'd go mad! If it wasn't for his valet Davis, who'd faithfully accompanied him from England, he didn't know how he could have put up with the annoyances of life in this gloomy and more than a little drafty cavern.

In the great hall Davis was trying his best to lay out his master's damp cloak so that it could dry unwrinkled before the fire. Disturbed from his task by a timid knock on the front door and annoyed at having been interrupted, he refused to be hurried, and the knock was repeated twice more before he finished at last and drew back the bolt, pulling the thick door open. Looking down he saw before him the most bedraggled individual he had ever seen, her cloak, completely covered with mud, clinging wetly to her small form. Golden hair clung in sodden tangles to her face, and rainwater dripped off the rim of her soaking, half-melted hat onto her slim, upturned nose.

Wide blue eyes regarded him without blinking and he asked frostily, "You wish?"

In a small voice she replied, "I should like to see the Marquis."

"I beg your pardon," the old valet replied with obvious hostility, "Lord Montague is not overseeing the hiring of servants. I am."

The tilted blue eyes widened even more and he noticed for the first time how large and vivid they were in the pale, heart-shaped face and how they were tilted at the corners and heavily framed with dark lashes.

"I'm not applying for a position as a servant," the piteous creature informed him, her tone suddenly no warmer than his. "I am Merewyn MacAilis, sister of the MacAilis laird, and I'm here to see Lord Montague on business."

Davis stared down at her mud-streaked cloak and soaking hem. "I find that rather hard to believe."

"Why, you arrogant old man!" she cried, startling him with her unexpected outburst, her hollow cheeks growing red. "How dare you speak to me like that!"

Davis considered himself totally underserving of a tongue-lashing by this belligerent child, and stepped back so that he could close the door in her face. Merewyn, outraged by such blatant bad manners, threw herself against it, and there followed a rather noisy struggle, Davis ordering her to desist with her actions and take herself off while she kept her small booted foot between the jamb and the heavy wood, beating with her palms against the iron bracings, protesting loudly and threatening him with all sorts of hideous violence.

"What in blazes is going on here?"

The ringing question, carrying a heavy threat of its own, brought an instant halt to the struggle, Davis stepping back so quickly, growing red-faced at having lost his control for the first time in his life, that Merewyn, the door flying backwards unexpectedly, pitched forward and found herself falling heavily against a hard, immovable object.

Lord Montague, feeling her soaking wet and shivering body land against his clean clothing, grabbed her thin arms in an iron grip and forced her away; she would have fallen had he not continued to hold her.

"Davis?" he asked ominously, his gray eyes narrowing as he looked at his shame-faced valet.

"Pray, forgive me, m'lord," Davis moaned. "I wanted to save you a confrontation with this—this little heathen." His faded eyes gazed distastefully down at the bewildered waif still held captive in the Marquis's powerful hands. "I've never seen anything like it! She actually tried to force her way in!"

The long fingers that held her small wrists tightened painfully and she felt herself being shaken. "What's the meaning of this, girl?" a booming voice in precise, hated English demanded.

Merewyn looked up and her heart skipped a beat, confused and astonished by the sight of her captor. He was by far the tallest man she'd ever seen although she

was accustomed since birth to the powerfully built Highlanders who farmed her brother's land. Beneath his
dark, unpowdered hair burned a pair of steely gray eyes
that were studying her coldly, the annoyance within
them almost palpable in its intensity. She barely came
beyond his massive chest and had to tilt back her head
in order to look fully into his arrogant face. He was ex-
traordinarily handsome, his aristocratic features
chiseled to the point of flawlessness, the mouth full-
lipped, the nose sharp and gracefully Roman, the chin
square and angrily set.

"Y-you can't be the Marquis of M-Montague!" she
quavered, regaining the use of her voice, her words thin
and unsure.

An ugly smile curved the sensual lips. "I can't?"

"No! You're not nearly old enough!" She was totally
confused, her wide indigo eyes mirroring bewilderment
as well as pain as she became aware of how tightly he
was holding her. Trying to pull herself free she found
that she could not and began to struggle in earnest.

"Let me go!" she panted, turning this way and that
but to no avail, his iron-clad fingers digging into the soft
flesh of her wrists.

"Only if you promise to behave," he replied, and the
mockery in his deep voice infuriated her. No one had
ever treated her like this before!

Her small booted foot lashed out and she kicked him
as hard as she could in the knee. She heard him expel air,
and then was jerked against his hard chest; he was forcing back her head, one strong hand beneath her small
chin, cruelly twisting her neck so that her face was inches from his.

"Damn you, you little brat," he rasped. She tried to
look away from the burning anger in his dark eyes, but
found that she couldn't move her head at all. She could
feel his heart beating beneath the rigid muscles of his

chest and burned with shame and embarrassment, tears
of frustration welling in her eyes.

Lord Montague could read the dark fear within them,
his own so close that he could see their indigo depths
flecked with a startlingly beautiful shade of gold. She
was very young, he noticed for the first time, studying
the delicately molded features that were visible beneath
the soggy brim of her hat. Becoming aware that she was
making him wet as her small but surprisingly soft body
was pressed against him, he let her go abruptly. She
staggered backwards, then stood glaring at him, the
tilted eyes flashing with indignation. He was amazed
that she had the courage to hold her ground.

"Perhaps you're willing to behave more civilly now?"
he asked.

"I suppose I should pattern my manners after you?"
she challenged.

His brows rose. "May I remind you that you came
here uninvited? I'd treat every intruder in my home the
same way."

"Your home!" she repeated, incredulous, color flooding to her face—and with the waning of its paleness he
began to realize how truly beautiful she was.

"My lord," Davis groaned, indicating with disbelief
the spreading puddle of muddy water on the marble
floor beneath the urchin's soaking boots.

Lord Montague shrugged, losing interest. "I don't
particularly care to have her in my employ, Davis, but if
you can beat some sense into her—"

"Do you think I came here to apply for a position?"
Merewyn shouted at him disbelievingly. "Who do you
think I am?"

"I haven't the vaguest idea," he retorted mildly, rocking slightly on his heels as he gazed down at her from his
great height. "But I'm sure I can guess the name. I imagine 'twill be MacSomething or MacSomeone—your

Highland names all sound alike to me."

Merewyn was sputtering with rage, unable to force coherent words from her lips. "You—you—!" she choked. Who was this arrogant blackguard? If only she had a dirk with her, she'd slash him right across his handsome face!

Lord Montague shrugged and glanced wearily at his valet. "I think I've insulted her. 'Tis infinitely tiresome, this fierce Scots pride. They blindly worship their chiefs, dead or alive, drunkard or tyrant, care for naught save their blood and their kin, and have no other interests save killing and feuding. I'm amazed the country has survived as long as it has." He eyed the furious beauty with sudden impatience, shaking his dark head decisively. "No, my girl, I don't think you'll do. I suggest you look elsewhere for work."

He was unprepared for her sudden onrush and was only just able to pin her flailing arms as she flew at him, intent only on inflicting pain anywhere she could. Before he could pack her firmly, she had kicked him again, and this time her little boot connected with his manhood, and though her aim was off-center he was nonetheless forced to drop her as pain exploded in his loins, making his senses reel.

"Justly met, sir!" Merewyn cried as he staggered down to his knees. "I hope 'twill take down your pride a notch or two because I warrant I've wounded you where you pride yourself the most!"

Davis, exhibiting more prowess than he had shown in almost forty years, flung himself upon her just as she was prepared to fly again at his fallen master. Seizing one of her slender arms he forced it behind her back and applied enough pressure to paralyze her without snapping it in two. He was surprised at how quickly she grew still, her entire body trembling, her breast heaving, and he kept a firm grip on her while Lord Montague, breathing heavily, straightened with a groan and came forward.

Merewyn's hat had fallen off in the struggle and a great tangled mass of wet curls tumbled to her waist. The Marquis seized a thick strand of it and wrapped it about one large fist, yanking her out of Davis's grasp and back against his hard chest. Through her cold, sodden clothing Merewyn could feel the heat of his body and she felt her mouth grow dry as she looked up into his gray eyes, their depths smoldering with a rage she had never before witnessed in any man's.

For a moment there was utter silence save for their labored breathing, Merewyn's heart pounding so loudly in her ears that she felt certain he could hear it. She couldn't believe she'd been so brutally treated by these two madmen, the most frightening of all this towering giant before her whose grip on her hair was becoming increasingly painful.

"I've heard stories of how savage Highlanders are," he said at last, his tone so cold that she felt her heart skip a beat before resuming its mad race, "but I never expected 'twould include the women as well. My advice to you, girl, is to leave this house before I break that long neck of yours in two."

She swallowed before speaking, unable to move her head or escape the burning intensity of his eyes. "I-I'm not a girl," she whispered at last, hating to be addressed as a member of the lower class.

Surprise and growing antagonism registered in the gray eyes. "You still refuse to drop that arrogance?" he asked, an unpleasant smile twisting his full lips. "Would you prefer to have me beat it out of you?"

"Y-you wouldn't dare!"

"Don't challenge me," he warned. "You'll only end up losing."

She tried to twist free of his hold, but as he jerked her

about as she broke away she heard him inhale sharply, the gray eyes growing dark with momentary pain. A slow smile curved her soft lips and her tone was as cold as his.

"Are you so certain I'd lose, sir? 'Twould seem I've already scored better than I intended."

Lord Montague found himself in danger of losing utter control of his temper. He was unaccustomed to the rude tongue of this little feisty creature, unaccustomed to seeing anything but sickly fear in the eyes of anyone who broached his anger, unaccustomed, especially, to being treated in such an outrageous manner by a lowly working-class wench. One of his powerful hands wrapped itself about her slender neck, his thumb resting at her throat where he could feel the madly racing pulse.

"I've no quarrel with you, my dear," he said silkily, his lean face only inches from hers, "but I've a mind that you needs be taught some manners."

His huge hand began to tighten, effectively closing off the passage of air to her lungs, and for the first time she knew genuine fear, her blue eyes opened wide, the stricken look within them reminding him suddenly of a frightened fawn he'd found lying in the fields of his English estate years ago. He'd not seen it at first because of its camouflaging coat, but when it raised its head to look at him he had come to an abrupt halt, unable to credit that anything could be so young and defenseless.

But there was nothing defenseless about this young hellion, he reminded himself, angry at the sudden pity that clouded his determination to punish her. She deserved to be soundly flogged until the arrogance in those enormous eyes turned to quivering fear and placidity. His loins still ached with every movement he made and for that insult alone she ought to be locked for at least a week in his root cellar.

He released her abruptly, deciding that she'd had enough, but still could not resist tormenting her. "Are you ready for a thrashing?" he asked pleasantly.

"Haven't you d-done enough?" she breathed as he
loosened his hold on her throat and she gasped gratefully for air.

He smiled cruelly, construing the fearful catch in her
soft voice as evidence of his victory. "I don't believe so,
my dear. You must admit you deserve one after doing
your best to destroy my—what did you term it?" The
cold gray eyes were again very close. "My proudest
possession?"

"If my brother were here he'd kill you," she countered
bravely, and the thought of Alexander brought sudden
panic to her heart. Alex! She'd come here for his sake, to
try and appeal to the Marquis to spare Cairnlach further
hardships and had instead been confronted by this ill-
tempered, fierce individual, by far the largest and most
intimidating man she'd ever seen, and had brawled with
him like a common street waif!

Suppose he was the Marquis's son? she thought in
panic. But no, he was too old for that, being thirty, at
least. But he might be his brother or perhaps a friend
whose opinions, she thought dismally, might mean quite
a bit to Lord Montague!

Her vivid blue eyes faltered, confronted with this
wretched realization, and her body slumped against the
towering man who still held her with one big fist gripping her hair; he took this as a sign that she had admitted defeat. Uncoiling the thick strands of damp hair
from his long fingers he let her go and stepped back.

"Davis, will you show her out, please?" he commanded quietly.

Merewyn felt the old man who had been standing behind her pack her by the collar of her cape and begin
dragging her towards the door. This last humiliation
was too much for her and her temper flared again.

"Go to blazes, you filthy Sassenachs!" she shouted,
flailing at him with her small fists. He warded her off

almost as easily as his master had done and then she
found herself being tossed into the air, landing with a
painful thump on her small rear in the mud and hearing
the great oak door being slammed behind her.

For a moment she lay there, too stunned to move,
then rose painfully to her feet, wiping away with her
grimy hand, the hot tears that coursed down her cheeks.
Catching sight of her wrist and seeing that it was dis-
colored, red marks from the giant's fingers still im-
printed on her soft skin, she burst into fresh tears of
helpless rage and began to run, not stopping until the
castle had fallen out of sight behind a grassy rise.

Only then she turned, her small breast heaving as she
gasped for breath, her red-rimmed eyes filled with burning hatred as she glared back at the solitary turret. She
had no idea who those men had been, but she intended
to find out, and once she did she would extract her revenge and, by God, 'twould be terrible to behold!

In silence she rowed herself back across the river, her
entire body bruised and aching, refusing to accept the
fact that she had been handled so callously. Never in her
sheltered life had anyone ever lifted a hand against her,
except Alexander, who had taken a switch to her only
twice: once when she had rowed by herself to Lieagh
Dubh, her beloved island in the Minch, a transgression
that had angered him bitterly because of the dangerous
currents, and then again when she had followed him to
hounds at the age of twelve after he had expressly told
her she was too young to join the hunt. She had fallen
from her horse and injured herself badly, thrown headlong against a tree root, and had lain unconscious for
two hours in the mist on the wet ground before they had
found her. Alexander had meted out her punishment
with his careworn visage grimly set, and she had not
been aware of the pain tearing at his heart for having to
lift a hand against her.

"I am a MacAilis," she whispered to herself as she

pulled with all her might against the oars, the boat knifing through the water in response to her frenzied rowing, "and no MacAilis will tolerate such treatment!"

The worst part of it, she reflected as she guided the punt towards the opposite shore, was that she could not tell Alexander and Malcolm what had happened, for they would be appalled at the fact that she had gone to Castle Montague alone.

Wearily, she pulled the boat up onto the beach and turned it over, then rubbed her aching derriere, scowling ill-temperedly. How dearly she'd love to take Romulus back there and give him the order to attack, to watch with a smile of pleasure as the deerhound's gleaming fangs imbedded themselves in the huge one's royal arse!

By the time she had reached the castle grounds her anger had begun to fade, replaced with puzzlement and a growing sense of unease. The old man had addressed the tall one as "my lord" when he'd first come onto the scene, but that couldn't have meant he was Lord Montague! Who was he, then, and did his presence there have something to do with the fact that the waterway had been closed?

CHAPTER TWO

"Miss Merewyn, Miss Merewyn, they be here! The saumot be here tae spawn!"

Sitting on the brick terrace with a bonnet shading her eyes from the strong rays of the spring sun that shone occasionally through the layer of clouds, Merewyn looked up quickly at the excited cry of Jemmie Kew, the ten-year-old son of the stablemaster John. Redheaded like his father, his eyes glowing in his young face, he raced with sturdy legs across the green stretch of lawn toward the slender girl in white lace-trimmed muslin who descended the terrace steps, the breeze stirring the golden tendrils of shining gold that peeked out from beneath the beribboned bonnet.

"Did you see them?" she demanded eagerly as he came to a panting halt before her, his upturned face revealing a great number of freckles.

"Oh, aye, miss! They be down i' the river, they be, an' Faither says ye maun hurry if ye wish tae see 'em. They be gang upstream richt fast!"

Merewyn tossed aside her book and hurried with him down the narrow path to the shore, the round black pebbles feeling smooth beneath her slippers. John Kew was standing close to the water's edge, hands deep in the pockets of his trews, his eyes searching the deep blue water before him.

44

"Are they really here, John?" she asked, coming to a breathless halt beside him.

He nodded his head. "Aye, miss. Never come quite at the same time each year, do they?"

"No, but they come every single year and that's what really matters." She leaned forward, taking care not to dirty the hem of her creamy white gown, knowing Annie would berate her heartily if she did. The coming of the salmon every year up the cold, deep waters of the Lieagh marked for Cairnlach the true advent of spring, which, though it was a rainy and often quite chilly season, heralded the end of the savage winter storms. Though sometimes the salmon's arrival was delayed until late May or June, Cairnlach legend had it that once they arrived there would be no more snowfall until next winter and most of the crofters planned their planting by the first sighting.

"Oh, there they are!" Merewyn cried as she caught sight of a flashing silver belly not too far from shore. Within seconds the clear water was teeming with them, some of them of immense size, and she wondered worriedly how they would manage to hurl themselves over the jutting boulders in the upper Lieagh if they weighed so very much.

"I wish I could see them jump the rapids," she sighed wistfully, her indigo eyes glowing nonetheless as she watched the passing school. At the age of seven Alexander had gone with his father to Castle Montague to watch the salmon make their final run, spawning with their last bit of strength far above the castle in an icy crystal pool where the melting snow from Ben Cailach fed into the turbulent river.

Alexander had described the sight to Merewyn many times, the memory still clear in his mind's eye despite the long years, evoking a strong desire in his young sister to witness the same, her interest fired by his description of the huge creatures leaping tirelessly into the foaming cataracts only to be forced back by a churning wall of water, trying again and again until they had succeeded.

"They came so close when I climbed onto a jutting rock," Alexander recalled, his brown eyes twinkling with the memory, "that one of them jumped right over my foot! I could have caught any number of them with my hand."

Every year when the salmon ran, Merewyn was again seized with the desire to witness their dying struggle, fascinated by the brown and silver bodies that fled so silently through the deep water before her. But MacAilises were no longer in possession of Cairnlach's sister castle, and she had never dared row over by herself for a look, afraid that Edward Villiers would arrest her for trespassing.

"Ooh, Faither, 'tis a grand ane!" wee Jemmie was shouting, pointing with a chubby finger into the water while John kept a firm grip on the lad's collar to prevent his tumbling in. Smacking his lips appreciatively he begged, "Can we eat ane?"

John smiled and shook his head. "These be old, Jem, an' near dying. I'd rather see ye tackle a piece of leather."

"Besides, they're going to have bairns," Merewyn added, stepping closer as she shook her thoughts free of the past.

Jemmie's eyes grew round. "Bairns? When? I want tae see!"

" 'Tisn't for us to witness," his father informed him. " 'Tis why they come here, lad. They've got themselves a bonnie nursery upriver, the same place where they were born."

Merewyn's tilted eyes danced beneath the brim of her bonnet. "Do you still want to eat one, Jem?"

"Och, never! Not when they be havin' wee anes!"

John laughed with her. "Next time he's got a big piece

of healthy pink fillet on his plate he'll forget that promise."

"Naturally," Merewyn responded with a smile.

Though the navigational rights to the river belonged to the Marquis of Montague, his private fishing rights extended only to the wide turn the river took near the MacAilis docks, though poaching was not uncommon there, Merewyn knew. The people of the glen were free to angle down to the Mich itself, however, sometimes bringing home enough to feed half the populace of the village. She herself had once tried her hand with the gaff and net, a patient Malcolm her tutor, and though the thrashing little fish she'd landed had been too tiny to make even a meal for the family cat, she'd been delighted with her luck.

"That seems to be the last of 'em," John remarked, the dark expanse of water emptying as quickly of the flashing creatures as it had filled with them moments before.

"There'll be more," Merewyn assured Jem, catching sight of his disappointed expression. "Come down again tomorrow and look. Meanwhile, I think I'll tell Malcolm the good news."

She bid farewell to the head groom and his small son and raced back up the path, holding her skirts aloft so as not to stumble over them. A week had passed since her ill-fated trip to the castle across the river, and Alexander had been gone since then to meet with the Marquis in Inverlochy. Merewyn dreaded his return, certain that she would be punished for her rash behavior, for there was little doubt in her mind that the Marquis had already been informed of her terrible deeds and would not hesitate to give Alexander a detailed account.

Merewyn tried to force these unpleasant thoughts from her mind as she sped across the fragrant earth towards the byre where she knew she would find Malcolm at the paddocks, examining the flocks, tallying the new-

born lambs with Norman Flint, and preparing to move
the older herds up toward the northern grazing sites after shearing. Here the more experienced sheep would
find sufficient grass upon the sparsely covered slopes to
keep them until summer, when they would be driven
high into braes by the shepherds and would not be seen
again until fall. Grasping her flopping bonnet with one
hand, Merewyn scampered across the green grass, her
worries already forgotten, laughing as she watched the
lambs frolicking behind the low stone fences, the sun
warming their backs and bringing an exuberance to their
young limbs.

Apparently the young were not the only ones sub-
jected to fits of boundless energy on this spring day,
Merewyn saw, as she neared the wooden byre where she
caught sight of her brother Malcolm struggling to hold
in the big Clydesdale Drummond, who was kicking up
his heels in an astonishing display of defiance.

"I didn't think that old beast had so much life left in
him," she called out as she approached, giggling at the
look of annoyance on her brother's face.

Norman Flint was leaning against the gate, his
graying hair blowing in the breeze, a smile on his craggy
face as he watched the battle between rider and drafter,
unsure of the outcome although he appeared to be enjoying himself enormously. Drummond had succeeded
in taking the bit between his long yellow teeth and, lowering his massive head, used his thick neck muscles to
wrest the reins from Malcolm's hands. There followed a
brisk and agonizing struggle to recapture them, during
which Malcolm's handsome face grew red with exertion,
the chords in his neck taut, his teeth clenched into a
grimace.

"You'll never hold him in," Norman remarked as the
Clydesdale began to buck.

"Do get off and let him roll," Merewyn called out,

coming to a halt beside the steward. " 'Tis all he wants
to do."

"And I think he's planning tae whether ye let him or
no, Master Colm," Norman Flint agreed, removing his
pipe from his mouth to speak.

Malcolm, deciding it wisest to abandon any attempts
to quiet his eager mount, slid from the animal's back
and pulled the bridle off his head as he did so. "Go on
then, you ill-tempered longshanks," he grumbled, and
the Clydesdale trotted off down the slope towards the
grazing sheep who, unconcerned by his presence, moved
aside so that he could go down on his knees and roll
about at his leisure, snorting in contentment.

Norman and Merewyn were still laughing heartily,
much to Malcolm's annoyance.

"I bet I could make a hunter out of him if I really put
my mind to it."

"You'd take him over jumps?" Norman Flint demanded, shaking with silent mirth, his bristling
mustache twitching. "Lord, Master Colm, that be a
sight I'd like tae see!"

"I doubt we ever shall," Merewyn stated sadly, giving
her brother a look that carried a warning nonetheless.
"A well-schooled plow like Drummond is harder to
come by than a hunter."

Malcolm held up his hands in mock resignation.
"Never fear, I've no intention of trying to work with
that rotten mule ever again."

The steward chuckled and turned back to the sheep,
watching with a lingering smile on his face as the tiny
lambs suckled their mothers, their small woolen tails
wagging with pleasure. "How many markers do we have
ready for Ben Cairn, Master Colm?"

"Oh, please, wait just a minute before you start talking about sheep," Merewyn begged, tugging impatiently
at her brother's shirt-sleeve.

Malcolm looked down at her sternly, but his expression softened despite himself as he gazed into her pleading indigo eyes, her small face even more delicate and innocently beautiful beneath the brim of her bonnet, the ribbons neatly tied beneath her firm little chin. "We've much to do, lass," he told her gently.

"But 'tis the salmon," she said in a rush, "they're running at last. I don't think the school's ever been this big before."

Norman Flint nodded his grizzled head. "Aye, 'tis guid tae hear! The more saumot comin' tae spawn, the more we'll be pullin' fra the waters for our tables!"

Malcolm stared down the slope towards the river far below. The paddocks were built upon a stretch of pasture that lay between the rolling moors and the knoll upon which Cairnlach Castle stood. From here one could take in the islands on the Minch and the southern exposure of the castle in an uninterrupted panorama of immense grandeur. The beauty of the landscape continued beyond the Lieagh to the rolling hills belonging to Montague, the foaming blue water having etched a winding path towards the castle deep into the face of the fragrant earth.

"So the salmon have come again," he murmured to himself, his clear brown eyes filled with pride as he looked about him at MacAilis land. "I gather we'll have no more snow, then." He reached down and patted Merewyn's small rump as though she were a child. " 'Tis grand news, but you'd better run along now. We've much to do."

Obediently, she started down the slope but his voice stopped her as she prepared to scoot under the fence. "Don't go running off anywhere," he warned. "Alex just got home and he has something very important to discuss with you."

"Did he say what it was about?" she asked, her heart thumping.

Malcolm shrugged and said with an evasive grin, "I've no idea."

"Oh, but you do!" she protested, wondering at his levity. But he had already dismissed her and was deep in conversation with Norman Flint. She fled silently back to the castle, her thoughts in a panic. Sweet Christ, what damage had she done to Alexander's efforts to have the waterway reopened?

"Well, I'm not going to let him scare me," she promised herself as she hurried up the long drive. "And no matter what that horrible stranger told Lord Montague about me, both Alexander and his high-and-mighty lordship will have to agree that I was very shabbily treated!"

Hurrying across the cobblestones she was intercepted by Morag, who came after her from the arched doorway leading to the kitchens, her mob cap almost flying from her head in her haste.

"Oh, Miss Merewyn, where've ye been?" she demanded breathlessly. "The laird's retairned and he's been askin' after ye for near an hour!"

Merewyn frowned at the maid who came to a panting halt before her, trying to straighten her cap with clumsy fingers. "Where is the laird?" she asked faintly.

"In the study, miss."

"Please tell him I'll be down shortly," Merewyn began, but Morag's eyes grew round.

"Och, no miss, 'twill never do! He said ye were tae see him soon as ye retairned!"

Merewyn scowled and heaved a sigh of resignation. "I suppose I ought to get it over with," she murmured to herself. "Thank you, Morag."

As she crossed the stone floor of the entrance hall, her slippered feet making no sound, she lifted her small chin and tried to tell herself that everything was well. Though Alexander was a harsh administrator he was never given to punishing her despite the enormity of some of her transgressions, save on those two occasions when he had taken the whip to her. Still, she thought to herself as she knocked somewhat timidly on the closed study door, it wasn't the punishment she feared, it was more the feeling of dread that overwhelmed her when she considered how much she might have damaged Cairnlach's chances of reconciliation with Edward Villiers.

Alexander was sitting at his desk attired in his traveling clothes, a leather haversack of folders and documents spread out before him. To Merewyn's surprise he looked up and smiled at her kindly when she entered, his brown eyes twinkling, seeming not the least bit angry.

"Well, here you are at last. Where've you been?"

"Down at the river," Merewyn replied in a subdued voice. "The salmon are here."

"Ah. And how does it look this year?"

"John thinks there may be more than last year," Merewyn replied warily, wondering at his apparent good humor.

"Excellent." He leaned back in his chair and stared thoughtfully out the window while she waited impatiently, dreading what was coming yet wishing he'd hurry and mete it out so that 'twould be over with quickly.

"I guess we'll have to send the herds up," he said after a moment, his brown eyes narrowed with concentrating. Merewyn had no doubt that he was seeing before him not the scenic beauty of the hills beyond the windowpanes, but his ledger books and the figures concerning his summer herds. "After all, we won't be having anymore snowfall, will we?"

A frown knit Merewyn's fine brows together. Unable to bear this amiable small talk any longer, she decided to bring up the subject herself. "Did you see Lord Montague in Inverlochy?" she asked hesitantly, hopping nervously from one small foot to another, hands clasped behind her back like a child awaiting its punishment. "Did he tell you where he's been all this time?"

"I saw him," Alex replied, recalling himself to the present, "and he was very prompt in agreeing to my suggestion that we should meet. We had a long and interesting talk and worked out some arrangements I'd like to discuss with you. I went over them briefly with Malcolm before he went up to the byres with Norman, but he's in total agreement with me."

"I saw him up there a few minutes ago," Merewyn informed him.

Alexander's brown eyes regarded her sharply. "He didn't tell you anything, did he?"

She shook her head in bewilderment. "What is it, Alex? Is the waterway—"

"Opened again, but that's not what I wanted to see you about."

Merewyn hung her head, suddenly deeply ashamed of herself, forgetting how much she had longed to hear those words. "I'm sorry, Alex," she whispered. "I was thinking only of Cairnlach. I didn't mean to do any harm. I shouldn't have gone, I know, but—"

"What in blazes?" he demanded in astonishment. "You're blathering like an idiot!"

"But Alex, I want to explain why I did it!"

"Whist! I don't know what it is you're talking about and I don't care. Listen to me, Merewyn. While I was in Inverlochy, I struck up a deal with Lord Montague that will end once and for all the conflicts between Cairnlach and Montague. You see—"

"You didn't sell out to him!" Merewyn wailed in sudden panic.

To her amazement she saw that Alexander was laughing at her, for all practical purposes a gay and carefree young man without the weight of beleaguered mills upon his shoulders. What on earth was the matter with him?

"Calm down," he told her lightly when he could speak. "I'd never do such a thing and you're daft to

suggest it. No, we've worked out another plan, something entirely different, and one that I'm certain you'll
approve of. You see, it has to do with Edward Villiers
himself."

"I don't want to hear anything about him," Merewyn
objected hurriedly, hoping to keep the conversation
away from her transgressions as long as possible. She
didn't dare hope that Alex knew nothing of her visit to
Montague, but why, then, didn't he appear angry with
her? What in the name of God was going on?

Alexander heaved a long-suffering sigh and regarded
her with feigned impatience. "Very well," he warned,
"but you're going to pay for your haste. The best news
will have to wait until last. First off, let me tell you the
terms of the new agreement. Because Lord Montague
knows so little about sheep husbandry and because his
forte lies in business, I've agreed to turn over control of
the mills to him entirely in exchange for the grazing
rights to all of his lands and total possession of his
herds. That means that Cairnlach will do the actual
farming, to wit, the production of the wool, and the
Marquis will manage the mills."

Merewyn's hands flew to her hot cheeks as she stared
at her brother aghast. "You've approved of this mad
scheme?" she whispered at last, the implications horri-
fying her.

Alexander's expression grew sober, seeing how much
his news had upset her. "Merewyn, you don't understand. It isn't as terrible as it sounds. I should have explained to you right away, but you wouldn't listen. Lord
Montague isn't the same—"

"Aye, I do understand!" she shouted tearfully.
"You're sacrificing everything we own for the one
foolish chance that this will make peace between us! Oh,
how he must have honeyed his words to make you agree
to this insanity!" Her voice broke and she couldn't go
on.

Alexander's tone grew annoyed. "Merewyn, will you please let me explain! Edward Villiers is—"

"I don't care!" she cried, beside herself with grief at his betrayal, feeling for the first time in her life that she hated him. "Oh, Alex, how could you! How could you!"

She turned and fled from the room, ignoring him as he called after her, wanting to hear no more about his insane plan. There was only one thing to do, she decided frantically as she fled up the winding staircase to her room. She'd confront Edward Villiers face to face as she should have done the first time, and demand that he keep out of Cairnlach's affairs once and for all. 'Twould have to be up to her to do it, she decided, for she seemed to be the only sane one left in the family! Alexander's voice was still calling to her from below, but she paid no heed, slipping quickly into her room to gather her belongings before he could come after her. She was afraid of what she'd say to him if she saw him again.

A hazy sunrise heralded the beginning of another day in the crowded city of Glasgow. Its burgeoning population had been increasing steadily since the Treaty of Unity between England and Scotland had opened up trade between both countries. A brisk tobacco business with the colonies and an increasing output of linen was rapidly making Glasgow one of the largest export cities in Great Britain. It was an old and, to some, an unattractive city, with narrow, tiwsting streets and blackened buildings. Redcoated tobacco lords, lowly laymen, and bitterly poor hard-drinking workers mingled daily on the crowded cobbled streets, a curious assortment of individuals as diverse as Glasgow itself.

Here, too, were located not far from the banks of the River Clyde Cairnlach's mills and offices. Several years ago engineers had begun widening the Clyde, making it deeper to enable larger cargo ships to sail directly from Glasgow to the Atlantic, and Alexander had already added two brigantines to Cairnlach's small merchant fleet.

Merewyn MacAilis, stepping down off the stagecoach before a seedy-looking inn, the courtyard teeming with workers in rough homespun clothing and merchants in flowing capes and spangled shoes, could not exactly remember how to get to the mills, for she had been there only twice before in her life. She stood in the center of the chaos in the inn yard clutching her small valise in one hand, gazing about her with a lost expression on her small face, her gown of dark russet velvet travel stained and hopelessly wrinkled. She was hungry and tired, dark circles staining the smooth skin beneath her tilted blue eyes, and her small nose sniffed longingly at the smell of roasting meat that came from the noisy depths of the inn before her.

Hungry as she was, she had no intentions of going inside. 'Twas far too crowded and doubtless filled with all sorts of unsavory characters, the stagecoach obviously having deposited her in the least fashionable part of town. She sighed as she stared about her at the tall brick buildings visible through the sooty air. The Cairnlach mills were her present goal, and only after she'd seen the Marquis would she seek out a more pleasant place to eat and rest.

He'd not elude her this time, Merewyn told herself fiercely, if only to bolster her own flagging morale. Wait and see if she wouldn't give him the proper set-to he'd been deserving all these years!

"Pardon me, miss, are you looking for someone in particular?"

She shrank from the unexpected voice, then relaxed as she found herself confronted by a middle-aged man dressed in a fashionable coat and breeches, his expression kind. "No one, actually," she confessed, gazing up at him with a timid smile. "I'm trying to find the Cairnlach mills."

Curiosity registered on the sharp features, but the slightly overweight gentleman was too polite to ask questions. " 'Tisn't far from here," he told the young girl with the untidy golden hair. "All the way down this street," he added, gesturing with a gloved hand, "then left to the water. Are you meaning to walk?"

Merewyn nodded and he eyed her doubtfully. " 'Tis no richt good neighborhood for the likes of you, miss."

"I'll be fine," she assured him, thanked him politely, and slipped away before he could respond. Hurrying down the sidewalk she was mindful of the stinking puddles in the gutter and alert for other possible dangers, especially from the windows of the tall stone buildings above, whose inhabitants were known to dump their refuse down on the streets, unmindful of the pedestrians below.

To her relief no one spoke to her at all, the people hurrying past intent mainly upon the coming day's work. The air was chilly and the vast majority of them moved down the street with downcast eyes, collars turned up against the dampness.

Merewyn walked quickly along the described route, and as she turned the corner she suddenly saw the tall brick buildings belonging to the mills, which she recognized from her earlier visits. The smell from the river was stronger here and she pulled her cloak more tightly about her slim body, burying her nose in the soft fur that trimmed the collar.

The big wrought iron gates were closed and locked and she put down her valise and shook them in a vain attempt to force them open. The yard beyond was empty and the low stone building that held the main office was dark, the shutters closed and tightly secured. Merewyn rattled again at the gates, hoping the noise would attract someone, and then, growing impatient, began to shout. Not long afterwards one of the doors to the office building opened and a feeble light appeared on the stoop.

Seconds later a short, balding man in a dark blue frock coat and ill-fitting trousers was hurrying towards her.

"Here, now, stop that, I say!"

He came to a halt before her, peering myopically through the bars and Merewyn found herself thinking irritably that Alexander had picked himself a fine watchman indeed, for the man was most assuredly half-blind.

"Wha 'ee be wantin'?" he demanded querulously, his voice high pitched and unfriendly.

"I've come to see the Marquis of Montague," Merewyn replied politely. "My name is Merewyn MacAilis."

"Wha? MacAilis?" He peered closer, his long nose thrust between the cold metal bars.

"Alexander MacAilis is my brother. Please open the gate. I'd like to see the Marquis."

"I canna do that," he replied. "Tain't no ane here."

Merewyn began to grow annoyed. It was chilly, she was shivering and bone tired, and she disliked talking to this queer old man through a locked gate. "Please let me in," she repeated less warmly than before. "I'll wait for him in the office."

He shook his hairless head apologetically. "I canna, miss. I canna let unauthorized persons in."

"I told you I am Alexander's sister!"

He squinted at her keenly. "Aye, there be a resemblance frae wha I can see wi' me weak een, but I canna take your word on't, miss."

"Why, how dare you, you doddard!" Merewyn burst out, her temper flaring. "I'm tired and I want to come in!"

The old watchman retreated to a safe distance at her words, half expecting her to fly at him in her rage. "I canna, miss," he repeated stubbornly. " 'Tis against the rules."

Merewyn forced herself to remain calm although she would have liked nothing better than to shake the little man until his few remaining teeth rattled in his empty head. "Very well," she said loftily, "will you please tell me when the Marquis is expected? I'll come back later."

"He willna be comin' back, miss," the watchman informed her reluctantly, certain that his words would bring on another fit of bad temper. "He's gang awa."

But Merewyn's temper had vanished as quickly as it had come and she stared at him in dismay, grasping at the metal bars for support. "Gone away?" she echoed. "But—but they told me in Inverlochy he'd gone to Glasgow!"

"Aye, he was here until yestreen. But the noo he be gang an' willna retairn."

"Did he go back home?" Merewyn's voice was suddenly very thin and the old man felt sympathy replacing his fear. She stood forlornly before the gate with her hands hanging at her sides and her head bowed, no longer proudly held as a moment before, and from what his misty vision could make out she seemed bonnie indeed and very young.

"I heard tell he was off tae London," he said, hating to disappoint her.

Merewyn was silent for so long that he began to worry. "Miss?"

She made no reply, for she hadn't even heard him. She was staring down at the wet pavement below her shoes, wondering miserably what she should do. How could she go home when she was ashamed to face Alexander, ashamed at having run off and causing him such terrible worry? Her plans had, as usual, been foolishly executed, and had come to naught, and she had succeeded only in bringing undeserved worry to her brothers. She should have known Lord Montague would elude her! Why, oh, why did she always have to act on such mad impulses and rush things through without thinking them over?

"Miss? Miss!"

She heard his quivering voice at last and looked up at

him, her blue eyes filled with resignation. "Aye?"

"Would 'ee care tae wait inside? Mr. Bancroft should be comin' in an hour or twa. I think I can bend the rules this once, especially if 'ee really be Master MacAilis' sister." He laughed nervously. "I wouldna want tae put that gentleman i' a fash, nay, nay!"

Merewyn shook her head and smiled at him thinly. "Thank you, no. I believe I'll find an inn and take the next coach home."

"But I dinna think—miss!" he called, for she had picked up her valise and was walking away. "Will 'ee no come in and wait?"

"I'm going home," she repeated, and he watched nervously as she disappeared down the narrow street, thin shoulders hunched against the rising wind.

"I do wonder if she really was the MacAilises' sister?" the watchman mumbled to himself as he walked reluctantly across the yard towards the warmth of his cubbyhole.

Merewyn's shoes echoed hollowly as she hurried down the empty street, praying there was still time to procure passage homeward on the northbound stage, for she saw now what a total fool she had been. If only her stupidity had been obvious sooner, before she'd even left for Inverlochy!

"Oh, Alex, I'm so sorry," she whispered, tears welling in her eyes. She knew then how tired she really was, for she rarely cried at silly things like the mere image of her brother's rough-hewn face before her eyes, but she suddenly realized that she missed both him and Malcolm terribly. What a fool she'd been, what a stupid, contemptible idiot! Why hadn't she waited for her anger to cool, then gone downstairs and talked to Alexander reasonably? After all, they'd never been confronted in the past by a problem too great for them to solve through calm discussion, and he had made every effort to be reasonable with her. She just hadn't listened!

'Twas all her fault, Merewyn told herself miserably. She deserved to be thrashed for running away and causing her brothers so much worry. Perhaps that horrible giant at Castle Montague had been right in saying that she was uncivilized and foul-tempered!

"Oh!"

"Here, now, what's the meaning of this?"

Taking no notice of her surroundings, her eyes downcast to the stones beneath her feet, Merewyn had barreled directly into the chest of a tall, thin man who had abruptly rounded the corner and stepped in front of her. The accident was not entirely her fault; he had been carrying his long nose far too arrogantly in the air and hadn't managed to see her in time. Now his bony fingers with their heavy gold rings were digging into her arms and Merewyn's head snapped back as he shook her irritably, enabling him to look fully into her face.

Her startling beauty hit him with considerable impact —delicately molded cheeks flushed with embarrassment; dark lashes framing the indigo depths of her wide, tilted eyes; her soft lips parted to reveal small, even white teeth. His rough handling had pushed her bonnet askew and in the pale sunlight the exposed golden curls radiated a light of their own, one soft tendril clinging to the smooth line of her jaw before she reached up and brushed it away.

"Pray, forgive me, sir," she murmured, her gentle tone with its soft Highland burr clearly befitting her delicate beauty. "I wasn't watching where I was going."

"Nonsense! 'Twas entirely my fault!"

She looked up, surprised by this sudden change in him. He was about Malcolm's age, she saw, a cocksure young gentleman with heavy black brows and a long, curling mustache. His clothes were very expensive, but Merewyn began to wonder if perhaps he might not be a member of the emerging middle class Alexander had told her about, too rich to be peasants but certainly not individuals of title and blood, their place in society earned through wealth alone.

He couldn't be born to the Quality, Merewyn thought to herself, warned by the roughness of his speech that even his careful enunciation could not hide, and by a callousness in his countenance that made her wonder what he was like when he didn't have such finely tailored clothes to attest to his success. His eyes were brown, like her brothers', but they were small and calculating, and she suddently didn't care at all for the gleam in them.

"Excuse me again," she murmured, and tried to move past him only to have him step quickly to the right, effectively blocking her path, and as she tried to pass him in the other direction he countered again. Merewyn looked up at him with annoyance, and he decided at once that she was far more beautiful than he'd originally thought, now that some spirit was reflected in her flashing eyes.

"Will you let me pass, sir?" she asked frostily.

A slow smile spread across the thin lips. "I've no intention of hindering you, miss."

"Good day, then," she replied and would have brushed by him except that he moved again to block her path, standing with his long, thin legs spread apart, his rings flashing as he planted his hands firmly on his narrow hips and stood smiling down at her with a somewhat less pleasant smile.

Merewyn was too angry to know fear. How dare this pompous oaf with his put-on airs detain her when she was in such a hurry to get back to the inn? What stupid game was he playing? "If you please," she said through clenched teeth, determined to remain civil.

"Oh, aye, I please," he replied indulgently, grinning at her as his glinting eyes began to rove slowly over her slim form, the rounded curve of her breasts plainly visible beneath the folds of her cloak.

Merewyn's anger faded into apprehension. She didn't

like the way he was staring at her as though he were mentally undressing her, and she tightened her hold on her valise, intent on making an unexpected dash past him. He outguessed her move, however, and as she leaped forward she felt him grab her, one sinuous arm sliding about her small waist, the other, incredibly, moving past her shoulders, his hand forcing its way between her cloak to the heavy breasts that he could feel through the smooth material of her bodice.

He pushed her back against the wet bricks of the building behind her, his moist lips coming down on hers, and Merewyn could feel the heat from his loins as he pressed his body against hers, his fingers digging cruelly into her flesh. She struggled to push him away but he was far stronger than she suspected, and she moaned in terror as his tongue snaked between her aching lips and into her mouth. This couldn't be happening to her! One didn't simply get attacked in broad daylight in the middle of the street, especially not in crowded Glasgow!

By now his hand had slid down the neckline of her gown and Merewyn gasped as she felt his cold touch on her bare breast. His mouth continued to cover hers as his roving fingers began to caress the soft nipples that had never been violated by any man, and she suddenly felt anger and disgust exploding like a tempest within her.

With unbelievable strength she managed to twist away from him, freeing one of her arms as she did so, and a tiny balled fist flew full force into the lust-contorted features. He yelped with pain and grabbed her shoulders, jerking her backwards so that her head struck the brick wall behind her. The pain fanned her fury and she kicked out at him while screaming at the top of her lungs for help.

"Shut up, you goddamned whore!" He was shaking her frantically, causing her head to snap back and forth on her slender neck while she struck at him with her fists, unaware that she was still screaming and that spectators had gathered from all directions although none of them cared to lend their assistance.

"Here now, here now, stop it!"

A uniformed constable with a long, bony face appeared on the scene and the milling crowd parted so that he could make his way to the struggling couple locked in combat on the walk, forcing them briskly apart while repeating loudly that they were to halt instantly with their unruliness. Merewyn, her head spinning, her lips bruised by her assailant's kisses, looked up with a dazed expression in her dark blue eyes as the constable's uniform swam before her.

"Oh, thank God you've come," she whispered as she recognized what he was.

"Officer, arrest this woman at once!" The ringing command came from the disheveled, panting man before her and was accompanied by a shakily pointed index finger at Merewyn's slender, unsteadily swaying figure pressed against the brick wall. "She tried to entice me, she did, and when I refused to accept the little slut's offer she attacked me and tried to steal my jewelry!" He held up his hands to confirm his story, the rings flashing on his bony fingers, the cool, controlled outrage in his impassive face lending credence to his accusation.

"I don't think—" the constable began in confusion, but was interrupted by the irate gentleman who raised a clenched fist threateningly in Merewyn's direction.

"My father happens to be John Rawlings, sir! What do you suppose he'll say when he learns I've been accosted by a disgusting little prostitute here in your jurisdiction?"

The constable's long face grew even longer and he licked nervously at his lips. "Aye, you're right, Master William. I'm sorry, I didna recognize ye. 'Tis an unfortunate situation, but then, the streets be teemin' with 'em." He stared down at Merewyn's expressionless face with growing antagonism. "Guess it wouldna hurt to take her in."

William Rawlings dusted off his coat with mild unconcern. "Good. I suggest you do so. What is your name, sir?"

"Mine?" The constable looked startled. "R-Randolph Widgett, sir."

The thin lips curled into a smile. "Well, Officer Widgett, I'll be sure to mention to my father that you handled the situation promptly and courteously."

Officer Widgett beamed. "Why, thank ye right kindly, sir!" He watched admiringly as William Rawlings turned and vanished into the respectfully parted crowd, then made a great show of taking Merewyn's arm, saying gruffly, "Ye'll come with me, then."

"I—" she began, but the world was whirling dizzily about her. She stumbled as blackness descended and would have fallen if the constable hadn't reached out and caught her in time.

"Ye'll have tae carry 'er all the way, Randy!" came a heckling voice from the watching throng. "Mind ye dinna drop 'er i' the gutter!"

"Can 'ee manage?" another voice guffawed.

"Aye, sure 'ee can," someone else laughed. "She's a wee tyke, ain't she? Like tae ride 'er meself if she weren't fainted dead away!"

"Gae on," snorted the first heckler contemptuously. "She be much tae bonnie fer the likes o' ye, Angus Alpin! Ye'd not hae the money she'd want fer takin' on yer filthy carcass!"

The constable ignored them, his bearing dignified as he lifted Merewyn into his arms though he loathed above everything the women and lasses who sold themselves on the Glasgow streets. 'Twas hard to believe they started this young, the wee thing in his arms barely weighing anything at all. She reminded him a mite of his daughter Janet, but as the thought entered his head he

made a disgusted sound deep in his throat. Janet was a
gentle, bonnie lass loved by all who knew her and this
. . . this was naught but a God-cursed prostitute, young
though she may be, and God alone kenned how many
men she had lain with before!

When Merewyn finally awoke it was to a world of
darkness, her eyelids fluttering open unexpectedly to
find herself lying on a wet stone floor with the dank,
fetid smell of filthy air assailing her nostrils. Her head
was aching miserably, and when she reached up to touch
it she found a large, tender lump at the base of her skull.
How had it gotten there? she asked herself in confusion.
She could remember only a few things like the bumpy
coach ride to town and the man behind the iron gate at
Alexander's mill.

Had she gone in to see the Marquis? she asked herself.
'Twould seem she could remember instead a dark-haired
stranger with a mustache who had—had done what?
He'd attacked her, hadn't he, and struck her head
against the brick wall when she'd tried to fight back!

Merewyn sat up as her memory slowly returned,
clutching her shaking hands to her breast. He'd called
her a whore, she remembered now, and had told the
constable who had come to her aid that she had proposi-
tioned him and tried to rob him.

"Dear God," she whispered and rose uncertainly to
her feet to look around her. The dim light of a flickering
torch cast eerie patterns on the slime-covered walls that
surrounded her, and as she turned to look out into the
narrow corridor she found herself facing a row of similar walls with square-cut openings lined with bars and
heavily braced wooden doors. She could hear murmuring, muffled laughter and subdued snoring going on
around her and realized that she must be surrounded by
a great number of people despite the fact that she could
see no one.

Where in the name of God was she? Merewyn moved

forward to touch the heavy, rusted bars that covered the opening in the wall before her, and as her eyes grew more accustomed and she could make out the dimensions of the room in which she stood, the horrible realization came at last.

"They've thrown me in gaol!" she whispered, her words sounding strange to her own ears.

"So ye be awake at last, dearie!"

She recoiled from the thick, slurred voice that floated to her from a corner of the cell, not having suspected that she wasn't alone. There was a moment of silence while the quiet noises about her from the other prisoners continued. Closer at hand Merewyn could hear water dripping steadily onto the stones at her feet and then the ragged breathing of her cell mate.

"I ast if yer was awake." The voice was no less slurred but sounded decidedly less friendly.

"Aye," Merewyn replied cautiously. "Who are you? Where are you?"

"Over here."

A movement in one corner drew her eyes to a huge bulk that, as her eyes grew accustomed to the weak light, turned out to be a fat woman with enormous breasts and blowsy brown hair, her bulbous nose reddened with drink. Bleary eyes studied her with lively interest as she smiled and revealed a great number of gaps between her yellowed teeth.

"C'mere, me girl."

Merewyn moved forward reluctantly and an unsteady hand reached out and pulled her down to the floor. "Dinna worry about gettin' wet," the thick voice advised when Merewyn resisted. "Yer already soaked enough."

'Twas true, Merewyn decided as she collapsed onto the floor. While she was unconscious they must have laid her right down into the water, for her gown felt damp and uncomfortable. She was tired and felt ill, but

was grateful for the numbness that still enveloped her—
otherwise she'd go mad with the realization of where she
actually was.

"There's been a mistake," she told her companion,
the words spilling from her lips as her mind began to
clear. "I've been falsely accused of—of—well, 'tis no
real matter. I must speak to the guard or someone, whoever is in charge! They've got to let me out!"

The fat woman chuckled and Merewyn wrinkled her
nose at the pungent smell of gin that wafted to her on
the musty air. "Ain't no use in that! No ane'd believe
ye!" She snorted derisively. "Way some of ye talk ye'd
think ye've never committed a sin i' yer lives!"

"But I never have done anything wrong before!"
Merewyn persisted, straining to see her companion's
face in the gloom. "They've no reason to keep me here!"

The fat woman's voice was suddenly weary. "Och, gae
on, dearie! 'Tis a grand performance, I'll grant ye that,
but wasted on the likes o' me. Save it for the magistrate." She belched ruminatively, then added admiringly, "Still, ye sound believable wi' that soft-bred voice of
yers. Maun attract the customers, I'm thinkin'."

The white, bloated mass of flesh before her seemed to
undulate as the world spun dizzily before Merewyn's
eyes. Had she gone mad? Was this Bedlam instead of
some stinking prison in Glasgow? This sort of thing
didn't happen to decent people! It couldn't!

"When do you think the magistrate will see me?" Her
voice sounded thin and unreal to her own ears.

"I dinna ken. No ane does. Ye'll have tae wait until he
gets time tae see ye."

"You sound as though you've been here a while,"
Merewyn commented, studying the older woman with
wide eyes.

She waved a pudgy hand noncommittally. "A lot o'
short whiles, too, dearie. Catch me a lot, they do."

"But what do you do that's so wrong?" Merewyn

asked. Squatting in the damp, gloomy confines of her cell she couldn't comprehend how anyone could possibly commit a crime that they knew might cause them to be thrown into gaol!

A rough cackle startled her. "I canna believe ye be that innocent, lass, or ye'd no be here!" A thick finger poked Merewyn in the ribs. "Skinny, ain't ye? Do ye get enough men wi' them bones? But, aye, ye be bonnie enough, I sawd that when they brung ye in. Caught me the same way they did ye, but me, I ain't got the wits I used to. Guess I'm at the bottle too much." She cackled again and wiped her thick lips with the back of her hand. "Needs it, though, I do."

Merewyn stared down at the fat woman in horror. This bloated, drunken mess was a prostitute? How could anyone possibly mistake herself for someone of that ilk? "I-I'm not what you think I am," she began, but the fat woman interrupted.

"I ain't in no mood to be listenin' to yer confessions, dearie. Ye'll have yer chance with the magistrate."

"But you said you didn't know when he'd see me!" Merewyn cried, her despair turning slowly to anger. She'd set that man straight when she saw him, she would, and when Alexander learned she'd been falsely accused of selling herself—she sobbed a little, unable to keep her emotions in check as she thought of her predicament.

And as for that disgusting man Rawlings, who had been the instrument of her arrest, she'd see to it that he paid, paid horribly for putting her in this black and stinking dungeon!

She felt the fat woman's thick hand pat her arm and heard a more kindly voice say, "There, there, dearie, dinna greet. 'Tis yer first time, I can see, but dinna yer worry. The magistrate has a soft heart for bonnie faces."

"But when will he see me?" Merewyn repeated pathetically, self-pity engulfing her and snuffing out her anger. She was cold and tired and so very hungry!

"I dinna ken," the fat woman replied unconcernedly. "Name's Maggie. What be yers?"

"Merewyn." She rubbed her tear-filled eyes with the back of her hand. "Merewyn MacAilis." As soon as she uttered her name she could have groaned at her stupidity, ashamed to tell this fat prostitute her real identity. But Maggie said nothing at all, and after a few minutes her deep, rhythmic snoring echoed within the damp stone walls of the cell.

Merewyn moved as far away from her as possible, huddling in one corner with her arms about her knees, her head leaning against the hard stones, and closed her eyes. She was exhausted but sleep refused to come. She could think only of her brothers and how horrified they'd be if they knew where she was. How in God's name was she going to get out of here?

The creaking of a door somewhere down the passage awakened her from a fitful doze some time later, and she jumped up, ignoring the pain in her cramped limbs and the unpleasant tingling sensation as blood returned to her frozen feet. Straining her eyes she could make out two men coming down the poorly lit aisle, one of them in a proper wig and a fur-lined cloak slung over his narrow shoulders. The other was short and curly headed and carried a great ring of jingling keys tied to his belt. Merewyn noticed that both men were armed.

None of the other prisoners seemed to be aware of them or even bothered to look up at their passage, and in the flickering lantern light Merewyn could at last see the faces of her fellow inmates. They were all women, many of them grotesquely ugly and even more overweight than Maggie, others far younger and prettier; but all of them were ill-kempt and poorly clothed, some of them with fever spots burning in their hollow cheeks, others with hideous pox scars on their disinterested faces.

As the two men hurried past her cell, Merewyn held out her hands imploringly, but they brushed by her without sparing her even a glance.

"Please, sir, help me!" she called after them.

"Shut up, will ye?" came a shrill voice from one of the cells further down the aisle.

Startled by this hostile command, Merewyn fell silent although she continued to lean on the bars, peering with luminous eyes at the two men who had paused before one of the doors, the taller one staring off into space while the guard unlocked it. His expression, Merewyn noticed, was resigned, as though he was accustomed to coming here often.

A moment later the guard emerged from the cell with a middle-aged woman pinioned at his side. She was well dressed as far as Merewyn could tell, her gown made of relatively expensive material, and skillfully embroidered although the full skirts were stained with dark blotches that appeared to be wine. There were bags under her eyes and her face was streaked with dirt and curiously mottled, but she must have been beautiful once.

"I kenned ye'd come for me, darlin'," she breathed at the tall man, her moist lips parted, her red hair clinging to her sallow face, smiling up at him drunkenly.

"Hey, Master Jim, 'ee shoulda picked yersel' a wife that doesna drink!" came a cackling voice from somewhere in the darkness.

The tall man said nothing, his face expressionless. Gripping the drunken woman's arm, he propelled her forward.

"Ouch, yer hurtin' me!" she accused, trying to wrench free. "Is that any way tae treat yer ain true love?"

Merewyn was so astonished at the scene going on before her, never having suspected that people such as this existed, that she forgot her resolve to appeal to them for help. She watched silently as they hurried past her cell, and her wide blue eyes briefly met the grimly narrowed

ones of the cloaked gentleman. For a moment their
glances held, and his stony expression changed slowly to
surprise at seeing such a beautiful girl before him; then
he turned his head abruptly and continued on without a
word, the redheaded woman firmly in tow.

"Wait!" Merewyn cried after him, suddenly remembering her own predicament. Her hands shot from between the bars in a vain attempt to catch at his sleeve,
but her efforts were rewarded only with a ringing blow
across her upturned, beseeching palms by the following
guard. Merewyn had not seen the short wooden stick he
carried until it cracked against her soft flesh and she
cried out and collapsed on the floor, nursing her burning
hands as tears coursed down her cheeks.

"That'll teach 'ee!" came a triumphant voice from
across the aisle.

"Och, leave the lass be!" Maggie shouted irritably
into the darkness.

"The day I take orders frae 'ee, Maggie McShane, be
the day 'ee be crowned Queen of England!"

Raucous laughter and snide comments followed this
remark, but Maggie ignored them all. "Rotten bitches,"
she muttered beneath her breath to Merewyn who was
still huddled in the corner. "Dinna pay them no mind!"

Silence fell quickly, the heckling women across the
aisle already having lost interest in trading insults with
Merewyn's cell mate, and no one disturbed the gloomy
confines again until late that evening, not even when a
squabble broke out between the two women in the cell
directly opposite Merewyn's.

The fight began with hostile threats and howled oaths,
and Maggie, who had been awakened by the first shout,
advised Merewyn to ignore the shrieking women as the
other prisoners were doing. Merewyn couldn't help but
be horrified by their loud blows and abuses, unable to
comprehend the fact that two women could behave so
violently toward one another. Men were supposed to

fight, not women, and she'd seen some of the brawniest in the village have a go at each other outside the pub on occasion, but never had she seen such a hate-filled display of punching, biting, and scratching between members of her own sex.

"They'll stop soon's they be tired," Maggie remarked when Merewyn made a disgusted comment and seated herself beside the fat woman on the floor.

"What are they fighting about?"

Maggie shrugged her heavy shoulders. "Who kens? I'm believin' they've forgotten, too. Always at each other, Isabelle and Moll. They be sisters, ye ken."

"They're sisters?" Merewyn echoed in amazement, turning to look at the brawling young women as they continued to assault each other. The older one, a hefty brunette with a livid birthmark on her left cheek, had succeeded in tearing the bodice of the other one's thin gown, exposing flat, unattractive breasts while her sister, ignoring her revealed condition, pummeled at the older one with her fists.

"I'd never, ever treat my sister that way if I had one," Merewyn remarked emphatically, deliberately turning away.

"Och, bairns, they be meant to fight," Maggie told her with great wisdom. " 'Twas all Coll an' me ever did when I was hame."

Merewyn was silent. She'd never in her life laid a hand on her brothers or they on her, at least not out of anger. Oh, aye, the three of them had argued many times, lost their tempers, flared at each other, but any confrontations had always ended with apologies and were resolved and quickly forgotten.

Merewyn stifled a choked sob, not wanting Maggie to hear, and laid her head in her arms. She wanted nothing more at the moment than to be home with Alex and Malcolm, to tell them how much she loved them and how sorry she was to have caused them so much worry.

Hot tears coursed down her grimy cheeks and she cried silently, hunger gnawing at her as much as the misery that engulfed her.

Supper was served by two weary guards, one of them carrying a blackened pot from which he ladled what appeared to be a pasty stew into small bowls with a bent spoon, the other one standing behind him and keeping a watchful eye on the women. Maggie, irritable now that the effects of the alcohol were wearing off, pushed her heavily jowled face against the bars and watched with parted lips and an intimidating scowl as her portion was doled out.

"Dinna worry, Maggie, me love," laughed the guard with the soup, the same one who had slapped Merewyn's hands earlier, "ye'll be gettin' all ye need. 'Twill take the gin oot o' yer system."

Maggie's reply was a guttural growl and the guard laughed again. "And, me fine girl, dinna ye be stealin' the wee lass's either," he admonished, holding out a bowl for Merewyn.

As she came forward quickly to accept it, she reached out and gripped his sleeve with desperately clutching fingers, tugging at it appealingly. "Please, sir, you've no right to keep me here!"

"Hey, leave go me coat!" he cried and tried to pull himself free without spilling the contents of his pot.

Merewyn's hold tightened. "You don't understand! My brother is Alexander MacAilis, laird of Cairnlach Castle!"

The older guard started, his eyes narrowing speculatively. "Not the MacAilis who makes wool?"

Merewyn's heart gave a joyful leap. "Aye! Aye! The same!"

"Sure, an' I'm the Prince of Wales," retorted the smaller guard, freeing himself with a jerk from the slender fingers that still clutched at his coat sleeve.

Merewyn's eyes were fastened on the older guard.

"Please believe me," she implored, certain that she could reason with him if she only had enough time!

"Gae on, ye filthy slut," the smaller one said.

The taller one moved closer to the bars. "No, wait a minute, Andy." He could clearly see the rising hope within Merewyn's indigo eyes. Her heart-shaped face was flushed and her soft lips were parted, scarcely daring to breathe, afraid he'd turn away again. "What's your name, lass?"

"Merewyn MacAilis." Her voice sounded thin and far away to her own ears and she fought to still the dizzying race of her heart. "M-my brother is Alexander MacAilis," she repeated, her soft lips trembling slightly as she stared up into the curious eyes of the guard, desperate to make him understand. "I was attacked on the street by a man who—who said I was trying to steal his rings. 'Tis simply not true!"

"Quit listenin' to that drivel!" Andy called out impatiently. He had moved further down the line with his soup pot, but when he saw that his companion was listening with obvious interest to the young prisoner's tale, he hurried back and lifted his balled fist as though intending to strike her.

"I said shut up, damn you!" he shouted at her.

Merewyn shrank back with a fearful exclamation.

"C'mon, Davie, dinna listen to her," Andy repeated irritably. "She's doin' a number on ye, she is. After ye've been here a while ye'll ken what I mean. Aye, she be bonnie enough for a stinkin' whore, but do ye ken wham she tried to rob! Squire John Rawlings's son, an' ye ken damned well he'd not lie about summat like that!"

Merewyn's blue eyes glittered feverishly and she could have wept when she saw the expression in the taller guard's face change slowly from friendliness to hostility. "Aye, you're right, Andy," he said, turning his back on her.

"Oh, please wait!" Merewyn cried tearfully, rattling

despairingly at the bars.

"One more word out o' ye," Andy shot back hatefully, "an' I'll beat the blazes out o' ye!"

Merewyn withdrew, sobbing, while both guards
moved off to feed the rest of the women who were complaining loudly about the delay in being served. She
watched them solemnly, tears coursing down her cheeks,
until they had completed their task. The taller one
turned towards her as he exited through the doorway
and Merewyn thought she detected an inkling of sympathy in his eyes.

"You'll have a turn with the magistrate in the
mornin', lass," he told her kindly.

The heavy door clanged shut, the key turned in the
lock, and Merewyn stood for a moment with her slim,
grimy form pressed against the bars, the bowl of stew in
one shaking hand, her thin shoulders hunched dejectedly. How could she possibly survive another night in this
nightmarish cell?

"Will ye be wantin' yer stew, dearie?" Maggie had
appeared at her side, her eyes gleaming hungrily when
she saw the untouched contents of Merewyn's bowl.
Merewyn stared down into the colorless liquid with its
unsavory lumps of gray meat and felt her stomach turn
over, her hunger vanishing abruptly.

"You can have it," she said wearily, extending the
bowl to Maggie, who took it eagerly and lifted it to her
lips.

Merewyn retreated into the corner, sickened by the
sounds the fat woman made while she ate, reminding her
of the hogs in the byre with their sucking, grunting, and
smacking. Tucking her feet under her skirts she buried
her hot face in her hands, the tears again dangerously
close. She made no movement or sound as Maggie finished eating and settled down nearby, wiping her greasy
lips with the back of her hand. Subdued whispers and
occasional coughs could be heard from the others in the

gloomy cavern, but the small cell that housed the
overweight, faded prostitute and the slender young girl
remained silent.

A great weariness gradually descended upon
Merewyn and her eyes grew heavy, but she found that
blessed sleep eluded her. She was shivering despite the
fact that she had wrapped her cloak tightly about her,
for it was wet and offered little warmth. She sat with her
head nodding, her golden hair damp and covered with
cobwebs, unable to find much needed rest.

Two rats soon emerged from their hiding places and
began fighting over the leftover contents of the stew
bowls, and Merewyn watched them for a time, too
weary and numb to feel the least bit of fear or revulsion.
At long last she closed her eyes and slept.

The jingling of keys and the groaning of the door as it
was opened awoke Merewyn hours later. Not a single
ray of sunlight filtered through the cracks along the
slime-covered walls and she had no idea what time it
was, blinking uncertainly as a lantern was thrust in her
face.

"Aye, that be the one."

She rose hesitantly to her feet and saw before her the
small guard named Andy who had been so unkind to her
yesterday, and another man, one whom she had never
seen before, his thin, unshaven face devoid of expression. She found herself recoiling, disliking the way
he was studying her intently, nodding his head to himself as though pleased by what he saw. His eyes met the
suspicious blue ones and he smiled suddenly.

"I am Edmund Unsworth, miss. I'm here to take you
to the magistrate."

She staggered a little and would have fallen had he not
put out his hand to catch her by the elbow. "Oh, thank
God," she breathed.

"You'll have to sign the release papers, first," Andy
had entered the cell behind Edmund Unsworth and was

fumbling about in his breast pocket, from which he withdrew a folded packet.

"Here, what's this about release papers?" Maggie demanded, sniffing like a hound as she pulled herself erect. "I never had to sign none before. Let me see 'em."

The little guard snatched them away from her eaching hand. "Ye canna even read, me love," he reminded her in a nasty voice. "Gae on wi' ye!"

Maggie retreated obediently to her corner, shaking her frizzy head of hair back and forth and muttering beneath her breath.

"What sort of papers are they?" Merewyn asked as they were held towards her, scarcely daring to hope that she was really on her way to see the magistrate.

"A mere formality," Mr. Unsworth assured her. "We keep records on every prisoner brought in here as to the day they were arrested, when they were released, the charges against them."

"Maggie's signed 'em before," Andy put in, casting a contemptuous look in the fat woman's direction. "She was just too fou to remember!"

"Yer a swine, Andy," she replied evenly, then squealed in pained surprise as his booted toe caught her square in one well-padded thigh.

"Shut up, you horse-faced bitch!"

"Please, give me the papers," Merewyn pleaded, anxious to put an end to their bickering and suddenly desperately eager to be out in the fresh air and sunlight.

The guard handed them over without ceremony and produced a pen, which she used to scratch her name with a shaky hand on the line Mr. Unsworth indicated. Then she extended them to him and he smiled graciously as he tucked them inside his coat.

"Shall we go?" he asked politely.

A tired but elated smile passed across Merewyn's soft lips and her blue eyes shone. "Aye," she said softly.

"Out with ye, then," Andy rasped, assuming an authoritative air, but as he reached out his hand to seize her, Merewyn slapped it away.

"I can walk myself," she told him icily, determined to see that he lost his job once the magistrate learned how badly he had treated her!

"I like that one's spirit," Edmund Unsworth said to no one in particular. Merewyn glanced at him curiously in the stronger light of the passageway. He was short and heavy set, she noticed, his arms powerful and well muscled. Long black hair was tied in a queue with a velvet ribbon, and a velvet cape hung from his thick shoulders.

Andy, his lips set in an angry line, prodded her from behind as she hesitated. "Move along there," he told her crisply. "No lagging!"

"Good luck, dearie!" came Maggie's cheerful voice from behind them, but Merewyn had no time to answer before she was ushered up a flight of worn stone steps and into an anteroom no larger than the cell she had just left behind.

A smoking candle stub burned on the rough-hewn table standing in the center of the room and cast eerie shadows on the cobwebbed ceiling. The air was thick and musty but Merewyn scarcely noticed, her heart singing with the realization that she was free at last.

"Am I to meet the magistrate here?" she asked Mr. Unsworth curiously as he followed her inside.

He smiled kindly into her upturned face. "No, my dear, we're going to meet him in his home."

A frown wrinkled her smooth brow. "Then why are we here?"

He smiled again and she noticed how white his teeth were against the unshaven darkness of his thin face. "May I remind you that you've just spent the night in gaol? If you want to make a good impression on the magistrate you'd better not see him looking the way you do." He coughed delicately. "If you'll forgive me for putting it so tactlessly."

Merewyn's hand came up unconsciously to touch the golden curls that were arranged in an untidy fashion and covered with dust, then stared at the grime on her up-turned palms. "I didn't know—" she stammered help-lessly.

"I thought you might like to wash and tidy yourself up a bit," Edmund Unsworth added as the door behind him opened. A sullen Andy entered slowly, carrying a kettle of steaming water and a washbowl, towel, a small bar of soap, and a comb.

Merewyn's blue eyes glowed as she looked up at Ed-mund Unsworth, comprehending at last the kindness he was bestowing upon her. "Oh, sir, I can't tell you what this means to me after the terrible way I've been treated here!" As she spoke she cast a venomous glance at the guard who withdrew without comment.

"Please take your time," Edmund Unsworth invited. He retreated to the doorway where he leaned against the jamb, watching as she lathered her face and hands and rinsed them with the hot water. Andy had laid the comb and a small, cracked mirror on the table and she un-pinned her hair and began to work out the snarls with practiced fingers, ignoring the short man behind her al-though normally she would have felt self-conscious about performing her toilette before a stranger.

At the moment she had no thoughts at all about pro-priety. She was determined to look her best when she went before the magistrate, certain that he would tend to believe her story more if she looked at least a little like a lady and not some filthy gutter child. The tangles were soon worked free and her long hair fell in shining strands below her waist, a vigorous combing having re-moved most of the dust. Merewyn plaited it quickly and then looked about for extra pins, realizing for the first time that she had lost her bonnet and valise during the struggle with William Rawlings the day before.

Had it been only yesterday? She felt as though she'd lived a thousand lifetimes in between, and she turned and gave Edmund Unsworth an apologetic smile. "I'm afraid I've lost my valise. There were clean clothes inside and extra pins for my hair."

Unsworth, who had been admiring the shining braid she had fashioned, was quick to assure her that, although she would have to fasten the heavy coil with what few pins she had left, she looked extremely presentable.

"But I still can't do anything about my gown," she lamented, staring down at the russet velvet, which was still slightly damp and clung to her slim frame beneath the stained and wrinkled cloak.

"I seriously doubt the magistrate will look down his nose at you," Edmund Unsworth assured her. "After all, you did spend the night in gaol. He'll take that into consideration. I wanted to give you the chance to wash the grime off your face and tidy your hair." He smiled at her encouragingly. "Besides, what you have to say is more important than how you look."

Merewyn returned his smile gratefully. "Thank you, Mr. Unsworth. You've eased my mind considerably."

"I'm relieved to hear it. Shall we go?"

They encountered no one at all as they left the anteroom and passed down the dingy corridor towards the main entrance except for Andy, who appeared from an alcove in time to show them out. Merewyn thought it rather odd that no other guards were about, but forgot her silent musings as she stepped out onto the street and saw that it was nighttime, the stars shining down through a hazy canopy of black upon the darkened buildings.

Lights burned in some of the windows that had been left unshuttered, and most of the doorways were crowded with the poor who huddled on the stoops for protection from the brisk north wind that was whipping

like ice across the cobblestones. Merewyn, who had expected it to be morning, was momentarily disoriented,
and as her steps faltered she felt Edmund Unsworth's
hand steady her.

"Miss MacAilis, are you unwell?"

" 'Tis evening," she murmured weakly, gazing about
her in confusion.

"Not evening," Edmund Unsworth corrected her.
" 'Tis almost three o'clock."

Her tilted blue eyes were black in the darkness as she
stared up at him, more bewildered than ever. "And
we're going to see the magistrate at this hour?"

Mr. Unsworth nodded amiably. "Sir Clive is expecting us. He read your arrest report during dinner and
something rang false to him about the circumstances
surrounding your incarceration. Rather than permit you
to spend another night in gaol, he ordered me to fetch
you at once. It took some time, I'm afraid, but I have
you now and, as I've said, Sir Clive is waiting for us."

"But how could he tell from the report that a mistake
had been made?" She looked up at him, suddenly eager.
" 'Twas my name, wasn't it! Does he know my
brother?"

Edmund Unsworth looked at her oddly. "Your
brother?"

Merewyn's confidence faltered at his sharp tone.
"Aye. That is, he—" Suddenly she was terribly afraid
that her release might only be temporary. Obviously Sir
Clive hadn't sent for her because he had recognized her
name. What, then, had prompted him to send for her at
such an odd hour?

"C-can we go, please?" she begged. "I must see him!"

"Certainly." His willing tone reassured her and she
allowed him to propel her through the chilly night, oblivious to the shadows that emerged from darkened
doorways and alleys to stare curiously after them.

"Please, can we stop a moment?" Merewyn panted

after her escort had hurried her along over a mile. Her head was spinning and she felt ill, not an unusual circumstance considering that she had eaten nothing in almost two days.

"We really can't afford to delay," Edmund Unsworth began, but Merewyn had already collapsed on the low stone wall that bordered the garden of a tall frame house facing the narrow street.

"Just for a minute," she pleaded, and found herself wondering irritably why the venerable Sir Clive hadn't sent a carriage for her. Edmund Unsworth was standing over her impatiently, his hands thrust deep in the pockets of his trousers while Merewyn tried in vain to catch her breath.

"Very well," he agreed reluctantly.

Merewyn sighed gratefully and let her aching head droop, the heavy lashes fluttering as her eyes closed, a great weariness overwhelming her. "Y-you're very kind," she murmured thickly.

Above her Edmund Unsworth had grown very still. Turning like a cat on the balls of his feet he sent a searching glance in every direction to assure himself that the street was deserted. The hand that was resting in his left pocket emerged slowly with a sinister-looking cudgel that he held in an experienced fashion, his fingers curling familiarly about its smooth surface.

Edmund Unsworth had been a member of an impressment gang for years and had learned to wield it expertly. 'Twouldn't take much of a blow to knock out the young girl who sat slumped on the wall before him, her head in her hands. A mere tap should do the trick, he decided, and she'd have only a small lump to show for her troubles when she came round.

'Twas something of a shame, actually, he thought to himself as he looked down at her thin shoulders and listened to her touching efforts to still her erratic breathing. Sympathy was an emotion he'd rarely experienced before and he was surprised to feel it now, after all he'd done in his life. He'd better act quickly before he had the chance to think of growing soft—and he lifted his arm and deftly brought down the cudgel on the back of the golden head.

Merewyn made no sound as she crumpled together in a piteously small heap, and Edmund moved quickly to catch her before she landed on the walk. Then he threw her without ceremony over one powerful shoulder and cast one last, wary look about him before he set off in an unswerving course for the river, where he knew he was expected.

Louis Kincaid, captain of the three-masted barkentine *Highlander*, stood with squat legs planted firmly apart on the quarterdeck, his narrowed eyes searching the darkened heavens above the network of rigging and furled sails, the late winter constellations plainly visible despite the many lights burning on the dock below and bobbing on the other ships moored about him. Unable to find sleep, he'd come on deck about an hour ago and had relieved the astonished watch by ordering him below. Now he prowled restlessly about his ship as does a man who is troubled in spirit, although Kincaid was a man of little conscience.

Water lapped against the hull and the pilings of the wharf, the *Highlander* dipping slightly in response, her timber creaking in the freshening breeze. The dock below was deserted although Kincaid knew that there were watches posted on each of the ships laying at anchor in Glasgow's crowded harbor. From an inn near the waterfront came the muted sounds of laughter and singing and the clanking of pewter ale mugs against wood.

The *Highlander* was ready to sail on tomorrow's tide, most of the crew already aboard. Louis Kincaid gave no thought to the hapless passengers who were already holed up in steerage despite how cold it would be below with the chilly spring air—damp as it came in from the river, penetrating the hull and enveloping them as they tried to sleep in the musty straw.

For the past eight months, since the threat of attack had lessened as the warring nations moved closer towards the treaty that had finally been signed in Paris in February, the *Highlander* had been making the Atlantic crossing with her holds full of human cargo en route to the Americas, and returning with the same holds groaning with rum, tobacco, molasses, and timber. A merchant vessel owned by a prominent Englishman, the *Highlander* transported only legally bonded servants, and the trim barkentine had earned herself the reputation of being a fleet and serviceable vessel above all suspicion.

This was a reputation of which Captain Kincaid was proud and that he exercised the utmost discretion to maintain. Those individuals he carried over every voyage who had been coerced or otherwise illegally converted into indentured slaves were handled with the same secrecy as the extra casks of rum or molasses or crates of tobacco that Kincaid brought back to England without entering on his records.

Adept at smuggling and far too shrewd to risk his impeccable qualifications, Kincaid had set up his business network with a few carefully selected men who were completely loyal and extremely well paid. All of them were assigned responsibilities that usually enabled him to remain totally uninvolved in the actual execution of the crimes, and leaving him also, should one of these men happen to be caught—and thus far none had—totally above suspicion or blame.

Leaning against the taffrail, Kincaid pulled out his watch, glanced at the ornate face, and returned it with a slight frown to his pocket. The frown changed to a look of relief as his keen eyes detected movement on the wharf below. Descending the stairs as quickly as his short legs would allow he crossed the main deck just as a panting Edmund Unsworth stepped aboard, dropping the limp bundle in his arms onto the ship's floor.

"Anyone see you?" the small man asked quietly.

"Course not." Unsworth lowered the still figure in the rumpled velvet to the deck and straightened, flexing his powerful muscles tiredly. "Damn, she's a wee thing, but 'tis a long way from the gaol to the river."

"You could have waited until you were closer before —incapacitating her," Kincaid pointed out, standing with his squat legs spread apart, hands clasped behind his back, looking down with a thoughtful expression at what his henchman had brought him.

Edmund Unsworth shrugged. "The timing was good and I didn't want to waste the chance."

"Let me have a look at her."

The toe of Unsworth's boot nudged Merewyn's slight form, rolling her over on her back so that her pale face lay exposed to the dark night sky. The long black lashes lay against the translucent skin beneath her eyes and the hollow cheekbones were sharply defined, giving her delicate features a mature beauty accentuated by the rounded swell of her firm breasts as they rose and fell with her regular breathing.

"Not bad," Kincaid murmured to himself, admiring in particular the thick coil of golden hair. "I'll have to see she don't lose those looks during the voyage. She ought to fetch a right fair price." His narrowed eyes gleamed. "A right fair price indeed. Do you have the papers?"

Edmund Unsworth handed them to him. "Signed proper as you can see. She won't be able to contest them."

The captain shook his head as he studied the neatly written name at the bottom of the parchment. "Signing under duress is a ruse some have tried too often.

Nobody'd believe her. I'll sign the other side in my cabin. Better get her below before anyone sees her."

As Unsworth stooped to pick her up Captain Kincaid muttered thoughtfully, "MacAilis. 'Tis a name I've heard before."

"Probably thinkin' of the Cairnlach MacAilises," Edmund replied as he straightened with Merewyn's still form in his powerful arms. "The ones who have the wool mills here in the city."

"Oh, aye." Kincaid glanced sharply at the small face half visible against Edmund Unsworth's chest. "No kin, is she?"

Unsworth laughed. "Christ, do you honestly believe a MacAilis female'd be whoring in Glasgow?"

Kincaid's thin lips parted in a humorless smile. "Reckon not. Wouldn't want her aboard if 'twere true. Dealing with the upper class is too risky even for me."

"Andy said the charges against her were thievery and whorin'. It couldn't be true," Edmund Unsworth assured his employer, then vanished with a loud laugh across the dark deck.

The captain watched him disappear down the hatch before striding to his cabin. He'd sign the papers and return them to the MacAilis lass only after they had cast their mooring lines and were out on the open sea. A satisfied smile tugged at the corners of his mouth. She'd be needing them in the colonies, she would.

Shortly after dawn the order to cast off was given by Captain Kincaid and, the hawsers released, the *Highlander* slipped soundlessly from its mooring and turned towards the sea, its rudder knifing through the still waters of the Clyde, heeling slightly as the rising morning breeze filled the sails. With its bow facing west, the trim, square-rigged vessel left the sleeping city behind to begin its long voyage across the Atlantic to Wilmington and North Carolina's rich tobacco lands where the demand for slaves and indentured servants was inexhaustible.

CHAPTER THREE

"C'mon, now, up wi' ye!"

Merewyn heard the words as though from far away and she fought against rising consciousness, preferring the dark world that had held her captive for so long.

"C'mon, girl!"

Someone was shaking her roughly and shouting impatiently, and she tried to turn her face away from the unwelcome noise, hoping to hide by burying it in the sweet softness of her down pillow. Was it Malcolm or Alex standing above her, she wondered groggily, and what did they want from her so late at night?

"Here, wake up, will ye?"

The hand was rougher now, jerking her back and forth, and she suddenly became aware of the fact that her face was not pressed against the smooth, clean-smelling satin that covered her bed at Cairnlach, but against something coarse that felt like straw. It was so musty that her small nose wrinkled and she sneezed impulsively and was suddenly awake.

" 'Bout time, ye lazy wench," came an unfamiliar and slightly hostile voice from above her.

She rolled over quickly and sat up, her hands flying to her head as a wave of dizziness overwhelmed her. Pain mingled with growing confusion as she opened her eyes and found a burly, bearded stranger carrying a lantern standing over her, a fierce scowl drawing his heavy brows together. The swaying light fell only in a small circle around her, making it impossible to guess at the size of the strange, cavernous room she found herself in, but Merewyn could hear groans and frightened whispers in the black reaches beyond her and the alien sound of creaking timber.

"Where am I?" she asked uncertainly, her voice strained. "Back in gaol?"

"Ye might as well be," came the rough, laughing reply. "C'mon now, the cap'n doesna like bein' kept waitin'."

"The captain?" She was more bewildered now than ever and the slow spinning of her head was beginning to make her feel ill.

"Aye, the cap'n. Come on!"

A hairy hand wrapped itself about her arm and jerked her to her feet. She staggered and fell against a thick chest and heard him laugh again, his reeking breath in her face. Disgusted, she pushed herself away and stood glaring up at him, her hands balled into small fists.

"Leave me alone!"

The bearded crewman bared his teeth in a leering grin and eyed her appraisingly, moving the lantern so close to her face that she would feel its heat. "A real firebrand, ain't ye? I wonder if the cap'n bargained for that? Come on, now, up wi' ye!"

Merewyn remained where she was, her hands still held protectively before her trembling form. Who was this bearded man with the rotting teeth, what did he want from her, and where on earth had Edmund Unsworth brought her? Common sense told her she couldn't be back in gaol, couldn't even be on solid ground for that matter. Now that her dizziness was gone she realized that everything around her continued to sway, and the disgusting man before her who smelt as though he hadn't had a bath in weeks had mentioned a captain. Was she on board a ship, then? Dear God, if so, where was she bound?

"Will ye be comin'?" the crewman demanded roughly, finally losing patience with her. Without waiting for her reply, he seized her slender arm in his big hand and propelled her to the hatchway, pushing her through with as much ceremony as if he were loading a sack of oats into a grain bin.

Seconds later Merewyn was standing up on deck blinking in the glaring light of day, half blinded by the sun reflecting on the deep green water that rolled beyond her field of vision. Above her she could hear the taut canvas snapping in the stiff breeze and could smell the salty tang to the air. The deck heaved gently beneath her feet and she stumbled as a feeling of faintness overwhelmed her. She put up no resistance as she was dragged across the polished wood and through a narrow passage that ended before a closed door.

"I brought the girl," her captor called out after rapping his hairy kunckles against the thick wood.

"Bring her in," came a perfunctory voice from the other side.

Merewyn found herself thrust inside a surprisingly roomy cabin containing finely carved furniture and a bunk covered with thick woolen blankets. At a table standing beneath the polished pane windows sat a short man in a lawn shirt opened at the throat, his hazel eyes narrowed as he studied her. Short cropped brown hair covered a wide and bony forehead and his thin lips were coated with grease, which he dabbed away with a linen napkin.

Merewyn had forgotten everything as her indigo eyes fastened themselves to the huge plate standing on the table before the captain. Her attention was claimed by a plump roasting hen covered with glazed vegetables, giving off a most tantalizing odor. For a moment her surroundings faded away and she was aware only of the gnawing hunger within her, remembering faintly that she had eaten nothing at all since the evening before she had arrived in Glasgow on the coach. How long ago had that been? Two days? Three? Even more?

"Would you care for some meat, Miss MacAilis?"

She jumped at the question, her wide blue eyes fastening themselves to the hazel ones before her. "You know me?"

The thin lips parted into a complacent smile. "In a manner of speaking, aye." To the bearded sailor who lingered in the doorway he added sternly, " 'Twill be all, Barrows."

Merewyn scarcely heard the door close behind the muttering crewman, concentrating instead on gathering her wits about her while struggling against the desire for food that was rising to blot out all other thoughts. "What am I doing here?" she demanded, forcing herself to look away from the steaming contents of the platter.

"All in good time," came the nonchalant reply. "You must eat first."

She waited without breathing while he broke off a drumstick and a thick slab of breast meat and poured a fresh glass of wine from the bottle at his elbow. "Sit down," he ordered as he extended them to her while indicating a huge seaman's chest standing against the bunk, and she lowered herself without replying, already occupied with tearing the succulent flash from the bone with her slender fingers.

For the moment Merewyn had forgotten everything else. Although she tried her best to keep from wolfing down her food, she gave up at last, hunger having done away with all restraints, and Captain Kincaid smiled to himself as he watched the famished girl eat, studying with approval the smooth cheeks and large blue eyes, the sunlight from the windows behind him reflecting within their cobalt depths and highlighting therein flecks of purest gold. Heavy black lashes emphasized their tilted corners, making them seem even larger, and both perfectly proportioned on either side of a small and charmingly upturned nose.

A fair price indeed, Captain Kincaid thought to himself, unable to control his glee, and he'd see to it that she stayed well fed and cared for during the voyage so as not to risk her looks.

"More wine?" he inquired politely, seeing that she had drained her glass.

"Thank you, no," she replied in her soft Highland burr. Now that the desperate, half starved look was gone from her eyes they seemed larger than ever, and he noticed that the hunger within them had been replaced with suspicion and growing fear.

Kincaid helped himself to another drumstick, then offered her a pie that she also declined. "I see you've had your fill," he commented, laying it back on the plate. "Now we can talk."

"I'd like to know where I am and who you are and where you're taking me," she began at once, trying to sound brave although he detected a trembling to the soft lips.

"Please, please, Miss MacAilis," he begged, holding up his hands. "One at a time. I am Louis Kincaid, captain of the *Highlander,* and we're bound for Wilmington, North Carolina."

"You mean the colonies?" Merewyn whispered, the rosy flush brought on by the wine she had gulped fading into paleness.

"Of course. Do you know of any other North Carolina?"

"But I don't understand," she protested, the darkening depths of her tilted eyes giving him an indication of the extent of the turmoil going on within her. "Why are you taking me there? Who are you?"

"I've already told you who I am," he remarked with

a smile. "The *Highlander* is a trade ship. We deal in exported New World commodities such as sugar, molasses, rum, tobacco, whatever we can find to fill our holds. On our return voyage from England we take along passengers, mostly in the form of indentured servants. Do you know what those are?"

"I'm not really sure," Merewyn murmured in confusion, massaging her aching temples. "They're no better than slaves, actually, people who are in debt or imprisoned, who've no way of gaining their freedom except to sign themselves away for a specific period of time to a master who buys them overseas."

"An excellent description for one who isn't sure," Captain Kincaid complimented her, raising his wine glass as a toast.

"But what does that have to do with me?"

"My dear Miss MacAilis, you answered the question yourself."

"I-I don't understand."

"Come now, a lass of your intelligence? Think a moment." He smiled as he stared into the bewildered blue eyes and saw the dawning realization appear in them.

"Surely you're not saying that I—that you plan to sell me in the colonies! Why, I didn't sign any indenture papers!"

"Think again, Miss MacAilis."

"I haven't," she repeated, her fear replaced with anger. "You've made a terrible mistake, sir, and I demand that you take me back to Glasgow at once!"

Captain Kincaid seemed unruffled by her outburst. "Are you certain you haven't signed anything in the recent past?"

Impatiently, she thought back to the harrowing hours she'd spent in the foul prison cell, though memories were oddly blurred together. "No, of course not," she said irritably. "Except the papers Mr. Unsworth—the release papers—he said 'twas just a formality . . ." Her words trailed away and her young face took on an ashen hue. "Y-you tricked me!"

Captain Kincaid smiled approvingly. "I'm pleased you figured that out yourself."

"But—" Merewyn broke off, wondering when she would awaken from this nightmare. She closed her eyes, hoping it would all go away, but when she opened them again she still found herself in Captain Kincaid's spacious cabin with the floor tilting slightly beneath her feet as much from dizziness as with the movement of the ship.

"The shock will wear off soon," Captain Kincaid assured her matter-of-factly. "Have no fear, Miss MacAilis. You'll be well treated, I promise."

"You despicable monster!" Merewyn flared at him, something seeming to snap deep inside of her. "I'll see you and your cohorts in Glasgow hanging by your necks! You'll pay for this and all the other crimes you've doubtless committed in your glorious career as a knave!"

The captain had grown very still at her words and now his thin lips were taut, the hazel eyes narrowed, his expression unpleasant. "You'd better have a care how you speak to me, Miss MacAilis. I'm the one who owns you at the moment and I can do with you as I please."

"Is that supposed to frighten me?" she cried bravely, her cheeks burning feverishly. "As soon as we reach Wilmington I'll go to the authorities, tell them who I am and what you've done to me, and then, sir, then—"

"Then you'll be sold on the market place like a common breeding sow," Captain Kincaid replied, his silky voice cutting through her loud tirade. " 'Tis the fate of all indentured servants upon disembarkation. No one will believe your story, Miss MacAilis. Not as long as I have these." He held up the folded documents she recognized as having signed in gaol, and waved them languidly in the air. Her eyes followed their passage back and forth before her pale face and he smiled as he laid them down on the table between them.

"I'll tell them how I was tricked into signing them," Merewyn said thickly.

He spread his hands in total unconcern. "I'm sorry, my dear, but with your signature on these papers you're lost, quite lost."

His words sounded like a death knell and she fought against the rising depression that threatened to overwhelm her.

"You'll get your half when we dock," he added conversationally, swallowing the last bit of wine in his glass. "The other half is mine to keep and will be turned over to your new owner."

Merewyn's soft lips trembled. She would never belong to anyone, never! Before the *Highlander* docked in Wilmington she would have those papers in her possession, no matter what lengths she'd have to go to get them!

"Everythin' all right, cap'n?"

Merewyn turned to see Barrows peering through the opened door, his eyes gleaming curiously beneath his bushy brows.

"Naught's amiss," Captain Kincaid replied nonchalantly, "but now that you're here you may as well take Miss MacAilis back to her quarters." His smile made her tremble. "We'll talk again, my dear."

Crewman Barrows scarcely waited for the hatch to be properly opened before he shoved his young captive inside, where she landed in a crumpled heap at the bottom of the ladder. On her hands and knees she crawled in the utter bleakness to a deserted corner in the straw. There she buried her face in her hands and let the hot tears course down her cheeks, sobbing in misery, terrified of what the future would hold for her. She was at the mercy

of a madman and she knew that without the indenture
papers she'd have no chance at all of regaining her freedom.

In the days that followed the passengers aboard the
Highlander were granted time on deck whenever the
weather permitted. Though late winter and early spring
were stormy times on the North Atlantic, the *Highlander*
encountered surprisingly few of them. More often than
not the hatch leading to the steerage was thrown open
and those below were able to walk about at their leisure.

Merewyn was astonished at the number of people
who emerged from the darkness their first time out, feeling a great deal of sympathy for the thin, shoddily
dressed individuals with their pinched faces, their
hollow eyes in sunken sockets for the most part bereft of
hope. Most of them spoke in thick Lowland accents but
she detected among a few the familiar and beloved Highland lilt and even some Gaelic. Yet when she tried to
speak or make any overtures of friendship she was
greeted with stony silence or, more disturbing, outward
displays of fear.

Soon she gave up all attempts at conversation and
spent the blessed hours in the chilly sunshine pacing
about briskly to exercise her stiff limbs, afraid of growing weak, knowing she'd need every ounce of her
strength in battling against her captors once the *Highlander* reached the colonies. The thought of possessing
and then destroying the copies of her indenture papers
was never far from her mind, and Merewyn was determined to see that the unpleasant captain and his band
of thieves were brought to justice.

She had no doubts that she was only one of many
hapless individuals who had been taken to the colonies
against their will, and helpless rage burned within her
heart whenever she thought of the wealth Louis Kincaid
had accrued from the hardships of others.

Not long afterwards a severe storm kept the passengers in the steerage for an endless stretch of time. Unable to keep track of the days in the constant murkiness within her prison, Merewyn grew sick at heart and longed to go topside. The pitch black compartment with its foul, reeking air was filled with the moans of the ill and she herself was bruised and exhausted from being flung time and again against an unyielding beam.

Rats that shared the living quarters below deck scampered unconcerned amid the straw as they foraged for food, and Merewyn had to contend not only with the keeling and turbulent movements of the ship in the towering waves, but also with the boldness of these disgusting rodents who dared approach her small supply of moldy bannocks and try to steal them despite her efforts to keep them away. She had hoarded the pitiful stash of food against the chance that a storm might keep them captive below, and thus far she had managed to stave off the hunger pangs successfully.

Wind roared beyond the thick hull and thunder cracked overhead with unbelievable intensity. Merewyn, kicking at one of the bolder furry creatures with her small foot, could feel her strength ebbing away, her determination to endure replaced with utter despair. She found it difficult to believe as she sat in the damp, rat-infested straw with the moans and fearful screams of the others about her, that she had ever known a warm and beautiful place like Cairnlach Castle. Even Alexander's rough-hewn face and Malcolm's boyish expression seemed fuzzy in her memory, and she found herself beginning to wish that the *Highlander* would founder and that an end to this hellish existence would come quickly.

And what sort of nonsense was that? she asked herself, suddenly irritable. She was a MacAilis, after all, and the MacAilis clan was a fighting clan, the Gaelic motto, roughly translated, being: *Surrender not even in death*. All right, then, she told herself in a brave attempt to bolster her spirits, if the *Highlander* sank she'd have

only a coward's excuse for giving in. The least she owed
Alexander and Malcolm was an explanation of what
had happened to her and she intended to survive the
crossing at all costs.

Gradually, the fearful pitching of the floundering
vessel subsided somewhat and Merewyn sat upright, listening attentively. She could no longer hear the gale
roaring outside nor the explosive crash of waves against
the hull. In the darkness around her some of the other
passengers began whispering to one another in less fearful tones as they sensed that the storm was passing.

A relieved smile passed across the weary young features although no one saw it. She hadn't really wanted
to drown after all, she told herself as she nibbled at one
of the crusty bannocks. Oh, no. She wanted to see Alex
and Malcolm again, and Annie and even her mare—
every familiar, intrinsic part of Cairnlach that she so
dearly loved.

"This I swear to you, Alex," she whispered to herself
as she curled up in a small ball to sleep, her hunger ap-
peased, "I'll come home, but not until Kincaid and his
men have paid for what they've done to me!"

When she awoke she felt more refreshed, and from the
subdued conversations going on about her she guessed
that the other passengers had overcome their seasickness
at last. The now familiar creaking of wood as the hatch
was thrown back made her look up eagerly, and the
rough voice calling down to those who wished to come
up brought immediate response.

As Merewyn came up on deck she could scarcely believe how placid the rolling blue waters were after the
tempest that had swept over them earlier. Billowy white
clouds filled the azure sky and the breeze that stirred the
golden tendrils at her temples was warm. She raised her
small face to the sun, taking strength from its welcoming
rays. Her weariness seemed to vanish, giving her young,

strong body a new vigor as she began her customary pacing about the deck, her faded russet gown billowing in the breeze.

"Miss MacAilis?"

She turned questioningly to the bos'n, by now a familiar figure to most of the steering passengers. He was younger than the other officers and seemed, in Merewyn's opinion, more polite and better educated than the rest of the *Highlander*'s crew. He was of average height, possessing pleasant features and a calm, unruffled manner that bespoke strength of character and honesty.

Merewyn had often wondered, seeing him busy on deck sending aloft the hands to adjust the rigging and the sails, if he knew of Captain Kincaid's criminal practices. Sometimes she was certain that he was an honest man and that he would be shocked by the truth, but she didn't dare approach him on the matter, unsure of her feelings and frightened of the risk she'd be taking in trying to gain his confidence.

He had rarely addressed her since their departure from Scotland, but he had nodded to her on occasion and even once given her a friendly smile.

"Mr. Winston?" she asked, gazing up into his clean-shaven face, her tilted blue eyes questioning.

"Captain Kincaid asked for you. He's in his cabin."

Merewyn swallowed hard. "D-did he say what he wanted?"

The bos'n looked puzzled. "Why, no, miss. That should wait until you come, don't you think?"

Merewyn's soft lips tightened. "I imagine so."

Carl Winston stood staring down at her thoughtfully, wondering at the cause for the fear and helpless resignation that sprang into the enormous dark eyes. Though he made it a point not to mingle with any of the passengers, he'd been aware of Merewyn MacAilis ever since the first time she'd come up on deck. Though bedraggled and obviously frightened, she'd nonetheless struck him as a proud and indomitable young lady, the arrogant carriage of her golden head reminding him of the titled women he'd often seen in London driving past in their expensive carriages.

He'd especially liked the way she'd shaken off that imbecilic sailor Barrow's hold before vanishing down the companionway to the captain's quarters, dusting off the velvet sleeve with one small hand as though Barrows had dirtied it with his touch. Since then the bos'n had watched her whenever she was out in the open air, striding back and forth on the main deck with a purposeful set to her delicate features, seemingly unaware of anyone else.

Though her reddish-brown velvet gown was stained and wrinkled he could see that it was finely tailored and guessed that she had been wealthy at some time in her life and had, perhaps through the death of her parents, fallen from grace and been forced to sign her life away. 'Twas a crying shame when you thought about it, he told himself often, but what could be done?

"Mr. Winston?"

He shook himself out of his reverie, shamefully aware that he had forgotten all else while admiring the tilted blue eyes with their shining depths of purest gold and the slim, upturned nose, as well as the soft, parted red lips.

"Eh? Did you say something, miss?"

"I asked if the captain wanted to see me right now." Merewyn spoke with a contrite smile, striving to conceal her impatience. She'd asked the man twice, now, and he just kept on staring at her like a sheep on the butcher block, his jaw hanging slack, his brown eyes wide and expressionless. What in blazes was the matter with him?

The bos'n blushed furiously beneath the candid gaze.

"Er . . . ah, aye, of course, Miss MacAilis. He's waiting for you."

She thanked him politely and turned away, forgetting him in the very next moment as other worries began to plague her. What did Kincaid want from her now? Her mouth was dry as she knocked quietly on the cabin door and received curt permission to enter.

Captain Kincaid was again reclining at his table, addressing himself to another elegant meal, but this time Merewyn was able to conquer the hunger that rose within her at the sight of so much appetizing food. She was still angry at herself for her poor display of self-control at her first meeting with the captain, and declined his offer to dine with him now with a small smile of triumph.

"You're amused, Miss MacAilis," Kincaid observed, studying her keenly. "Why?"

"You wouldn't understand," she responded coolly.

His tone was no less pleasant. "I see you've managed to retain your spirits after all these weeks. I only hope you can weather the rest of the voyage as well."

Merewyn's haughty demeanor faded at his words. "How long has it been?" she asked hesitantly.

"Five weeks." He laughed as he saw her shocked expression and languidly peeled the skin off a succulent lime. "Surely you aren't saying the time has flown by unnoticed," he chided.

" 'Tis difficult to measure day and night when you're forced to live in utter darkness," she informed him with a scowl.

"I apologize for your accommodations," he responded with another smile so smug that she had to grapple with the urge to slap him, "but while I'm determined to keep you looking well I'm not going to give you my quarters. Ah, that reminds me of something I've been meaning to ask you. You are certain, aren't you, that you're still a virgin?"

Merewyn's hollow cheeks flooded with color, forcing the captain to laugh, his hazel eyes filled with genuine amusement.

"Excellent. 'Twill help increase your value."

"What would it matter that I-I—" Merewyn choked out.

The captain shrugged, still occupied with peeling the fruit in his hand. " 'Twill matter to the right man who buys you." The hazel eyes met hers and she turned away from the cruel merriment within his, terrified of the implications he'd made. Could it be true that the man who bought her might try to . . . would demand. . . . Her hands flew to her hot cheeks and she moaned in anguish.

"Och, don't take it so hard," Kincaid advised her mildly. "I never thought for a moment that you were the prostitute Edmund claimed you were. Not the type for it, and believe me," his eyes gleamed, "I've known enough in my time to tell one from the other. Still, you weren't above stealing from a gentleman, so how could I be sure?"

Merewyn stared at him uncomprehendingly, her blue eyes glittering feverishly.

"You know damned well what I'm talking about," Captain Kincaid went on impatiently, taking a bite of the lime and making a face as the tart juice touched his lips. "William Rawlings. You tried to steal his rings."

"How do you know so much about me?" Merewyn asked in a whisper, retreating towards the cabin door, suddenly unnerved by the thickset, grinning man seated before her.

"I know about every prisoner that goes in and out of most of the gaols in Scotland and even some in England, including Newgate. A shrewd businessman deals over a large geographical area."

"You're a monster," Merewyn breathed, struggling

against the numb terror that was building within her.

"You've told me that before," he replied, unperturbed. Suddenly bored with the conversation he said unexpectedly, "I want you to become my cook."

"What?"

"I said you're to become the *Highlander*'s cook."

"Why, you're daft!" she cried, thinking that he was.

He shook his head with its closely cropped dark hair back and forth. "Oh, I assure you I am not. I lost my steward during the storm last night. He washed overboard. 'Twas a pity, actually, he made excellent consommé."

"Surely there are others among the crew who can—"

He waved her words away impatiently. "Naturally, I don't expect you to prepare meals for all of us. Just for the officers and myself. I can't think of anything I'd enjoy more than eating a meal I know you've fashioned with your own little hands."

Merewyn felt her stomach churn at the tone of his voice. "I couldn't possibly—"

"Of course you can, and you will. I've been wanting you to spend more time topside and this will solve the problem for me. You do look thinner and more pale than when we cast off in Glasgow."

"I won't do it!" Merewyn cried stubbornly. "You can't force me to work like a—like a common slave!"

He bared his teeth in a ghastly smile. "I suggest you get used to it, my dear Miss MacAilis."

She said nothing, her small face turned away from him as he rose and came around the table towards her. She tried to stand her ground, her small chin firmly set, but her lips trembled dangerously and she flinched as one of his hands reached out to touch the soft golden braid that was pinned to the nape of her neck.

"No reason to fear me," he assured her. "I've no intentions of lowering the quality of my merchandise. I expect top money for you, my dear."

She turned her face away again, shaking uncontrollably.

"May I count on your cooperation in the galley, Miss MacAilis?"

When she made no reply he took her pointed little chin in his hand and forced her head around so that she was staring up into his hard eyes, her own wide with fear. "Miss MacAilis?" he repeated dangerously.

"Aye," she choked out.

"Excellent."

He let her go and went to the door, opening it and calling down the companionway while Merwyn retreated to a safe distance, trying to overcome the feeling of nausea that had overwhelmed her at his nearness.

Now that the shock of his proposal was beginning to wear off she could see the benefits it might entail. Longer hours out of the bilge-saturated steerage, for one thing, and close contact with the food preserves . . . Her mouth began to water as she thought of the tantalizing dishes she would set aside for herself to be eaten then and there or saved for later. After the meager rations she'd received during the past few weeks the thought of helping herself to daily meals of the same quality she'd observed Kincaid consume made her feel weak with longing.

"Take Miss MacAilis to the galley."

Merewyn turned and found herself staring into Crewman Barrow's grinning, bearded face. She groaned inwardly, hating the filthy bull-necked man who always seemed to be present whenever she was out on deck, leering at her with his half-closed eyes, his lips moist with drool. 'Twas enough to make anyone feel ill.

Following Barrow's shuffling footsteps down the narrow companionway, Merewyn fought to still the tremendous excitement surging within her. Now that she was expected to cook for the captain she felt certain she'd be spending a lot of her time in his cabin and was convinced that she'd eventually find her indentureship papers.

She scarcely heard Barrow's tedious explanation of the captain's dining schedule, nor noticed anything more about the galley itself than that it appeared almost as well equipped as the cavernous kitchens in Cairnlach. Her mind was racing over possibilities as she considered where the most likely hiding place might be. There was a gleeful smile on her lips as she nodded her head in agreement with everything the bearded crewman said to her and she didn't notice at all that his bloodshot eyes strayed constantly to the neckline of her russet gown, which revealed the firm swell of her breasts.

Tomorrow, she exulted, she would begin her search, and if all went well she would have the papers within her possession by the time they docked in Wilmington. Without them Captain Louis wouldn't be able to discredit her story of kidnapping and blackmail.

"Miss MacAilis, I must compliment you on your soup."

The words belonged to the boatswain Winston, whose youthful face took on a self-conscious blush as Merewyn responded with a grateful smile.

"Thank you, Mr. Winston. I'm surprised myself, if the truth must be told. At home I rarely set foot inside the kitchen."

"And where was that?" the first mate asked conversationally. Both he and the bos'n were guests of Captain Kincaid that evening and were seated with the short, stocky gentleman at the table in his cabin elegantly draped with a linen cloth. The three of them had just finished the clear broth Merewyn had prepared for the occasion, and though it was her first effort at cooking she had been surprised and rather pleased at the results.

She froze in the process of removing the soup bowls

from the table, startled by the first mate's unexpected question, reluctant to disclose anything about her home and her real identity. Let Louis Kincaid go on believing she was a whore or a thief, for she planned to use her name as a weapon against him when the time came.

"In Glasgow, Mr. Ames," she replied hurriedly. "There were so many in my family that someone else always prepared the meals."

Thankfully, the first mate seemed disinclined to pursue the topic and conversation between the three men turned to nautical matters that Merewyn ignored. While clearing the table she let her eyes rove the cabin, surreptitiously searching for likely hiding places.

Captain Kincaid's quarters were neat and simply furnished. Besides the table at which he took his meals he possessed only a cabinet, which stood across from his bunk and the big seaman's chest. The cabinet, Merewyn knew from a previous visit, contained brandy bottles and, in the bottom compartment, some clothing. It was kept locked, doubtless to keep the fine liquor from the hands of his crew, and Merewyn wondered if the papers might be there as well.

She chafed with impatience for the opportunity to look, her urgency becoming greater as the hours went by, and still the captain showed no inclination of dismissing his officers and going topside. Wordlessly, she served the remainder of the meal, withdrawing in silence so that the three of them could eat, and retreated to the small galley where she helped the shy cabin boy wash the dishes, although it was not a part of her designated duties.

Merewyn liked the curly-headed, fourteen-year-old lad. David Brown had served as a powder monkey on board a heavily armed British frigate that had waged numerous assaults on the French during the Seven Years' War. In 1756, at the age of eight, he'd participated in several significant sea battles, the telling of which made Merewyn shake with terror. During the last one he had lost several fingers on his right hand to a jammed cannon, but had easily overcome the disappointment of knowing he'd never become a sea captain without the ability of tying all the important rigging knots and working up on the yardarms.

"I really don't mind if I stay a cabin boy the rest of my life, Miss Merewyn," he'd told her on numerous occasions when they worked side by side at the big wooden table. "Long's I can be out on the sea an' gae places, I'm happy."

"You're a lucky lad, David," Merewyn replied sadly. "There aren't many of us who can claim they're happy in what they do."

"Och, 'twill be nice i' the colonies," he assured her hastily, hating to see the sorrow on her small face, for he had already grown very fond of the golden-haired, unsmiling girl since the captain had assigned her to take old Martin Barne's place.

David had despised the pipe-smoking, oath-hurling little man who had served as Captain Kincaid's steward. Though an excellent chef, Martin Barnes had had the disposition of a bad-tempered bear and David had learned early on to avoid his cuffs and bruises. Martin had also shown an unmistakeable penchant for lads, which, though David only vaguely understood such things, he found totally abhorrent. He had spent every voyage living in constant fear that the balding old man would come after him.

"I imagine they'll be done eating now," he commented to Merewyn as he rubbed the last of the heavy cooking pots dry with a cloth and hung it on a peg beside the others. "I'll get the dishes."

"Oh, 'tis kind of you," Merewyn said with a smile as she reached out and took the large wooden tray out of his hands, "but I don't mind doing it."

David eyed her with a slight frown. "They'll be heavy,

they will. You ken there were three of 'em eating to-night."

"I'll be all right," Merewyn assured him hastily, her words drifting back to him as she vanished with sweeping skirts through the door. Heart hammering with eager anticipation she tiptoed into the captain's quarters only to force down a groan of disappointment when she saw him lounging alone at the table, his wine glass half full.

"Why, where are Mr. Winston and Mr. Ames?" she asked, feigning polite curiosity as she set down her tray.

"Topside," Captain Kincaid replied lazily. "Always rushing off after they've eaten." He shook his head disapprovingly. "Some men have no idea how to savor a good meal."

"Thank you," she replied, dropping her eyes from his and hoping she sounded docile enough, knowing that he had meant to compliment her. How she hated the under-sized, smug little runt! Someday. . . .

She forced herself to remain calm, taking her time as he drained his glass and stretched, belching appreciative-ly. She could tell by the dull glaze of his puffy eyes that he had drunk more than usual, but she was relieved to see that he appeared oblivious to her presence, fully aware of what alcohol could do to a man. Much as he insisted that he would deliver her to the colonies with her virginity intact, she didn't trust him one measure, nor his filthy, leering crew, and moved cautiously as she began stacking the china onto the tray.

Captain Kincaid pushed back his chair abruptly and rose to his feet, reaching for the coat he had tossed onto his bunk. Hope mingled with fear as she watched him move with slightly uneven steps towards the door.

"Captain," she began in a high, unnatural voice, then swallowed heavily as he turned, trying to speak more calmly, "you'll be wanting naught else?"

A surprisingly gracious smile spread across the thin

lips. "That will be all, Miss MacAilis. I'm going up to the helm."

"Aye, sir," she replied politely, hoping he would not see the excitement surging into her dark eyes. No sooner had the door closed behind him than she was at the cabinet, her slender fingers trembling slightly as she worked at the brass fastenings.

She could scarcely believe her good fortune when the carved door opened with only a slight tug. Pushing aside the assortment of bottles, she rummaged hurriedly behind them, then tried the garment drawers only to come up empty-handed. Bitterly disappointed, she turned to survey the cabin thoroughly, wondering where to look next, desperately afraid that she'd not have enough time before the captain returned.

Merewyn's eyes fell on the big seaman's chest and she went down on her knees before it, pulling frantically on the heavy lid only to find that she could not raise it. A small brass lock secured it tightly, she saw, and she could have wept when she saw that the key was missing. The papers had to be inside, she told herself frantically, and abandoned the rest of the furnishings in the room, concentrating on finding the key. Merewyn opened every drawer, searched inside every pocket in the coats and breeches she came across in the small clothespress, and even looked under the blankets on the bunk, but found nothing at all. Almost weeping with frustration she forced herself to stop after having exhausted every likely hiding place, convinced that the captain carried the key on his person.

In silence she returned to her previous task, the china clinking as she heaped it hurriedly onto the tray. What was she to do now? How could she ever get her hands on that key if it was constantly in the captain's possession? The *Highlander* would be docking in Wilmington all too soon, and if she didn't have the papers by then she didn't know what she would do. The situation clearly called for desperate measures, but she had no idea what kind or how she was to execute them.

For the next few days she kept a close watch on the captain, raking the outline of his pockets with her eyes for the telltale bulge of a key ring. She even tried to surprise him in the companionway in the hopes of catching him in the act of removing them from his coat, but never came away with any indication that he really had them anywhere on his person.

Hope waned into frustration and she grew thin and nervous, dark circles forming under her large eyes. The whereabouts of the keys plagued her constantly and she became snappish even with young David Brown, who tried to counter her irritable comments with an eager smile, hoping in vain to change her dark moods into gayer ones.

"Oh, Miss Merewyn, what be it?" he asked despairingly one afternoon after she'd chastised him sharply for dropping and breaking a serving bowl and then burst into tears before his astonished eyes, her head drooping onto her thin arms as she collapsed against the table.

"I'm so unhappy, David," she confessed in a muffled voice, refusing to look at him.

He stood helplessly at her side, wanting to comfort her but afraid to do so while her slender shoulders shook, her frail body racked with sobs. "I didn't mean to break it," he assured her in a small voice.

This time he was rewarded with a tremulous smile, the blue eyes filled with tears that she reached up to dash away with the back of her hand. "Oh, David, I don't care about the bowl!"

"Then why are you crying?" he demanded worriedly.

Merewyn's sobs subsided as she looked into his freckled face with its wide, concerned eyes and quelled the impulse to reach out and ruffle the curly hair, knowing David was always hotly embarrassed by any signs of affection. She sighed deeply and accepted with another thin smile the handkerchief he extended.

" 'Tis clean," he assured her.

"You're very sweet, David," she answered and he blushed and turned away while she dried her eyes. "I'm sorry I shouted at you. 'Twas my fault. I-I haven't been feeling too well lately."

He nodded forlornly. "I wish there was summat I could do to help you, miss."

"I wish there was, too. But 'tis between the captain and myself. He has something that belongs to me and I can't get it back."

David's expression grew puzzled. "Did he steal summat from you?"

Merewyn nodded, beginning to feel ashamed of having lost control of herself before the impressionable lad. " 'Tis nothing, actually. I'm crying because he's locked it in his chest and I've no idea where he keeps the key."

"Why, that's no great secret!" David cried eagerly much to her astonishment. " 'Tis kept inside his log."

Merwyn had grown very still, her dark blue eyes fastened on his small face. "His log?" she repeated in a whisper.

"Aye. The big book in the cabinet."

"Have you seen it before? Are you sure?" She found herself suddenly feeling faint and had to clutch at the tabletop for support.

"Aye, 'tis there," he replied with a firmness that erased all doubt from her mind. "I've seen it myself."

Merewyn closed her eyes for a moment, struggling to control her elation. She mustn't let David see how much his words had affected her. Resisting the impulse to throw her arms about him and cover his freckled face with kisses she merely said in a choked voice, "Thank you, David."

He grinned unabashedly. "No need to thank me! I dinna care too much for the cap'n and I especially dinna like that he's taken summat from you." His voice dropped to a whisper. "You willna be telling him I said that?"

Merewyn laughed and deposited a hearty kiss on both his thin cheeks after all, unable to contain her happiness. "Of course not! We'll keep that a secret, and the fact that you told me where the key is, too."

David grinned happily at the thought of being able to share a secret with the young girl who had treated him so very kindly since he'd been ordered to help her in the galley. "I'll not tell anyone!" he vowed.

The log book and the brandy cabinet began to occupy almost all of Merewyn's thoughts thereafter. She wandered about the deck oblivious to the other passengers and crewmen, the expression on her small face shuttered and far away. Most of the others who shared the hold with her had come to accept their fate as the journey neared its end and had begun making friends. They mingled in groups of twos and threes during their hours in the fresh air, talking together in low tones, but Merewyn ignored them, shunning their companionship, seeming to have forgotten that in the beginning she had desperately tried to nurture it herself only to be rebuffed.

Nothing else seemed important to her any more than obtaining the indenture papers and on the days she served the captain in his quarters she could scarcely keep her eyes from the brandy cabinet. At night it haunted her dreams until she felt certain she would go mad waiting for the chance to look inside.

One warm afternoon, her work finished for the day, Merewyn wandered to the rail and stood leaning against it, her haunted blue eyes searching the horizon before her. The *Highlander*'s sails had been trimmed to take advantage of the stiff breeze and her bow surged through the swells, the water reflecting the sunshine with blinding radiance. High above, the canvas was bathed in golden light, and for the first time Merewyn found herself responding to the sights and sounds around her, an appreciation for nature's beauty warming her heart. Suddenly she could afford to think of life and its infinite loveliness again.

Soon they would be docking in North Carolina and she would be free of the nightmare that had gripped her for so long, free because she had no intentions of disembarking without the indenture papers in her possession. Aye, she even felt a wee bit happy today, and it made her realize that she hadn't felt this way since she'd first left for Glasgow to find the notorious Marquis of Montague.

Lord Montague! Merewyn's heart lurched. To tell the truth she hadn't thought of him once in all these long weeks although she'd dwelled on memories of Alexander and Malcolm and Cairnlach for hours upon tortured hour. Somehow the fuzzy image of the man she'd never seen, who had indirectly been the instrument of her abduction, did not frighten her as it once had. Oh, aye, she thought, with a prim smile playing on her soft lips and a determined glow in her dark eyes that would have made her brothers groan with dread could they but see it, after she'd dealt effectively with Captain Louis Kincaid she'd take on the Marquis of Montague. 'Twould be child's play after all of this!

Turning around she glanced up at the quarterdeck and saw that the afternoon watch had been set and became aware that the hour was late. The sun was beginning its downward descent and as evening approached, she waited until the golden light changed subtly to crimson before going below.

Dawn brought the start of a busy morning for Merewyn, who was occupied in the galley with preparing the eggs David had brought her from the fowl that were housed up on deck. The cheerful lad had left sever-

al minutes ago with the captain's coffee, Kincaid enjoying a strong, black potful every morning while he
dressed.

With deft fingers Merewyn broke the shells and
poured the rich, yolky contents into the sizzling pan. As
she stirred them with a wooden spoon a faint, wistful
smile curved her soft lips and her tired eyes glowed with
longing. How surprised Annie would be when her young
charge returned to Cairnlach and exhibited her culinary
prowess! But the smile faded quickly, for she felt certain
that her long ordeal had changed her in some subtle way
and she was concerned that Alexander, Annie, and
Malcolm might not like what they saw when she came
back.

"Perhaps I haven't changed that much," she whispered to herself as she transferred the eggs to a chafing
dish, although she knew deep in her heart that somehow
nothing would be the same again when she returned.

"Nonsense!" she said aloud, some of the old spirit
surging back into the tilted eyes. "I'm growing soft in
my old age!"

"Did you say summat?"

She turned with a guilty smile as David came in. "Just
talking to myself like a daft old woman," she confessed,
then frowned as she saw the steaming coffee on the lad's
tray. "Didn't the captain care for that this morning?"

David shrugged. "He's drunk, miss."

Merewyn watched him set the tray down, a frown
drawing her smooth brows together. "Drunk?"

"Aye. Happens every now and then, it does."

"But how do you know he's drunk? Did he tell you?"

"He's sleepin' it off," David replied with the wisdom
of experience. "I shook him a few times to make sure."

"And he didn't move?" Merewyn demanded breathlessly, her heart skipping a beat.

"Nay. He willna be up for a while." David pointed at
the eggs and grinned hungrily. "We should eat those

afore they get cold. You'll just have to make more later anyway."

Merewyn nodded vaguely. "Aye, David, eat them if you want to. I've got something to do."

"What?" the lad asked curiously as he seated himself at the table.

"Nothing in particular," she responded, untying the apron from her small waist, reluctant to involve him in her mad plan. Silently, she hurried to the captain's quarters where she knocked boldly, casting nervous glances over her shoulder to make sure the companionway was empty. When no answer was forthcoming she opened the door and peered inside to find the shutters fastened and the room only dimly lit. From the bunk in the corner came sonorous snoring and as Merewyn's eyes adjusted she could make out Louis Kincaid's prone form buried beneath the blankets.

Heart hammering, she tiptoed inside and closed the narrow door softly behind her. Noiselessly, she moved towards the brandy cabinet and pulled open the door. Her breath caught in her throat as it creaked alarmingly and she cast a swift glance at the still figure on the bunk, then sighed in relief as she saw that it hadn't stirred.

As the loud snoring continued, she lifted out the heavy leather volume in the bottom drawer and carried it to the table where she threw back the front cover. There, lying in the center of the first page, lay a tiny brass key.

Merewyn picked it up with trembling fingers and hurried to the seaman's chest, fumbling desperately with the lock, the blood pounding in her ears. After an endless moment the lock dropped open with a faint click and she laid it aside, slowly raising the heavy lid. Inside she found a vast assortment of articles, mostly masculine items: a silver-backed hairbrush and shaving implements, several fine lawn shirts with lace-trimmed sleeves, even a bolt of expensive silk that Kincaid doubtless intended to have tailored into something for himself, Merewyn decided as she tossed it unceremoniously to the floor.

A small leather satchel lay beneath the silk and she lifted it out, her fingers working nervously at the small clasp until she had it open, finding within a great number of documents. Sorting through them she saw immediately that they were all papers similar to the ones she had signed, doubtless belonging to the other passengers, but she set them aside, intent only on finding her own familiar handwriting on one of them. She found it quickly, for it was the only one that hadn't been torn in two, and clutched it disbelievingly to her breast, tears of relief welling in her tilted eyes.

"Ah, have you found it?"

A frightened cry fell from her lips and she whirled about to find Louis Kincaid standing over her, looking not in the least bit drunk, a dangerous smile playing on his thin lips.

"You t-tricked me," Merewyn whispered, gazing up at him, her wide blue eyes filled with dismay.

"I had no choice," he replied calmly. "I suspected you were up to something. You behaved so curiously whenever you came in here with my meals, but I didn't know what you were after. It soon occurred to me that you wanted your indenture papers but I wanted to make sure."

He bent down and prized them from her stiff fingers, returning them to their proper place in the leather pouch. "Poor, disillusioned lass," he murmured with a sorrowful shake of his closely cropped head. "Didn't you realize you'd still be my prisoner without them?"

"That's not true!" Merewyn cried, her voice thin and strained.

He grabbed her arm and pulled her roughly to her feet so that they were facing each other, the captain only an inch or two taller than she. "I'm afraid you're going to

regret this, Miss MacAilis," he told her in a tone that
sent shivers of apprehension down her spine. "I believe
'twill be worth the risk of damaging those ravishing
good looks."

"What do you mean?" Fear was clogging her ability
to reason and she began to shake as she stared into his
narrowed hazel eyes.

"I intend to punish you for what you've done, of
course." He moved away from her to cross the floor and
throw open the shutters, allowing the sunlight to stream
inside. "But to show you what a merciful man I can be
I'll permit you to pick the method."

"I-I don't understand." Merewyn's heart-shaped face
was pale, her eyes glittering feverishly. "Please—"

Kincaid came around the table towads her, his eyes
never leaving her face as he paused to kick the still
opened chest shut with his foot. "Someone told you
where that key was," he continued pleasantly, but
Merewyn's heart only pounded harder at his tone. "I'll
gladly stay your punishment if you tell me who it was."

"Never!" she cried immediately, and he spread his
hands.

"Very well, as you wish. I've a suspect or two in mind
anyway, and I'll find out soon enough."

He lowered himself into his chair, propping his hands
behind his head and gazed at her with the same pleasant
smile on his lips. "Even you, Miss MacAilis, must admit
that I can't allow the passengers to behave in such a
criminal fashion. Wrongdoings must be punished and I
intend to use you as an example in case anyone else is
tempted to try the same thing. Tsk, tsk, 'tis a shame,
actually. The voyage had been so peaceful thus far."

He held up his hand, plowing ruthlessly through her
protests. "Here are a list of your choices, my dear: you
can spend the remainder of the voyage locked in one of
the storage compartments, and I assure you they're dark
and very, very tiny; you can take twenty lashes tied to

the mast; or you can spend the night with me."

Merewyn stared at him, the color draining even further from her cheeks so that her face took on a chalky hue, her lips working soundlessly, her breasts within the russet velvet heaving. "You're mad!"

"Am I? I expect you're thinking of my promise that your purity would not be tainted." The lips parted to reveal small, eneven teeth and Merewyn was reminded of the snarl of a foaming wolf. "I stand by my word, my dear. You will leave this ship a virgin even if you agree to spend the night with me."

He laughed, thoroughly enjoying the look of utter terror in her heart-shaped face. "Aye, indeed, it can be done, Miss MacAilis. There are ways which you can pleasure me—and I you—without risking your treasured maidenhead."

Merewyn's hands flew to her cheeks in horror. She did not understand at all how he intended to achieve this end but suspected that his methods would be bizarre and terrifying. "I'd rather die!" she cried.

"Come come, 'twouldn't be that terrible, but since you so obviously abhor my suggestion I believe we'll opt for the twenty lashes." His eyes gleamed. "I think the hands would get more enjoyment out of that since they'll be able to witness it."

"You wouldn't dare!" Merewyn cried in panic.

His smile vanished to leave a grimness more cruel and frightening than anything she'd ever witnessed before in a man's expression. "If you think that then you don't know me very well, my dear."

"Cap'n, sir," came an unexpected voice through the thick wood of the door, startling both of them.

"Come in," Kincaid called impatiently while giving Merewyn a warning glance to remain silent.

She bit back a horrified gasp as she saw the bearded moron Barrows enter the cabin with young David Brown firmly in tow. The lad was very pale, his freckles standing out in the whiteness of his face, and his brown eyes widened as he saw Merewyn standing in the center of the spacious cabin, tears glistening in her dark blue eyes.

"Ah, so you've brought me the culprit," Kincaid remarked approvingly as the thickset sailor pushed the boy inside, causing him to land sprawling at Merewyn's feet. She bent down quickly to help him up and stood with her arm about him, the two frightened young faces confronting Kincaid, reminding him momentarily that both were actually barely older than children. His expression grew dark at this unexpected stirring of pity and he snarled a curt dismissal at Barrows, who withdrew without speaking.

Captain Kincaid rose and wandered towards them, hands clasped behind his back, shaking his head sorrowfully to and fro. "David, David," he sighed, "I'm disappointed in you. After all our voyages together how can you betray me like this?"

David's eyes fairly bulged from his head. "Me, cap'n? What did I do?"

"Why, you told Miss MacAilis where I keep the key to my chest."

"I only thought—" David began, but Merewyn swiftly clamped her small hand over his mouth.

"Don't speak!" she cried, flashing a look of hatred at the captain. "He doesn't know!"

"Ah, but 'tis too late," Kincaid informed her smoothly. "I suspected the lad all along. I should have known he'd be gullible to your charms."

David shook himself free of Merewyn's fierce hold and drew himself erect before the short figure before him. "I wanted to help her get back what you stole from her!" he cried bravely. "I dinna feel I've done summat wrong!"

Captain Kincaid sighed again. "That's where you're mistaken, lad. You should know by now that serving your captain is your foremost duty. You've betrayed me, lad, and for that you must be punished."

"You'll not touch him!" Merewyn cried, her voice quivering despite her efforts to exhibit outward calm. "I tricked him into telling me! You can't blame him for being fooled by my lies!"

"All the more reason the lad should be thrashed," Kincaid replied, his tone as cold as ice. " 'Twill teach him to be duped by a bloody wench and show the rest of the crew that they'd better think twice before doing the same."

Merewyn doubted she had ever seen so much cruelty in any man's eyes before. Dear God, she thought frantically, the man was insane. His cultivated accents, his seeming honesty, and his kindness to the passengers were all façades to confuse the average person so that no one would suspect that within him lurked the perverse and twisted mind of a madman.

"You wouldn't dare publicly whip David or myself," she threatened with as much boldness as she could muster, hoping to reason with him somehow. "Your crew seems decent enough, they'd never allow it!"

"Ah, but you're wrong, my dear," he replied, his tone effectively crushing her hopes. "They've been with me a long time and they trust my word explicitly. If I tell them you've both committed crimes worthy of a flogging they'll not demur."

"But we haven't!" Merewyn cried. "In the name of God, sir! I've been enslaved against my will and David was following his kind heart in trying to help me!"

Captain Kincaid rubbed his chin thoughtfully, and both of them moved closer together, David's healthy hand seeking and finding Merewyn's small one, which closed firmly about his own.

The innocent gesture kindled the captain's anger and he said firmly, "A flogging is what you'll get—you, David, to teach you the meaning of loyalty, and you,

Miss MacAilis, because I believe your new master will be more satisfied with a pliant, obedient young lady and not a willful hellcat. You'd be surprised how effectively a whipping can cure someone of excessive spirit!" He strode to the cabin door and was about to open it when it swung inwards seemingly of its own accord, almost striking him down in the process.

"Damn you, Barrows," he snarled at the bearded crewman. "What is it?"

The crewman's bloodshot eyes glinted. "I thought yer might be ready to call for me, sir. I figured ye'd be plannin' summat wi' the lad." His rotten teeth were revealed in a hideous grin as his eager gaze swept both David and Merewyn.

"You were listening at the door, you scum!" Kincaid sounded more amused than angry. "I should have you flogged, too, to teach you some manners."

"I wasn't, cap'n, I wasn't," Barrows assured him, and Merewyn was reminded of a groveling dog fearful of his master's punitive hand. Sick with fear she closed her eyes to block out the two hated men from view.

"Of course you were," Kincaid's tone was oily smooth. "You wouldn't know how to 'figure' anything in your head at all. But no matter. Assemble the crew on the main deck and all the passengers, too. I want to be sure they're taught a valuable lesson in obedience that will carry them through the rest of this voyage and perhaps their years of indenture as well."

"No!" Merewyn cried as the grinning crewman hurried off. "They won't allow you to go through with it! Both Mr. Winston and Mr. Ames seem to be decent men —they'll stop you, I know it!"

His smile made her stomach churn. "Indeed not, Miss MacAilis. They follow the captain's orders unquestioningly and unerringly. 'Tis the law of the sea."

As their hands were bound behind their backs and they were propelled up onto the deck, Merewyn's tear streaked face bent close to David's. "I'm so sorry," she whispered.

He tried to smile at her bravely. " 'Tisn't your fault, miss. Dinna worry. I've been beaten before and 'tisn't so bad. The pain goes by and by."

Merewyn found no comfort in his words, aware that his voice was shaking, and she gasped as she was pushed out into the bright sunshine and saw the half circle of curious and apprehensive faces gathered about the main mast. She didn't know what would be worse, the actual beating or the pain of its public humiliation. She moved numbly at David's side, part of her still refusing to believe that this was happening to her. Someone would stop Kincaid from going through with this, she told herself over and over again. They couldn't all be such animals!

Carl Winston came hurrying towards them, his expression filled with worried disbelief, and Merewyn's heart leaped as he called out, "Captain, you can't do this! Barrows says you're goin to—to flog a woman!"

Kincaid's tone stopped him in midstride. "Stand to, Mr. Winston, or you'll join them!"

"But, sir!"

The small man's twisted features were thrust close into the sweating bos'n's face. "Are you questioning my orders, Winston?"

"I can't let you go through with it, sir!"

The pleasant young man appeared to be in an agony of doubt. Though he had little liking for the *Highlander*'s captain he had served him for many years and knew that his judgments were always sound, his books always in order, his men's wages always faithfully paid out. Oh, he'd witnessed whippings on board the ship before, but that had been a matter between the captain and the offending crewman, not a beautiful young woman whose slender body would never endure the blows of the whip!

"You can't let me go through with it?" Kincaid

echoed, his words dripping contempt. "Do I catch wind of mutiny, Winston?"

"No, captain, I—"

"Hold your tongue!" The words cracked in the still air and curious faces turned their way. "I've always liked you, Winston," Kincaid hissed, "so I'll overlook this transgression, but unless you desist this moment you'll join Master Brown and Miss MacAilis at the mast."

"But what has she done?" the bos'n questioned with wide eyes while Merewyn moaned involuntarily, having heard the courage and conviction in his voice changing to quavering uncertainty.

"What have they done?"

Now the captain was speaking loud enough for the gathered throng to hear, the crewmen's faces grim, the passengers' fearful. "Miss MacAilis," he continued, grabbing her arm and dragging her with him into the center of the cirle, "has been charged with attempted theft. I awoke this morning to find her in my cabin rifling through my belongings. I've no doubt she was going to cheat me out of the money I paid for her so that she could slip away in Wilmington free and clear with no indenture papers to show that I supplied her passage across!"

There was dead silence. Overhead, the wind snapped in the taut sails and the beams creaked but no one paid any attention; all eyes were riveted to the pale, trembling girl standing with her golden head bowed. On the faces of some of the sailors there was an inkling of sympathy, but among the passengers there was only veiled hostility, the captain's words striking home their own desperate plights.

"I believe Miss Mac Ailis should be punished in order to teach her to accept her lot as the rest of you have done!"

Now there were murmurs of approval and Merewyn, eyes fastened to the deck, listened with pounding heart, unable to believe that this was happening to her and wishing that she would faint dead away before she was forced to endure any more.

"What about the rest of you?" Kincaid's loud voice demanded, obviously addressing the crew. "Do you have no objections?"

"Beat the wench!" came an excited voice Merewyn couldn't recognize.

"Aye, 'tis a proud little bitch she is!" came Barrow's triumphant shout.

Merewyn's head snapped up and her eyes flew opened in disbelief at the blood lust she heard in the excited voices around her.

"Cowards!" she screamed suddenly, her cobalt eyes sweeping every face with blazing hatred. "Are you so pitiable that you derive pleasure from watching an innocent woman being flogged?"

"Sir, she willna endure twenty lashes." The quiet voice was that of Seaman Askew, who spent most of his time in the lookout high overhead, having learned from the sobbing David the severity of the expected punishment.

Captain Kincaid stared thoughtfully at Merewyn's thin shoulders. "Perhaps you're right," he agreed unpleasantly. "We'll reduce the number to ten." He turned back to his crew. "Ten lashes, lad, what do you say?"

No one answered, Merewyn's taunting words having sobered them all, but as hope rose within her it was abruptly dashed by the sight of the heavyset Barrows stalking towards her bared to the waist, carrying in one hand a thick leather thong with a knotted tip. He flicked it at her menacingly and laughed as she cowered back.

"Come on, then," Kincaid shouted impatiently, "bring the lad on first! I want Miss MacAilis to appreciate what her deed has cost another!"

As David was dragged forward, his face chalky white, Merewyn tried to run towards him, but Seaman Bergh, the sailmaker who had cheered aloud at the prospect of her beating, thrust out his heavy foot and she tripped over it, sprawling on the deck with her hands tied behind her back. With a laugh the powerful man lifted her up, and she stood with her head spinning, her knees scraped and bruised. Raising her pale face she saw that David had been lashed securely to the mast and she could hear his labored breathing from where she stood, his shoulders hunched as he awaited the first stinging blow.

"Ten for Master Brown as well," Captain Kincaid ordered, and the thong whistled through the air, the first blow cutting the boy's chambray shirt to ribbons. The second drew blood and Merewyn moaned as she saw it stain the fabric and trickle down his back. 'Twas her fault that the lad was suffering and she felt she couldn't bear that knowledge, certain that it would haunt her far longer than the pain she herself would shortly receive.

"Stop! Stop!" she screamed as David cried out, his head lolling.

No one heard her. Gazing frantically about she saw that most of the passengers were watching transfixed, the hostility they had displayed earlier having faded into disbelieving horror. The women were covering their faces with their hands, some of them having turned away altogether, but the crew was watching stoically, most of them without expression, for they had witnessed many such beatings in the past and some of them had endured them themselves as well.

Merewyn detected pity in the faces of some, but knew then that Kincaid had been right. None of them would help her. They would obey the captain's orders no matter how unjust they might seem. Doubtless they'd seen enough floggings during their years as sailors to grow indifferent to them.

"Ten! 'Tis enough, Mr. Barrows!"

Kincaid's gleeful voice penetrated her foggy consciousness and she turned to see David collapsed against the mast, his back bleeding, his flesh torn in several places. A soft moan escaped her lips and she ran forward as he was taken down. No one stopped her this time, and she went down on her knees before his still form, straining at her bindings so that she could touch him.

"David! David!" she cried as two sailors hoisted him upright.

His eyes fluttered open and he smiled weakly, but she could tell that he didn't recognize her.

"Take him away," the captain ordered. "Lock him in irons 'til he comes round, then let him be. He'll have learned his lesson. Mr. Barrows, if you will, secure the next prisoner."

She fought against the hands that jerked her upright, kicking and biting, but she was no match for the powerful crewman, and could only sob helplessly as her arms were raised and her hands tied tightly to the hard wood. Captain Kincaid's grinning face floated before her vision and she felt his hands at the neckline of her gown, ripping it so that the creamy white skin of her back was exposed. She bowed her head, tears of anguish running down her thin cheeks as she awaited the first blow.

"All right, Mr. Barrows, begin!"

"One!"

She scarcely heard the sailor as the leather snapped like a pistol shot in her ears. White hot pain seared her back and she screamed, never having endured anything so agonizing in her life although she had sworn to herself she'd display no weakness.

"Two!"

She screamed again, her body jerking as the leather thong left a deep red welt across the creamy whiteness of her back.

"Three!"

"Harder, Mr. Barrows!"

"Four!"

"Sails to larboard stern!"

Merewyn did not hear the lookout's cry nor the excited babble of voices that followed. Pandemonium broke loose abruptly, crewmen scampering aloft while Captain Kincaid, the swooning girl momentarily forgotten, hurried up the ladder to the upper deck, a spyglass in one hand. Barrows could not resist one final lash before he, too, abandoned the main deck and scurried into the rigging.

Merewyn did not know how long she stood slumped against the polished wood base of the mast, her wrists tightly bound, her senses filled with consuming pain, until she felt a gentle tugging motion on the leather thongs that cut so cruelly into her wrists.

"I'll have you down in a moment, miss."

She thought she recognized the bos'n's voice and as she opened her eyes she could see the glint of a blade as it sawed through the leather that secured her arms. The tough hide snapped free unexpectedly and she tumbled to the hard deck, momentarily losing consciousness when unbearable pain shot through her ravaged back.

Carl Winston's face was pale, his brow covered with sweat as he tried to feel for a pulse, desperately afraid that she might be dead. Relieved to feel that her heart was beating, he gently pulled the velvet gown back up over her shoulders, gallantly avoiding a glance at the firm breasts that were momentarily revealed when he turned her over. Merewyn stirred but did not open her eyes, and the bos'n hurried off for a pail of sea water, certain it would help bring her around.

As he came racing back across the deck with the sloshing bucket he felt a heavy hand clamp down on his shoulder and a deep voice command, "Give me that."

Gulping as he looked up at the speaker, so busy with his task that he hadn't realized that the *Highlander* had already been boarded, he hastily complied.

Merewyn fretfully pushed away the hand that was wiping her face with a wet cloth, afraid that whoever was bending over her intended to drown her. She was drifting in and out of consciousness, praying that blackness would emerge the winner so that she could escape from the searing agony that consumed her.

"Merewyn, can you hear me?"

She struggled to recognize the harsh voice, certain that she had heard it before. Opening her eyes she moaned again and found herself looking up into a lean face that floated fuzzily before her misty vision. Steely gray eyes met hers and she tried to focus, her gaze wandering from their cold depths to the long, Roman nose and the full, rage-twisted lips.

"Y-you!" she whispered, her voice barely audible. She saw the handsome face bend closer, the expression less harsh. Was she dreaming or did she really recognize this man above her as the one who had treated her so abominably in Castle Montague weeks ago?

The full lips parted into a mocking smile. "I see you know me," came the deep voice. " 'Twould seem I have a penchant for catching you at a disadvantage, ma'am, or is it that you always make it a habit of looking like a guttersnipe?"

"C-curse you, you b-bloody Sassenach," she whispered and tried to say more, the soft lips moving soundlessly; but then her eyelids fluttered shut and the black lashes came to rest against the translucent skin beneath her eyes, and welcome darkness claimed her.

CHAPTER FOUR

Merewyn awoke thinking to herself, "I'm still aboard the *Highlander*."

Abruptly, she opened her eyes to find herself lying on her side in a roomy bed, soft covers draped over her naked body. From where she lay she could see that she was in a spacious cabin, the walls richly paneled, a huge armoire standing beside a desk liberally strewn with books. Closer to the bed stood a chair with a washbasin upon it, the water inside smelling strangely of herbs.

The gentle swaying of the floor beneath her was something Merewyn had become familiar with during her long weeks at sea, confirming her first waking belief that she was still on the water. But this couldn't be the *Highlander,* she thought to herself, throwing off the covers and attempting to rise. The movement brought instant pain and, although it was not severe, she fell back onto the sheets as memories of the last harrowing minutes before she'd lost consciousness returned.

She'd been flogged, she recalled, and tortured with pain and humiliation, left half swooning against the mast until someone—she thought it might have been Carl Winston—had cut her free. But the face that appeared above hers when she'd opened her eyes had not been the pleasant young bos'n's but the handsome, forbidding visage of the hated behemoth who'd been so cruel to her in Scotland. She must have been delirious, she told herself. How on earth could it really have been the same man?

Fretfully, she pushed the confused thoughts from her mind, concentrating on the pain in her back, relieved to find that it was not severe. Touching it with one shaking hand, she found the skin smooth and soft to the touch, no scars to bear evidence to the terrible crime that had occurred. Gingerly, she got out of bed, tiptoeing nervously on bare feet past the door, afraid that someone would burst in and find her prancing about the room with nothing on at all.

A large mirror hung on one paneled wall and she walked over to it to look upon the image she hadn't seen for months. She was shocked at how thin she had grown, dark circles etched beneath the blue eyes that looked larger than ever in the wanness of her face. Her high cheekbones were more sharply defined than before, the hollows beneath them deeply shadowed. Her ribs, she was dismayed to see, protruded sharply from beneath her skin and she sighed sorrowfully, thinking how horrified Annie would be to see her young charge so wasted away.

Turning slightly, she craned her slender neck to look at her back and was pleased to see that the red welts were almost gone. It was then that she noticed that her hair hung in a long, golden mass to her waist, thoroughly washed and painstakingly combed, the filtered sunlight from the curtained stern windows giving it a radiance that had been lacking since her imprisonment.

Who had been caring for her? she wondered. And where was she? Perhaps if she went topside someone could answer her questions.

Glancing about the spacious cabin her eyes fell upon her russet gown, which was draped clean and neatly pressed over the back of a chair. Folded in a small pile beside it were her stockings and chemise, and with a glad cry she hurridly picked them up, dressing carefully so as not to brush the material against her back, which was still exceedingly tender.

Footsteps sounded in the corridor outside as she fumbled with the buttons in the back, and she whirled about as the door opened unexpectedly, revealing the towering frame of the man she had encountered only once before in her life in a meeting she would have cheerfully erased from both their memories if only that were possible. His piercing gray eyes registered surprise as he saw her standing defiantly before him, the thick golden hair spilling to her slender waist, an indignant flush creeping to her cheeks.

"Don't you believe in knocking?" she demanded, her voice trembling despite the arrogant toss of her head.

Ian Villiers, Marquis of Montague, did not reply immediately. Twice before when he'd seen her she had been inconvenienced, to say the least, and though he had suspected that the tart-tongued, bedraggled urchin who had attacked him at the castle had been beautiful, he could not credit how indescribably lovely she really was. Weeks of hardship had given her heart-shaped face a pinched look that only accentuated the sharply defined cheekbones and her enormous indigo eyes, their tilted slant adding an almost Oriental mystery to the delicate countenance. The heavy velvet gown covered the sparseness of her thin frame so that she looked ethereally slim, and when she moved closer to him he had the distinct impression that she might float away at any moment.

"I asked you if you believed in knocking," she repeated, the sweet voice tinged with a trace of that mature hauteur he'd come to think belonged only to older women.

A slow smile curved the sensual lips. "Forgive me, ma'am," he mocked. "I didn't expect you to be up. Please remember that during the past few days you've been dead to the world and made no objections to my uninvited presence."

A faint flush tinged the finely molded cheekbones and she gazed up at him with eyes so wide that he could clearly see the gold glittering in their depths. "Y-you tended me while I was ill?" The soft voice was unsure now, the arrogance gone.

Lord Montague stepped inside and came to a halt before her, looking down into the upturned young face, his long legs planted firmly apart, his powerful arms folded across his massive chest. "Does the thought appeal to you?"

"Certainly not! I'd been hoping I only imagined seeing you before me after. . ." Her words trailed away as a fleeting expression of anguish passed across the lovely features.

"I'm pleased to see that none of your spirit has been damaged in the ordeal," Lord Montague remarked flippantly in an attempt to goad her back into her original mood so that she might forget the memories he knew she was reliving.

As she whirled about to glare at him, her blue eyes beginning to flash, he added mildly, "When I first met you, you had the temperament of an aging termagant. I see you still do." He strolled leisurely about the room while she watched him distrustfully, the sunlight shining in her golden hair as she moved hastily to keep him in her field of vision.

Seeing the dark scowl upon her face, he told her obligingly, "Mrs. Janet MacCrary has been caring for you. She looked after your wounds and bathed you while you were ill. Aye, you had a fever, a high one at that."

Merewyn shook her head. "No, 'twasn't what I wanted to ask. Who is Mrs. MacCrary? One of the women from the other ship?"

"She's the innkeeper's wife." Seeing the look of utter bewilderment creep over the lovely features he asked in surprise, "Did you think we were still on board the *Highlander*?"

"No, I thought, at least I assumed—" Her words trailed off as she stared at him in confusion. "Where are we?"

"In Boston. What made you think we were still out to sea?"

"The floor tilted so when I awoke. I thought—" She fell silent, unable to grasp the fact that she was on solid ground, and in the colonies, no less.

"Doubtless a dizzy spell," he remarked. "We've been in Boston for three days now."

Merewyn's voice was faint and she wavered on her feet, looking about her as though seeking support from some unknown source. "I-I don't understand. I just don't understand anything."

For a moment the Marquis' heart was filled with pity as he looked down into the little face with its touchingly lost expression. What was it about her, he wondered, that made her seem so vulnerable when in truth she was one of the most passionate firebrands he'd ever come across? Once before she'd managed to soften his feelings toward her with that defenseless demeanor and he'd hated her for it, wanting very much to thrash her for the pain she'd inflicted on him with her small booted foot.

"Perhaps I can explain," he suggested, his tone more gentle, and Merewyn looked at him searchingly, immediately on the defensive.

"Who are you?" she demanded suspiciously, ignoring his offer. "I don't even know your name."

He gave her an insolent smile, the gray eyes filled with amusement. "I am Ian Villiers, ma'am, Marquis of Montague."

"But you can't be!" she breathed, echoing the same words of denial she'd uttered weeks ago while he had been shaking her dripping wet body to and fro.

"Oh, but I am," he assured her. "My uncle Edward

died in March after a fall from his horse. I was his sole heir.''

"Then it was you who closed our waterway!'' Merewyn cried, everything falling into place at last.

He shrugged his massive shoulders. '' 'Twas my uncle's last suggestion and I thought 'twould be a wise precaution until I learned what sort of partners you MacAilises were.'' He grinned unabashedly. "Edward told me quite a bit about the lot of you but I took it for granted that his views were somewhat prejudiced. Don't look so murderous, ma'am. You'll recall that I opened the waterway again without demanding the price increase my uncle sought.''

"And it was you,'' Merewyn continued as though he hadn't spoken, her voice shaking, "who schemed against Alexander to take total control of the mills. Now I understand what he was trying to tell me that day.'' The blue eyes smoldered with accusation. "Oh, how thoroughly you must have tricked him with your honesty and let's-bury-the-past attitude! I've an idea why you came after me, too! To claim me as your bride, no doubt, in order to further your control over Alex. I can assure you, sir, I'd rather be fed to the sharks!''

She turned her back on him and was startled when his deep, rumbling laugh rang out behind her.

"Wait, my dear,'' he told her, coming across the room toward her, "the first thing you'd better learn to do is dress properly. Your buttons are undone.''

"Don't touch me,'' she threatened, whirling about to face him, feeling angry and helpless as she tilted back her head in order to look into his eyes. Why did he have to be so—so cursed large?

"I mean no harm,'' he assured her, his aristocratic countenance filled with mild unconcern. "You can't do them yourself, can you? Allow me.''

She turned reluctantly, lifting the heavy mass of hair

out of the way and heard him whistle softly as he saw the faint red welts on her skin.

"Are they so very ugly?" she choked, scarlet with embarrassment.

His tone was oddly gentle. "Not at all. Mrs. MacCrary's herbal ointment seems to have worked well."

She waited in an agony of self-consciousness as he fastened her gown, trembling as his strong fingers brushed her skin, loathing him for making her feel so impotent. As soon as he was finished she let her hair tumble down and moved away from him, her dark eyes flashing with dislike.

"So you really are the Marquis of Montague," she said bitterly. "I wish I'd known that day I came to see you. I would have run a dirk right through that black heart of yours."

"Compassionate little beast, aren't you?" he asked, infuriating her by smiling unaffectedly. "Why on earth did you go to Glasgow? I assume you were tricked into signing the indenture papers and taken aboard the *Highlander* there."

"How did you know?" Merewyn demanded, the soft voice filled with sudden fear. Above all she didn't want him to know that she had been thrown in gaol as a suspected prostitute! Dear God, how he'd mock her for that and she knew she wouldn't be able to bear it!

He shrugged his broad shoulders, regarding her intently, curious at her sudden change from icy hauteur to uncertainty. " 'Twasn't difficult to guess. Did Alexander take you down to Glasgow?"

She hung her head in shame. "I came alone," she admitted. "To see you. Your uncle, I mean."

His surprise was evident in his tone. "Alone? Why?"

"I've an impetuous nature," she confessed honestly, and hurried on before he had time to make the disparaging remark she felt certain he would, "and I wanted to try and put an end to the nonsense Alexander had agreed to."

"And how did you expect to achieve this end once you met Lord Montague? By kicking him in the groin? I gather 'tis your specialty."

The golden head snapped up and Merewyn flew at him, her small fists drawn back to strike, her temper boiling over. "Y-you impudent dog! Someone should have beaten that arrogance out of you long ago!"

"And I expect you're going to try?" he demanded mildly, easily catching the flailing fists in his strong hands, pulling her against him so that she was unable to move, tears of helplessness brimming in her large eyes. "I cannot understand what it is about me, ma'am," came his deep voice close to her ear, "that makes you want to inflict physical punishment whenever we meet."

" 'Tis the very least you deserve!" she panted, struggling to no avail to free herself, finding it difficult to breathe as he crushed her against his hard chest, his powerful arms tightening about her, one large hand painfully securing both of her wrists, the other about her small waist as he half lifted her off the ground in an effort to keep her from kicking at him.

"Let me go!" she gasped.

"Not until you promise to behave," he replied, sounding not the least bit concerned by the fact that he was attempting to subdue the raging little vixen beneath him.

"Never!"

"You should have learned your lesson by now," he reminded her. "You didn't exactly emerge victorious from our last altercation."

"Nor did you manage to come away totally unscathed," she retorted, twisting her head away from the fine lawn shirt against which it had been pressed in order to look up at him, her lips parted, her small teeth bared so that he was reminded momentarily of a raging wolf cub.

His own temper began to rise. "Damn you, you little bitch," he rasped, "were you a man I'd have laid the glove to you by now."

"Are you so certain you'd win that duel?" she demanded in a mocking tone, her voice no warmer than his.

He shook her angrily and was startled to hear her cry out, pain evident in her deep-set blue eyes as her small head rolled to one side, the thin shoulders drooping; and, suddenly remembering that she was recovering from a vicious whipping, he was aware that he had probably hurt her badly. Again he felt that twinge of pity in his heart and he gently loosened his hold, concerned by her ghastly paleness.

"Are you all right?" he asked, staring intently down into the ashen little face.

Her eyes fluttered open, the indigo depths burning with hatred, but her voice was faint and it trembled as she spoke. "A p-pox take you, you Sassenach b-brute!"

The door to Merewyn's room burst opened unexpectedly and an elderly woman with hawkish features, her graying hair pulled severely from her high forehead and tied in a knot at the nape of her neck, strode authoritatively inside. Faded green eyes surveyed the battling couple before her with disbelief, misconstruing the angry glitter in the towering Marquis' eyes as passion, for he held the swaying girl in his arms as though he had been embracing her ardently, Merewyn's soft red lips parted as though in response to his kisses.

"I canna believe my eyes!" came an outraged voice heavily laced with a Scots burr. "Couldn't you wait until the lassie was fully recovered before falling upon her this way? And unattended in her bedroom! I really don't know what to say, m'lord!''

Lord Montague responded with a slow smile to her shocked accusations, his handsome countenance registering considerable amusement. "Believe me, Mrs. MacCrary,'' he assured her, lifting the helpless girl effortlessly into his arms and carrying her to the bed, "kissing this young devil's spawn is the last thing I'd want to do.''

"Put me down, you muck-eating blackguard,'' Merewyn whispered weakly as his lean face came close to hers, her choice words startling even a hardened man like the Marquis who, as he deposited her more gently than he would have liked on the thick blankets, was relieved that the pious Mrs. MacCrary hadn't heard what the pain-racked, seemingly innocent angel had said. Statements like that better served beggars on a London street.

"I assure you 'twas not as it seemed,'' he added, straightening from his task and turning to face the wrath of Janet MacCrary whose impatiently tapping toe indicated clearly that she expected an explanation. "I came in to see how Miss MacAilis was faring and found her attempting to go downstairs. You can see that she had even dressed herself.''

The russet gown that covered Merewyn's slender body lent credence to the story, but the elderly woman still looked unconvinced.

"When I tried to pursuade her that she should return to her bed,'' the Marquis continued insolently, "she could not be reasoned with and I was in the process of forcefully returning her there when you arrived.''

The sharp green eyes studied the impassive features lying against the downy pillows—the indigo eyes closed, Merewyn having drifted off to sleep, exhausted by her encounter with the Marquis—and the old woman's unrelenting expression softened as she looked down into the delicate face, and reached out to brush a golden tendril from the smooth forehead with unexpected gentleness.

"Thank you for your help, m'lord," she said with a sharp glance into the Marquis's handsome face, "but now that the lassie's better I dinna think you should be coming up here nae more."

The full lips tightened. "I assure you, Mrs. MacCrary, I've no intentions of returning to this wild creature's lair."

He strolled casually out of the door and Mrs. Mac-Crary shook her head as his large frame disappeared from view. He was an arrogant scoundrel, that one, she thought, as she busied herself with loosening the bodice of the velvet gown to make her sleeping patient more comfortable. Handsome as the snow tigers she'd seen in Nepal in her youth, but just as dangerous.

When Merewyn awoke again it was to find the gray-haired woman forcing open the door with her foot to enter the room with a wooden tray in her bony hands. The tantalizing smell of broth and freshly baked bread wafted through the room and Merewyn opened her eyes, her small nose twitching in response.

"Aye, and I was thinkin' this'd wake you."

She looked up quickly, vaguely remembering the sharp-featured woman in the plain brown dress, the sleeves and neckline unadorned, no hint of lace or embroidery to be seen. "Are you Mrs. MacCrary?" she hazarded.

The stern features softened for a fraction of a second when she saw the confusion in the wide blue eyes. "Aye, 'tis who I am. Are you hungry, lass?"

Merewyn's expression cleared. "Why, you're Scots!"

"Of course I am," Mrs. MacCrary retorted good naturedly, setting the tray down on a chair and extending the bowl of soup to Merewyn, who accepted it eagerly, her belly growling. "Though 'tis been years since I've seen it."

"How long?" Merewyn asked curiously as she chomped industriously on a thickly buttered slice of bread.

"Nearly two score years," she replied, pulling up the chair and seating herself, the tray transferred to her lap. "After my Allen died I went home wantin' naught but to spend the rest of my days in dear Aberdeen, but then the bonnie Prince did come and I'm sure you ken what happened then, though you look a wee bit young to have been there yourself."

"I was born several months before Culloden," Merewyn explained. "My father died there." She swallowed another spoonful of the bracing broth. "What did your husband do?" she asked curiously, assuming Mrs. MacCrary had been married to the Allen she had so casually mentioned.

"He was with the British East India Company," Janet replied, always eager for the opportunity to talk about her late, beloved husband. "When we first arrived in India when I was a wee lass no older than yourself there wasn't much of a British establishment there at the time." The severe expression softened with memories. " 'Twas a good time, lass, and one I'll always remember with a fond heart. We traveled everywhere, Allen and I, to Tibet, Nepal and almost into China though the natives were reportedly hostile. Still, we never had any trouble. Not the way they did in the Battle of Plassey in '57. I knew Robert Clive, I did, for he was an acquaintance of Allen's, but by the time he led the company into war my Allen was long dead."

"What happened?" Merewyn asked softly, hearing the yearning behind those simple words.

"A fever. 'Twas common in India. Took a matter of days, that's all."

"I'm sorry," Merewyn said.

The green eyes fastened themselves on the heart-shaped face, regarding her intently for a few moments before the old woman said wonderingly, "I really think you are."

" 'Tis hard to lose someone you care for," Merewyn added, her voice soft with a longing of her own, thinking of the mother she had lost while so very young and the father she had never seen, although Alexander had told her so much about him that she felt deep in her heart that she had known him well. Tears welled in her eyes and she dashed them away, embarrassed by her weakness.

"There, there, lass." Janet MacCrary was patting her small hand comfortingly. " 'Tis the sickness you've had. No reason to blush so just because you've shed a few tears. What's amiss?"

"I was thinking about my brothers," Merewyn explained, sniffling shamefacedly. "I haven't seen them for so long and they must be terribly worried about me."

"Sir Robert told me how you'd been kidnapped," the old woman informed her sympathetically. " 'Twas dreadful, I'm sure, but 'tis over now and you'll be home again soon enough."

"Sir Robert?" The tear-filled eyes were wide with curiosity.

"Aye. Captain of the ship that rescued you."

Merewyn digested this news in silence, suddenly aware of how little she really did know about the few days that had elapsed since Louis Kincaid had ordered her so heinously beaten. She'd wanted to ask the Marquis to explain everything to her but had ended up quarreling with him instead. 'Twas to be expected, she told herself with a contemptuous curl to her red lower lip. That hard-bitten brute was too arrogant to get along with anyone.

"How did I get here?" Merewyn asked, helping herself to another slice of bread.

"Sir Robert and the Marquis brought you," Mrs.
MacCrary explained, delighted to see her young patient
exhibit such a healthy appetite and determined to answer all her questions in the hopes that she'd continue to
eat while she spoke. How thin the wee lassie was! "HMS
Columbia, Sir Robert's ship, chased down the one you
were on."

"The *Highlander.*"

"Aye, the *Highlander.* Can't see how I'd forget a name
like that. 'Twould seem, according to what Sir Robert
told me the night they brought you here, they'd arrested
a man in Glasgow who was trying to smuggle some
women aboard another ship, and when they questioned
him and threatened him, he finally gave the names of
others he'd tricked into bonding during the past few
years."

She shook her head in disgust. "Foul business. The
man should be hanged."

"Was his name Edmund Unsworth?" Merewyn demanded.

The green eyes narrowed thoughtfully. "It seems to
me that's what Sir Robert said. Anyway, 'twould seem
he and that captain, Kincaid, was it?"

Merewyn shuddered, nodding her head vigorously.

"Kincaid, then, had been under suspicion for some
time. They only needed proof. That Unsworth fellow
provided it along with the names of the people he'd kidnapped in the past. Lord Montague happened to be in
Glasgow and when he learned yours was on that list he
came aboard *Columbia* and said he was going with them
to fetch you."

" 'Twould have been better for all concerned,"
Merewyn remarked with considerable asperity, "if his
lordship hadn't done my brother the favor and left such
work to Sir Robert and his crew."

"I fancy you've no liking for the man," Janet Mac-

Crary observed shrewdly, studying Merewyn's firmly set little chin.

"Well, I don't," she retorted.

"He's certainly handsome," the older woman pointed out.

"Do you think so?" Merewyn asked coldly, turning a blank expression toward her that left Janet no doubt in her mind as to the girl's true feelings for the well-built giant.

"Aye, but I'd not like to be dealing with that one," she confessed, and was amused to see that her young patient seemed relieved, as though it was important to her than no one else liked the Marquis either.

"And how did we happen to come to Boston?" Merewyn asked in a much warmer tone, determined to thrust the image of the hated Ian Villiers from her thoughts and bring Janet MacCrary's attention back to the subject at hand.

"To take on fresh provisions, of course," came the prompt reply, "and to give you time to recover before you set sail again for England."

Merewyn's brow darkened, disliking the thought of enduring another long voyage. But Alexander, Malcolm, and Cairnlach, not enslavement and despair, lay at the end of this one, she told herself, her heart warming.

"There, I've said enough," the old woman stated, seeing the excited flush that crept to Merewyn's hollow cheeks, believing it due to overexertion. "Lord love us, lass, I don't believe I've gossiped this much in years."

She bent down and picked up the tray, then started for the door. "I'll have my husband fetch up the bath for you tomorrow," she added as she paused on the threshold. "I imagine you'll be wantin' to have one more good wash before you board that ship again."

Merewyn stared at her curiously. "I thought you said

your husband was dead."

The green eyes held only a trace of wistfulness. "Aye, my Allen's gone. But a woman has to make her way somehow, lass. When I came to Boston I had naught but the clothes on my back and a wee bit of siller in my hand. Didn't take too long until I found Mr. MacCrary, from Inverness originally, and he was setting up this ale house here. I started working at the bar, one thing led to another and. . ." She smiled briefly before adding, " 'Tis how you came to be here, lass. He and Sir Robert are cousins of sorts."

What a strange woman, Merewyn thought to herself when she had gone, spending her youth in colorful places that she herself had never even heard of. Though her speech and dress indicated that Janet MacCrary was somewhat puritanical, she had nonetheless followed the man she loved through strange, exotic, and doubtless primitive countries, then relocated in the colonies where she'd shunned propriety to work in a public ale house! But then, as Janet herself had admitted, poverty and need made strange bedfellows of some.

Feeling unexpectedly restless, Merewyn tossed back the covers and got out of bed, shaking out the wrinkles in her gown and padding in stocking feet to the window where she drew back the curtains to peer curiously out. Twilight was falling over the city and she could see the rough silhouettes of numerous buildings, most of them elegant houses made of brick or other stone. A broad river wound its way past her window, and when she followed it with her eyes she could make out wharves and a tangle of masts belonging to ships moored not too far from the MacCrarys' inn.

She sighed as she let the curtains fall back into place and turned away from the beauty of the gold and violet sunset. If only she was already home in Cairnlach! She felt a great weariness replacing her earlier high spirits and her thin shoulders drooped as loneliness weighed heavily upon her, self-pity threatened to engulf her, and tears smarted in her eyes anew. Reaching up to wipe them away she felt a sharp twinge in her back and was reminded of the injuries Janet MacCrary had tried so patiently to heal.

Where was Louis Kincaid at the moment? Merewyn wondered, rising to pace the room, her skirts rustling. Had Sir Robert managed to arrest him, too? Would he be taken back to England to stand trial? She shivered at the thought, hoping 'twould not be on the same ship she'd be traveling on! She never wanted to lay eyes on that vile little man again unless it was to see him swinging from the gallows. Aye, he deserved to be hung for the beatings she and David had received! David. . . .

Dear God, David! Merewyn's heart stopped. Had anyone done anything to help David while she herself had been ill? A vision of his lacerated back, his face ashen as they carried him below, brought dread to her heart and she hurriedly drew on her shoes, then pulled her cape from the peg near the door, not even noticing that it, too, had been thoroughly cleaned for her. All her thoughts were centered on the young boy who had tried so hard to help her, only to end up paying so horribly for his kindness.

The landing was only dimly illuminated by light filtering from the taproom below and Merewyn carefully felt her way down the creaking stairs, skirting the smoke-filled room from which the sounds of laughter and the smell of food told her that the MacCrarys had a full house on their hands. She had no desire to meet up with the domineering, iron-haired woman, certain that she'd be sent back to bed, nor did she wish to encounter the Marquis if he was indeed staying here at the inn. She wanted to see David, and nothing else mattered.

Feeling certain that the boy would still be aboard the *Highlander,* and convinced, too, that the barkentine was somewhere in the harbor, she stepped outside, turning up her fur-trimmed collar against the crispness of the night air, the fading daylight still outlining the soaring masts of the same ships she had seen from her window. The narrow, twisting street was deserted and Merewyn found nothing to detain her as she left the cobblestones behind and set off along the wharves, skirting the crates and barrels that were stacked neatly on the uneven wooden planking.

A few solitary strollers moved along the bridge that spanned the river not too far downstream, but Merewyn ignored them, her eyes straining through the darkness to read the names of the ships which she passed, the bobbing lights making it difficult to see. There were a great number of ships here, she realized, many more than in Glasgow, the pier stretching all the way downriver, and she wondered how far she would have to go before she found the *Highlander*.

Two seamen, obviously drunk, came tottering off the gangplank of one of the sloops as she passed, one of them colliding solidly with her as he staggered unexpectedly, his great weight almost knocking her down.

" 'ey Jim!" he called as he regained his balance, Merewyn's arm firmly clasped in his pudgy hand, blinking as he stared down at her. "See what I got 'ere!"

"Let me go!" Merewyn demanded, trying to pull free as the red-snouted Jim staggered over to join his companion, his bloodshot eyes attempting to focus on the protesting beauty before him. His thick lips spread into a leering grin.

"Aye, Dan'l, 'tis a fine one yer got." His words were interspersed with hiccoughs.

"Better'n any two-penny whore I seed back 'ome," Dan'l agreed, reeling slightly as Merewyn pushed against his voluminous paunch, one small elbow digging painfully into his ribs.

"Unhand me, you drunken beggar!"

Her angry words brought a chortle of glee from Jim.

"She be a 'ot one, she be! Too much woman for yer alone, Dan'l me lad!"

"Shut up yer mouth yer bleedin' buggar!" Dan'l retorted, irritated because Merewyn's small fists had begun pummeling him relentlessly.

" 'Tisn't no way to talk to yer friend!" Jim protested in a wounded tone. "Yer a perishin' foul-mouthed cuss, Dan'l Fred'ricks!"

"An' yer a drunken liar!"

Merewyn's temper flared, disgusted by their foolish argument and the stale smell of gin that seemed to ooze out of every pore. She had no fear for her own personal safety, neither of the two men seeming capable of doing anything other than standing on their own two feet, and even that accomplishment was proven doubtful when she pushed Dan'l again, causing him to reel and let go of her, falling heavily on his fat rump on the hard wooden pier.

" 'Ere, now, what'd yer do to me friend?" demanded Jim in a nasty tone, advancing menacingly towards Merewyn while the dumb-founded Dan sat gazing up at her with hurt-filled eyes.

"I'll do the same to you if you touch me!" Merewyn threatened, her blue eyes flashing, only to retreat a hasty step, sensing that Seaman Jim was not as helpless as his companion. She disliked, too, the gleam in his beady eyes as he looked her up and down appraisingly.

"Not bad, not bad," he murmured, licking his lips as he took in the thick golden rope of hair pinned to the nape of her slender neck. "Too much wench for Dan'l but not so for me!"

He took another deliberate step towards her and Merewyn moved quickly away. Behind her the confused Daniel was rising slowly to his feet, shaking himself like a wet dog, and Merewyn realized with sudden panic that she was trapped.

"Stay away from me!" she said bravely, measuring

the distance between the approaching Jim and the end of the wharf, wondering if she could squeeze by him without tumbling into the water.

"Don't yer be frightened," Jim soothed her with another leer. "Ol' Jim'll—"

A deep, polite voice from behind drowned out his words. "Do you need help, ma'am?"

Merewyn's heart leaped as she turned and saw Lord Montague's large frame loom from the darkness, although she never would have confessed aloud that she was glad to see him. He came to a halt directly behind the wavering Jim, powerful arms crossed over his broad chest, his gray eyes holding hers, a pleasant smile playing on his full lips.

Jim's eyes fairly bulged from his head as he turned and craned his thick neck to look up into the towering Marquis's face. Fear flickered on the ruddy features and he nervously moistened his lips with the tip of his tongue.

"We was just havin' us a bit of fun wi' the lady," he explained, his voice strained and unnaturally high. "Didn't mean nothin' by it, sir."

"See that it doesn't happen again," Lord Montague responded, still smiling pleasantly though there was an unmistakably hard edge to his tone that sent a shiver down even Merewyn's spine.

"Aye, sir, aye."

The Marquis looked after them as they hobbled away in the darkness, leaning against each other for support. His handsome features impassive, he then turned back to Merewyn and gazed down at her questioningly.

She tilted back her head to look up at him, her own expression defiant. "Doubtless you expect thanks for helping me. Well, I don't intend to say anything! I didn't need you at all!"

"Well, then, next time I'll just remember to leave the reins in your hands," he assured her. "As for the moment, if you think you can handle the rest of the riffraff on these docks I'll leave you to your business." He turned and strode away, leaving Merewyn alone, making her realize as soon as he vanished in the darkness that she felt much safer in his presence after all.

"Wait!" she called, lifting her skirts and breaking into a run, catching up with him near the street where she caught hold of his muscular arm, tugging impatiently until he looked down at her inquiringly. He made no effort to check his stride, however, and she was forced to run to keep up with him.

"Blast you, Villiers!" she panted at last, scowling at him ill-temperedly. "*Will* you stop!"

He obliged, seeing that she looked extremely pale and that her small chest was heaving as she gasped for air. He'd forgotten that she'd had a high fever only two days before and felt some of his annoyance fade with the thought. Yet he refused to exhibit any softening towards her on his part and demanded coldly.

"Is there a reason for bellowing after me like some barnyard calf?"

She bit back her angry retort. "I-I'm sorry," she forced herself to say contritely. " 'Twas very k-kind of you to help me back there."

His deep laugh rumbled in his chest and he propped his hands on his narrow hips, looking down at her bowed head with a knowing smile. "I'd warrant you'd rather have cut out your tongue than say that, but I suspect you want something from me. What is it?"

She looked up at him and he was surprised to see the humble expression on her small face. "Will you take me to the *Highlander,* please?"

Something in her soft voice made him ask more kindly, "What is it, lass? Does Mrs. MacCrary know you're out here? Never mind, I know she doesn't. She'd never permit you to go out on the docks alone."

"I have to get on board the *Highlander*," Merewyn

repeated stubbornly. "If you won't take me at least let me go. Don't take me back to the inn."

"I'll take you," he replied, ignoring the antagonism that was returning to her eyes. In the dim lantern light they appeared almost black and seemed to take up almost half of her finely proportioned face. The stiff breeze from the river and the tussle with the sailors had loosened some of the golden curls that were blowing about her temples, but her disheveled appearance only made her incredible loveliness seem all the more unique. He found himself thinking again that it was a pity that such unbelievable beauty could be found in a young girl of such contrary nature.

"You're lucky I happened along when I did," he commented. "Don't scowl at me, lass, 'tis done. Now," he added, starting back in the direction they'd come, "why don't you tell me why 'tis so important for you to go aboard the *Highlander*?"

" 'Tis because of David," she explained as she hurried along at his side. "I'm terribly worried about him."

Lord Montague came to an abrupt halt and seized her arm roughly. "What are you saying?" he demanded, his gray eyes so forbidding that she recoiled, trying in vain to free herself from his iron grip. "You've got some sort of assignation with one of the crew?"

"There isn't time to tell you everything," she snapped, pulling free at last and starting up the wharf in the direction he had been leading her. "Will you take me or not?"

"Aye, I will," he responded through clenched teeth, telling himself that Alexander MacAilis was a total fool if he believed his sister to be the innocent angel he had so worshipfully described at their first meeting in Inverlochy. What sort of family was this MacAilis clan? Had his first impression of Alexander been a mistaken one? Though he had sensed the young laird's distrust and antagonism during that first meeting, Lord Montague had been tolerant, fully aware that his uncle had done little to enhance any friendship between himself and the MacAilises.

Ian himself, listening to his uncle ramble on his deathbed, had been led to believe they were weak-willed, sniveling barbarians, as he'd thought all Highlanders were, but after spending some time with the quiet, intelligent MacAilis chieftain, he'd realized that his uncle's prejudice had been based on misguided sentiment. Lord Montague was a sound and, above all, swift judge of character. He'd dealt with enough good and bad men in his time to see through all of them, and had needed only a few days with Alexander MacAilis, while going over the books and ledgers, to change his opinion about Cairnlach's inhabitants. He had decided he'd try to do what he could to make the business profitable for both.

But now he found himself wondering if he'd not made a mistake after all, especially in giving up the comforts of his new home in Scotland or the quick trip to London he'd promised himself to go chasing after this tart-tongued wench as a favor to his new business partner. Ian Villiers was not often given to making mistakes and his nature was wrathful at best when that rare moment came, and so it was with a considerably bruising grip that he pulled the panting young MacAilis lass up the gangway onto the *Highlander*'s deck.

Lieutenant Harold Spencer, standing watch on board the moored barkentine, came striding forward to meet them, having recognized the tall, dark-headed Marquis immediately. "Anything amiss, my lord?" he asked, curiously taking in the utterly spent young lass at the frowning man's side, his expression registering considerable surprise as he recognized the wan face with its enormous tilted eyes. "Isn't that the young lady, my lord?"

"Aye, 'tis Miss MacAilis," the Marquis replied impatiently, thinking that 'young lady' was scarcely an apt description for the little betraying monster beside him.

"She has an appointment to meet one of the crew members." His expression was contemptuous as he thrust Merewyn forward.

Lieutenant Spencer shook his head. "Not all of them are here, miss. Captain Sir Robert has taken most of them into custody."

Merewyn had looked up at the sound of the polite, educated voice and found herself confronted by a man not much older than Malcolm and whose looks were surprisingly similar. His hair beneath the tricorn hat was thick and chestnut brown in color, his eyes the same shade, and she felt an instant liking for him—an empathy he seemed to feel, for he suddenly flushed self-consciously and gave her an awkward bow.

"I'm Lieutenant Harold Spencer, miss. I'll be sailing the *Highlander* back to England."

Merewyn's answering smile was warm, and Lord Montague, watching her keenly, found himself surprised by it, never having suspected that she possessed anything more than vast stores of hostility for her fellow beings. "I'm happy to make your acquaintance, Lieutenant. I seriously doubt you've imprisoned the crewman I want to see." A strained expression entered the guileless blue eyes that, Spencer noticed with growing admiration, were remarkable in their size and color, the darkness within interspersed with shining gold.

"His name is David Brown and he—I'm afraid he may be badly hurt. Captain Kincaid had him flogged, too."

Lieutenant Spencer felt he couldn't bear to look at the pain in her delicate countenance any longer. "We've put him in one of the officer's cabins," he informed her quickly.

"Then he's all right?" Merewyn breathed.

"We're tending to him, miss," came the evasive reply.

"I'd like to see him."

"I don't think—"

"I'd like to see him," Merewyn repeated, and Lord Montague was forced to smile when he saw how quickly the young Lieutenant hurried to comply, leading them briskly across the deck to the companionway.

Merewyn had never been inside the cabin to which Lieutenant Spencer brought her—sparsely furnished quarters much smaller than Captain Kincaid's—and she guessed that it had belonged to the first mate or Carl Winston, the bos'n. But she forgot all else when she saw David lying in the bunk, tossing feverishly among the rough blankets, naked to the waist, the ragged lacerations on his back open and oozing, and she bit back a cry of alarm.

"Oh, David!"

Quickly she sank to her knees beside him, taking his hot hand in hers, tears welling in her eyes. "David, 'tis Merewyn. Can you hear me?"

He moaned as he looked at her, but she could tell by his glazed expression that he did not recognize her. Still she persisted, softly uttering his name, trying to lure him back to a more lucid state, her small hand cool and soothing as she touched his burning forehead.

"David, please," she begged, not really sure what she expected of him but desperate to elicit some sort of reply.

"Merewyn, there's no use in this."

She looked up, dimly aware that the Marquis had spoken to her. He was bending down, his lean face close to hers, and she thought she detected sympathy in the forbidding gray eyes. "Why didn't you bring him to Mrs. MacCrary's?" she blazed at him, all of her anger and fear directed at this towering individual who always seemed to be responsible for everyone else's troubles.

Something flickered in the compelling eyes as he saw the hatred burning in hers. "I wasn't informed of the lad's existence," he told her coldly. Reaching out his hand he tried to pull her to her feet, but she resisted.

"I want to stay with him."

"You can't. You're barely recovered from a fever yourself."

She gazed beseechingly at Lieutenant Spencer. "Can't you help him?"

"We've been trying, miss," he replied uncomfortably, unable to meet the accusing indigo eyes.

"But he's dreadfully ill!" she cried, turning back to the babbling boy. "And his wounds, they're not healing as they should!"

"Merewyn, come away." The command in the deep voice was unmistakable.

"I tell you I won't!" she shouted.

"Please, miss, don't upset yourself," Lieutenant Spencer implored, convinced that the dainty young lady was prepared to have an attack of the vapors.

"We have to do something!" she countered, anger and despair mingling on her comely features. Turning to the Marquis, whose dark eyes were regarding her with exasperation, she demanded, "Can't you do anything?"

"Aye," he replied and she felt relief wash over her at his calm tone. "I'll have some of Mrs. MacCrary's herbal ointment sent over." He glanced thoughtfully at the thrashing figure on the bunk. "I also think we should bring in a physician."

The heart-shaped face glowed with gratitude. "Oh, would you?" Merewyn breathed.

Lord Montague had never been the recipient of her warmest smile and forgot for a brief moment that he disliked her. "I'll do what I can," he promised more kindly, "but I want you to go back to the inn."

She shook her head. "I'm going to stay here until David gets well."

This stubborn expression was one he was far more familiar with by now and he knew also that it would be futile to argue with her. Motioning to Lieutenant Spencer he drew the younger man out into the narrow corridor. "I'll get the physician myself. Mrs. MacCrary ought to know where one can be found. The lad looks bad. See if you can't find some cold water to sponge him with to bring that fever down—and I doubt you'll be able to, but try to convince Miss MacAilis to have someone take her back to the inn."

"I'll do my best, my lord," Lieutenant Spencer replied with determination. But Ian knew as he went on deck that the lieutenant's best simply wouldn't be good enough where Merewyn MacAilis was concerned.

When he returned a scant half-hour later with Janet MacCrary in tow, he found Merewyn still huddled beside the bunk, gently applying a cold compress to the burning forehead while David lay moaning on his side. She looked up hopelessly as he entered, heaving a great sigh of relief as she saw Janet MacCrary behind him.

"Oh, thank God you've come!" she cried, addressing the older woman. "Did you bring the doctor?"

"We won't be needing one," Mrs. MacCrary informed her tartly, setting down the small satchel she had brought with her and rolling up her sleeves in a businesslike fashion. "Those barbarians know naught of medicine. First thing they'd want to do is bleed him. Ha! The poor laddie needs to keep the wee strength he's got. I learned my medicine from the Sherpahs, lass, and they've been healing themselves for thousands of years without a university clown to confuse them!"

Merewyn's answering smile was tremulous and rather bewildered, finding the domineering woman a little intimidating, but she was relieved that knowledgeable and seemingly competent help had come at last. "Is there anything I can do to help?"

"You can go topside and give me room here," the gray-haired woman suggested not unkindly.

"What will you do to him?" Merewyn asked as she rose to her feet, her eyes lingering worriedly on David's flushed face.

"Clean those wounds and pack my ointment into it. Wrap him up good and sweat the fever out of him."

Merewyn would have liked to stay a moment longer, but she felt the Marquis's insistent hand on her arm and followed him obediently up onto the large deck, drawing her cloak about her as she stepped out into the chilly air. "Do you think he'll make it?" she asked worriedly, her large eyes hopefully fastened to his impassive face.

Lord Montague leaned his tall frame against the railing. "I think so."

"I don't believe I'll be able to bear it if something happens to him," Merewyn said with a catch in her soft voice. " 'Twas my fault he was f-flogged."

"Are you certain?"

She hung her head, nodding miserably. "I tried to steal my indenture papers back from Captain Kincaid. David helped me by telling me where he kept the key to his chest. The captain caught me, of course, and said I was to be punished to set an example for the others. David was whipped because he'd betrayed the captain's trust." Her soft lips trembled and she wrung her hands together. " 'Tis all my fault!"

"He'll be fine," Ian assured her gently, striving to keep his murderous anger at Louis Kincaid in check. Sniveling bastard! How he wished now that he'd choked the fellow to death when he'd first boarded the *Highlander,* before Merewyn's sagging form at the mast had claimed his disbelieving attention.

"I owe you an apology, ma'am," he told her now.

In the dim lantern light he could see that her upturned face was filled with astonishment. "You do?"

"Aye. For accusing you of dallying with the hands. I thought David Brown was someone you'd developed a fondness for."

Merewyn's clear laugh rang in the still night air. "For David? He's just a wee lad!"

"At the time I didn't know," Lord Montague reminded her.

Her smile lingered nonetheless. "Oh, but I am fond of
him," she admitted, "and once he gets well I'm going to
take him back to Cairnlach with me."

The Marquis was startled to hear this. "What for?"

"He can't spend the rest of his days as a cabin boy,"
Merewyn replied firmly. "No one will ever give him the
chance to become something more because of his crippled hand. I intend to see that Alex finds work for him
on one of Cairnlach's transport ships. Perhaps as a cox-
swain or something similar, and I don't see why he can't
eventually take on a command of his own." She smiled
sheepishly. "Of course, I can't force him. He's free to
make his own choice."

Lord Montague had to admit to himself that he would
never have expected such a generous gesture from the
irascible young girl standing before him. How could she
be such an odd mix of conflicting emotions? he wondered. She had the manners of a gutter child, the beauty
and rearing of a lady of quality, the temper of a hot-
headed curmudgeon and, on occasion, a surprisingly
warm and loving heart. He shook his dark head, not
understanding her at all.

"What happened to the other passengers?" Merewyn
asked, bringing him from his reverie.

"I believe they've been sent to Wilmington on another
ship."

"And Sir Robert? Where is he? I should like very
much to meet him."

"Doubtless aboard *Columbia* at the moment." Lord
Montague indicated a trim brigantine, bristling with
guns, that bobbed serenely in the water not too far
away. "Now that you're well I imagine he'll make prep-
arations to set sail."

"And I'm to go aboard the *Columbia*?" Merewyn

asked. At his nod she shook her head. "I'm not going to leave David. Lieutenant Spencer said he'd be commanding the *Highlander* back, didn't he? Well, I'll remain aboard. What difference does it make if I go home on one ship or the other?"

The Marquis stared at her irritably. "Damn you, woman," he cursed softly, "do you think you're a law unto yourself? You cannot parade among us like Her Royal Majesty telling us what you will or will not do."

The blue eyes flashed as she rose to his bait. "I can't? 'Twould seem the shoe is on the other foot, my lord." The title sounded like a mocking insult as it fell from her lips. "I'm certain Sir Robert will agree from the kindness of his heart to permit me to remain with David, who happens to be my friend. So, I ask, what right do you have in telling me that I can not?"

The coldness of his gaze might have frightened her if she hadn't been so incensed with anger at his pompous airs, impossible to ignore; every arrogant word he uttered goaded her into retaliation. Aye, she was familiar enough with his kind to know him through and through: handsome, och, maybe she'd go so far as to admit he was; wealthy, no doubt respected, and highly revered all his life, he was accustomed to getting what he wanted and making any men who stood in his way quail with fear. She knew nothing of his past, but no matter how high and mighty he had been in England he was naught but a Sassenach usurper to her and she wasn't about to let him gain any quarter where the MacAilises were concerned.

"I know your kind, my lord," she told him, her words vibrating with dislike, her slim body taut with anger. "And I know what it is you're after. You want everything Cairnlach has, but you're not going to get it. Not one wee bit!"

"You remind me of an incessantly whining insect," he remarked blandly, his unconcern belied by the blackness of his expression, "and I could squash you just as easily."

"You may," she admitted, much to his surprise, displaying no outward sign of fear though he suspected the effort was costing her plenty, for he had seen the color draining from her delicate cheeks at his calm threat. "But you're underestimating the MacAilis clan and the Highland pride you so wrongly condemned when I first met you. We are indomitable, sir, and you'd do well to remember it."

" 'Tis amusing how you give such importance to your trivial little world," he mocked, annoyed at the grudging respect he was beginning to feel for her as she stood squarely before him, determined to stand her ground as he towered above her. "You're mistaken if you believe all I want is your silly mill. There's more to life, ma'am, than sheep and wool, and your foolish insistence that Cairnlach is the hub of creation begins to bore me. Perhaps, in your naive little mind, it may be true."

"I don't have to listen to this," Merewyn cried, "and I won't!" She turned heel and stalked away, sweeping across the deck with her small head proudly carried. But Lord Montague had eyes only for the unconscious sway of her rounded hips, thinking to himself, not for the first time, that she had a body that was too alluring for such a disagreeable creature.

A freshening wind caught the taut canvas, filling them and sending the *Highlander*'s bowsprit plunging through the waves. The barkentine was London bound, three days out of Boston Harbor, following the same channels through which HMS *Columbia* had passed only two days ahead of her. The weather was fair, the sun standing high on the horizon, the ocean below a deep emerald green. A salty tang hung in the crisp morning air and a far-traveling sea gull wheeled overhead, its raucous cry filled with a strangely haunting beauty.

Merewyn came wearily from the passageway, her first time up since the *Highlander* had cleared the Charles River. There were dark circles beneath her tired eyes, but she was smiling to herself as she leaned against the rail, turning her small face to the welcoming warmth of the sun. David's fever had broken some time during the night, and when she had looked in on him towards dawn she had found him sleeping peacefully, his forehead damp, his fretful tossing and turning finally ended. She had tended him tirelessly the past three days, following Janet MacCrary's instructions unerringly. Desperately determined that the lad should live, she knew she'd have his death on her conscience if he didn't.

"How's the lad, miss?"

She turned as Carl Winston addressed her, his boyish expression hopeful as he leaned closer to catch her tired but elated words. "Better at last, I'm glad to say."

"Ah, I knew it! I could tell by the look on your face when you came up. 'Twas all your doing, miss."

"Oh, no," she said hastily. "We've Mrs. MacCrary to thank."

"But it was you who tended the lad all this time," he reminded her.

She smiled again, too tired to reply, missing the worshipful look in his eyes as he studied the averted profile and the smooth line of her jaw, the hollows beneath her soft cheeks clearly defined. He had been thoroughly delighted when he'd discovered that Captain Sir Robert Lindsey had granted her permission to return to England aboard the *Highlander,* Merewyn having assured the kindly naval officer that she had no intention of leaving David until he was out of danger.

The youthful bos'n had done his best to help with the nursing, urging the exhausted girl to sleep whenever it was his turn to stay with David, bathing the hot forehead and applying new ointment to the wounded back that was beginning to show signs of healing. Merewyn had taken all her meals in the cabin where David lay, and Carl Winston had faithfully carried them down to her three times a day on a wooden tray, gallantly overlooking her distracted thanks, content to do what he could to ease her burden.

Lieutenant Harold Spencer, commanding the *Highlander* under Sir Robert's orders, had also shown himself eager to share Merewyn's task, and Carl's heart always swelled with jealousy whenever he entered the small cabin to find the handsome young officer sharing vigil at Merewyn's side.

"You should go below and rest," he said with a great show of manly concern, hoping to gain an advantage over the lieutenant who was presently occupied elsewhere. "You look tired."

"I'm not," Merewyn assured him. "I want to stay up here for a while. The air feels so good and the sun so warm."

"Aye, that it is," the bos'n agreed. " 'Tis a blessing that it shines," he added, admiring the soft golden curls that framed the delicate face, the sunlight giving them a radiance he found breathtaking.

Lieutenant Spencer, coming down the ladder from the upper deck and observing the two heads, one dark and one fair, bent close together as though they were sharing intimate secrets, strode quickly toward them while trying to hide his haste. It was clearly obvious to Lord Montague, however, watching from the helm with a cynical twist to his full lips, and he shook his dark head, never having seen such a besotted display of competitive courtship in his entire life. He himself had seen nothing of Merewyn MacAilis the past three days, save for an occasional encounter in the companionway when she had given him a tight nod before brushing past, but he had noticed how drawn she looked, the strain evident in the luminous blue eyes. Doubtless she was feeling responsible for the young cabin boy's condition, and Lord

Montague found himself pitying her, aware that she was carrying a large burden of guilt on her slender shoulders.

Watching her briefly as she smiled and laughed in response to the young men's banter as they vied for her attention, he noticed that she appeared gay and free of cares and guessed that David's fever must have broken at last. Abruptly, he dismissed her from his mind, his gray eyes wandering over the tightly trimmed sails and the intricate rigging, his strong hands sure and experienced on the wheel. Almost a dozen years had passed since he'd last been at the helm of a ship, but he hadn't forgotten the stir of excitement when the vessel heeled gently in response to his hands, and his long legs braced themselves for the ever changing tilt to the polished deck, his stance that of a man as comfortable there on the sea as on land.

The muffled sound of soft laughter drifted to him from below, breaking into his thoughts, and he glanced down to see that Merewyn was responding to something Lieutenant Spencer had said to her, her tilted eyes sparkling, soft lips parted, the lieutenant's handsome face wreathed in smiles while the glowering bos'n looked jealously on.

Aye, she was a first-class trollop, Ian thought to himself, turning disinterestedly away. She had enough beauty to pull any man about by the heartstrings and the wit and skill to accomplish it. Where had she developed this talent for flirting sequestered her entire life within the protective walls of Cairnlach Castle? She had the flair and poise of a much older, experienced woman, and damned if he knew how she managed it.

No matter, he decided with a faint shrug. The sooner they were back in Scotland the better, for he couldn't wait to turn this difficult handful of young womanhood back over to her brother. Thereafter he intended to keep his relationship with the MacAilises strickly on a business level. He frowned thoughtfully, remembering the insulting comment he'd made to Merewyn about the mills being of little importance. He'd been lying to her, of course, though she'd been too angry to realize it. The mills were earning s staggering amount of yearly revenue and had the potential of expanding even further into the market, a business challenge Ian found difficult to ignore.

Naive little chit, he thought irritably, glancing down at Merewyn's trim back while she leaned against the rail, one admirer on either side. Did she honestly believe he viewed his inheritance as insignificant?

Relieved at the helm by Lieutenant Spencer not long afterwards, he sauntered leisurely across the deck, hands clasped behind his broad back, taking the recently vacated place at the railing beside the solitary figure in russet velvet, her skirts billowing in the light afternoon breeze. "I see your court has retired, ma'am, or did you wrathfully dismiss them for some innocently committed crime?"

She ignored him, her little nose pointed haughtily into the air.

"Fie on you," he continued mildly. "Don't you realize both of them worship the very ground you stand on?"

"If you're trying to start an argument," came her soft, warning reply, "you'll have to look elsewhere. I'm not going to speak to you any more."

"In that case 'twill be an exceptionally lonely voyage for me," he mocked, his lean face close as he bent down to look into her eyes and saw the expected fury flashing in them. How easy she was to manipulate, he thought to himself, her quicksilver moods responding to any carefully chosen word he cared to utter. Womanly in graces, aye, but still a child who could be twisted quite easily about his finger.

"You seem to take great delight in tormenting me," she remarked, gazing up at him questioningly, more perplexed than angry. "Why?"

He shrugged his broad shoulders. "No other diversion on hand, I imagine." Sensing the tart retort on her lips, he added before she could speak, "May I also remind you that you and I have an old score to settle? For your brother's sake I won't give you the thrashing you deserve, but I've no intentions of letting you go unscathed."

"What is it I've done?" Merewyn demanded irritably, finding the towering man before her more exasperating than anyone she'd ever met. Really, his arrogance was unbelievable!

The gray eyes were filled with derisive laughter. "Do you honestly mean to tell me you've forgotten our little altercation? I'm accustomed to abuse from high-spirited women—'tis all a part of the game—but yours bordered on the insulting and I don't take kindly to insults."

Merewyn was prepared to make a jeering retort, but the cruel glint in his eyes warned her that he meant what he said. There was a definite limit to which he could be goaded, and she suspected that she had stepped over that line when she'd kicked him in that so-delicate spot, and then made it worse by standing over him and hurling abuses that must have angered him no end.

"I see you've nothing to say," he commented as she remained silent, her small face averted. "I'm almost led to believe that you intend to become obedient."

The soft lips tightened, but still she said nothing.

"In that case, perhaps 'tis possible that you may even apologize to me for your crude treatment."

"Now you're pushing me too far!" she cried, aware that he had done so deliberately, but not caring anymore. Her contemptuous gaze fastened itself on his handsome face. "I simply cannot fathom your bottomless supply of conceit! If I'd kicked you anywhere else you would never have taken it so personally. Truly, my lord, I'm beginning to suspect that men such as yourself are governed by the content of their breeches alone!"

Flushed with anger she whirled about and vanished below decks, leaving Lord Montague to stare after her, somewhat astonished by her outburst. Was there no limit to the things she'd say when she was angry? He doubted he'd ever come across a more ill-mannered, foul-tongued wench in his life. But then his full lips began to twitch and he surprised himself by throwing back his head and giving vent to a great gale of amused laughter.

Merewyn herself was feeling a trifle ashamed of her words as she headed towards David's cabin, unable to understand why the Marquis and his mocking comments aroused in her such terrible rage. Naturally, she hated and resented him for being a Villiers, but her antagonism seemed to go deeper than that. She felt she'd never encountered a more conceited, swell-headed brute in her entire life and was chafing for the opportunity to give him a proper set-to, certain that no one else had succeeded thus far.

Quietly, she pushed open the cabin door, the dark scowl on her face giving way to a relieved smile when she found David still sleeping peacefully, his breathing deep and regular. As she tiptoed to the bunk and smoothed his hair from his brow he startled her by opening his eyes, glinking in an effort to focus his blurred vision.

"Merewyn?"

"Aye, David, I'm here."

"What happened? Have I been ill?" His voice was faint and confused.

"Aye, and your wounds took bad, but you're better now."

He licked his dry lips. "I remember them cutting me loose from the mast. . ." Terror overwhelmed him and he attempted to rise. "The captain—"

Merewyn gently pushed him back. "Lie still!"

Her heart went out to him as he winced. Well did she

know the agony such movement brought! "Lie still," she repeated softly, "and don't roll over on your back. Stay on your side. Captain Kincaid has been arrested, David. 'Tis a long story and I won't tell it to you now. First you must sleep."

"I'll try," he promised weakly as his eyelids fluttered shut.

A great wave of exhaustion seemed to settle over Merewyn as she turned away from the sleeping boy, and she bowed her head, finding it terribly hard of a sudden to carry it upright. With slumped shoulders, she closed the narrow door softly behind her and moved like a sleepwalker down the passageway toward her own cabin. Too tired to be startled, she turned slowly and reluctantly as she heard the Marquis's deep voice address her unexpectedly from behind.

"You'd better retire, ma'am. You need rest."

"I'm capable of making my own decisions, my lord," she responded, but her words lacked their usual asperity and he looked at her keenly, seeing the shadows beneath her fatigue-darkened eyes. She tried to glare at him fiercely but succeeded only in looking even more defensively young, her expression dazed and helpless.

"You aren't well," he added harshly. "Let me take you to your cabin." His strong hand was beneath her elbow, supporting her, but she shook it off impatiently.

"I can go myself, thank you," she declared, but she wavered as she spoke and he was quick to step forward so that she fell against his chest as weariness overcame her. For a moment she leaned against him, her face buried in the softness of his shirt, and he could feel the pliant curves of her body press against his muscular one. His strong arms came around her to steady her, and as his lean cheek brushed by accident against her shining curls he could smell some sweet fragrance there and was startled by the impact it had on him, and by the unexpected tenderness that overwhelmed him as he held the slender girl to him.

Merewyn, dimly aware that she had stumbled and had landed against the hated Marquis' powerful body, thrust herself away, her cheeks rosy with embarrassment, forcing away with a groan of denial the realization that she had found comfort in those few seconds he had held her —a feeling of security she hadn't known for a long time now.

"A pleasant night to you, Lord Sassenach," she fumed, recovering herself and vanishing through her cabin door with an indignant swirl of velvet skirts. The towering Marquis stood looking after her, scarcely aware of her insulting farewell, a thoughtful frown on his handsome, finely chiseled face.

The sun was setting in a vast panorama of colors, the huge, blood-red ball descending into a golden sea, the shimmering whitecaps glinting fire. To the east night was rapidly falling, and the white canvas sails, scarlet as they caught the last dying rays, glowed agaist the rich violet backdrop of descending darkness. The *Highlander* rolled like a playful porpoise through the waves, her bowsprit surging ever onward, her speed undiminished in the gathering twilight.

Merewyn stood against the taffrail, savoring the feeling of peace that came with the tranquil evening. The cool breeze stirred the soft tendrils of shining hair that framed her heart-shaped face, while the golden depths of her indigo eyes caught and reflected the lingering fingers of sunlight that streaked across the heavens. She sighed softly, immersed in admiration for nature's spectacular show, feeling that even the majesty of a Highland sunset was hard put to match this moment.

How different this voyage was from the despairing journey to the colonies! With her own comfortable

cabin and plenty to eat, she found that she could enjoy
the sheer exhiliration of being on the open sea, her time
occupied with learning all sorts of nautical facts from
both Lieutenant Spencer and Carl Winston, who hovered about her whenever she came on deck. Even David,
his recovery rapid with the waning of his fever, had
joined her several times during the past few days before
she ordered him below again, concerned by the lingering
paleness of his freckled face.

Aye, she thought with a faint smile curving her soft
lips, 'twould be a perfect voyage if only the Marquis of
Montague were not aboard. The smile faded as she
thought of him, replaced with a puzzled frown. Ever
since their brief encounter in the narrow companionway
scarcely a week ago they had spoken not at all. Merewyn
avoided him as best she could, but she had been aware
of his pensive, compelling eyes resting upon her often.

She could not understand the disturbing, never-
before-experienced emotion that had risen within her
momentarily when she found herself in his arms, and
though she agonized over the mishap she could not see
her way clear to explain why—though she knew she still
hated him—she had felt so strange with her face pressed
against his broad chest, his lean, handsome features
close to her own. She flushed hotly whenever she recalled how hard yet uncommnly yielding his body had
been, her soft thighs touching his muscular ones, every
curve and part of her seeming to fit against him.

" 'Tis fair weather we've been having."

Merewyn jumped at the sound of Carl Winston's
voice, color flooding to her cheeks, afraid that he could
read some of her thoughts on her face. "Aye," she stammered.

"I don't believe I've ever encountered fewer storms
than on this voyage," he added, coming to a halt beside
her, his experienced eyes roving the dark sky above
where the first stars were beginning to twinkle and a

crescent moon ascended on the horizon.

"We've been fortunate," Merewyn agreed, recovering herself. Propping her slender arms on the rail she stared out beyond the gently dipping bow. " 'Twill be late summer when we return. I can't believe how quickly the time has gone."

"You were cruelly robbed of spring," Carl said to her, his voice husky with emotion. "My dear Miss MacAilis, when I think of what that monster Kincaid put you through, and how I let him lay the lash to you, I could kill myself for my cowardice!"

"You were obeying orders," Merewyn soothed him, thinking how very remote that event seemed in her mind, how far removed from the beauty of the velvet evening, though it had taken place aboard this very ship, there at the mast directly in front of her. She'd come almost full circle, she decided thoughtfully, feeling almost as happy tonight as she'd last been at Cairnlach before any of this had happened. 'Twas strange what a magical evening like this could do!

"I shouldn't have allowed such a barbarous event to take place!" The bos'n's impassioned voice broke into her thoughts. "Can you ever forgive me?"

She hid her smile, his woebegone eyes reminding her fleetingly of her hound Remus when he begged for food. "Of course, Mr. Winston. I've never held you responsible."

"I still can't help feeling the crew, myself especially, should have done something to prevent it."

"The crew could not disobey Captain Kincaid's orders any more than you could," Merewyn reminded him patiently. "And both Seaman Bergh and Mr. Barrows are in custody with him aboard the *Columbia*."

Carl Winston sighed deeply, moving a little closer, his calloused hands coming to rest beside her small ones on the rail. "I'm a fool for never suspecting Kincaid of wrongdoings. I've served him nigh on seven years now,

through the war and all, and though I can't confess to
have had personal feelings for him I did respect him."

"He was a master at seeming that which he was not,"
Merewyn remarked, surreptitiously moving away in an
attempt to increase the distance between them. Never
had she known the bos'n to be so bold.

"Can't you understand?" he demanded mournfully,
seizing both her hands in his in an impetuous gesture. "I
should have realized at once you weren't some common
working lass forced to sign her life away. I suspected so,
but I didn't want to believe it. Miss MacAilis—" His
voice throbbed with emotion. "My feelings—"

"Don't matter at all," she finished hastily. "Please
don't plague yourself with guilt! 'Tis more than I can
bear to see!"

He released her hands, ashamed of his forwardness,
"Aye. That is, I—I suppose I should see the new watch
is set."

He did not see the relief that crossed her small face in
the darkness, Merewyn having feared that he was prepared to make some sort of romantic disclosure she
would have had to denounce. She liked Carl Winston
well enough, but didn't want to hurt his feelings by telling him that she felt none of the ardent yearning for him
that he appeared to feel for her.

"We ought to be making fair time to London with the
westerlies to our stern," he added, his voice filled with
embarrassment at having lost his steely self-control of
which he so prided himself, and had forced himself upon
the hapless young woman before him. God strike him
dead for his lack of manners!

Merewyn inhaled sharply and seized his arm in disbelief. "London! But we're bound for Glasgow!"

"Glasgow?" The pleasant features were filled with
perplexity. "You're mistaken, Miss MacAilis. We set
the course for London. I thought you knew."

"Whatever are we going there for?" she demanded,

annoyed and confused. She didn't want to make a stop-over there, she wanted to go home!

"We'll be meeting HMS *Columbia* there," the bos'n explained, puzzled by her reaction. " 'Tis possible we may be called on to testify against Captain Kincaid." At Merewyn's soft cry of dismay he added hastily, "Not you. They wouldn't expose you to anything like that, never fear."

"I don't mind," she responded weakly. "I'm willing to do whatever I can to see that bloody swine hanged, but I thought 'twould all be done in Glasgow." She fell silent, not wanting to add that she needed the comforting presence of her brothers there with her if she was expected to get up before the authorities and tell them everything that had happened to her.

Somewhat shocked by her choice of words, the bos'n merely shook his head, telling himself that she'd endured a great deal of suffering and that the only gallant thing he could do was overlook them.

"I want to go home," Merewyn persisted. "Is Lieutenant Spencer in his quarters?"

"Aye, but there's naught he can do," the bos'n assured her, disliking the idea of Merewyn going alone to the handsome young officer's cabin.

The soft lips tightened with determination. "Perhaps there is."

He watched her slim form vanish through the darkness and sighed unhappily. 'Twas difficult to be so enamoured while the object of one's affections remained totally oblivious to one's feelings!

Merewyn knocked on the door to Captain Kincaid's quarters, entering boldly without waiting for an invitation, too concerned about the matters at hand to worry about decorum. As she stepped inside and saw the familiar furnishings, everything the same except for the absence of the big sea chest beside the bunk, she faltered, the memories she was reliving clearly showing in the timorous expression on the heart-shaped face. How well she could remember the sick dread that had churned in her stomach when she and David had cowered before the diabolically grinning captain, Barrow's little pig's eyes gleaming with blood lust behind him.

"You look as though you've seen a ghost."

Merewyn started at the sound of the deep voice, turning fearfully, half expecting for one wild moment to find the swaggering little sea captain before her. Instead, it was the Marquis of Montague whose towering frame filled her line of vision, and the tilted blue eyes grew hostile.

"What are you doing here?"

A cynical smile twisted the full lips. "These are my quarters."

"I thought Lieutenant Spencer was staying here!"

The cold gray eyes narrowed. "He's bunking in David's former quarters now that the lad is in the great cabin again. If you want to see him I suggest you go there."

She ignored the obvious implications in his harsh tone. " 'Tis just like you to take the best for yourself," she accused, glad that her old dislike for him had risen within her as he stood insolently before her, long legs planted wide apart, powerful arms crossed before his broad chest. 'Twas only weariness that had made her behave so oddly that night in the passageway, she realized with vast relief, and not some mysterious sway the Marquis held over her.

"Lieutenant Spencer insisted I take the captain's quarters," he informed her with another mocking smile. "I would gladly have let you have them, Your Highness, but I'm afraid no other bunk on this ship would suit me."

"Aye, you're a colossal longshanks," she retorted, "and I wouldn't expect you to make sacrifices on my behalf even if you were small enough to sleep in the scuppers."

"Because you want no favors at all from me," he finished, echoing her previous, impassioned vows. "No quarter taken from the despised Lord Montague. A Villiers is to be hated and treated like lowly vermin."

She said nothing, not caring at all for the glint that had entered the intimidating gray eyes.

"I suppose 'tis just my first taste of clan rivalry," he observed, turning his broad back on her and striding to the brandy cabinet from which he removed a bottle of wine. "But I recall that even enemies are not above sharing a dram of good Highland scotch together now and then. I don't have whiskey, but may I convince you to have a glass of canary with me? Sir Robert made this bottle a gift to me and I must admit 'tis excellent."

"Thank you, no," Merewyn replied sourly. She had no desire at all of making this a cozy visit. "I really must see Lieutenant Spencer."

"I see I've been replaced in your affections," he remarked insolently, the gleam again entering his gray eyes. "Though I will be fair and admit that the young lieutenant has many admirable qualities."

"Quite unlike yourself," Merewyn retorted, unable to resist taunting him as he stood so confidently before her, the wine bottle still in his hand.

His handsome visage grew hard. "May I remind you, ma'am, that in verbal warfare between the two of us you rarely emerge victorious? I suggest you stop prancing before me like a cockerel with hackles raised. I'm in no mood to trade insults with you this evening."

He filled two glasses with the clear wine, his aristocratic profile illuminated by the flickering lamp burning on the table, his dark hair gleaming, his full lips twisted in the same mocking smile that was always there whenever Merewyn was in his presence. Striding across the floor he extended a glass to her and she accepted it reluctantly—jerking her hand away as his strong fingers touched hers then biting her lower lip angrily at the answering laughter in the keen gray eyes.

"Suppose you tell me," he invited, retreating behind the table and lounging comfortably in the chair, "what you want to see Lieutenant Spencer about."

"Why are we going to London?" she countered, looking down at him accusingly. "Why am I not being taken to Glasgow?"

"It couldn't be helped," he responded curtly.

"You seem monstrously pleased by the fact that we're going."

His answering smile infuriated her. "I am. I've been intending to make a trip there myself. This way 'twill save me some time."

She found curiosity getting the better of her. "Why do you want to go to London?"

He twirled the stem of his wine glass absently in one long-fingered hand, but his eyes regarded her shrewdly. "You're beginning to realize, I suspect, that you know precious little about this Villiers. I approve of your curiosity, ma'am. 'Tis wise to learn all you can about your enemies before you set out to destroy them."

Draining his glass in one long swallow he leaned forward to refill it. "Don't look so outraged, I know very well you're plotting deviously to get rid of me."

"I'm not making any secret about it," she contradicted tartly, still standing before the table with her glass, looking down at him with a sneering curl to her soft lips. "I know exactly what sort of man you really are even though you've somehow managed to fool my brother, who isn't easily taken in."

"I believe I should take that as a compliment," he

remarked with the same maddening smile that always fanned her temper.

"Take it any way you please, you conceited Sassenach, but bear in mind that great Goliath was felled by wee David!"

"God's teeth, you impertinent little wench, are you threatening me?" he asked, truly incredulous.

"I told you that I intend to do all I can to ensure that Cairnlach doesn't fall into your hands," she replied with as much courage as she could muster, although she retreated a step as he rose and came around the table towards her, towering above her so that she had to tilt back her head to look up into his intimidating face.

"I never realized I was up against such a determined little lion cub," he said, his tone silky and dangerous. "While I concede that your heart isn't faint I must point out to you, ma'am, for your own good, that you can't possibly hope to succeed in your battle against me."

As he spoke his strong hands shot out, closing about her slender neck, his fingers tightening ever so slightly around her throat. "Do you remember our first meeting, my dear? You had second thoughts then, too, when it occurred to you that perhaps you'd taken on too much after all."

The long fingers closed a little tighter, the pressure beginning to grow, and Merewyn found it becoming difficult to breathe. She refused to acknowledge that she was afraid, however, though her large blue eyes had grown dark with fear as she stared up at him. She thought of her beloved Cairnlach, of Alexander riding proudly about his land, and told herself that she would never, never permit this hated rogue to take that away from the MacAilises no matter what sort of scare tactics he used. She would stand her ground before this grim giant who seemed bent on choking the life out of her, and she would defeat him in any way she could. She must!

Lord Montague could see the dark fear within her tilted eyes, but saw also the grimly compressed lips and could sense the struggle in her taut little body to retain her courage. He released her abruptly, stepping back so unexpectedly that she stumbled and almost fell.

"A pox take you, you blackhearted knave," she gasped, recovering her balance, her cheeks flushed.

" 'Twould seem I was wrong in assuming I could break you easily," he remarked, hiding his grudging respect beneath a forbidding demeanor, her refusal to become cowed in his presence further fanning his anger. Where had the chit come by her courage? Was she such a fool that she refused to back down from such hopelessly stacked odds? Or was this an example of the Gaelic hardheadedness his uncle had so ranted about as he lay dying in his bed, his body twisted and broken from his accident?

Difficult, contrary breed, these Highlanders, Ian Villiers thought contemptuously to himself. Twice they'd risked everything to see their adored Stuart King returned to the throne, and even the Duke of Cumberland's butchery after Culloden and the staggering price on the fugitive Prince's head hadn't swayed them to betray their loyalty. Nor had the Disarming Act done much to break them, though he had heard that the Scots took fanatical pride in pipe playing and displaying their tartans, pleasures denied them in the face of King George's stiffly imposed laws.

'Twas a hard and savage land and Ian was beginning to realize that its people were just like the earth from whose rugged bosom they had been nurtured. Aye, they were probably all as deuced stubborn and fearless as the proud young girl standing before him, her blue eyes filled with a defiant hatred that left him little doubt that she'd promptly slit his belly with a dirk or claymore given half the chance. Little wonder indeed that the Hanoverian King and the English people were so eager to rid themselves of their unwanted northern neighbor!

Even his tight-lipped servants, Ian recalled, had chosen freedom from hated Villiers rule rather than accept the lucrative wages he had offered them. Devil take them all! He was tired of their bleating patriotism!

But how to rid himself of this tiresome wench who was rapidly becoming a thorn in his side? Worse still was the fact that he wanted her, an unpleasant discovery he'd made that night when her firm young body had been pressed against his, the scent of her soft hair filling his senses. He disliked her, aye, but found himself unable to ignore the desire her alluring beauty and the sensuous curves of her slender form aroused within him.

Merewyn had not idea what caused his long silence, but she didn't like the sadistic gleam that suddenly entered his gray eyes. "You'll never be able to 'break me' as you term it," she told him fiercely as he glanced down at her thoughtfully. "I won't give up, not until I see you out of our lives forever."

"That, I'm afraid, is quite impossible," he replied nonchalantly, his eyes lingering on her parted lips. "I've made Castle Montague my home and no one, not even you, my dear, can evict me."

He turned away from her to refill his wine glass a third time while she stared distrustfully at his tall frame, her blue eyes wide with dislike.

"I can, however," he added, setting the bottle aside, "be persuaded to withdraw my proposal of taking over management of the mills."

Merewyn was not placated by this startling comment. "I don't believe you."

He came to a halt before her, his brows mockingly

lifted. "You, ma'am, hold the power of persuading me in that decision."

"How?" she asked warily, retreating a step, disliking him so near.

The corners of his mouth twitched as he observed her involuntary movement. "I am willing to make an exchange. Control of the mills goes back to your brother in return for a night you spend with me."

There was utter silence in the cabin save for the creaking of the beams as the *Highlander* listed in response to the changing winds. Merewyn had grown very pale although two spots of rosy color burned feverishly in her delicate cheeks. Her tilted blue eyes had darkened so that they appeared almost black, the golden flecks within them no longer visible.

"You're mad!" she whispered at last, her voice breaking with barely controlled fury. "You c-can't mean it!"

He seemed nonplussed. "But I do, my dear. 'Tis quite a lucrative offer, I must say, and one you should think over carefully before you turn it down."

He watched as the color spread across the remainder of her finely molded features, flaming over the smooth brow, her soft lips parted as she struggled to find appropriate words. "What kind of monster are you?"

He made as if to move towards her and she jerked back, her small fists threateningly raised. "Don't touch me! If you so much as lay a a hand on me I'll—I'll make you rue the day you ever laid eyes on me!"

"I already do, my dear," he assured her mildly, but made no attempt to move away, towering over her, his nearness making her quake with fright.

"I'd sooner l-lie with s-swine, and if you try to t-take me against my will I'll scratch your face to shreds!" She held up her hands menacingly, fingernails presented to fly at him, but he startled her by laughing, the deep sound rumbling in his chest.

"I've never received a more charming proposal, my

dear." The gray eyes were filled with guileless mirth. "But there are other ways to gain what I seek without using violence."

"What do you mean?" Merewyn breathed. She backed up another step only to find herself pressed against the cabin wall and as she looked behind her, distracted, she felt her wrists seized in Lord Montague's powerful hands, one muscular thigh crushing both her slender legs beneath it so that she could not kick at him.

He forced her back even harder against the paneling, his lean face so close that she could look deep into the gray eyes and read the untoward emotions within them. Despite her fear she had to admit that his visage was arrestingly handsome, but even as the thought passed fleetingly through her mind she uttered a stifled moan of protest and tried to twist away from him, finding to her horror that she could not move at all. His sinewy body was leaning into hers and her small breast heaved as she gasped for air, finding it impossible to breathe while forced against his hard chest.

Lord Montague could sense the fear within her, but the soft body arched against his had driven all other thoughts from his mind. Her indigo eyes were wide as she gazed beseechingly up into his, the long lashes, surprisingly dark for one so fair, fluttering against the delicate skin beneath the delicately curved brows. His hungry eyes traveled from their violet depths down the slim, upturned nose to the softly pouting lips that were partially opened as she gasped for air, and he bent down suddenly and pressed his own to them, feeling a familiar but unexpectedly strong stirring in his loins as he felt the warmth of her mouth beneath his.

Merewyn was cruelly reminded of another kiss, the circumstances almost the same, when an odious, bony-featured man named Rawlings had forced her up against the brick wall of the building in Glasgow, pinning her arms just like this so that she was unable to fight him.

But where his touch had brought revulsion, this one was beginning to bring a quickening sensation that mingled with her fear and heightened its compelling intensity.

The Marquis's lips were hot with passion, teasing her as she tried to avert her face so that she didn't have the will to turn away. He pulled her even closer, the curves of her pliant body molded against his, and Merewyn could feel his manhood hardening against her soft thighs. Never had she experienced the heat that seemed to rise from him, engulfing her, his tongue forcing its way between her small teeth, his lips bruisingly painful as they covered her own.

He was seducing her with his kiss, she realized, drawing from her a response she did not want to give—but she found herself powerless, unable to resist her growing excitement. A flame had leaped deep within her at the first touch of his lips and she had suddenly become a stranger to her own body as it responded seemingly with a will of its own, drawing inexorably towards some secret end she could not even begin to guess at.

Suddenly, she was frightened of this terrifying loss of control, no longer in command of her faculties, and she began to struggle desperately to regain them. With strength born of desperation she managed to twist her face away, hoping that her display of unwillingness would calm his ardour. To her dismay she felt his lips seek undaunted the hollow of her throat, his breath warm against her skin as his strong hands slid caressingly over her taut breasts that felt firm beneath the smooth velvet bodice of her gown.

Merewyn moaned as his lips hungrily sought and found hers again, seemingly unable to get enough of their sweetness, kissing her deeply, his senses filling with the scent of her. Ian had forgotten his determination to prove his superiority over this stubborn girl, to show her that he could elicit whatever response he wanted merely from his sure, experienced touch.

The moment he had felt her soft and, aye, yielding lips beneath his, all thoughts had left him save for the need to have this ravishing creature, to kindle in her un-tutored body the passion he sensed she was capable of giving. He burned with desire to possess her, to slake his need deep within her, the sensuous quivering of her flesh as he molded her against him fanning the flame until he was certain it would consume him altogether.

"You plague-ridden s-scum!"

The impassioned, tremulous cry was accompanied by a stinging pain as she sank her little teeth deeply into one muscular shoulder, the pain bringing instant clarity to his clouded senses.

"Let . . . me . . . go . . . at . . . once!"

The words were interspersed with breathless gasps as Merewyn struggled to free herself, still pinned between the wall and his massive chest, trying her best to force him away.

"I'll let you go this time," he said, his hated voice slightly breathless itself, "but you will be mine, Merewyn, I swear it."

"No! I'd rather be dead!"

She was crying now, the tears streaming down her flushed cheeks, their salty wetness mingling in her mouth with the taste of him and she uttered a choked cry and was gone, giving him one last tantalizing glimpse of her golden hair and trim back before she disappeared through the door.

Back in the safety of her own cabin she threw herself on the narrow bunk, her thin shoulders shaking as she buried her hot face in the soft blankets. Where had that devil's spawn acquired such intimate powers, rendering her helpless by the mere touch of his lips on her own? She'd been kissed once before in her life, that time too against her will, but had not felt anything resembling that odd, breathless stirring within her. Dear God, was she really some cheap penny whore to respond so rapidly to a man's kiss despite her hatred for him?

"I'm not!" she whispered furiously to herself, tears brimming afresh in her dark eyes. Lord Montague was naught but a flagrant roué who fancied he could control a woman as easily as a skilled coachman gaining response from his horses with only the slightest touch. Doubtless he'd practiced on countless females in the past, and the thought brought a self-loathing sneer to Merewyn's soft but painfully bruised lips.

Though she had tried her best to fight the mysterious awakening within her she knew damned well that Montague had sensed it as well, remembering with an outraged groan the answering fire she'd seen smoldering in his eyes and had felt in his hardening loins.

"He'll not get the mills through me!" she cried stormily, pounding her balled fists on the blankets. "He'll not! He'll not! No matter what an accomplished lover he thinks he is!"

But her anger quickly faded to be replaced with grave misgivings. She could not deny that the Marquis had touched a vulnerable spot within her, and she was frightened that he might try to use that against her, proving disastrous to them all.

CHAPTER FIVE

"You'll not be doing it, I tell you!"

"Oh, aye, you can't stop me!"

"I'll tie you to the capstan if I have to!"

"You don't own me!"

"No, thank God for that! I'd have died of apoplexy by now!"

The heated argument that took place in the late afternoon on the *Highlander*'s main deck involved a red-faced Carl Winston and a determined Merewyn, the object of their disagreement being Merewyn's unswerving decision to climb up to the lookout for a taste of adventure.

"You'll be killed if you fall!" Carl Winston cried, his voice louder than she had ever heard it. "I've seen it happen even among the best-trained men!"

"I've been climbing larches in Scotland since I was a wee bairn," Merewyn countered, "and some of them were three times as high."

The bos'n ran a nervous hand through his thick brown hair. "I won't permit it, Miss MacAilis, and if you won't listen to me I'll call Lord Montague up here to stop you!"

The thought of the Marquis made Merewyn all the more determined to go through with her plan. Bored and restless after a month at sea she was desperate for distraction and had been seized by the sudden urge to see what the ship looked like from high in the crow's nest. Suggesting her plan to the bos'n who had come on deck behind her had brought instant conflict.

"How can you climb in that gown?" he demanded, gazing disbelievingly at her voluminous skirts. "You'd never make it past the mainsail before you got tangled up in the ropes!"

"At least let me try," Merewyn begged.

"No!"

She was surprised at the bos'n's stubbornness, accustomed to his displays of genteel gallantry, always treating her as though she were made of delicate porcelain. Nevertheless, she could not forget her plan; her body was filled with such restless energy that she felt sure only a rigorous climb aloft could dissipate it.

"You haven't any conception of the distance," Carl added, entreating her to come to her senses with upturned hands. "One misplaced foot and you'll land on the deck. A fall from that high up will kill you!"

"I won't fall," Merewyn said obstinately, viewing the climb as a challenge. "I've watched the crew enough to know how to do it safely."

"You can't be serious! Even if you were wearing breeches 'twould be difficult enough." He eyed her slender form despairingly. "There aren't any handholds either and you don't even have the strength to hoist yourself up. Besides, the wind can pluck you right off the rigging if you don't know exactly what you're doing!"

"See if I don't!" Merewyn cried mischievously, and he looked on helplessly as she whisked up the rat ropes before he could stop her, giving him a tempting glimpse of firm white calves and slender ankles as she ascended nimbly overhead.

"Miss MacAilis, come down this instant!"

"I'm fine," she assured him, her small face filled with excitement as she looked down to find the azure sea rolling almost directly beneath her. With sure movements she scaled towards the first yardarm where she pulled herself aloft, balancing precariously on the narrow footrope while she leaned against the yard as she had seen the crewmen do, listening to the rhythmic cracking of the heavy canvas.

Looking down from the crosstree where she stood she saw that she was much higher than she had imagined, the bos'n's frantic gestures and shouted words almost unintelligible. Clutching firmly to a taut halyard she craned her neck to look at the crow's nest high above her, the square, astonished face of Seaman Askew peering down at her. 'Twas really too high for her, Merewyn decided reluctantly, as she peered up at Askew's precarious perch. Still, now that she was up here she intended to enjoy the view.

The *Highlander* was traveling northeast through calm waters, the sun glaring off the smooth surface, and Merewyn was slightly disappointed as she looked about her to see nothing but the rolling ocean stretching far beyond the horizon. What had she honestly been expecting to see? The White Cliffs of Dover shimmering before her? 'Twould be weeks yet before they sighted land, and she was an ass to have hoped otherwise.

As for the climb up here, Carl Winston had been wrong in saying that 'twould be far too difficult for her. Malcolm had taught her to climb when she still wore pantalettes and they had scaled even the tallest larches that grew far down in the glen below Cairnlach. Her fear of heights had lessened every time she and her adventurous brother had scrambled up yet another ancient larch, its branches reaching high into the windy skies. It had been years since she'd last attempted a stunt like this, Merewyn thought to herself, but 'twas refreshing exercise, and besides, she'd been through enough the past few months not to feel that a madcap act like this was justified.

A commotion on the deck below brought her attention back to Carl Winston who, she saw, was shouting and gesticulating frantically at David, who had come up to lounge about on deck, his freckled face filling with astonishment as he looked up at her. The lad had a vastly good life, Merewyn decided with an almost maternal smile, waving at him casually. Aye, she'd grown devilishly fond of David, her only complaint being that he had taken to fetching this and that for the exalted Lord Montague as though he considered him his sovereign.

Looking down again Merewyn saw that David had disappeared, and she decided suddenly that she'd had enough. Cautiously, she began to lower herself, her small foot searching for a toehold, then began clambering downward as skillfully as a monkey. As she neared the end of her climb she suddenly heard the Marquis's furious voice shouting at her.

"Merewyn, are you mad? Come down this instant!"

Annoyed at his authoritative tone she paused in her descent and looked down at him, her feet almost level with the top of his dark head.

"If you aren't on this deck in three seconds I'll come after you," he threatened, and she saw that he was genuinely angry, his handsome features so forbidding that she began to feel apprehensive. But she was safely out of reach and could not resist taunting him.

"You couldn't climb to save your own worthless hide, you Sassenach booby!"

Carl Winston's jaw dropped at her unexpected attack and David, standing behind the towering Marquis, clapped his hand over his mouth, though Merewyn suspected he was trying more to hide a snicker than subdue a gasp of horror. David worshipped the intimidating Marquis, much to Merewyn's secret disgust, but he was not above finding humor at anyone's expense, laughing often at Merewyn's caustic comments concerning the long-legged Englishman.

Determined not to risk a repetition of what had happened between them in his cabin that night, Merewyn had taken to ignoring the Marquis altogether, avoiding him with surprising luck on so small a vessel so that she rarely saw him at all. Lord Montague seemed content to tolerate her sullen silences whenever they did meet, but Merewyn was not at all mollified by his change of character, distrusting him too much to believe he didn't have something new hidden up his sleeve.

"You little bitch!" The Marquis's temper was barely in check as he stared up at her with a black expression, ignoring those gathered around him. "Do you think you're safe from me up there?"

"I imagine you'd haul me down if you were angry enough," she admitted, propping herself up more comfortably, enjoying herself enormously.

"Are you trying to kill yourself?" Ian demanded, the unpleasantness of his tone warning her that perhaps she had gone too far after all, and that she'd better go down before he really came after her. But still she lingered, savoring this victory, for she knew that she had him at a disadvantage for the first time since she'd made his annoying acquaintance.

"What on earth are you trying to prove? His enraged question brought her attention back to his angry countenance. "That you're as good as a man? I'm beginning to believe you should have been born one, because your behavior certainly tends to lean towards the masculine gender."

His rough words stung, for Alexander had also accused her too often of being a hoyden, and the laughter in Merewyn's slanted eyes gave way to defensiveness. "You have no right to speak to me like that merely because I don't conform to your standards of decorum!"

"I suppose I shouldn't have expected Highland

wenches to behave like civilized Englishwomen, either," he responded icily, rocking slightly on his heels, his long legs spread as he looked up at her, the wind blowing through his dark curls. "Highlanders are called barbarians and I can understand why now, seeing how you display the characteristics of a monkey."

There were assorted laughs and guffaws from the crewmen who had gathered, obviously enjoying the verbal duel going on between the towering Marquis standing on the deck and the slip of a girl clinging so precariously to the rigging above. Merewyn's heart-shaped face was flushed, aware that he had scored and that she had nothing suitable to say in reply. Before she could think of a fitting retort his impatient voice came again.

"Merewyn, I'm coming up there now and I warn you that I intend to drag you down by your hair."

She scowled, her large blue eyes thoughtful as she stared down into his hard expression, wondering if he really meant to carry out his threat. Lieutenant Spencer, she suddenly noticed, had come down from the helm to see what was happening, the officer's brown eyes widening with astonishment as he saw the slender young girl swinging a good twenty feet above his head.

"Miss MacAilis! Whatever are you doing?"

"I was seized with the urge to test my climbing skills," she replied, smiling down at him so sweetly that the watching Carl Winston scowled furiously.

"Please come down," the lieutenant begged. "I'm afraid you may hurt yourself. 'Twould be on my conscience as I am captain of this ship."

"I'll happily comply to such a kind request," Merewyn responded obligingly, giving Lord Montague an acid glance as she swung effortlessly down. No sooner had her feet touched the deck than she felt herself being lifted by the lace embroidered velvet at the nape of her neck and dragged forward so that her face was only inches from the Marquis's livid countenance. She recoiled, never having seen him look so angry or so frightening.

"You little fool," he snarled at her. "You bloody little fool! Were you trying to kill yourself?"

"How dare you! Let me go!" she cried, trying to retain what little dignity she had with her feet swinging helplessly several inches above the deck as he shook her to and fro.

"No," he replied and a shiver went down her spine at his tone. "I think this time, ma'am, you've gone a bit too far."

"What are you going to do to me?" she demanded, her tone quavering despite itself as he hauled her over to the capstan where he sweated himself, tossing her effortlessly across his muscular thighs. "What—" she began, outraged, her words changing to a yelp of pain as his large hand came down to deliver a stinging blow on her small rump.

"If you insist on behaving like a child, then you'll be treated like one," he told her, not pausing in his task as she struggled and kicked her legs.

"Stop! Let me go!"

To her utter mortification she saw that the crew had gathered even closer round, some grinning, others laughing openly—even David. Only Carl Winston managed to look affronted by this outrageous display, though he lacked the courage to intervene, not caring at all for the glint in the intimidating Marquis's gray eyes.

Merewyn continued to struggle, squirming in vain to avoid the heavy hand and the humiliating spanking it dealt, her derrière on fire, Lord Montague making no effort to soften his blows.

" 'Ere, your lordship, 'tis enough," came the laughter-quivering voice of Seaman Askew, who had shinned down the mast in order to take a closer look at the festivities going on below. Though he liked and admired the young MacAilis lass, he had decided from the first that she was a spirited creature in need of a firm disciplining, and he had to admit that she deserved it after such a dangerous act like climbing into the rigging. The other ladies of quality he remembered meeting in the past had always been refined and genteel, but then, he decided with a sorrowful shake of his head, the world was forever changing.

"Now then," said Lord Montague, not even out of breath after subduing the fuming girl, "are you going to behave?" As he spoke he gripped her upper arms and lifted her as though she weighed nothing, turning her around so that she was sitting on his lap, her small face so close to his that their lips were almost touching.

Merewyn's reply was a smart slap to his lean cheek that cracked like a pistol shot over the crowded deck. Without speaking she slid off his lap and stormed below, the Marquis looking after her with a faint smile tugging at the corners of his mouth.

"That's a plaguey spirited wench!" Seaman Askew laughed despite himself.

"Aye, but too much cheek for me!" came the amused reply from the man beside him.

"You should have seen her when Kincaid had her bound for the flayin'," Askew informed the young crewman who had signed aboard in Boston to replace the arrested Barrows. "She was spitting like a wildcat and—" He broke off abruptly, looking ashamed of himself, recalling how that terrible event had torn at his heart, the courage in the young girl's defiant stance having touched him deeply. "Wasn't all that important," he muttered and hurried aloft before anyone else could comment.

Lord Montague's smile had changed to a scowl at the crewman's words and he rose to his great height, staring speculatively at the doorway through which Merewyn had just vanished.

"Hope you taught her a lesson, m'lord," young quartermaster Hammond said soberly in the ensuing silence. " 'Tis no place for a woman up there."

Lord Montague nodded. "I'm afraid Miss MacAilis doesn't always know what's good for her."

In her cabin Merewyn was stalking to and fro, pausing often to rub her stinging rear, her face on fire, eyes flashing with rage. Stinking bloody Sassenach! What right did he have to discipline her? No right at all! He wasn't her guardian, thank God for that, and no one, not even Alexander, had ever punished her in such a humiliating way! She'd get even, she vowed, just wait and see if she didn't!

"Hulking longshanks!" she fumed, picking up a book lying on the small table near her bunk and sending it hurling to the floor. A candleholder quickly followed. "Arrogant swine!" Truly he must think himself a deity among men, making his own laws, living for his own pleasure, manipulating others at his whim. And as for his conceited assurance that he was the one man every woman swooned for, bringing them groveling at his feet with the crook of his finger merely to taste his lovemaking. . . .

"Oooh! I hate him!"

The days of pretending he didn't exist were over! She was prepared to wage full-blown war to bring him to his knees. She tapped her lip thoughtfully with one rosy fingertip. Now, if she could only come up with a suitable means of achieving this end. . . .

Vengeance aside, it was late evening before Merewyn ventured topside, so embarrassed by her humiliation that she wanted to meet no one, and so it was only under cover of darkness that she dared to go out. The moon hung low on the skyline, a pale yellow orb casting its silvery light on the black water so that the waves sparkled like diamonds.

Merewyn wandered to the rail, breathing deeply of

the fresh night air, her spirits lifting as the gentle breeze caressed her bare skin. 'Twas simple to forget her hardships on nights such as these. How she had come to love them, the air heavy with the smell of salt, the *Highlander* rolling placidly through the waves, her sails taut and cracking overhead.

"You mustn't take everything so to heart, miss."

Lieutenant Spencer had come up behind her in time to catch her sigh, misconstruing it as a sign of lingering self-pity. "Lord Montague did what he thought was right."

"And do you think it was?" she countered darkly, turning to face him. A smile curved her soft lips as he hesitated. "Oh, devil take you, sir, I can see that you do."

"I believed his methods rather extreme," he explained hastily, the brown eyes lighting with boyish amusement when he saw that she was teasing him. "But certainly effective. You won't be trying anything so foolish again?"

"No," she admitted, looking up at the sails high above. "But not because the venerable Marquis forbade it. 'Twas a momentary madness. I was bored and searching for distraction."

Lieutenant Spencer shook his dark head. "I don't understand you, Miss MacAilis. You're so unlike any other woman I've ever known. Do you do such . . . er . . . madcap things often?"

Merewyn's clear laugh rang softly through the still night air. "I'm dreadfully immature," she confessed. "My brothers are forever accusing me of behaving like a child." Her face fell suddenly as longing for Alex and Malcolm overwhelmed her.

"What is it?" the young officer asked, sensing her sadness although he could not see her expression.

"A pang of homesickness, that's all," she replied quickly—but her soft voice trembled.

Lieutenant Spencer felt his heart fill with sympathy. Unlike the obstinate Carl Winston, he'd long ago decided to bury his feelings for the beautiful young girl, sensing in some instinctive but little understood way that he was not the man to awaken the budding womanhood within her. He had to confess that she was also too difficult for him, despite her dainty looks and gentle ways, and today's episode with the rigging only confirmed his suspicions. Still, he could not entirely ignore the persistent tug at his heartstrings, especially not when her large dark eyes filled with such sadness as she cast a curious glance at him, wondering at his silence.

Impulsively, he reached out and took her small hands in his, stepping closer so that he could peer down into her delicate face. "You'll be home before you know it," he assured her heartily. "Sir Robert sent a message to Glasgow even before we departed from Boston and I've no doubt 'twill only be a matter of days before your brothers learn you are well."

"Do you think so?" she asked hopefully, the indigo eyes suddenly bright.

"Aye."

For a moment they stood close together smiling at each other, his hands still holding hers, appearing, to any casual observer, engrossed in the most intimate of conversations. Absorbed in their own private thoughts, both were oblivious to the Marquis of Montague, who leaned indolently against the rail nearby, his narrowed eyes studying them dispassionately although his square chin was harshly set. . . .

By morning the fair weather had abruptly changed and the glass was dropping rapidly as Merewyn came on deck. Lifting her small face anxiously she saw that the low gray sky was filled with an icy wind driven from the north. The ocean was a sullen mass of heaving water beneath the leaden skies and Merewyn could feel a heaviness in the air similar to the thick blanket of humidity that, when it descended, always heralded a brewing storm for Cairnlach.

"We're in for it," David remarked to her as she met him descending the ladder from the upper deck with an empty coffee mug in his hands. Lieutenant Spencer thinks 'tmay be a wild one."

"I hope not," Merewyn murmured, crossing her slender arms to warm herself as a chilly blast of wind tugged at her gown and hair.

"Scared, are you?" David asked with a teasing grin.

Her reply was a haughty sniff, the slim little nose pointed skyward.

"Wouldn't be nothing like the great squall we hit in the South Seas near the Tonga Islands on my first time out," David assured her. "The waves was higher than houses, miss, an' I thought we'd founder for sure, we took on that much water. Lost three men overboard, we did."

He paused thoughtfully, testing the air like a hound sniffing a scent on the wind. "Southwesterly breeze and northerly wind. 'Tis sure call for a change in the weather."

A loud hammering noise brought both their heads around to Crewman Askew, who was busy fastening deadbolts to the tightly shuttered cabin windows. Everyone seemed occupied with preparing for the storm, Merewyn noticed, watching the hands moving about battening hatches and securing loose articles on deck. Even the wooden crates housing the chickens were tightly lashed down, the brightly colored hens squawking indignantly at their rough treatment, loose feathers hurling skyward in the wind.

Crewmen were scrambling aloft via the shrouds to secure the sails with gaskets, others attaching lifelines they would be using in the event the waves would be driven high enough to wash over the decks. All of them seemed cheerful, Merewyn noticed, shouting insults at one an-

other as they worked, no one seeming the least bit concerned about the pending storm.

"The winds'll be blowin' like mad bulls," David told
her, still scanning the skies, his brown eyes watching her
covertly for an indication of fear.

Merewyn tossed her head haughtily. "I don't care
how bad 'twill be. We endured enough of them on the
way over, remember? I think I'll lock myself in my cabin
until you tell me 'tis safe to come out."

"No dancing about i' the rigging?" David demanded
with feigned astonishment.

"Be quiet," she said haughtily, "or I'll have Lieutenant Spencer string you up by the thumbs."

"Aye, that one'd do as you ask," David agreed with a
grin, pouring the last few drops of coffee from the mug
down into the scupper, watching it run off with seeming
concentration. "Not at all like the Marquis, is he? You
canna go leading that one about by the nose though I've
a feeling you'd like to."

"You rude little knave!" Merewyn burst out. "Where
did you get such awful manners?"

"Don't look so huffy," David added. " 'Tis your own
fault. You go out of your way to make him mad."

"You don't understand a thing about it," Merewyn
retorted, resisting the urge to give his backside a good
swift kick. "You're too wise for your age, I see, but not
smart enough to know when to hold your flapping
tongue!"

"And if you'd behave more your age, miss," David
pointed out, his boyish grin softening his words, "you'd
not be getting into hot water with the Marquis so
much."

"Worthless lout," she answered good-naturedly. "Are
you going to the galley with that dirty mug? I think I'll
go with you and get myself something to eat. If the
storm lasts too long we may not have the chance to eat
dinner."

"You just canna admit that you're fair starving because you didna come up for meals yesterday. I think
you were too ashamed after that thrashing his lordship
gave you."

Merewyn did not even deign to grace him with a
haughty glance, her slender shoulders stiff as he followed her below. "You're an ignorant lad," was her
final comment, but David heard her giggle as she said it.

The lantern hanging from the center beam in her
cabin was swaying precariously when Merewyn entered,
her arms filled with almost a dozen crisp bannocks and
a huge wedge of savory cheese, one small hand wrapped
firmly about a bottle of wine. Depositing her booty on
the table that occupied almost half of her tiny living
space, she took the lantern down as a precaution, setting
it beside her food supply. David had assured her that the
storm wouldn't last long, but she wasn't about to take
the chance, hating the thought of growing any hungrier
than she already was.

Thunder cracked overhead, startling her, and she
could smell the faintly acrid scent of sulphur as lightning
seared the sky. Hail began to drum deafeningly upon the
decks above, drowning out the crashing of the waves as
they battered the barkentine's hull. David had been
right, Merewyn decided, uncorking the bottle and pouring herself a small glass—ocean squalls came and went
surprisingly fast.

She would have preferred lemonade or even water to
drink, but neither had been available, the galley
amidships already tightly packed up, but she had managed to cajole a bottle from Carl Winston, an avid col-
lector of spirits and a self-proclaimed wine connoisseur
who kept his own supply in his quarters.

" 'Tis one of my best clarets!" he'd called after her,
watching her stagger slightly between the bulkheads in
the darkened companionway as the ship lurched, winc-
ing at the possibility that she might drop and break it,

spilling the precious ruby contents on the planking.

"I'll be sure to enjoy it," Merewyn had replied over one dainty shoulder, disappearing from sight.

Actually, 'twas an excellent vintage, she told herself, sipping experimentally from her glass as she seated herself on her bunk, slender legs stretched out before her, small slippered feet tapping restlessly together. How long would she have to sit here, she wondered, until it was safe to go topside? She'd spent all day yesterday confined to her quarters, after all, because of Lord Montague's callous treatment, and she didn't like the prospect of more hours of confinement.

Merewyn's gold-flecked eyes narrowed. She'd sworn to avenge herself for the shame the hated Marquis had brought upon her, and gain Cairnlach's freedom at the same time. Had her brother also suffered such helpless bouts of rage in dealing with Ian's predecessor Edward? She suspected that he must have, firmly convinced that Edward and Ian Villiers were of the same conscienceless ilk.

"Poor Alex," she murmured to herself, her words lost to the noisily pounding rain beyond the cabin walls. " 'Tis for you I drink this toast, and for all the years you had to put up with the pox-eaten Villiers while Malcolm and I could only guess at what you were going through!"

The narrow cabin door opened unexpectedly and the towering object of Merewyn's dislike was suddenly there in her quarters, coming to an abrupt halt as he stared down in astonishment at the collation spread out on the small table before him. His harsh gaze traveled to the bunk where Merewyn was sitting, a half-empty wine glass in one small hand, one slender ankle peeping out from beneath her russet skirts. Her luminous eyes were fastened on his face, rosy color flooding to her cheeks at the unexpected sight of him glowering above her.

"What are you doing here?" she demanded rudely.

"Making sure you weren't parading about on deck in this weather. I wouldn't put anything past you after yesterday's idiotic display."

"That doesn't give you any right to burst in here without knocking," she retorted.

He propped himself casually against the wall, arms folded across his broad chest, shaking his dark head slowly in disbelief. "I see you've made yourself quite comfortable," he remarked, his gray eyes resting on the wine glass.

"I was hungry," Merewyn said, feeling foolish beneath his mocking gaze although she didn't know why. "If you recall I had little to eat yesterday."

"Don't look so accusing. 'Twasn't my fault you felt too ashamed to show yourself at mealtime."

She tossed her golden head defiantly. "I wasn't ashamed. I was afraid of what I might do to you if I saw you again too soon."

A deep laugh rumbled in his chest. "Am I to quake with fear at such a violent threat?" Though her haughty words would normally have irritated him, he was paying them scant attention, his gaze arrested on her slim form as she sat before him on the bunk, her features flushed with the effects of the wine, the flickering lamplight turning the indigo depths of her eyes to purest gold, which was matched in radiance only by the softly gleaming hair arranged in a flawlessly beautiful chignon at the nape of her long neck, accentuating the smooth cheeks and ivory temples.

" 'Tis no idle threat, m'lord, I assure you." Merewyn had set the wine glass aside and was scrambling to her feet, a tiny bundle of quivering fury as she stood before him, the tilted eyes barely level with his clefted chin. "I honestly intend to see you vanquished!"

"Such brave words from so small a lion cub," he mocked.

Their glances tightly locked, both of them were unprepared when the *Highlander* listed beneath the onslaught of a great surging wall of water, where she hovered for several terrifying seconds on her beam ends before righting herself with loudly groaning timber. The mishap had thrown Merewyn against the Marquis's broad chest and he had caught her to keep her from falling, barely managing to retain his own balance as the battered vessel righted herself violently.

Lifting her eyes, Merewyn found herself looking up at the finely chiseled features of the handsome face not inches from hers, the forbidding look in the compelling gray eyes giving way swiftly to another she recognized and especially feared. She dropped her gaze swiftly only to find it fastened instead to his full lips, remembering despite herself the mysterious sensation their fiery touch had aroused within her.

Ian could feel her heart racing as her small form was pressed against the rigid muscles of his chest and, thinking it was from fear, he sought to comfort her, aware that she was very pale. " 'Tis a well built vessel," he assured her. "We're in no danger of foundering."

"I think that a pity," she retorted unexpectedly in that proud, unyielding voice he had come to know well, her palms pressed flat against his hard torso as she tried to push him away. " 'Twould certainly solve all my problems if you were drowned, my lord."

"But you'd die with me," he reminded her, and was surprised when a slow smiled curved the soft red lips.

"Aye. 'Tis worth the price to regain Cairnlach's freedom from Villiers tyranny."

"You'd rather die for Cairnlach's sake than accept my simple offer to end the conflicts between us?" he asked disbelievingly.

"What you are asking," Merewyn said, her words quavering slightly as his arms slid even more tightly about her slender waist, "would mean that I would submit to you, and MacAilises do not surrender. Death is far more honorable."

"I find it hard to believe you'd go so far," he told her, his dark eyes lingering on her lips, refusing to let her go, the seductive length of her thighs pressed tightly against his muscular ones, arousing in him the same desire to possess her he had experienced before.

"Then you don't know me very well," she retorted bravely, lifting her large eyes to look into his but finding that a mistake, for she could easily read the smoldering desire in their darkening depths. A pulse began to beat nervously in one soft temple and she renewed her efforts to detach herself from his strong hands, although every struggling movement she made caused her body to touch his more intimately, his hardness making it obvious how much he wanted her.

"Let me go!" she panted, trying to arch away from him but finding it impossible, his arms tightening even more about her. She shrank away as she felt his strong fingers beneath her chin, forcing her face upwards so that she was gazing into his fiery eyes.

"Your words tell me one thing, Merewyn," he said, his breathing ragged, "but your body tells me another. You want me as much as I want you."

"N-no," she moaned, despising herself as she realized that it was true. There was searing heat wherever they touched, his manhood meeting and joining the womanly softness between her slender thighs, their bodies fitting together as inevitably as though they had been made for each other.

His mouth was covering hers, his lips teasing, demanding a response, and she could not turn away, his hold punishingly strong. Her palms were still pressed against the hardness of his chest and she could feel his heart beating rapidly, a pounding race that made her feel weak, unable to credit that his desire for her could be so great. His lips were on fire as they tested the unyielding hardness of her own, seeking with unquenchable determination to elicit from them the softening that told him she had capitulated, that he had awakened the feelings she had experienced the last time into a desire as strong and unfulfilled as his.

His large hands slipped about her soft, curving rear, pulling her even closer to him, molding her quivering though strangely pliant body against his hardness as he half lifted her off the floor in his desire to feel every soft, desirable part of her. Though he wanted to taste every inch of her smooth flesh he persisted, his mouth covering hers—exploring, tasting, demanding a response Merewyn felt she could no longer withhold.

A dizzying thrill shot through him as he sensed the soft lips yielding beneath his kiss, her arms moving almost timidly to slide about his corded neck so that he was finally able to hold the length of her completely against him, her taut breasts burning him with their touch. Effortlessly, he lifted her into his arms and carried her to the bunk, his mouth still upon hers, his tongue teasing and bold, making her feel weak with sudden longing.

Merewyn opened her eyes as she felt him lay her gently back onto the soft bedclothes and looked up to see him leaning over her, his handsome features shadowed in the flickering lantern light, giving them the impression of being more sharply defined than ever; his dark curls gleaming; his gray eyes alive with emotions as he effortlessly pulled off the russet gown and tossed it aside. She was wearing nothing underneath save a thin petticoat and chemise. These followed swiftly so that she was soon lying naked before him, her body of flawless ivory silky smooth in the dim light, far more slender and seductive than he had ever dreamed possible. Her slanted eyes were soft with yearning as she gazed up at him, and Ian, never having seen anything in them for him save hostility and antagonism, could not credit the compelling effect they had upon him.

With a groan he pulled her to him, covering the length of her firm body with his, letting her feel the heat and hardness of him so that she was aware again of how much he wanted her. His hungry lips moved from her mouth to the smooth curve of her throat, caressing the silken skin there before tasting the sweetness of her rounded breasts, his gentle touch arousing within her a passion that soon matched his own. Her hands moved over the broad expanse of his back, the muscles rigid beneath his chambray shirt, her fingers entwined in his dark curls as he roved her body with growing need, determined to know every mysterious part of her before slaking his desperate thirst within her. Ian was barely able to hold his passion in check although he forced himself to wait, wanting to savor every enticing inch of her before he was finished.

Though Merewyn had never lain in a man's arms before, she sensed in some little understood way that she was heightening Ian's pleasure merely by responding to her own, pressing her soft lips eagerly to his as he sought their taste again. An almost feverish excitement had gripped her when she first felt his hard body upon hers, the sensation growing as he shed his own clothing and lay above her, his flesh almost searing her with its heat.

Her fingers caressed him in imitation, wanting to please him as he had her, and she felt him shudder as she touched his burning hardness, a wondering expression in her large eyes as she realized how easily she could achieve this end.

"Merewyn," he whispered, her name sounding like a caress as it fell from his lips. "My fiery little nemesis."

"Is that how you see me?" she asked softly, dimpling as his lips traced the smoothness of her firm little jaw. "As an antagonist?"

"We're too much alike to be that," he contradicted,

his voice husky, his tongue teasing her breasts so that the nipples rose taut. "Even though you are fair as sunlight and I dark as night. You had to let me love you, Merewyn. 'Twas inevitable. Don't deny you weren't drawn to me from the first."

His hungry mouth covered hers so that she could not reply, and all memory of his words were wiped clear from her mind as she let his passion consume her, the taste and smell of him filling her senses. She clung to him as his kisses grew deeper, drawing her from herself so that she felt a part of him, sharing his need to satisfy the passion that had been born, innocently enough, in their first, heated confrontation. The fervent anger they had felt toward each other now tempered into desire, although the intensity of their emotions was the same.

Merewyn's soft thighs parted almost of their own volition as he hovered for a timeless moment above her. She grew very still, waiting, her eyes soft with yearning, never having looked more beautiful to him.

"Merewyn," he groaned, a triumphant light in his dark eyes, savoring every moment of this conquest.

"Miss MacAilis!"

The abrupt pounding on the cabin door startled both of them and Ian froze instantly above her, his breathing ragged, while Merewyn bit back a moan of fear.

"Miss MacAilis?" came the voice again, more uncertain this time.

Merewyn struggled to free herself from the Marquis's body, which still pinned hers to the blankets. "Aye?"

" 'Tis John Hammond. Lieutenant Spencer asked me to inform you that you may come up now. The storm's passed."

"Thank you," she murmured, and felt dizzy with relief as she heard his footsteps retreat down the passageway. The Marquis's great weight abruptly lifted and she looked up at him fearfully, not caring for the ugly gleam that had entered his gray eyes as he began pulling his breeches over his muscular thighs.

"You'd better not keep the lieutenant waiting," he suggested, his tone silky and dangerous, making her draw back against the wall, hugging the covers protectively over her slight form. "Suppose he grows suspicious about your absence and comes down himself?"

Deliberately ignoring the pain he saw in the dark, gold-flecked eyes, he reached down and grabbed her chin in his big hand, forcing her small face towards him, the ominous expression in the handsome visage making her quiver with fear. "I'll not be sharing you with some twaddling Navy officer, ma'am. I intend to have you next time, and you'll belong only to me."

Merewyn felt anger beginning to dull her fear, her shame increasing as she realized that she was still aching with want and need and suspected from his harsh breathing that Ian felt the same. She despised herself for desiring him and for the sickening ease with which he had seduced her, wanting to strike out at him and hurt him as he had her.

"You, sir," she said coldly, "have no right to tell me whose company I may keep. You don't own me."

His smile was grim. "I find that rather difficult to believe considering how quickly you were willing to give yourself to me."

"That may be true," Merewyn admitted, her tone cutting, "but I don't intend to allow you the opportunity of trying to seduce me again."

His laughter was derisive. "And how do you propose to get rid of me? We'll be in London soon, ma'am, where no one can stop me, not Carl Winston or your dashing lieutenant." His dark eyes roved her half-covered body with frightening deliberation. "I'll have you before long, Merewyn, and I'll taste the pleasures of your body whenever I wish, and you'll be begging me to do so."

"*No I won't!*" she cried, tears of pain and frustration

starting in her eyes as he twisted her neck cruelly.

"Aye, you will. You're mine now, Merewyn, despite how much you may think you hate me."

"I loathe you!" she choked, and Ian could feel his conscience stirring at her lost expression, her anger gone completely, her soft lips trembling as she strove to keep from shedding humiliating tears before him.

He released her so abruptly that she banged her head against the paneling, the helpless tears flowing faster while she averted her face and closed her eyes to shut out his hated image as he towered over her. "You overlooked one thing in dealing with me, my dear." His tone made the tears flow faster. "I'm not a gentleman at all."

The door slammed behind him and she pressed her hand to her mouth to control her sobs. She was lost, she told herself, lost! In almost giving herself to him she had shown him how easily he could control her body and her mind, and she was terrified of the power he had over her, afraid that he would force her to betray Alexander and Malcolm despite her efforts to stop him.

Lord Montague was startled to hear muffled sobs coming from the other side of the thin door and felt a momentary softening within him as the pitiful sounds continued. Then he steeled himself and strode away, his vision suddenly haunted by the image he had seen last night of the handsome young officer and the golden-haired girl standing with clasped hands beneath the shining light of the moon, smiling tenderly at one another.

The *Highlander* sailed serenely down the Thames River on high tide, the port of London spread out in a vast network of wharves, docks, and warehouses before her. Merewyn, standing breathlessly on the fore deck, could scarcely believe the city's immense size, dwarfing Glasgow so thoroughly that it seemed as insignificant as the tiny village that lay below the castle in Glen Cairn.

Tall buildings of limestone and houses of red brick lined the waterfront, while throngs of horses, people, and carriages filled the crowded streets and gave the city an alien air to Merewyn, accustomed as she was to the sparsely populated Highlands.

The brackish smell from the river was strong and she wrinkled her small nose, causing David, who had joined her at the railing, to laugh unaffectedly. " 'Twill grow worse," he promised. "Wait til you have a look at what floats in the street gutters."

"I'll thank you to keep your comments to yourself," she replied tartly, but he only laughed again. "Have you been to London before, David?"

He shrugged his narrow shoulders. "A few times, aye. More since I've been shippin' out of here on the *Highlander*."

"Then you know your way around the city?"

He grinned. "Aye, to places where a lady willna go."

Merewyn shook her head in exasperation. "Honestly, David, sometimes I think you behave more like a man of forty than a lad of fourteen. And don't you dare tell me about those places," she warned as he opened his mouth to speak.

"And what is it you want to see in London?" he asked curiously, aware that her lighthearted manner was largely assumed.

"I want to know how to get home," she admitted, casting a nervous glance over one shoulder to assure herself that Lord Montague was nowhere within hearing. She relaxed when she saw his tall form lounging casually on the deck above, his narrowed eyes wandering over the crowded wharves before him. "I don't have any money and I've no idea how to get there."

"His lordship told me he was going to take us to Scotland," David reminded her, puzzled by her concern.

Merewyn hesitated, wondering if she was doing the right thing in confiding to David her plans to escape from the Marquis as soon as she could. She knew the young lad worshipped the arrogant giant, and fleetingly questioned his loyalty to her. Though Ian had spoken little to her during the remainder of the voyage she felt certain that he intended to hold his promise of abusing her, and she was desperate to flee before that happened.

"Well, then, David, are you ready to disembark?"

She jumped as she heard his deep voice behind her, unaware that he had descended the ladder and had sauntered across the deck to join them. His gray eyes mocked her as she stared up at him indignantly, resenting his presence.

"And you, Merewyn? Are you ready to join the huddled masses of Europe's most infamous city?"

"I'm going to take the first coach I can find heading north," she informed him tartly, her blue eyes flashing with dislike.

He threw back his head and laughed while Merewyn regarded him with a scowl on her small face. "My dear, your ignorance constantly amazes me," he told her when he could speak, grinning down at her insolently from his great height. "At times I believe you a fey creature from another world with your wisdom and sharp tongue, and at other times I'm led to believe you don't have the common sense of a child. How do you propose to travel north without money? Do you have any conception at all of the distance between London and Scotland?"

"I—"

"And what of the dangers that lurk around every bend? Highwaymen and unscrupulous characters ready to take advantage of a helpless young beauty traveling alone?"

"I can take care of myself, damn you!" she breathed angrily, aware that he was deliberately trying to make her look foolish.

"Oh, I see how well you can take care of yourself," he

remarked cynically, his eyes darkening for a moment as they lingered on her parted lips.

Merewyn turned away abruptly, scowling fiercely. Damn him, he was right. She would have to depend on him whether she liked it or not, for he was the only person at the moment who had the means of bringing her back home.

"Will we be going to Scotland soon?" David asked timidly, disliking the tension that hovered between them, and angry, too, because he saw that in some way he didn't really understand, the towering Marquis had hurt Merewyn.

The gray eyes were kind as he looked down into his freckled face. "Aye, lad, but there are a few things I must attend to before we can go."

"What things?" David asked, his curiosity getting the better of him.

"First, I have to make sure the matter with Louis Kincaid has been settled," the Marquis replied obligingly while his eyes lingered on Merewyn's stiff back. "And then there are personal matters that require my attention. I had to leave London very unexpectedly when word of my uncle's accident reached me."

He saw the slender shoulders stiffen even more at this, and a cruel smile twisted his full lips. "Neither do I expect Miss MacAilis to proceed directly from a long sea voyage to a lengthy, exhausting stagecoach ride. I believe her constitution too delicate for that."

Merewyn's defiant expression when she whirled about to face him attested to the opposite. But she said nothing at all, though her indigo eyes were accusing, making no mistake of her true feelings for him.

"If you'll excuse me," he added with a mocking nod in her direction, "I'll have someone procure a vehicle for us, and then we'll be off."

"Oh, miss, 'twill be grand being here as his lordship's guests!" David cried excitedly.

Merewyn hated to dash his enthusiasm but felt that
'guests' was hardly a fitting description for them. Somehow the term 'prisoners' seemed more apt. Just you
wait, my lord Monster, she fumed after his broad back.
As soon as I get home I'll see that you pay for this!

To Merewyn's surprise it was not a simple carriage
that met them at the wharf but a well-sprung coach-and-
six, a liveried driver perched high on the seat, a postil-
lion in matching uniform holding the lead horse's nervously tossing head. The elegant black and gold vehicle
was embossed with a lavish coat-of-arms and Lord
Montague, seeing Merewyn's curious look as she was
handed inside, informed her evenly, " 'Tis the Villiers'
coat-of-arms, ma'am."

"Oh?" She gazed up at him with wide, guileless eyes.
"I didn't realize your family was old enough to have
established one. 'Twas said Edward was born on the
wrong side of the blanket, after all."

His lips tightened ominously and she felt a small
twinge of fear within her heart, but felt confident
enough that he wouldn't dare strike her with so many
people milling about. Abruptly, he pushed away the
coachman's politely assisting hand and grabbed her
roughly, forcing her inside where he threw her against
the richly upholstered cushions, his expression filled
with barely controlled rage.

David, oblivious to their furious encounter, took advantage of the Marquis's preoccupied attention and
clambered quickly up beside the driver, his eyes bright
with excitement. At an impatient signal from the Marquis, the large vehicle lurched off down the narrow
street, jockeying its way past the blackened buildings towards the inner city.

Merewyn sat with her small face pressed against the
window, forgetting the Marquis who sat glowering
beside her his hard thigh just barely brushing against
hers. What a fascinating city, she thought excitedly, un-

able to get her fill of the well-dressed gentlemen in their frocks and spangled shoes and the elegantly attired women whose colorful gowns made her sigh enviously, reminding her that she had been wearing the same threadbare velvet for months. Beggars clustered about the coach as it moved slowly through the choked streets, their dirty hands raised beseechingly, and Merewyn turned appealingly to the Marquis, her large indgo eyes filled with pity.

"Can't we help them?"

"We could toss them a few coins," he replied coldly, "but 'twould gain them little. They'd spend it on ale, get drunk, go home and abuse their wives and children."

"Oh, how can you be so callous?" Merewyn demanded.

Ian shrugged his broad shoulders. "I'm afraid that's the truth."

She turned away from the window, having lost interest in her surroundings, her heart aching for the thin faces and the hopeless eyes that stared back at her. London teemed with both the fashionable and the crude, the wealthy and the destitute, she remembered Alexander telling her after describing his first visit there. How right he'd been, Merewyn thought, and even the beauty of Mayfair and the sight of the elegant houses facing Hyde Park did little to shake her from her somber musing.

Not long afterwards the coach bore sharply to the right and turned up a meandering drive towards a large mansion of rosy brick, a wide flight of marble steps leading up to the carved wooden doors before which the coach eventually drew to a halt. Birds sang in the shady trees overhead and flowers bloomed along the trimmed walks leading off toward the garden, and Merewyn shook her head disbelievingly as she accepted the Marquis's proffered arm and stepped to the ground.

" 'Twas warm on the river," she murmured, looking about her at the lush greenery, "but it didn't really hit me until now. I left Cairnlach in the last throes of winter and return to England with summer in full bloom!''

The Marquis was forced to laugh as he looked down and saw her bewildered expression. "I imagine the change is somewhat difficult to adjust to. You'll be fine tomorrow.''

"Where are we?" Merewyn asked suspiciously as he led her up the flight of steps towards the bowing majordomo who awaited them in the doorway. "Whose house is this?"

Ian's lips curved. "Mine.''

She hung back and stared up at him in astonishment. "Yours?" she choked. "Don't tell me I'm staying here with you!"

He made no reply, his strong hand at her elbow propelling her forward, and she found she couldn't pull herself free without causing a scene.

"Welcome home, m'lord," said the majordomo, his long face showing nothing but mild unconcern, his attention centered on the towering man before him, all but ignoring the furious girl who was pinioned at his side. "I was expecting you sooner, my lord. We were worried something had happened to you." His precise enunciation proclaimed him a gentleman's gentleman of the first order.

"I was unexpectedly detained," Lord Montague replied without a trace of sympathy for his faithful servant's concern. "I had to make a quick trip to Boston.''

The majordomo's eyes widened. "Boston, m'lord?" Then, annoyed that his curiosity had gotten the better of him, he let his countenance grow as expressionless as before. Wordlessly, he turned and opened the door wide to allow them to enter.

Ian forced the reluctant girl inside, Merewyn forgetting her anger as she stood gaping at the fine imported tile floor and the opulence of the entrance hall. "I meant colonial Boston," the Marquis told the old man with a wicked smile, well aware that Francis, after his initial blunder, would show no more interest in the subject regardless of what it cost him. Unlike his valet Davis, who had tried over the years to manipulate his master's unmanageable character, Francis had built around him a protective shell so that he rarely reacted at all to the Marquis's often hair-raising deeds. Hence, he hadn't lifted an eyebrow at the sight of the ravishing creature at his master's side. Although Francis was accustomed to having them in the house, he had to admit that this one was by far the loveliest his lordship had ever brought home with him—faded, tattered gown notwithstanding.

"I'll see to your things, m'lord," Francis began, but the Marquis waved his words impatiently aside.

"I didn't bring much with me and the young lady has nothing at all."

Francis's carefully arranged features sagged with utter astonishment as Merewyn said crisply, " 'Twouldn't matter if I did. I don't intend to stay."

No, he thought, this was too much. She was Scots, the lady was, no mistaking the soft burr in her voice! Lord help him, he didn't care at all for the glint in her slanted blue eyes and, for that matter, neither did his lordship, who was glowering at her impatiently, their locked glances hinting at an antagonism that seemed to have been forged rather deeply.

"Where do you propose to go?" Ian asked conversationally, and Francis, knowing him well, was not fooled by his casual tone. More often than not it boded ill for someone, and he wouldn't care to see his master's temper unleashed towards the golden-haired beauty standing defiantly before him.

"I don't know," she replied, her tone no warmer than his, "but I won't stay here with you!"

"Since when are you so concerned with propriety?"

the Marquis asked, and Francis could tell by the young lady's stricken expression that he had somehow touched a tender nerve. Pity stirred within his heart as he stared down into her heart-shaped face, far more comely than any he had ever seen, and he moved forward to step between the towering man and the young girl standing before him.

"You'll be hungry, I imagine," he said to her, tactfully blocking the Marquis's intimidating form from view, drawing her attention to his kindly face. "A pot of strong tea and a piece of my cherry cake would sit well with you, my lady."

He hurried off before Merewyn could correct him as to his mode of address, then riveted her furious gaze back to the Marquis's handsome face, her expression fierce enough to crush the will of a lesser man. "I'm not staying here," she repeated firmly, "and you can't force me to."

"I won't," he assured her with a mocking smile. "You're free to go if you wish. I won't stop you."

"Why are you doing this to me?" she demanded, her slender shoulders slumping as she realized that she didn't have the strength anymore to fight him. She was tired of constantly being on her guard, tired of their incessant verbal battles, and she wanted to go home.

Lord Montague was not outwardly affected by her piteous expression. "Surely I don't have to explain to you why," he said coldly, his gray eyes gleaming as he looked down at her. "I've taken more abuse from you, ma'am, than from anyone in my wide circle of acquaintances, and I might add that some of them are less than savory. I did not take lightly your well-aimed kick the first time we met, but I was willing to overlook that in the heat of the moment. Since then, however, you have tongue lashed me, goaded me into losing my temper, called me a bastard, and slapped me publicly."

His ominous tone made her shiver with apprehension.

"Obviously, you can't be chastened with a few simple rebukes or a mild spanking, but I will make you pay, my dear, never fear."

"You can't be so heartless!" she protested, her trembling voice telling him that she believed just that. "Alex wouldn't—"

"Alexander is in Scotland," he reminded her harshly, "and you are here with me, Merewyn. You've no money and no way to get home until I see fit to take you."

"I'll run away!"

He shrugged. "Feel free to do so. Just remember that this time you may not be lucky enough to be rescued by the Royal Navy. Who knows where you'll end up."

A vision of the dank prison cell where she had spent such lonely hours unexpectedly came to mind and she shivered, tears smarting in her eyes. She was trapped and both of them knew it. Damn him and his bloody pride!

Unnoticed, Francis had reappeared in the hallway, and he coughed discreetly to announce his presence. His eyes darted uneasily to Lord Montague, never having seen such a black expression on his face before. There was trouble afoot from the look of it, and he didn't care for it at all.

"Your tea is ready, m'lord," he announced, his formal tone giving no indication at all of the serious doubts he was experiencing within.

"Miss MacAilis will have some," the Marquis informed him curtly. "See that she's made comfortable in the South Room, Francis, and that you feed the lad we brought with us."

"If you'll come this way, miss," Francis invited as Lord Montague turned and strode out. "I've laid everything out in the salon."

Merewyn nodded wordlessly and followed him there, an unnerving, haunted look in her tilted indigo eyes.

* * *

About the time that Merewyn was sipping tea in the home of the Marquis of Montague, a hired chaise was drawing up before a modest house off the Marylebone Road, its sole occupant being a weary, fastidiously attired gentleman, his fashionable clothing wrinkled from long hours of travel. Stepping down, he watched closely the unloading of his trunks and portmanteaus by a disinterested manservant, then pressed a coin into the hand of the driver and mounted the steps to the small stone house without a backwards glance.

"Will you be wanting something to eat, sir?" asked the round-faced housekeeper as she opened the door, anxious to please him.

"No. I'll be in my room and I do not wish to be disturbed."

Brushing past her and ignoring her startled look, he strode down the upper landing, peering into all of the rooms, and chose the largest and most elegant for himself. Here the heavy gold drapes were drawn across the windows, plunging the room into semidarkness, but its occupant made no move to open them as hc stepped inside and shut the door firmly behind him. Tossing his hat and gloves onto the large bed which stood in one corner, he drew a cheroot from his coat and lit it absently, his thoughts elsewhere as he began pacing restlessly about.

His muscles ached and his limbs felt stiff from the long hours in the carriage, for he had made it a point to rest little during the journey south. For the last two days they had stopped only for meals, and he had slept on the padded squabs while the coachman guided the weary horses through the darkness along the post road, jolting through unseen holes and lurching into the mud. Thank God that was all behind him!

Moving absently to the window he parted the drapes slightly so that he could peer down onto the street below. The chaise was already gone, he saw, but as he watched another more elegant one rolled by, the pair of perfectly matched bays moving at a high-stepping trot, their shod hooves echoing against the stones. Two pedestrians standing on the opposite side of the street, a middle-aged woman in ivory silk and a young boy in satin pantaloons, waited until the carriage had rumbled by before venturing across and disappearing through the gate of a house nearby.

Pigeons cooed in the eaves directly above the window, their mournful sounds reminding him of another room, far more shabby than this, where several of them had fluttered about on the sill. Light from the street had filtered through the torn curtains to reveal a narrow bed with dirty, rumpled blankets and a washbasin that stood in one corner, the water tepid and unclean.

Both the man and the woman had landed in that room innocently enough and certainly in the usual way, what with a proper offer and willing agreement. Actually, the girl had been quite beautiful although he knew her looks probably wouldn't carry her through but a few more winters. She was young with firm, high breasts and limpid green eyes, her hair red and gleaming in the flickering light from the smoking candle stub burning on the table. They had met on the steps of an alehouse, he slightly reeling, his vision misted, and she had approached him from the darkness as he stepped outside where she had been waiting patiently for a man like him.

Once inside the musty room he had kicked the door shut and pulled her to him, nuzzling her neck, his hand seeking her breasts while she giggled and pulled away from him, increasing his ardor with he feigned shyness. He had come after her, his heavy-lidded eyes still foggy with drink, and he grabbed her, his wet mouth coming down to cover hers. She did not move away this time and he could feel the tautness of her breasts as she pressed closer. Eagerly he pawed at them, his hand moving inside the bodice to tease the nipples until they rose beneath his touch; then he half dragged her to the bed and forced her down beside him, seeking clumsily to remove her gown.

"Here, wait," she protested, slapping away his hand as she heard the material rip. " 'Tis one of my best, dearie."

He watched impatiently as she removed it, leaning back on the lumpy mattress as she shook her long hair free, then planted his lips on her breast and began sucking eagerly until she laughed and pushed him away.

"You'll ruin them fine clothes, dearie. Here, let me." She undressed him with nimble fingers, playfully allowing her heavy breasts to sway above him, thinking to herself that they were fine clothes indeed and that she intended to have herself a look in his coat pockets once he was sound asleep.

"Ah, and I thought you'd be too fou to love your Nellie," she said to him as his clothes came away and revealed to her his hardness.

"Never too drunk for this," he told her roughly and kissed her deeply, leaving the bitter taste of ale in her mouth. Rolling her beneath him he pressed the length of him upon her, but she turned her head aside so that she could speak.

"Wait, dearie, you'll have to wash first."

He appeared not to have heard, intent on forcing her thighs apart, suddenly desperate to feel her close about him. One hand was stroking and squeezing her breast, the other moving down between her legs, but Nellie remained adamant.

"You'll have to wash," she repeated firmly. "Them's the rules!"

He ignored her, his mouth seeking hers, his tongue forcing its way between her teeth. Nellie found herself beginning to grow impatient. Lord, but drunkards were hard to reason with! One had to lead them like a bairn, one did! Better to take a firm stand, she decided, trying to slap his roving hand away. Unexpectedly, he seized the flesh of her inner thigh between his fingers and twisted cruelly, determined to part them with force, and she shrieked painfully, her cry further fanning his desire.

"Let me go!" Nellie cried angrily.

He pinched her again, her howl heightening his pleasure, then sank his teeth into the plump flesh of her breast. Nellie screamed more fearfully and tried to twist away from his sweating body.

"Come on, my bonnie," he rasped, "I won't hurt you."

Nellie had dealt with his kind often enough and knew that he would become passive once she inflicted pain of her own. Freeing her arms she flew at his face, her fingernails raking across his cheek. That was the point when white hot rage had consumed him. Aye, he could remember well how his hands had tightened about her slender neck, more and more, until her madly racing pulse seemed to travel up his fingers and arms and into his brain, the drumming making him dizzy so that he saw nothing but dull red behind his closed eyelids.

He couldn't remember if she had struggled, for apparently several minutes had elapsed before he came to his senses lying over her. Her face was chalky, her eyes closed, her throat covered with red welts, and he didn't have to bend his head to listen to her heart to know that she was dead. It had come to him only dimly, however, that he himself had strangled her.

For a moment he lay above her, wondering what had happened to him, but then cold fear began to seep through his alcoholic stupor. Suppose someone came through that door and found him lying in bed with a naked corpse? Had she screamed at all? He couldn't remember. He dressed quickly and splashed some water on his face to clear his mind. He was no longer drunk, his senses heightened by urgency, blood throbbing through his veins and giving him a feeling of utter power.

He would have to get rid of the body, he decided, staring down at the bed with a thoughtful expression. Bending down, he struggled to ease the limp form into the low-cut gown, sweat beading on his forehead, his breath whistling between his clenched teeth. Lifting her into his arms he stepped quietly out into the corridor and made his way stealthily down the creaking stairs. Muffled voices and low laughter filtered from the other rooms, but no one witnessed his departure with the lifeless form of Nellie Arling thrown over one shoulder.

The street outside was dark and deserted, the cobblestones glistening in the moonlight. A cat spat at him as he came down the steps, then dashed away, and he trudged intently towards the river, every sense alert for possible danger. He encountered no one at all, for most of the city's inhabitants had already secured themselves until morning behind tightly shuttered windows and firmly bolted doors.

He stood for a moment on the bulkhead, watching the swirling water below before dropping his bundle down and stepping back quickly to avoid being splashed. The heavy gown dragged her under surprisingly fast and he caught only one last glimpse of her long red hair and the eerie whiteness of an arm before she was gone. He lingered for another minute to assure himself that she would not resurface, and when she failed to do so, he turned away with a deep sigh of relief, pulling his handkerchief from his pocket to mop his brow.

As he started down the street he felt considerably better. Doubtless the body would turn up in a day or two, but even then, what did it matter? A cheap whore with no family or friends found drowned in the River Clyde was no cause for alarm, and the authorities would probably waste little time in investigating her death. Even so, he decided 'twould be better for him to go away for a while, just to ensure his safety, and he settled on London, a city whose anonymous, bustling size would stand him in good stead.

Puffing methodically on his cheroot, he turned away from the window as he recalled his thoughts to the present, dismissing the view of the tile rooftops of the other houses with a disinterested shrug. Now that he was here he intended to make his stay worthwhile, perhaps even find himself a suitable wife to further secure his position in society. After all, he was a wealthy man, well liked by friends and respected by acquaintances. Actually, now that he thought on it, he should have come to London some time ago, for here he would certainly find the social success that had somehow always eluded him back home. A satisfied grin curved the thin lips and his pale eyes gleamed. Perhaps poor little Nellie had done him a favor after all.

CHAPTER SIX

Merewyn jumped as she heard the sitting room door slam and hurried from the bedroom where she had been pacing back and forth on the elegant carpet. Her heart sank as she saw the intimidating figure of the Marquis step into the room, a bundle tied in jute carried in one long-fingered hand. He had changed his attire from the informal nankeen breeches and coat he had worn during most of the journey aboard the *Highlander* to fashionable knee breeches, stockings, a lawn shirt, and a richly embroidered coat of velvet puce. His dark curls were carefully tied in a queue with black ribbon, and Merewyn came to an abrupt halt, eyeing him with astonishment, unable to credit his transformation.

A knowing smile curved his full lips. "You seem taken aback by my dandified appearance," he commented nonchalantly. "Doubtless you'll come to realize soon enough that I'm at home in any situation."

"As a pirate, a blackguard, or an adventurer, aye," she agreed sourly, hating him for speaking the obvious truth, "but not as a gentleman."

His gray eyes gleamed. "I see you still seize every opportunity to insult me. That will end soon enough, my dear."

"What do you mean?" she demanded bravely, al-

221

though her small chin quivered, aware suddenly that she was now entirely at his mercy, for here in London there was no Alexander or even a Carl Winston to help her.

He clasped his hands behind his broad back and stood looking down at her. "I've no intention of ending your apprehension so soon by telling you what I have in mind," he informed her mockingly, then extended the package. "This is for you."

"What is it?" she asked suspiciously, her dark, accusing eyes never leaving his handsome face.

"You'll have to open it."

Reluctantly, she took it from him and untied the twine with fingers that trembled slightly, unnerved by the fact that she could feel his eyes resting intently upon her bent head. The wrapping fell away to reveal a gown of dark green velvet piped at the sleeves and along the full skirts in ivory, the neckline scooped and adorned with fine Bordeaux lace.

" 'Tis rather plain," the Marquis commented with an almost bored air as she held it aloft, her small face filled with wonder, "and I don't believe the color will suit you very well, but 'twas all I could find on such short notice."

"You couldn't have had this sewn for me!" Merewyn protested disbelievingly. "Why, we've only been in London a few hours!"

His tone was malicious. "Aye, you're right, ma'am. 'Twill be several days before the gowns I've commissioned for you are ready, though I had to pay double the price to have them so soon and without an initial fitting, but that one is intended to see you through until then."

"But where did you get it?" Merwyn asked, ignoring his words.

"Shall we say that a friend of mine was kind enough to donate it from her private collection?"

Merewyn's cheeks flamed and her slanted eyes widened with shock. "Do you mean this . . . this thing belongs to your mistress?"

"Aye. Or, rather one should say it was once her gown and she was once my mistress."

Merwyn uttered a strangled sound and threw the green velvet gown at him with all her might. "Do you honestly believe I'll consent to wear this foul piece of charity?"

Ian picked up the gown that had landed at his feet in a crumpled heap, and shook it out with deliberate unconcern. "I don't see why not. 'Tis rather becoming if a trifle outdated. Besides," he added, moving towards her so swiftly that she didn't have time to back away, "you must admit yours is no longer serviceable." Even as he spoke his hand shot out and seized the neckline of her worn russet traveling gown, and she cried out as he jerked downward, ripping the bodice almost to her narrow waist, revealing her smooth white shoulders and the chemise she wore underneath.

Tears came to her eyes as she stared up at him, their darkened depths filled with suffering, and he said harshly, "You may not agree with me, ma'am, but your gown was long past its prime. I'm sorry I frightened you, but there was no other way to convince you to accept this one. Now, are you going to put it on or will I have to do it for you?"

Above all, she loathed the thought of his intimate touch and quickly pulled the torn russet velvet from her body, seemingly unaware of his presence as she stared stonily past him although tears of humiliation trickled down her cheeks. The Marquis received only the briefest glimpse of her slender calves and ankles before the shimmering green velvet covered her, and he waited patiently while she fastened the hooks and eyes, studying her critically, his powerful arms crossed before his broad chest.

" 'Tis an admirable fit," he commented, surveying her intently as she stood before him, her golden head drooping in defeat. "Elizabeth has gained a bit here and there over the past few years but she was almost your size when that gown was made for her. 'Tis a bit long but 'twill do until Mrs. Ludley comes by to take it up for you."

"I'd rather burn it than wear it," Merwyn assured him, lifting her small face to glare at him, "but you've left me no other choice."

Ian was astonished at how well the color suited her after all. The flashing blue eyes had been transformed into glowing emeralds, her golden hair had taken on the warm hue of honey, and her skin appeared an even creamier white than before. The smooth velvet clung to her willowy figure, emphasizing her tiny waist and curving hips, her firm breasts clearly defined beneath the lace-trimmed bodice.

"You'll need some petticoats," Ian told her flatly. "I don't want you parading about town in such a revealing state."

"I don't intend to go anywhere!" The wide emerald eyes were so translucent that he had the brief impression he could see straight through them. "I refuse to leave this house until you take me home!"

His mocking smile infuriated her even more, making her aware of how helpless she was to combat his dangerous moods. "You have no choice, my dear. Elizabeth is no doubt intensely curious to know who that gown was intended for, and although I did not choose to enlighten her I daresay she'll ferret out the information soon enough. And Mrs. Ludley, the woman who is sewing your gowns, will undoubtedly spread word that I'be commissioned an entire wardrobe for a female." He shook his dark head. "No, you've no choice at all, ma'am, because I don't intend to let London's fashionable set go mad with curiosity."

"I refuse to accept anything from you, especially a wardrobe!" Merewyn shouted, stamping her small foot and giving him a tantalizing view of her slender buttocks as she turned her slim back on him and stormed to the window where she stood leaning her hot forehead against the cool pane. In the twilight below an elegant coach rumbled by, but she didn't even see it, too wrapped up in misery to care about anything at all.

"I will not permit you to attend social gatherings in the same gown, Merewyn," the Marquis informed her stiff back coldly. "What will people say if I permit you to be seen in public in anything less than the finest fashion creations?"

"And do you expect me to be seen in your company at balls?" she cried, beside herself with helpless rage, storming back across the distance between them and staring up into his finely chiseled face, her lips trembling.

"Of course."

"I won't! I refuse!"

"Then all of London will witness our fisticuffs," he retorted, "because I'll drag you where I see fit no matter how hard you try to resist me."

"Is this your plan, then?" she asked, her voice dropping to a whisper, the rage replaced with a dread that was clearly mirrored in the gold-flecked depths of her turquoise eyes. "To humiliate me publicly? To ruin my good name?"

"I believe you could stand a lesson in humility," Ian agreed. "Doubtless several."

"And what about your partnership with my brother, whom you claim to like and respect?" she asked in a quavering voice, struggling to check the flow of tears, hating to display such weakness before him. "The business must have meant something to you, otherwise you'd never have left London in the first place. Don't you realize you'll be finished with Cairnlach after Alex learns what you've done to me?"

"My, my, how quickly you change tack," Ian

mocked, looking down at her coldly. They were standing so close together that he could see the wildly beating
pulse in her throat and he was unexpectedly reminded of
the time he had lain above her, his body on fire wherever
she had touched him with hers. He had been almost mad
with the want of her and the feel of her, and so close to
conquering her, only to be cruelly thwarted in the one
moment before he had actually taken her. He could well
imagine how exciting she would feel to him now if he
only slid his hands about her tiny waist, her flesh no
doubt warm and supple beneath the smooth velvet.

With an effort he forced his attention back to the
words he had just uttered. "I recall," he finished
harshly, "that you vowed to destroy me and the partnership at all costs. Now you are begging for me to save it
all for your sake?"

"I still intend to destroy you," Merewyn replied tremulously, having seen the stirring of passion in his gray
eyes, frightened because she knew now what it meant
and aware, too, of how much she feared it. "Alex will
dissolve the partnership after I tell him how cruelly you
treated me and though you fancy yourself something of
a god here in London, you're naught but a despicable
cad to the MacAilises!" Her voice vibrated with passion
and hatred, and he was reminded again of the ineffectual
but bravely snarling little lion cub who had stood up to
him so many times before.

"We'll see," he shrugged unperturbed. "As of yet
Alexander knows nothing of your whereabouts and I
have only just begun with you, my dear. I daresay you'll
be whistling another tune before your time with me is
done."

"I don't believe you!" Merewyn retorted, but her
words lacked conviction and she could tell by his triumphant smile that he was aware of it.

"In that case I'm afraid you don't know me very
well." He turned and started for the door, but paused

there to address her over one massive shoulder. "Francis will see to your needs tonight and I've made it clear to the other servants that you're to have the utmost care and attention. I believe you'll find everything to your liking."

"Where are you going?" Merewyn asked suspiciously, his commend sounding like a dismissal.

The handsome features were devoid of mockery. "My dear Merewyn, surely you don't expect me to ruin your reputation all in one throw by staying in the same house with you?"

She made no reply, her expression touching in its bewilderment, and Ian added helpfully, "I'll be staying across town in the house my uncle left me, which is considered the official Montague residence."

Merewyn's tilted eyes mirrored her confusion. "I don't understand. I thought this was your home."

"And so it is. Before Edward's death I was known as the Earl of Ravensley. In addition to the family estate in Surrey I also owned this townhouse."

Merewyn refused to acknowledge that this information had come as a total surprise. "How fortunate that Edward had no other heirs," she said sarcastically. "You've gone from Earl to Marquis. What a pity you didn't marry an heirless Duke's daughter. Then you'd have it all."

"I once had a Duke's daughter," the Marquis informed her with a mocking smile, "but before I could marry her I grew bored with her. Good night, ma'am."

He was gone before she could reply, leaving her to stare at the closed door with an apprehensive frown on her small face. She was at the mercy of a heartless and bloodthirsty man. How on earth was she to escape him? Even if Alexander did know of her whereabouts by now, as Lieutenant Spencer had assured, her, how long would it take before he arrived? Even tomorrow might prove too late. She couldn't tolerate the thought of the

MacAilis name becoming a source of mockery for the people of London, a city where her brother's name was well known to some. After all, Cairnlach did handle a considerable amount of business here.

Merewyn's heart leaped. Of course! Why hadn't she thought of it sooner? Surely there must be a branch office somewhere here in the city, or at least someone who had dealt with her brother in the past and would be willing to help her! Tomorrow, she decided eagerly, she would order Francis to have the carriage brought round for her and drive down to the business district.

Merewyn slept peacefully that night, her worries relieved for the time being, the four-poster in which she lay luxuriously large compared to the narrow bunk where she had slept for so long. Oddly enough, she felt a little sad when she awoke, realizing she would miss the beautiful sunrises and golden afternoons aboard the ship that had been her home for almost a third of a year.

She sat up and sleepily rubbed her eyes, her pensive gaze growing cold as it fell upon the beautiful emerald gown hanging over a chair beside the bed. She would rather die than wear that tainted thing on her person, but Lord Montague had given her no other alternative after ripping her other one to shreds. As she slipped it on she wondered idly about this Elizabeth and what the Marquis could possibly have said to her in asking for the gown. Had he expressly requested it for his newest amour? Merewyn's soft cheeks flamed as she shamefully recalled how she had almost given herself willingly to the towering, impassioned Marquis that day of the storm at sea, doubly thankful now that they had been interrupted at the very last moment. She wasn't about to be numbered among his plentiful paramours and she swore on her father's grave that she'd never allow her emotions to run away with her like that again.

Angrily, she stalked to the dressing table and began brushing her hair with vicious strokes, then quickly plaited the long golden strands and pinned them to her head, not even bothering to secure them with her usual care. She wanted to get down to the business district as quickly as possible, and Lord help Francis if he stood in her way!

The majordomo, however, was nowhere to be seen, and Merewyn wondered irritably at this annoying lack of servants as she flung open the salon door to find it empty. Passing by the breakfast room she stopped short when the tantalizing odor of eggs, tomatoes, and kippers wafted out into the corridor. A swift glance inside revealed that the sideboard was piled high with chafing dishes and she ventured forward, deciding she had enough time for at least a quick meal.

"Good morning, miss. Will you be wanting coffee or tea?"

Francis had appeared in the doorway as he spoke, but he stopped abruptly at the sight of her, his jaw going slack as he saw the gown she was wearing. "God's blood, isn't that—" He caught himself in time and with a visible effort strove to wipe the ludicrous expression off his face. Never in his long years with Lord Montague had he received as many shocks as he had during the short time this ravishing creature had been in the house!

Here he was cursing like a drunken seaman before a lady, but, by God, he'd swear that gown belonged to Elizabeth Comerford! It had to! He'd never forget the last time she'd worn it here, when she had followed the Earl home one night from the Langdon ball. They'd ended up having an argument and he had tossed her out of the house stark naked at four in the morning. Her infuriated pounding on the door had awakened Francis and he had let her in, his cheeks flaming as he politely averted his eyes at the sight of her shockingly white body. The Earl had refused to let her back into his bedroom, forcing Francis to go in to retrieve the gown, and he could well remember exactly what it had looked like. It couldn't be another!

Lady Elizabeth had dressed in silence and promptly
fled, and Francis had never expected to see her again
after such a humiliation, but damn if she didn't show up
again two days later in order to beg the Earl's forgiveness. Francis could only shake his head, never quite
understanding the strange way the Marquis had of making women lose their sense of reason. Elizabeth's plead-
ings, however, had fallen on deaf ears, for his master
had already lost interest in her, and Francis was rather
pleased that she was no longer welcome in the house. He
had no liking for the cold, sharp-tongued woman at all.
Scarcely a month after the incident had come the news
of Edward Villiers's accident. The Earl had departed for
Scotland and that was the last Francis had ever thought
to see of her.

Recalling himself with an effort to the present and
wondering how he could possibly make up for his
blunder, he said ruefully to Merewyn, "Excuse me, miss,
I don't know what I'm talking about."

Her hauntingly beautiful eyes fastened themselves to
his face. "Of course you do. Obviously you recognize
this gown." She hesitated, then added pleadingly,
"Please believe that I'm ashamed to be seen in it, but I
don't have anything else to wear. Your kind master
ripped my only gown to shreds."

Francis coughed, not quite sure how to handle this
young girl whose directness he found unnerving. Suddenly she laughed, although it rang hollow in the air.

"I imagine those words sound terribly suspicious, but
I didn't mean that the Marquis and I—" Now she was
blushing almost as furiously as he. "We did not—we
haven't—"

"Yes, miss, I understand, miss." Desperate to flee, he
hurried to the sideboard and picked up a chafing dish.
"You need more kippers," he observed. "I'll get you
some."

"No, you don't understand at all!" Merewyn cried as he started for the door. "I'm being held here against my will! Lord Montague coerced me into coming here!"

Francis paused doubtfully in the doorway, the chafing dish in his hands. "His lordship wouldn't," he began, but Merewyn's anxious voice interrupted him.

"You know deuced well he would, and he has!" She was suddenly desperate to convince him that she was not another of Lord Montague's lovers, knowing that the faint contempt she saw in his eyes was totally unjust. She wasn't what he thought her to be! She wasn't!

"Miss, I don't believe—"

"Ah, Francis, here you are. I hope you don't mind that I let myself in."

The clear, tinkling voice cut through the majordomo's blustered comment, and Merewyn grew very still as a dark-haired woman in rose-colored silk with flounced skirts swept into the breakfast room. She was strikingly beautiful, her chestnut hair gleaming in the sunlight, eyes as pale as gooseberries set far apart in a perfect oval face, her red lips wide and sensuous. She came to an abrupt halt as she saw Merewyn sitting before her at the table, and for a timeless moment their glances locked and held.

Merewyn was unaware of how beautiful she appeared to Elizabeth Comerford, the sunshine streaming down on her golden hair and giving it the glowing aura of ripened wheat. The emerald gown transformed her indigo eyes to a startlingly clear turquoise and the color flooding to her hollow cheeks added depth and dimension to her delicate features so that they appeared even more flawless than usual. Elizabeth, some ten years her senior, paled in comparison to the young girl's innocent beauty, and she knew instinctively that even in her prime her looks had never compared to the Nordic perfection of Ian's newest plaything.

"Well," she purred, recovering herself with re-

markable ease, gliding gracefully towards the table, her
pale eyes never leaving Merewyn's flushed face, "I was
wondering what Ian had done with my green velvet.
Now I know."

Francis, the chafing dish scorching his fingers unnoticed, hurried back into the room, anxious to divert
the maelstrom he felt certain was coming. There was no
way his young charge could defend herself against a
woman of Elizabeth Comerford's expertise!

"Lord Montague isn't here," he said nervously. "He's
gone to Grosvenor Street."

"That's quite all right, Francis," Elizabeth soothed
without giving him so much as a glance. "I'll keep Miss
What's-Her-Name company until he returns."

Merewyn didn't care at all for the malicious glint in
the gooseberry eyes. Jealous women were the most dangerous of all and she suspected strongly that this one
wore her iron claws only thinly sheathed in velvet
gloves.

"My name," she said quietly, "is Merewyn
MacAilis."

The tinkling laugh came again, this time edged with
obvious contempt. "Why, you're Scotch, aren't you?
How utterly quaint!"

"Perhaps you'd care to leave a message for the Marquis?" Francis tried again.

Elizabeth rounded on him, her words as sharp as the
lash of a whip. "I said I'd wait here, you doddard. Get
out."

For all his experience Francis was not one to take on
a formidable opponent like Lady Comerford. Reason-
ining that Merewyn could fend for herself, he exited
from the room as fast as his short legs would take him,
pausing in the kitchen to dispatch a messenger immediately for Grosvenor Street in the hopes that the Marquis
could be summoned before disaster occurred.

Alone with the striking older woman, Merewyn did

her best to remain calm, refusing to be drawn into a verbal battle of jealousy over a man the likes of the Marquis of Montague. For all she cared Elizabeth Comerford was more than welcome to him and she told herself heartily that they were certainly well suited to each other.

"Have you known Ian long?" Elizabeth asked, seating herself at the table and pouring a cup of tea with the air of one who felt perfectly at home as hostess in the Marquis's breakfast room.

Merewyn refused to be baited. "There's no need to interrogate me, madame. I'm quite willing to tell you everything you want to know."

"I am Lady Elizabeth Comerford," the older woman corrected icily, Merewyn's mode of address having made her feel like an aging matron.

Merewyn met her cold gaze squarely. "Please excuse me, Lady Comerford. Being as we were not formally introduced I had no idea who you were."

"Why, you impertinent little chit!" Elizabeth cried, losing her temper, her hatred for this golden-haired beauty increasing as she realized that this was no untried child. Where had Ian come up with such a clever prize, and how on earth could she herself possibly hope to compete against this precocious novelty?

"Do you have any idea who I am?" she added with a quelling frown.

"I'm afraid not," Merewyn replied apologetically, reaching for the butter and spreading it thickly across a biscuit, hoping Lady Comerford would not see that her fingers were trembling. "Lord Montague has mentioned you only once to me, and that was briefly last night."

Elizabeth was quick to seize an advantage. " 'Lord Montague' you call him?" she asked with a haughty toss of her head. "My, my, aren't you formal with him!" She watched as Merewyn replaced the silver butter dish, biting her lips to keep from shrieking as the lace at the edge of her slender wrist trailed through the crock of jam standing nearby. She herself was fastidious to the point of madness and couldn't bear to see the lovely velvet gown ruined by this ill-mannered wench.

Merewyn, well aware of the reason for the strangled expression on the older woman's face, gave her a guileless smile, her heart-shaped face radiating nothing but polite dismay. "I'm sorry, I forgot 'twas your gown," she apologized sweetly, dabbing the jam away with her napkin. "The sleeves are rather long, don't you think?"

Lady Elizabeth struggled with her temper. "Why is it you address Ian by his title?" she demanded through clenched teeth.

Merewyn shrugged. " 'Tis simply that I don't believe I know him well enough to be more familiar with him."

Elizabeth did not know what to make of this mysterious young beauty. Was she trying to make a fool of her with her feigned innocence, or had she really misconstrued the child's presence here? Was she not Ian's latest paramour after all? God's teeth, but she had to be! Only a man like Ian Villiers would have the gall to publicly dally with an obviously innocent maiden, a Scottish one no less!

"I can see that you are curious about my presence here," Merewyn went on calmly, her fears lessening as Elizabeth's uncertainty grew. "Seeing as you were kind enough to lend me your gown I expect you should receive an explanation."

"It doesn't really matter who you are," Elizabeth said icily. "You'll never be able to hold on to Ian, even if you did follow him all the way from Scotland." She leaned forward, her pale green eyes glowing, her long fingers clutching the linen tablecloth so tightly that the knuckles turned white. "You're naught but a child, do you hear? And even if your innocence pleases him he'll tire of it soon enough, I swear it! He needs a real woman who can give him whatever he asks for. 'Twill only be a matter of time before he crushes a neophyte like you."

"I expect you believe yourself worthy of that challenge?" Merewyn countered blandly. " 'Twould seem, Lady Comerford, that you are growing too old to be playing such games."

Elizabeth sprang to her feet, upsetting her tea cup and sending the contents splashing upon the embroidered tablecloth. "You little bitch!" she breathed. "I should claw your eyes out for that!"

Merewyn rose also, worried that the furious woman intended to do just that. She didn't think she would be able to hold her own very well against this raging siren, and had no desire at the moment to test her own prowess at fist fighting. Dear God, Montague wasn't worth all this! She hated him with every fiber of her being, hated him all the more for subjecting her to this torture. Was this a sample of the revenge he had planned for her? How many others like Lady Comerford would she have to engage in verbal battle as though she were fighting to retain the man she loved, when in truth she despised his very being?

"Oh, heaven help me," she whispered, and Elizabeth, having overheard her plea, smiled arrogantly.

"You'll need more than divine intervention to keep Ian for yourself, dearie," she hissed. "He's been known to treat his playthings rather roughly. I only hope you'll be able to endure."

"Ah, Elizabeth, I see you've wasted no time in finding out what I wanted to do with your gown."

The forbidding voice was that of the Marquis, and Merewyn felt her heart sink as he strolled into the room wearing elegant dove-gray attire that suited him as well as the puce satin of yesterday. Seemingly oblivious to the tension in the air he allowed his indolent gaze to travel from Elizabeth's angry countenance to Merewyn's wide, bluish-green eyes and he nodded approvingly at her appearance, feeling certain that Elizabeth had been duly impressed with Merewyn's innocent beauty. The fact that her golden hair was disheveled and not as carefully arranged as usual pleased him even more, for it gave her a wanton air that Elizabeth would surely find maddening.

Merewyn saw the lingering anger in Lady Comerford's pale green eyes fade into such yearning that she felt embarrassed to be witness to it. The red lips parted and she suspected that Elizabeth would have gone to him but for Lord Montague's dour expression, which Elizabeth apparently knew quite well.

"I trust you slept well, Merewyn," Ian said, ignoring Elizabeth as he strolled further into the room and came to a halt before her.

Aware that he was toying with her to increase Elizabeth's jealousy, Merewyn refused to meet his gaze although she could feel his compelling eyes on her averted face. Busying herself with her breakfast she replied noncommittally, " 'Tis really of no interest to you, I imagine."

"Nonsense," he assured her, and she could tell by his tone that she had annoyed him with her refusal to join in his game. "I'm always concerned for the welfare of my house guests. Isn't that true, Elizabeth?"

"You were always very kind to me, Ian," Elizabeth responded huskily.

"I'm glad you have fond memories of the past," he told her, emphasizing the last word, his eyes lingering on Merewyn's profile, his lips twitching as he saw the rosy color creep to her hollow cheeks.

"You've been away so long," Elizabeth accused, her tone plaintive, not sounding at all like the haughty individual who had swept into the room not a half hour ago.

Sickened by this display of fawning weakness, Merewyn rose to her feet, a contemptuous scowl on her small face. "If you'll excuse me," she began, only to feel the Marquis' large hand on her shoulder, forcing her back down into her chair with a bruising grip.

"You haven't finished your tea," he said silkily and she quailed at his tone, aware that he had no intentions of letting her go so easily. To Elizabeth he added helpfully, "My return was delayed by an unexpected excursion to the colonies."

"The colonies!" she echoed, Merewyn's presence all but forgotten. "Whatever made you go there?"

Ian reached down and toyed playfully with a silken curl that lay against Merewyn's soft temple. "Let's just say that there was something there I had to bring back and didn't trust anyone else to do it for me."

It took all Merewyn's willpower to keep herself from jerking free of the hand that was caressing her, determined not to show Elizabeth Comerford her true feelings for the Marquis. Let the brazen bitch discover them for herself; she did not intend to help her.

A black scowl crossed Elizabeth's beautiful face and her pale green eyes followed as though hypnotized the strong fingers that stroked the shining gold curls. How well she knew the look on that handsome face, having been its recipient many times in the past but, oh, how long ago it seemed since he had looked at her that way! And yet it was obvious that his passion for the young girl was tempered by something Elizabeth could not quite place her finger on. Was it hatred or mistrust she saw in those compelling gray eyes, or the self-loathing of a man who has always been in firm control of his emotions but has finally found himself confronted by some damning mystery he could not understand?

And the girl! Elizabeth's eyes narrowed as she studied Merewyn's flushed face; saw the fear in the soft, tilted eyes as she struggled not to let her aversion show. Surely they could not be lovers, she thought triumphantly, not when the little wench appeared to dislike Ian so! Or were they nonetheless? she worried fretfully. Had Ian taken a fancy to the child in Scotland and brought her back here

238 ELLEN TANNER MARSH

against her wishes? There was something odd afoot, she told herself, and she was determined to get to the bottom of it.

"Well," she said with a forced smile that looked to Merewyn more like a grimace, "I imagine the two of you wish to be alone. I simply came to see what you'd done with my gown, Ian, and I'm satisfied that it's been put to good use." To Merewyn she added graciously, "I'll send over a few more, child. You can't be seen about town in the same old thing."

No sooner had the door closed behind her graceful figure than Ian burst into laughter. Merewyn, her dark eyes flashing, surveyed him mistrustfully. " 'Twould seem you've found yourself a patron," he told her when he could speak. "What did you say to endear yourself so?"

Merewyn made no reply, and the amused smile was replaced by a mocking one. "I don't believe for a moment that Elizabeth has had a change of heart. Doubtless she's scheming even now for ways to get rid of you. She's far too stubborn to give in so easily."

Merewyn's small shoulders slumped dejectedly and she rested her hot face in her hands. She felt tired and drained, confused by the exhausting scene that had just taken place. "So this is how you intend to extract your revenge," she said hopelessly, not lifting her face to look at him. "You'll drive me mad with these cat and mouse games."

"Are you willing to make peace with me, Merewyn?" he asked seriously.

She looked up quickly to find him regarding her with no trace of mockery on his handsome face. "I just want to go home," she replied, and he felt his conscience stirring as he looked down into her ravaged expression.

"I'll take you home if you agree to end this foolish clan rivalry between the Villiers and the MacAilises once and for all."

Merewyn's soft lips tightened obstinately. "I can't," she whispered, then drew herself up and tossed her small head arrogantly, her large eyes regarding him defiantly. "I can't and I won't! Somehow you've convinced Alexander that you're a faultless gentleman, which leaves only me to make sure you never gain control of Cairnlash because I know the truth about you! I won't agree to that partnership even if it means I'll have to take on every one of your fawning, drooling mistresses!"

Francis had shuffled inside in time to catch her impassioned words and the relieved smile he'd been wearing since Elizabeth Comerford's departure gave way to an uncertain frown. As Merewyn rose from her chair and brushed past him he through he caught the glimmer of tears in her eyes and he turned accusingly to the Marquis, who had moved to the window and was peering out, his broad back unyielding. It was not Francis's way to interfere in his master's business, but something the young girl had said had piqued his curiousity.

"You're not causing trouble in that wool business, my lord?" he asked cautiously, intent on dabbing up the dark stain Elizabeth had made on the tablecloth by upsetting her teacup.

The broad shoulders shook slightly as Lord Montague chuckled, but his tone was flat as he replied, "Causing trouble, Francis? Nay, I'd be more inclined to believe I've inherited it. 'Twould seem I stepped into a hornets' nest when I took over Edward's holdings."

"That young girl," Francis went on carefully, "is she one of those people you've become partners with?"

"Aye. Her older brother runs the business, but the way she fights for it you'd think 'twas hers alone."

Francis coughed uncomfortably. "Begging your pardon, my lord, but don't you think she has a right to be worried?" At the Marquis's black look he went on hurriedly, "I mean, from what I heard 'twould seem she's afraid that you plan to take it away from her family.

Wouldn't that mean she feels her home and way of life threatened?"

"You infer too much from the little you hear," Ian growled, and added cruelly, "and you're starting to sound just like Davis with your interfering comments."

Francis blanched at this greatest of insults and said nothing more, withdrawing silently with the dirtied tablecloth over one arm. Ian stood moodily at the window, regretting what he had said and well aware that he had hurt the faithful majordomo's feelings. But what could Francis possibly understand about the problems that had beset him since he'd made the cursed decision to take over Edward's business? Though Merewyn would never believe him, he had truly intended to base his partnership with Alexander on mutual trust and helpfulness. He was tired of her incessant meddling and grimly resolved to go through with his plan to keep her here at his mercy until some of the arrogance was forced out of her. Perhaps then he might continue his new life in Scotland in a peaceful manner.

"Excuse me, miss, his lordship says you're to wear this tonight."

Merewyn looked up from the small writing table where she had been composing a letter that David was to take to Bond Street later that afternoon. Since her arrival three days ago Lord Montague had forbidden her use of the carriage, enforcing a house arrest he had established after catching her trying to borrow money from a sympathetic manservant who had been rendered powerless by her beauty and the beseeching look in her indigo eyes. The hapless young man had been dismissed on the spot and no amount of pleading on Merewyn's part could sway the Marquis to reverse his heartless decision.

The shy little maid who had spoken to her was standing hesitantly in the sitting room doorway, holding a gown of azure damask in her hands, the flounced skirts caught up with gold ribbons and shot through with gold piping, the bodice lavishly embroidered with floss flowers. Merewyn's eyes widened, unable to believe that something so beautiful could be meant for her.

"I can't possibly wear anything this elegant to dine alone downstairs," she sighed, laying down her pen and crossing the room to take it wistfully from the blushing girl. Her dark eyes narrowed suddenly and she asked nervously, "His lordship isn't joining me for dinner, is he?"

"No, miss. He said 'twas for the ball."

"The ball?" Merewyn echoed, her heart sinking. "What ball?"

"At Lady Humphries', miss."

The name meant nothing at all to Merewyn, but the Marquis's intentions were all too painfully obvious. Doubtless he intended to humiliate her by parading her about in a crowded ballroom as his latest paramour.

She thrust the beautiful gown back into the maid's hands and told her curtly, "I'm not going to any balls, and you can tell the Marquis I've no intentions of accepting this . . . this thing!"

"I'd rather expected that reaction from you," the Marquis told her as he strolled casually into the room, towering over the defiant, golden-haired girl and the mousy little maid who was quaking in terror at the sight of the impatient look on his handsome face. "You may go, Betsy," he added bluntly, and the grateful girl bobbed a quick curtsy and vanished, the relief on her small face obvious to both of them.

"I'm not going," Merewyn repeated, collecting herself for the battle she knew was forthcoming. Tilting back her head so that she could look squarely into his face she trembled inwardly, unnerved just as Betsy had been by the intimidating set of the classic features. Still, she refused to let him see her fear and she was surprised when, instead of rebuking her, he sighed almost wearily.

"You always seem to take delight in being at odds with me, Merewyn."

"And I shall continue to do so as long as you try to force me against my will," she countered. "You know bloody well what people will think about me when I'm ushered into Lady Humphries's home as your escort!"

"How odd that you're suddenly so worried about convention," he commented darkly, staring thoughtfully at the gown Betsy had placed in his hands. " 'Twould seem in the past you cared not a whit for proper behavior."

"I'm not going," she repeated stubbornly, meeting his gray eyes staunchly.

His fingers shot out and clamped down painfully on her arm. "You will, Merewyn, if I have to bodily drag you. 'Tis time you learned obedience. I had Mrs. Ludley design this gown especially for you and I intend to see that you wear it."

His handsome face was inches from hers as he half lifted her off the floor, pulling her so close that she could see the angry pulse beating in his temple. "I've grown weary of your defiance, my dear, and you may as well face the fact that I will not take you home until you've learned to do as I tell you without question and without protest. I'm in no mood to spend the rest of my life trying to deal reasonably with Alexander while you harangue in the background about everything I do. You will not leave here until I am assured you will obey me!"

Merewyn's indigo eyes flashed at his arrogant speech, hating him with her entire being, wishing she were a man so that she could slash his handsome face with the point of a sword. She'd never obey him, never, and she intended to fight him as long as she had breath in her body, for Cairnlach's sake more than her own.

A contemptuous smile curved his sensual lips. "I can see from your expression that your thoughts are far from kind, ma'am. No matter. I've great reserves of patience." He set her down far more roughly than she deserved and she rubbed her aching arms, her expression mutinous as she glared up at him.

"You'll pay for this, you bloody swine," she choked through clenched teeth.

He shrugged his massive shoulders. "Comments of that nature are precisely what delay your return home, Merewyn, and I wish you'd have sense enough to realize it." Tossing the damask gown onto the chaise lounge beside him, he added, "I expect you to be ready at nine."

Merewyn stared after him, her eyes blazing, wishing she had a dagger so that she could plunge it into his broad Sassenach back. Blackguard! Swine! How she hated him! Did he think his brutal treatment would break her? Make her meek so that she would readily agree to accept him as manager of the Glasgow mills? A faint look of doubt crept into the golden depths of her tilted eyes. How far would he go in his dastardly threat to bodily drag her to the Humphries ball? Could she afford to disobey him in this?

Her gaze fell upon the beautiful gown and a hopeless scowl crossed her small face. God, how she hated him!

Francis was standing in the entrance foyer later that evening, meticulously dusting off Lord Montague's hat and searching among the many sets of gentleman's gloves for the proper pair when the Marquis strode through the front door, bareheaded and sans wig as Francis had expected. A swift glance assured the majordomo that nothing else in his attire was lacking, however. The Marquis had donned a coat of satin claret shot through with silver threads, and his knee breeches were champagne yellow, tailored so well that they seemed molded to his muscular thighs. His wrists foamed with lace and a dark ruby glittered in his neckcloth and Francis, a connoisseur of elegant garb, was forced to admit that he had never seen his lordship look more fashionable or arrestingly handsome.

"I believe I've found the proper hat and gloves, m'lord," he said proudly, extending them with a flourish.

"Thank you, Francis," Ian replied, accepting them absently. "Is Merewyn ready?"

"I'll send Betsy up to see," Francis said and started for the kitchen when Merewyn's voice brought his eyes to the landing above.

"That won't be necessary, Francis. Here I am."

The old servant's jaw dropped as he took in the breathtaking vision floating down the staircase towards him. The damask gown shimmered, the golden petticoats beneath rustled softly as Merewyn lifted them to descend the stairs, two tiny satin slippers peeping out from beneath the glittering hem. Her hair had been powdered and arranged on her head so that several ringlets fell enchantingly down to her smooth white shoulders, and her indigo eyes appeared larger and darker than ever, highlighted by the soft blue color of her gown.

Betsy had fasten a fragile gold necklace studded with sapphires and diamonds about her smooth throat, and her heart-shaped face seemed more delicate than usual, her powdered hair swept for emphasis from her temples. Betsy had insisted on rouging the soft cheeks, and the hollows beneath them took on an angular beauty that made her seem older than her seventeen years—a maturity made more intriguing by the childish pout to her soft red lips, a dimple appearing on either side as she smiled almost shyly in response to the majordomo's admiring stare.

"May I say that you look enchanting, miss?" Francis asked, hurrying forward to help her step down into the hallway, taking her hand as gingerly as though she were made of porcelain. "The gown is most becoming."

"You may thank Lord Montague for that," Merewyn replied, giving the Marquis who stood motionless in the foyer, his eyes narrowed as he studied her, a chilling glance. " 'Twas his choice."

"His lordship has always had an excellent eye for color," Francis agreed happily, unaware of their locked, antagonistic glances.

"I imagine 'tis because he's had so much experience in selecting women's wardrobes," Merewyn commented acidly.

Francis coughed self-consciously, realizing his mistake. Mournfully, he relinquished his hold of the small hand, noticing that the Marquis came forward to take it in his strong one with a bruising grip, although Merewyn gave no outward indication of the pain he caused her. The old servant shook his head sadly as he watched them descend the front steps towards the waiting coach, the Marquis towering over his slender captive, Merewyn's slim back proudly held, although Francis detected a dejected droop to the normally haughty carriage of her small head.

What, he wondered worriedly, did Lord Montague have in mind with her this evening? 'Twould set tongues a wagging if he took that young girl to Lady Humphries without a proper chaperone, especially since she hadn't been formally introduced into society as of yet. Francis sighed heavily. He didn't understand anything about Merewyn MacAilis's presence in London or why the Marquis had been acting so strangely towards her, as though obsessed with trying to cause her pain. Though it was not his way to interfere, he thought perhaps he might take it upon himself to ask the young lad David what mysterious role the Scottish lass played in Lord Montague's life.

As the coach rumbled off down the drive, Merewyn leaned back stiffly against the velvet cushions, trying her best to ignore the Marquis who sat close beside her, although she had to admit to herself that she had never seen him look so elegant or so handsome before. The

rocking motion of the vehicle threw her up against him
on occasion, and whenever her slender thigh came into
contact with his hard, muscular one, she was reminded
despite herself of the time when they had touched even
more intimately, the time he had lain above her, his lean
features softened with tenderness and passion, the heat
and hardness of his body arousing within her an excitement and longing for fulfillment that she could recapture, oddly enough, merely by his nearness tonight.

"Will you stop scowling so?" he ordered, his deep
voice startling her from her reverie.

Blushing furiously, afraid that he could read her
thoughts in her face, she turned her small nose into the
air and presented him with a beautiful, yet thoroughly
affronted profile. Laughter rumbled in his deep chest in
response to this haughty gesture, and his strong fingers
were under her chin, forcing her small face around so
that her smoldering blue eyes met his.

"You have the flirtatious skill of an accomplished
courtesan," he told her lightly, "and the beauty of Athe-
na. You're an enigma to me, Merewyn. How is it that an
ill-tempered, foul-tongued little brute can possess such
breathtaking fairness?"

She wanted to deliver a stinging retort but somehow
found the words dying on her lips as she stared up into
his dark eyes, never having seen the look of tender admiration in them before. Her heart began a nervous
tatoo, aware of how close they were sitting together in
the intimate confines of the coach, his hand still beneath
her chin, his fingers stroking her soft cheek almost without his being aware of it.

At that moment another coach coming from a darkened side alley, cut directly into their path as it swung
onto the main street, and forced the Montague
coachman to bring his animals to an abrupt halt; he
hurled a string of oaths after the offending vehicle before urging his stamping horses onward. The lurching
stop had thrown Merewyn against Ian's broad chest,

and as she put out her arms to steady herself she found them moving of their own volition to encircle his thick neck while his own slid about her small waist, pulling her so close against him that their lips were almost touching.

"I'm beginning to wonder why I have neglected you these past three days," he commented huskily. "Life is certainly sweeter when you choose to be kind to me, Merewyn."

"I'll never be kind to you," she vowed, her voice tremulous, her eyes drawn despite herself to his smiling, sensual mouth.

"What a liar you are," he told her mockingly. "No sooner do we find ourselves alone in the coach than you throw yourself at my head. You are indeed an enigma, ma'am. What makes you say one thing when your actions clearly indicate you desire the opposite?"

"Oh, how insufferable you are!" she cried, but she did not sound quite as angry as she should have, leading Ian to wonder in astonishment if she might be teasing him. Merewyn acting playful with him?

He couldn't credit that if it were true, but he found himself unable to resist replying in a bantering tone, " 'Tis perhaps the kindest label you have ever affixed to me."

"All the others were richly deserved," she responded somewhat breathlessly, unable to draw her eyes away from his.

He pulled her to him, finding it impossible to resist the pouting red lips any longer and his mouth came down hungrily to cover hers. She made no effort to push him away, her lips warm and alive beneath his, and he felt again the same heady passion that always engulfed him whenever she was close.

Merewyn's senses were reeling beneath his ardent kiss, and she had all but forgotten the purpose of their outing and how he had intended to humiliate her before London's fashionable folk. She was aware only of how handsome he appeared to her tonight in his exquisitely tailored attire, his dark hair tied in a queue, looking the true embodiment of a young girl's fancy. She felt as though she herself was enchanted this evening, the beautiful gown he had had made especially for her having transformed her into the highborn, beautiful lady she had often yearned to be in her childhood dreams when the MacAilises had still been desperately poor, a bitter time when Merewyn had possessed only two threadbare gowns to her name.

The coach lurched to a stop a second time, forcing them apart, and Merewyn, instantly mortified by her wanton behavior, moved as far away from Lord Montague as possible, pressing herself against the padded seat, her cheeks burning, her lips still on fire from his kiss.

To her dismay he chose to make mockery of the tenderness that had sprung up between them, commenting in the cryptic tone she hated, "What a pity you don't always throw yourself at me so eagerly. I sincerely regret I don't have the key that unlocks the other woman within you."

"Go to Hades," she choked, and his deep laughter filled the coach's interior.

"Your penchant for cursing never ceases to amaze me, ma'am. I'm willing to believe you even taught the seamen aboard the *Highlander* an oath or two."

The coach moved forward again and then came to another halt. Merewyn saw that they were nearing a fabulous estate that stood on the brow of a small hill, lanterns illuminating the circular drive that was filled with a procession of vehicles, each one awaiting a turn to discharge its richly attired occupants. Maroon-liveried footmen flanked the well-lit entrance, and at the sight of the number of guests milling in the entrance hall her mouth suddenly went dry and she grew very still.

Ian was instantly aware of her changing mood and

glanced at her sharply from beneath his dark brows to
see that her face was pale, the rouge on her cheeks the
only relief from her ghastly pallor. Her eyes glittered in
the flickering torch light; her soft lips, still reddened
from his kisses, slightly parted; and her small bosom was
rising and falling in rapid rhythm.

"I believe you're afraid," he observed, although for
some reason this discovery did not give him the satisfaction it should have.

She turned towards him, her achingly beautiful little
face filled with a mixture of fear and loathing. "Why
shouldn't I be? You're going to make a laughing stock
out of me."

"Come, come," Ian replied heartily, "I'm not going to
throw you to the lions."

"I wish I'd died that day Louis Kincaid ordered me
whipped," she murmured passionately. " 'Twould have
been far more merciful than enduring this!"

To his surprise he saw tears standing in the tilted blue
eyes and she pressed her shaking hand to her lips. "Oh,
Alex," she whispered, seeming all at once to have forgotten his presence, "pray, forgive me!"

Ian was taken aback by her fervent plea. Was her fear
not for herself, after all, but for her brothers? Was she
honestly fretting about what a scandal involving the
MacAilis name might do to Alexander? Had he perhaps
misjudged her entirely all along? Could it be true that it
was her love for Cairnlach and for her brothers that had
spurred her into trying to destroy him, rather than some
vendetta borne of her personal hatred for him?

Intriguing questions, these, and he had no answers for
any of them, nor was there time to dwell on them more
deeply, for the coach had drawn to a stop before the
marble steps and two footmen were approaching, one of
them opening the door and the other lowering the steps,
his hand held aloft to help Merewyn down. She
hesitated only for a second, wiping the tears from her

eyes with the back of her hand, a truly childlike gesture; and as she sniffled pathetically Lord Montague found himself stirred by unaccountable pity.

Even as he watched she steeled herself, the suffering in the indigo eyes turning slowly to determination until they had become two cold, glowing sapphires, devoid of emotion; the frozen smile on her lips so startling the footman with its beauty that he flushed and stammered a greeting as he helped her down. His own countenance expressionless, the Marquis followed. Taking her arm as they ascended the stairs, he became aware of the underlying hardness in the slender body that had only minutes before yielded so warmly to the insistent pressure of his arms. Turning his head, he looked down into her cold little face and would have been hard put to believe that she had been weeping seconds ago if he hadn't personally seen the tears.

Gaily conversing couples thronged the entrance hall greeting acquaintances, and Merewyn hung back for only a fraction of a second before going bravely forward at Ian's side to meet Sir George and Lady Humphries, the same expressionless smile still frozen to her lips.

"Why, Ian, you came back after all!" Lady Humphries, her black hair heavily powdered and her brown eyes lined with kohl, hurried forward as the tall Marquis stepped into the hall. She held her hands out to him and he took them in his automatically, bringing them to his lips. "I didn't think we'd ever see you again once you left for Scotland!"

"Did you think the wolves would eat me?" he asked, his gray eyes twinkling while Merewyn looked up at him in astonishment, never having seen him so unaffected and gay. Could this be a sampling of the infamous Villiers charm?

Lady Humphries laughed gaily. "Dear me, no! 'Twas the savages I was worried about! I was afraid they'd run you through with those fierce claymores George says they always carry."

"The King has forbidden them to bear arms," Ian informed her, the faint note of warning in his deep voice passing unnoticed over her elegantly coiffed head.

"Do you really think English law will stop those barbarians from doing anything they want to?" she asked coyly, deliberately turning one dainty shoulder to block Merewyn from her line of vision, her hands still clutching his. "Oh, Ian, I'm so happy you could come! George, here's Ian come all the way from the wilds of Scotland just to see us!"

A short, spindle-legged gentleman in a powdered wig came forward, his ruddy face wreathed in a welcome smile, seemingly oblivious to the hungry manner in which his wife was staring at the handsome Marquis. Merewyn smothered a giggle, amused, despite her anger at Lady Humphries' rude comments by the difference in height between the two men. Lord Montague was gravely polite as he bowed low before Sir George, whose bewigged head was barely on level with the Marquis's broad chest.

"Couldn't stay away from our English beauties for long, eh?" George Humphries asked with a knowing wink, his sunken eyes twinkling. "Can't say I blame you, old man! Highland lassies are reported to be deuced ugly. Whey-faced and horse-teethed, isn't that what your brother called 'em, Caroline?"

The Marquis's eyes instantly sought Merewyn's, and as he saw the renewed anger burning within hers he reached down and took her hand in his, pulling her to his side. "As a matter of fact I found one who doesn't quite fit that description," he remarked pleasantly. "Sir George, Lady Caroline, this is Miss Merewyn MacAilis of Cairnlach, Glen Cairn."

There was abrupt silence, not only from the Hum-

phries but from the other couples who had been close
enough to hear the Marquis's clear, carrying words.
Their curious stares unnerved Merewyn, who was unaware of how startlingly beautiful she looked, her tilted
eyes still flashing from the Humphries's unjust attack on
her beloved Highlands, her cheeks flaming, her soft lips
slightly parted. There was an arrogant tilt to her golden
head quite similar to that of the Marquis who stood
close at her side, his strong fingers still clasped about
hers. The protectiveness of his stance did not go unnoticed by Caroline Humphries, who finally stirred and
with obvious effort dragged her eyes away from the
striking beauty in cerulean blue.

"How quaint," she murmured to Ian, her tone no
longer warm. "You've brought one of them back for us
to admire."

"Nonsense, Caro," her husband put in heartily, moving forward to take Merewyn's cold hand in his. "Can't
you tell this isn't one of the creatures Teddy described?
Welcome to London, m'dear."

"Thank you," Merewyn replied cooly, frowning as
she regarded the couple standing before her. "I don't
believe—"

"Come along, Merewyn," Ian interrupted, wresting
her hand from George Humphries' eager grasp. "There
are others you must meet tonight."

"Yes, indeed," Lady Humphries added with feigned
brightness, her eyes lingering with ill-concealed jealousy
on Merewyn's heart-shaped face. "Show the girl what
sort of people a truly cultured society revolves around."

"I've already seen—" Merewyn began, but the Marquis interrupted her a second time, smiling so beguilingly at Lady Humphries that the woman grew pale, her
lips parting as her breath came faster, leaving no doubt
in Merewyn's mind as to her true feelings for the towering Marquis.

"I want Merewyn to be well-received tonight," he told

Caroline blandly, "not because this is her first visit to town, but because I expect to bring her here more often."

Lady Humphries swallowed with considerable effort. "Y-you do?"

"Oh, perhaps I forgot to mention," Ian added with the evil smile that to Merewyn had always heralded doom, "Miss MacAilis is my fiancée." With that he bowed and disappeared into the crowd, pulling a dumbstruck Merewyn bodily behind him.

"Don't say a word," he cautioned, becoming aware of her seething expression. "I didn't want your reputation ruined and decided naming you as my betrothed would be the best way out."

"What?" Merewyn cried, astounded. "Ruining my reputation is precisely what you had planned for me all along! And why tell such a blatant lie? Surely you must realize Lady Humphries will spread the news like wild-fire about this assembly!"

Ian's full lips twitched. "Doubtlessly."

"I don't understand you!" Merewyn protested loudly, causing several curious heads to turn their way. "What sort of game are you playing now, m'lord? Was it merely to provoke jealousy in your ex-mistress, or am I mistaken? Is Lady Humphries a current paramour?"

"She fancies herself in love with me," Ian responded lightly, "though you'll be pleased to know that I have never done anything to encourage her."

"I don't care who you choose to dally with, you unspeakable lout!" she hissed, ignoring the startled look on the face of a young buck who had been drawn irresistibly closer by her beauty, only to retreat hastily after overhearing her scathing words and becoming the recipient of a black scowl from the intimidating Marquis.

"Tut, tut, those are harsh words for a man who has just saved you from disgrace."

"I believe you incapable of making a kindhearted sacrifice for anyone, especially me," Merewyn retorted coldly. "More likely than not you'll use it to further my torment. What do you have in mind next? Do you intend to abandon me at the altar?"

"Damn it, Merewyn," he said irritably, controlling himself with visible effort although he would have liked to shake her until her teeth rattled. "Are you so thick that I have to explain my motives to you every time? You were crying in the coach because of Alexander and it made me realize for the first time that I have no quarrel with him and have no right to damage his name merely because he is saddled with an unmanageable sister!"

Ian's tone grew more forbidding, and she recoiled instinctively. "Whatever conflict exists between us, Merewyn, is ours alone, and I intend to resolve it between the two of us and no one else."

Merewyn was prepared to make a scathing reply when, over his broad shoulder, she saw Elizabeth Comerford bearing down upon them with a purposeful air, looking extremely beautiful in a gown of gleaming peach satin.

"I'm so glad you came, Ian," she murmured throatily to the Marquis, smiling up at him seductively, deliberately ignoring Merewyn, whose small face was rigid with anger. "They're forming a set for the first dance. Will you join me?"

"I don't see why not," he responded amiably, and Merewyn tried hard to pretend she didn't see the strong hand that slid intimately about Lady Comerford's waist in a brief caress, his gray eyes mocking as he watched her intently.

"Why, Ian," Elizabeth remarked, her gaze having followed his to Merewyn's stony countenance, "aren't those your jewels?" She was staring avidly at the diamonds and sapphires that adorned Merewyn's smooth throat, and when he nodded her expression grew hard, her lips tightening, and Merewyn could almost feel the palpable anger that radiated from her.

"Are you certain the child won't lose them?" she asked worriedly, giving Merewyn a condescending smile.

"I believe she's wise enough to hold on to them," the Marquis replied, seemingly enjoying the stricken look that entered the dark, tilted eyes at Lady Comerford's unkind words.

"Oh, listen, the musicians are striking up the melody!" Elizabeth cried eagerly, seizing his hands. "Hurry!"

Merewyn watched as they made their way onto the dance floor, the Marquis far taller than any man present, noticing, too, that almost all of the women turned their eyes longingly his way. Miserably, she skirted the milling crowd and exited through the tall French windows out onto the stone terrace, where she leaned against the balustrade and breathed deeply of the tranquil night air. The music wafted gently towards her on the faint summer breeze, but she was oblivious to its beauty and that of the gaily colored lanterns festooning the tall trees around the pleasant park.

Why did Ian take such pleasure in tormenting her? she wondered forlornly. He had displayed such kindness towards her in saving her reputation and rescuing her from Lady Humphries's shrewd and unkind perusal, only to revert instantly into the despicable monster she so despised—plunging a knife through her heart, as it were, by flirting so deliberately with Elizabeth Comerford, enjoying himself hugely as he twisted it cruelly.

She thought again of the kiss he had given her in the coach and her cheeks grew flushed as she remembered how exciting the touch of his lips had been and how eagerly she had responded. Faugh, but she was a weak, sniveling woman to show him how easily he could control her! Devil take him, she wasn't about to see him victorious!

A discreet cough from behind made her whirl about fearfully, but she relaxed when she found herself coming face to face with a pleasant young man in a periwig, his powder blue coat lavishly embroidered, a shy smile on his lips.

"Sir?" she prompted helpfully when he hesitated, his cheeks reddening and his courage fleeing now that he was actually gazing into the exquisite face.

"Excuse me, m-miss, I couldn't help noticing inside that your card was still empty. Would you c-care to dance with me?"

For a moment the dark lashes fluttered shut over the cobalt eyes as she struggled to throw off the memories that haunted her, and he felt disappointment overwhelm him, but then she graced him with such a dazzling smile that his heart hammered.

"I'd like that very much," she replied in a sweet voice, and he could scarcely credit his joy as he took her small hand in his and led her back inside.

On the dance floor Lord Montague and Lady Comerford were performing the prescribed dance steps with considerable skill, and as they came together Lady Comerford remarked acidly, "Really, Ian, you shouldn't have brought that unpolished wench with you! Just think what people will say!"

"I'm accustomed to being the favored topic of gossiping matrons," Ian replied unperturbed, his eyes sweeping the crowded room as though searching for someone. A small frown knit his brows together and Elizabeth, aware that she had lost his attention, tapped him lightly on the sleeve with her fan.

"Surely you must agree that a formal ball is no place for a rustic infant from the Highlands! I certainly hope no one leads her out. She'll doubtless perform a fling while the rest of us are dancing the minuet."

"I believe you're mistaken," Ian told her, and something in his tone caused her to whirl around, her pale green eyes searching the corner of the room in which he had fastened his speculative gaze. She gasped when she spotted Merewyn dancing with the youthful Earl of Denmont, her slender form, encased in shimmering azure damask, swaying in perfect time to the music, her slippered feet seeming to carry her several inches above the marble floor.

There was unmistakable beauty and grace in her movements and Elizabeth said flatly. "Apparently, they've heard of the minuet in your remote Highlands after all, Ian."

"Apparently," he agreed absently, his attention still claimed by the whirling, golden-haired nymph, noticing with a faint scowl that he was not the only man present who was watching her. Throughout the course of the evening he observed Merewyn being squired onto the floor by first one, then another beaming admirer, frowning as he noticed the heightened color in the delicately molded cheeks and the sparkle in her eyes that had never been there before. Nor had she ever looked at him in such a beguiling manner, a saucy smile on her red lips as though she were flirting to the hilt with every one of her partners.

"Your fiancée seems monstrously content to parade about on the arms of other men." This caustic comment came from Caroline Humphries, who was Ian's current partner.

" 'Tis a trait common to the female gender," he responded deliberately, and she dropped her gaze from the ominous gleam in his steely eyes.

"Have you decided on a wedding date?" she inquired nervously.

"Not yet." His smile was intimidating, quelling her to silence.

Merewyn was sitting on a richly upholstered chair

where her latest admirer had deposited her after the
dance had ended, gallantly offering to brave the crush of
the milling throng to fetch her a glass of *rattafia*. Watching the other couples whirl past, she sighed wearily, glad
for the chance to get off her feet. Unconsciously, she
searched the crowd for the towering man in wine-col-
ored satin she had been following with her eyes all evening, her soft lips tightening when she found him at last
dancing with the simpering Lady Humphries.

Doubtless he was enjoying himself, Merewyn thought
passionately, for he had danced with almost every woman present, young and old, and not once had he offered
to lead her out. Surely 'twas expected of a gentleman to
dance at least once with his fiancée! But then, she reflected angrily, Lord Montague was no gentleman and
she was definitely not his fiancée! As a matter of fact,
if he came to her this very moment and asked for her she
would flatly refuse him!

"You seem to be enjoying yourself, ma'am."

She jumped as she heard his deep voice and looked up
quickly into the glowering gray eyes. "I am," she responded warily, "but no more so than you."

"Ah, do I detect a faint note of jealousy?" he asked
pleasantly, leaning over her solicitously, one strong
hand resting on the back of her chair, for all appearances whispering intimacies into one perfect little ear.

"Don't lean over me so!" Merewyn hissed, disliking
to have him so close, hating the thrill that always shot
through her at his nearness.

He straightened immediately, his eyes growing cold.
"I beg your forgiveness, dear lady. 'Twould seem you
welcome the attentions of all men this evening save
mine."

"Can you wonder why?" she countered icily, her slim
little nose pointed haughtily skywards. "Do you expect
me to show you kindness after you've taken such pleasure in being cruel to me?"

"And have you warranted better treatment?" he shot back, annoyed. "You've done naught but made my life miserable since I first laid eyes on you."

Rather than the sharp retort he expected to hear, her reply was abrupt silence and, gazing quickly down at her, Ian saw her face turned towards the far end of the ballroom where a small group of men had just emerged from the gaming room and were standing together conversing in animated tones. She was breathing heavily, her lips parted, her face so pale that he thought she might faint, the cobalt eyes glassy and wide with shock.

"Mereywn?"

She made no reply and he bent closer, touching the hand that lay in her lap, startled to find it icy cold.

"Merewyn, are you ill?"

His deep voice, taut with concern, had no affect on her whatsoever. Ian swore beneath his breath and shook her gently, hoping to rouse her from her strange reverie. What the devil was ailing the lass? He'd swear that look on her face stemmed from passion, misconstruing the darkening of her eyes as yearning rather than fear. Turning his head he studied the group of men but could not tell which one among them she had singled out. Most of them had danced with her at one time or another. The little bitch, could she have agreed to a rendezvous with one of them?

"God's teeth, will you answer me, you stubborn wench?"

This time the steely anger in his tone roused Merewyn and she stirred, her small hand reaching up to clutch protectively at his muscular arm. "Ian?" she quavered.

"Merewyn, what is it?" he demanded, beside himself with impatience as she fell silent again.

She shook her head and sighed as deeply as though she were returning from a great distance, and then abruptly smiled up at him, her expression devoid of emotion. "I'm sorry," she said, laughing shakily. "I thought I recognized someone. I must have been mistaken."

Lord Montague was totally dissatisfied with her answer, certain that she was hiding something from him. "Who was it?" he demanded.

The indigo eyes shifted nervously away from the black countenance. "No one. I told you I made a mistake."

With an angry exclamation he jerked her upright, his iron fingers closing about her wrist. "I'm taking you home," he told her in a tone that brooked no argument. "If you've made plans for the evening that don't include me you may as well forget them."

Merewyn hung her head, too shaken to argue with him, and with tightened lips and a murderous expression, he propelled her out of the ballroom, not even bothering to bid farewell to Lord and Lady Humphries. With ill-concealed impatience he waited on the steps for his coach to be brought around, then thrust Merewyn roughly inside and sat regarding her intently, clearly expecting an explanation. Merewyn said nothing, her small face averted, and Ian gave up at last, feeling helpless, his rage barely in control.

Only when they were standing in the darkened hallway of the elegant townhouse did Merewyn turn to him, carefully unpinning the sapphire necklace and extending it with a wan smile. "Perhaps you ought to take this now," she said quietly. "Lady Comerford was right. I could very well lose it."

Ian stared down at her in exasperation, the necklace swinging in his hand, unable to find the proper words to deal with her, knowing that a show of anger would only cause her to withdraw even more. What in hell was wrong with her? If she didn't confide in him soon he'd twist her head right off her wretched neck.

"Thank you for letting me wear it. The jewels are truly beautiful."

The Marquis watched as she turned and climbed

wearily up the stairs, her slim shoulders bowed, a vision of haunted loveliness in the glittering damask gown. Not until he'd heard her bedroom door close softly did he turn away, an amused smile tugging at his sensual mouth despite his ill temper. Impertinent little chit, if he didn't know any better he'd have sworn that she had just dismissed him from his own house! Carelessly pocketing the expensive necklace, Ian returned to the waiting coach, curtly ordering the coachman to drive him to the Montague residence on Grosvenor Road, and as he settled with a sigh against the squabs he found his thoughts lingering on Merewyn and her inexplicable behaviour. If she still refused tomorrow to answer his questions he'd simply have to take matters into his own hands, he decided with a faint scowl.

The London streets were nearly empty this time of night and the elegant coach bearing the Villiers coat-of-arms made excellent time as it rumbled down the twisting streets that were normally choked with horses, carriages, and sedan chairs. Only one other vehicle passed them by as the silent coachman and his pensive passenger rolled down Park Lane, and if Lord Montague hadn't drawn his curtains he would have recognized one of its occupants as Lady Elizabeth Comerford.

Elizabeth herself took no notice of her surroundings, for she was in a nasty frame of mind, seething over the news Caroline Humphries had casually told her not twenty minutes ago. Lord Montague and that mealy-mouthed wench he'd brought back from Scotland with him were going to be married! Even now Elizabeth couldn't quite believe it. Why hadn't Ian told her right away? Why did she have to learn it from that flat-chested trollop Caroline Humphries? It couldn't be true! Ian had once been hers, and she could still remember how possessively he had bedded her, even now making her knees weak with longing merely at the thought of his experienced hands roving her body.

But that had been before his departure for Scotland, a disquieting voice in the back of her mind reminded her snidely. And since his return Ian had shown not the least bit of interest in her. No, he was far too occupied with that golden-haired strumpet he was reportedly be-trothed to! Elizabeth's lips tightened into an angry line. She'd put a stop to that wedding, she swore, if it cost every ounce of her strength, for there was definitely something wrong between Lord Montague and his little amour. She'd seen it with her own eyes that morning in the Marquis's townhouse, and was convinced that Ian wasn't marrying her for love.

"Your thoughts are troubled, m'lady."

Elizabeth jumped as the bony hand came to rest in-timately on her knee, having forgotten her companion's presence entirely. " 'Tis unimportant," she responded with a strained smile, suddenly wishing that she hadn't agreed to accompany him.

Actually, she'd only wanted to make Ian jealous, hav-ing planned her departure in the company of this gen-tleman to coincide with his own, but damned if Ian hadn't left unexpectedly early! One moment he'd been speaking intimately with his heathen bride-to-be, the next he'd simply vanished, leaving Elizabeth bound to her promise to this man who had whispered to her earlier that he resided not far away in a rented townhouse off Marylebone Road.

Oh, he was handsome enough, Elizabeth was forced to admit, with his piercing brown eyes, well-groomed mustache, and angular features, but it was Ian Villiers whom she wanted, whose very image made her heart cry out. Later, when they lay together, their naked bodies touching, Elizabeth's breath came faster for she could almost imagine that it was Ian who lay above her, Ian touching her with sure, experienced hands, and she cried out, almost certain that it was he.

CHAPTER SEVEN

"Now, my dear, suppose you tell me what came over you last night?"

Merewyn's heart skipped a beat and she looked up quickly as the Marquis sauntered into the breakfast room, no longer dressed as the personable dandy of the previous evening. In fact, he appeared more like the lord of his Highland estate, his long legs encased in brick-colored breeches and black boots, a simple buckskin coat tossed carelessly over his broad shoulders, his stock plain and unadorned with jewelry or lace. His finely chiseled features had a harsh set to them, however, and Merewyn felt her heart sink, recognizing the determined look in his eyes.

"I haven't the faintest idea what you mean," she responded weakly, deliberately focusing her attention on her breakfast, her golden head bent. But he had seen the flicker of fear in the slanted indigo eyes.

"Come, come," he said impatiently, halting in the center of the small room. "You know damned well what I'm talking about. You saw someone at the Humphries' last night whose presence disturbed you. Who was it?"

"Really, my lord," Merewyn protested, raising her head and giving him a guileless smile, "I simply don't know what you're talking about!"

Ian fought and conquered the softening in his heart as he looked down into her perfect, heart-shaped face, knowing her smile was intended to sway him. "You're a rotten liar, Merewyn."

She sighed resignedly. "Very well, if you must know, I saw a man in the ballroom who reminded me at first of an unscrupulous business partner Alex once had. The man in question was our solicitor's assistant and it was later discovered that he was skimming funds off the profits for his own use and entering them in the books as legitimate expenditures."

"Edward never mentioned him to me," Ian said warily, not sure if she was speaking the truth and finding it exasperatingly difficult to tell, what with the simple honesty radiating from her small face. Devil take it, maybe she was a good liar after all.

" 'Twas years ago," Merewyn informed him helpfully, busily spreading butter on a croissant. "I was still a wee lass, but I'll never forget what he looked like. He was sent to prison, of course, but I imagine enough years have elapsed since then for his sentence to have been served."

"So you believe he came to London after his release?" Merewyn didn't care for the suspicion she heard in his deep voice and strove to hide her extreme nervousness. "Perhaps he has," she replied with a shaky laugh, "but I must have been mistaken, for when I got a closer look at him I found he didn't resemble the man at all."

"But you were extremely upset," the Marquis pointed out, "even after we came home. Surely a case of mistaken identity doesn't warrant such a strong reaction."

He was watching her closely, his keen gray eyes fastened to her face and Merewyn managed a convincingly affronted scowl. "Surely you must admit I had had enough shocks that evening to find it difficult to cope with one more, however imagined. Your announcement of our pending marriage left me ill equipped to handle any more."

Ian ignored her rebuking tone and demanded harshly, "What was the man's name, Merewyn?"

Her clear little laugh annoyed him, for he was growing more and more unsure of the game she was playing and did not know at all how to handle her in this. "I certainly can't be expected to remember that, Ian! After all, 'twas years ago!"

"And yet you remember his face?"

Merewyn grew still, having realized her mistake, then laughed self-consciously. "I told you 'twas a vague resemblance and that later I realized I'd been wrong. Now, could we please talk about something else?"

For a moment the Marquis was silent, eyeing her thoughtfully; then he shrugged his massive shoulders as though he considered the matter closed. "Actually I came to ask if you'd care to ride out with me. 'Tis an uncommonly cool morning."

He was unprepared for the warmth of her smile as she sprang eagerly to her feet. "Oh, aye, I'd love to! Do you know I haven't been riding since .. . ."

She broke off abruptly, her face falling. How long ago had it been since she'd galloped her mare across the sundappled moors with Malcolm following behind on the lumbering Drummond? It seemed like years, now that she thought on it, and that laughing, happy Merewyn was somehow a stranger to her now. If only she had known back then that her life would shortly be ruined by a devilishly handsome but heartless giant by the name of Ian Villiers, she might have been able to prevent everything that had happened to her since she'd first laid eyes on him.

Suddenly, she was reluctant to ride out with him and said sullenly, "I don't have the proper attire."

Ian's smile was malicious, having observed the display

of hostile emotions that had passed across her small face. "Ah, but you do, my dear. Lady Comerford sent round some more of her gowns yesterday afternoon, and Francis informed me when I came in that one of them happened to be a habit."

Merewyn scowled and opened her mouth to tell him that she had no intention of accepting his mistress's gift when a gentle breeze wafted through the opened windows behind her, bringing with it the scent of flowers and the twittering of song birds. A heady desire to gallop overwhelmed her and she knew she couldn't combat the call of a summer morning any more than she could the determined gleam in Lord Montague's gray eyes.

"Very well," she agreed loftily, "I'll meet you outside."

The full lips twitched in response to her haughty tone. "Very good, madame."

As she ascended the stairs to her bedroom, the excitement died within her, remembering the heat conversation that had taken place between them minutes before. Though the Marquis did not suspect anything was amiss, her heart was deeply troubled, and fear had been her constant companion since leaving Lady Humphries' home last last night. She was convinced beyond a shadow of a doubt that one of the men she had seen conversing so amiably together in the crowded ballroom had been William Rawlings, whose charges in Glasgow had sent her to gaol as a thief and a prostitute.

Merewyn was certain that Rawlings hadn't seen her and prayed fervently that if he had he hadn't realized that the girl in the elegant damask gown had been the same disheveled traveler in the stained and wrinkled russet velvet he had encountered months ago. Unreasonable fears tormented her as she changed her attire, just as they had caused her to toss fitfully throughout the night. Suppose he had recognized her?

Suppose he found out her name and told everyone that the Marquis of Montague's 'fiancée' was in truth a cheap whore not above committing crimes like stealing a gentleman's rings? Dear God, and suppose the Marquis, in his thirst for revenge against her, took up the cry himself?

A low moan fell from Merewyn's soft lips and she struggled to keep back her tears, her fingers fumbling with the fastenings of the elegant dark brown habit Lady Comerford had given her. Surveying herself in the glass, she saw that she was deathly pale, her brimming eyes luminous, and she chewed her lips, striving valiantly to screw up her courage enough to face an outing with the Marquis as though nothing were amiss. Later, when she was alone, she would think of a way out of this dilemma and find a means of escaping from London as quickly as possible.

Lord Montague was waiting for her outside the carriage house, conversing with the head groom while tapping his muscular thigh absently with a bone-handled quirt, impatient to be off, exuding a vitality and restless energy that seemed to be shared by his mount, a heavily muscled black stallion that stamped and reared, nostrils flaring, refusing to be quieted by the soft-speaking man who held him.

"I don't believe I've ever seen one like him," Merewyn commented thoughtfully as she joined the Marquis, eyeing the big animal appraisingly. "He's not island bred, is he?"

"No, indeed," Ian assured her, smiling to himself as he watched her run an experienced eye over the stallion's sloping rump and long, sinewy legs. "He's a barb. I had him imported from Spain."

"Andalusian blood, no doubt," Merewyn murmured and whirled about indignantly when he laughed. "Is that so amusing?"

"Careful, your rustic breeding is showing," Ian

warned, adding to the head groom, "Miss MacAilis is more at home in the company of sheep and horses than fellow human beings."

"I warrant she has stauncher friends among the beasties, m'lord," the middle-aged man with the kindly face remarked unperturbed, his sympathies lying with the golden-haired girl who, talk at the house had it, was sweet and unassuming, but possessed enough spirit to take on a man the likes of the Marquis.

Unlike the majordomo Francis, Nick Holder heartily approved of her presence in the house, having wished for quite some time now that his master would show some sense and take himself a wife. Naturally, he'd already heard the news of the engagement from John Bolling, the Montague coachman, who'd heard it from the Humphries' footman last night. Nick smiled suddenly, his craggy face softening.

"Congratulations, m'lord."

The Marquis eyed him narrowly. "For what?"

Nick's confidence faltered beneath the hard gaze. "Why, on your betrothal to the lady, m'lord," he stammered, growing red.

Lord Montague raised an eyebrow. "You congratulate me, Nick? 'Twould be more appropriate if you offered me your condolences."

"I only thought—" Nick began, but Merewyn interrupted him coldly.

"I'm afraid you've made a mistake, sir. Lord Montague and I are not getting married."

Nick watched in bewilderment as she defiantly ignored the helping hand the Marquis extended, mounting without assistance the high-stepping gray mare that had been led out for her, her shoulders stiff as she settled into the saddle, her gloved hands expertly encircling the polished leather reins.

"Aye, I'd say you have your hands full, m'lord," Nick commented as he steadied the prancing barb in order for the Marquis to mount. "But they say the best marriages are forged from trouble. Strengthens the heart, it does."

"And since when are you an expert on matrimony, Nick?" the Marquis asked quietly, a warning glint in his eyes. "You're almost fifty and you've yet to take a wife."

"Aye, m'lord," Nick conceded reluctantly, not wishing to start an argument with the Marquis, an argument he would invariably lose. He watched pensively as the barb wheeled and broke into a trot at the lanky mare's side, champing nervously as he strained at the bit, Lord Montague holding him back with ease, his seat as always impeccable.

'Twas a right well-matched duo, Nick decided, meaning not only the high-strung beasts but their riders. He'd wondered throughout the years if his lordship would ever find a woman brave enough to take him on. Sure, and the Marquis had had his share of women, but none of them had had the backbone, in Nick Holder's opinion, to handle him properly. That little blonde beauty with the underlying core of iron appealed to him a great deal and he wondered, with a small smile playing on his lips as he watched her cut expertly in front of the Marquis and take off at a canter down the path leading towards the park, if perhaps his lordship had finally found his match.

Hyde Park, resplendent in full summer bloom, was a sea of striking green, its ancient trees crowned with leaves, the well-tended lanes flanked by thick manicured lawns. In the early morning hours, with the sun still shimmering through the mist, it was nearly deserted, and Merewyn found it hard to believe that such a bountiful, empty oasis could exist in the crowded city.

"I believe Madrigal should be taken through his paces," Ian told her, drawing alongside, the stallion's crested neck flecked with foam as he strained forward in his eagerness to run. "Are you afraid to gallop?"

"Afraid?" Merewyn shot back. "Me?"

A smile tugged at the corners of his mouth. " 'Twas foolish of me to ask," he agreed, and let the barb spring forward with no further urging than by loosening his reins.

Merewyn's mare was no slugabed, and as she pounded off in pursuit, Merewyn leaned low over the glossy mane, enjoying the feel of the warm wind fanning her face, the sound of hoofbeats echoing through the still morning air. The wide path was excellent turf for a fast run and the two animals charged headlong between the trees, seeming to enjoy the mad pace as much as their riders.

When the horses were winded at last they were slowed to a modest walk to let them blow, and Merewyn leaned back, her soft lips parted with excitement, the blood drumming in her veins, her golden hair disheveled beneath the rakishly tilted tricorn.

"I warrant there's nothing more exhilirating than a good hard gallop," Ian remarked as he brought the stallion closer so that he could look into her flushed and smiling face.

Merewyn nodded her head in agreement, savoring the intimacy that seemed to have sprung up between them at the enjoyment of something shared, wishing a trifle wistfully that it would last. How rarely did they speak to one another as friends, she realized sadly, remembering only the constant verbal battle that went on between them.

"You ride extremely well, Merewyn," Ian commented lazily, his handsome face averted as he stared off through the trees, not having observed the longing on her comely features. "I'm amazed to discover how well polished you are after all. You really surprised me last night with your drawing room skill."

"Doubtless you expected me to perform wild Highland reels and strathspeys rather than the courant," Merewyn replied a trifle coolly, and he was forced to think of Elizabeth's unkind comment to that very effect.

"Not I," he said truthfully, turning to look at her, his eyes narrowing as he saw her closed expression that moments before had seemed so free of cares. "You've a most determined gleam in your eye," he added, propping his strong hands on the stallion's thick withers and leaning back comfortably in the saddle. "More often than not such a look warns me to be on my guard. I wonder if it has anything to do with my mention of last night?"

" 'Tis nothing to tease about," Merewyn informed him soberly. "I want to know what you're going to do now that you've told Lady Humphries we're going to be married. 'Twas a damnable lie, we both know it, and yet your head groom has heard the news already. I wouldn't be surprised if you and I were the hottest salon topics at the moment, and I have visions of London streets crammed with carriages containing your former lovers on their way through Mayfair to spread the news."

Ian laughed in a purely unaffected manner, his deep chest rumbling with the sound, and when he could speak again he told her severely, "You musn't exaggerate my popularity, ma'am. 'Twill turn my head."

"You?" Merewyn asked with feigned astonishment. "Your head is already so enormously swelled that I wonder how you manage to fit it through the door."

"I should have cut that tart tongue of yours out long ago," he countered darkly.

But Merewyn could tell that he wasn't genuinely angry and was heartened enough to prompt, "Then what do you intend to do?"

"About our engagement?" He shrugged his broad shoulders disinterestedly. "Let the gossip hens squawk what they will. Either way your reputation remains unsoiled."

"But that is precisely why you took me to the Humphries' to begin with," Merewyn reminded him, con-

fused. "To ruin my name and teach me obedience."
Now the slanted eyes were flashing indignantly.

"There are other ways to achieve that end," Lord
Montague replied smoothly. Observing the loathing in
her small face, he moved his horse closer to hers until
their knees touched, reaching out with one strong hand
to grab the reins from her so that she couldn't move her
mount away.

"I want you, Merewyn," he informed her simply,
"and I will not rest until I have you. There is something
about you that stirs me more than any other woman I've
ever known and I intend to taste the sweet mysteries you
offer."

"I'd rather die!" Merewyn whispered, trying to tear
her gaze away from his and finding that she could not.

"You'll never convince me of that," Ian replied with
an infuriatingly confident smile, and he was once again
the evil ogre she feared and hated with all her being.
"You've given yourself to me willingly once before,
Merewyn, and only a timely intervention kept me from
possessing you. Oh, don't worry," he added smoothly as
she made a strangled sound and tried to wrest the reins
from his strong fingers, "I don't intent to take you by
force. What you gave me freely I found far more desirable than anything I could take for myself."

"Why are you so cruel to me?" Merewyn demanded
tearfully. As she gazed piteously into his lean face, he
saw that he had hurt her unexpectedly with his harsh
threats. "There are times when you can be so kind and
lead me to believe perhaps we'll mend the differences
between us, and then you suddenly change and take delight in catching me off guard so that you can be unkind."

"Is that what you honestly wish?" Ian demanded
sharply, his finely chiseled face only inches from hers,
the depths of his eyes burning with something she could

not recognize. "To mend these differences you say exist between us?"

"I'm so tired of our arguments," Merewyn confessed, "and I don't think I'm strong enough to fight you alone."

"So you're willing to make amends in order to bribe me into taking you back to Cairnlach where you'll recruit your brothers into full-blown clan war."

His voice was harsh and she drew away from his intimidating scowl.

"Damn it, Merewyn, can't you accept the fact that I'm not Edward Villiers and that I had no preconceived hatred towards you MacAilises when I first arrived?"

"So you're saying that everything is my fault?" she asked bitterly. "That I eroded the perfect friendship you had with my brother? Well, I don't believe for a moment that you intend to settle for half the business! You're too thirsty for power!"

"I'm sorry you believe that of me, Merewyn."

She was momentarily put out by the regret in his tone, then she steeled herself resolutely. "What else should I believe, Ian? You've yet to show me that there's another side to you. Ever since the day you closed down the waterway you've been nothing but trouble. You are rude, selfish, and arrogant and you took it upon yourself to take me to London against my will after all that I'd been through just so you could teach me a lesson." Her voice had begun trembling dangerously as she delivered this impassioned speech, her cheeks flushed, unaware that he was guiding both their mounts down the shady lane, his eyes resting intently on her bent head from his great height.

The Marquis was silent, never having considered her plight that way before. She was right in claiming that he hadn't taken into consideration the hardships she had endured since leaving home last spring. Damn it, he thought to himself, she needed to be punished for her own arrogance, needed to be taught that she couldn't lead him about by the nose despite everything that had happened to her!

"So you think yourself an innocently wronged individual," Ian remarked sharply. "What saving graces do you possess that should convince me to make peace with your family? You're equally as arrogant as I, Merewyn, and twice as ready to play the cutthroat. No, ma'am, when I return you to Scotland 'twill be to a life of serenity for me without a meddlesome wench constantly underfoot."

Merewyn turned away, biting her lips to keep from crying. Damn him! He was a liar and a rake who would take what he wanted, including herself, with no regard to anyone else's feelings. "You'll never have what you want the most, Ian Villiers," she hissed, her voice vibrating with hatred, her cobalt eyes as cold as ice. "I've told you before that I'd rather lie with swine."

Ian's big hands clenched into fists and the stallion reared at the unexpected pressure on the reins. Damn the contemptible brat, he thought savagely to himself, she was right, his desire to have her was standing in the way of everything. If only she didn't excite him so, he could easily dismiss her and crush the defiance out of her, and he hated himself for the softening he'd felt towards her last night, when he had foolishly told Caroline Humphries they were planning to be married. God's blood, he'd rather be emasculated than find himself wed to that foul-tempered bitch!

"If you speak to me like that again," Ian told her through clenched teeth, "I'll thrash you within an inch of your life."

"I'm impervious to beatings," Merewyn spat back, masking her fear behind anger. "Do whatever you please with me, m'lord, but I'll never make peace with you, never!"

Ian swore loudly, his temper snapping, and seized her with one hand by the neck, the other sliding around her waist, pulling her bodily from her horse so that she was sitting in the saddle before him, her small rear pressed against his thighs, gasping for air as he abruptly released her, his eyes blazing into hers. Grasping her arms he shook her mercilessly, causing her hat to tumble to the ground and her hair to come unpinned, the golden braid spilling down her back.

"I've had enough of your impertinence, you little brat," the Marquis breathed, beside himself with anger. "So you insist I'll never be rid of you despite my best efforts? No matter, I'll simply change my plans and make sure that you spend the rest of your life as miserable as I."

"What do you mean?" Merewyn whispered, her head spinning as he released her, falling dizzily against his hard chest, hot tears of fear and pain spilling onto the front of his coat.

"You'll see," he replied grimly, his square jaw clenched. "My patience is at an end."

Engrossed in their impassioned exchange, neither one of them had noticed the pair of riders approaching around a bend in the lane until both had drawn abreast of Merewyn's mare, now riderless and without proper control, who had ambled to the grassy roadside where she stood grazing unconcernedly. Merewyn's hat lay trampled beneath her trim hooves, and she herself was sitting in an intimate pose upon Lord Montague's lap, her small face pressed against his muscular chest, wanting to shut out the sight of him as she shed humiliating tears. The Marquis's big hands still gripped her arms, although his hold was not as painful as it had been moments before.

Having felt her slender shoulders shaking with suppressed sobs, his anger had vanished abruptly and even the murderous look upon his handsome face had eased somewhat as he leaned over her, admiring, despite himself, the golden curls that fell to her waist, breathing in their fragrance, his lean cheek almost touching the top of her head.

Lady Elizabeth Comerford, one of the perplexed witnesses to this scene, misconstrued the lingering fury in the Marquis's gray eyes as passion, and felt her heart grow cold, unable to believe that the Marquis could display so little self-control in pulling the girl onto his horse to embrace her in this solitary stretch of the park thinking no one would see! Why, he had even removed her hat and unpinned her hair and was burying his face in its shining softness as though preparing to bed her right then and there!

Elizabeth couldn't bear to watch any longer and pushed her mount forward, her reluctant companion waiting a good distance behind. "Why, Ian, that's rather forward, don't you think? Are you trying to make a public spectacle of yourself?"

Lord Montague cursed inwardly as he looked up and met Elizabeth's probing eyes, the jealousy in her sharp voice painfully obvious. But he contained himself with an affort and smiled at her mockingly.

"My dear Elizabeth, since when do you worry so much about appearances?" His eyes wandered past her to the soberly attired gentleman who waited uncomfortably beneath the spreading branches of a nearby chestnut tree. Dismissing him instantly, his hands stole about Merewyn's thin shoulders and he pressed her face against his coat, determined not to let Elizabeth see that she was weeping. To his relief Merewyn showed no inclination to struggle. In fact, a tremor had run through her slender body at the sound of Elizabeth's shrill voice and she had grown very still.

Elizabeth's pale eyes narrowed as she watched the muscular arms move protectively around the young girl, and she drew in her breath in an audible hiss. "If you're referring to my companion," she said with a faint shrug, "we're out for a morning ride. Surely even you, Ian, would call that respectable."

Merewyn could feel the Marquis's huge body shake with silent laughter. "Come, come, Elizabeth, I know damned well you couldn't resist sharing your bed with him, either."

"Jealous, Ian?" she asked cruelly, leaning forward expectantly, her pale green eyes filled with both hatred and yearning.

Lord Montague's voice was cutting. "My dear Elizabeth, you're simply not worth being jealous over."

"I expect your little chit is?" Elizabeth flared, thinking she'd scream if she had to look at the two of them locked in that cozy embrace another second.

"Perhaps," Ian replied, smiling as he lowered his dark head to touch his lips to the shining curls, enjoying the responding look of utter loathing that crossed Elizabeth's flawless features. "I can't bear to let Merewyn stray from me for long. Even the distance separating us on horseback was too maddeningly great for me."

The gentleman awaiting Elizabeth was growing impatient. "Are you ready to go on, Elizabeth?" he called out to her.

"I'm coming, darling," she responded, gracing him with a wan smile. "Ride on ahead."

He nodded obligingly and turned his mount in the direction they had come, vanishing behind a bend in the lane flanked by thick trees.

"You think you've caught yourself a fine fish, don't you, my dear Miss MacAilis?" Elizabeth cried, turning to face the couple before her, her fury engulfing both of them. "Well, he's naught but a scoundrel and a knave!"

Merewyn turned in the Marquis's arms, her tears gone, a faint smile playing on her soft lips. "I think him a fine fish, indeed, Lady Comerford. What a pity you let him slip off your hook before you could land him."

Elizabeth uttered a strangled sound and wheeled her horse so savagely that the unsuspecting animal reared before charging off at a mad gallop, the chestnut-haired woman clinging precariously to his back. Laughter rumbled in Ian's deep chest, but as he turned to look down at Merewyn, his gray eyes twinkling, she began to struggle in an effort to free herself from his hold.

"Let me go or I'll claw your eyes out!" she threatened.

Sobering, Lord Montague obliged her, releasing her so abruptly that she tumbled backwards unexpectedly. Before he could grab her she slipped from the horse's back, landing in a small heap in the dust dangerously close to the iron-shod hooves. Ian was instantly at her side, lifting her up against him, his eyes dark with concern.

"Are you hurt?" he asked, his voice strained. Merewyn took no notice, pushing him away and getting quickly to her feet, dusting off her habit with vicious strokes of her gloved hand while chewing her lips to control her tears. Without a word she walked away from him and seized the mare's reins, mounting and starting off in the direction they had come.

He caught up with her a short distance away, and his tone was sincere as he said, "I'm sorry, Merewyn. I didn't know you'd fall off."

She said nothing, her delicate profile unrelenting, and he tightened his lips in angry frustration.

When they reached the stableyard Merewyn dismounted and handed the reins to Nick, who came out to meet them, waiting expectantly to hear her evaluations of the mare he himself had schooled. His eager smile faded into a puzzled frown as she wordlessly turned her trim back on both him and the towering Lord Montague and marched through the garden, vanishing behind the thickly blooming rose bushes.

Nick cast a bewildered glance at the Marquis, wanting to ask what had put the young lady in such a bad frame of mind, but was forewarned by the similar look on his lordship's hawkish face. Without a word he took the stallion's reins and led the horses away without so much as a backwards glance. 'Twould be a roughshod marriage, he decided, if they were already going at one another like bantam cocks, and here the engagement not even officially announced.

At the far end of Hyde Park leading down along the Serpentine, Lady Comerford and her companion were riding at a slow trot, Elizabeth beside herself with anger, her entire being consumed with jealousy. How she hated Merewyn MacAilis! What power did the little wench have over Ian Villiers that made him behave like an infatuated schoolboy? Had Lord Montague developed some perverse penchant for cradle-robbing? Whatever the reason she was determined to put a stop to it.

"You're angry, my dear."

Elizabeth scowled irritably, for she had entirely forgotten William's presence, and heartily wished herself rid of him. He'd served her well enough last night, but she had no wish to see him again. There was only one man she wanted now and none other would do. "I'm tired," she responded curtly.

William smiled and moved his mount closer to hers. "I'm to thank for your lack of sleep," he reminded her, his breath hot against her cheek.

It took all Elizabeth's willpower not to jerk away. God's teeth, he was a swaggering oaf! Did he honestly believe he'd been that good? Her reply to his comment was a distracted smile.

"You've been upset ever since we met that couple back there," William observed after a moment of silence. "I've never seen anything like it, the two of them pawing at each other in broad daylight—on horseback, no less!''

"They were doing no such thing!" Elizabeth shrieked at him, her cheeks hot.

William Rawlings hid his astonishment at her outburst beneath a carefully controlled mask. "If you insist, my dear. Do you know the man?"

Elizabeth swallowed hard, struggling to regain control of herself. "Not very well."

Her tone was unconvincing, but no matter what her answer would have been he already knew exactly what her feelings for the large gentleman were. "Do you know his name?" he asked curiously.

"Ian Villiers," Elizabeth replied reluctantly.

William's heavy brows shot up in astonishment. "Not the Marquis of Montague?"

Elizabeth's pale green eyes were fastened to his face. "Do you know him, by chance? More recently he went by the title of Earl of Ravensley."

"I know him only as the Marquis of Montague, though I've never laid eyes on the man before. His inheritance caused quite a sensation back home."

"I should have realized you'd know him, William, coming from Glasgow yourself. Why is it," she added, hoping to turn the conversation away from the topic of Ian Villiers, "that you don't speak with one of those Scotch dialects?"

William laughed in response, although Elizabeth was too preoccupied with her own thoughts to see the bitterness in his bony face, his mustache twitching as his lips tightened angrily, the laughter abruptly gone. 'Twas better not to reveal one was Scots in a city that despised them. He'd been looked down upon his entire life, despite his wealth, for being lowborn and common, and had come to the bitter conclusion that money did not buy respect—especially in London where a title was often more important than well-lined pockets.

"What is Lord Montague doing back in England so soon?" he asked, evading Elizabeth's question.

"He's going to be married," she replied flatly.

"Married? How interesting. Who is the lucky bride?"

Pure hatred radiated in the green eyes. "I'd rather not talk about her."

William smiled placatingly. "As you wish, my dear."

He was moodily silent as they turned their horses homeward, Elizabeth sharing his silence, her dismay growing as her thoughts returned time and again to the disturbing sight that had met them when their horses rounded the bend: Ian Villiers astride his stallion, Merewyn MacAilis in his arms, tousled and reclining comfortably against him, her face averted, no doubt to hide from Elizabeth the blush that had crept to her hollow cheeks as a result of his kisses.

They parted with the briefest of farewells, Elizabeth returning to her modest townhouse that her late husband had left to her a year before, William Rawlings to his rented home near Marylebone where he found a visitor awaiting him in the parlor.

"Damned good to see you, Will," boomed Oswald Trantham in hearty greeting as the thin, pensive young man entered the room. "Been waiting since nine for you." He winked and gave the younger man a sly smile, the folds of fat in his jowls bulging. "Your housekeeper tells me you rode out at dawn with a strapping wench at your side."

"My housekeeper has too many eyes in her head," William retorted, making no effort to hide the fact that he cared little for the fat gentleman in the powdered wig reclining comfortably on the sofa, his periwinkle blue coat and satin breeches lavishly embroidered and far too frilly for William's countrified tastes.

"What brings you to London?" Oswald Trantham asked conversationally, ignoring William's impatient scowl. "And do sit down, will you? I can't tolerate craning my neck while I speak."

"I was bored with Glasgow," William replied nonchalantly, depositing himself in a chair, crossing his thin legs before him.

Oswald laughed heartily, the ruddy color of bad health and overindulgence flooding his round cheeks. "Doubtless the lassies offered you little diversion there. If you're hunting, by God, then London's the territory. We've plenty of roving ladies ripe for the taking."

"I was thinking more in terms of finding myself a wife," William informed him coolly, reaching for the brandy decanter that stood at his elbow.

Oswald laughed uproariously and slapped his pudgy thigh. "There, and now I've heard the impossible. You, Will? Looking for a wife?"

"I'm twenty-seven," William said stiffly. " 'Tis high time I married."

"And your father? Does the Squire approve of your search for a—what do you call us over there? Sassenach bride?"

William took a long swallow of the golden liquid before rising casually to fill Oswald's extended glass. "I am not a Highlander and I don't use such terms. My father is quite delighted that I've chosen to come here to take a wife. He has a touching wish for grandchildren in his old age."

"More likely than not he's hoping you'll reel in a title," Oswald observed shrewdly, laughing as he saw the prominent cheekbones grow flushed. "Been a sore point for you all your life, hasn't it, Will, to possess all that money and still not be accepted socially?"

"Money can buy me any place in the upper crust I wish," William struggled to keep from displaying the murderous rage that was beginning to build within him. He'd always hated Oswald Trantham, his mother's fat, disgusting brother, and was glad that long years had always elapsed between his uncle's visits to Glasgow.

Naturally, he had expected Oswald to look him up when he arrived in London, but frankly had been hoping for at least a few more days respite.

Oswald was a wealthy banker, married to Lord Arthur Pembroke's only child, a horse-faced, tired-looking woman as fat as he, and it was a constant source of amusement for William to see how impatiently Oswald was waiting for Lord Pembroke to die so that he would inherit the meager title the old man had assured him twenty years ago would be his if he married his daughter Dorothy. Oswald was now forty-three; Lord Pembroke seventy-nine and still as healthy as a horse, word had it, though William had never met the man himself.

"How did you know I was here?" he asked conversationally, feeling he should display at least token civility towards his uncle.

"One of Dorothy's friends overheard you being introduced at Lady Humphries' last night. You know deuced well how women are. They know the names of every member of your household and extended family, even your damned cat if you have one." Oswald belched loudly and helped himself to another glass of brandy while William scowled as he watched the alarming drop of the level in the cut-crystal decanter. "We were invited, but my gout was acting up. Pleased to say 'tis better today."

"I'm glad to hear it," William murmured.

Oswald's little eyes twinkled. "Ha! I'm sure you do, my boy. I know damned well there's little love lost between us. How did you happen to gain admission to Caroline's little rout?"

"I'm not unknown in the city," William boasted. "I'm surprised, however, that Dorothy's friend didn't introduce herself to me." He scowled again, not liking at all the idea of someone running to his aunt behind his back to inform her of his presence.

Oswald shrugged and fumbled in his pocket for his snuffbox. "Women love to spy and carry tales, you ought to know that by now, lad. Tell me, did you find a filly worthy of your stables?"

"No," William responded curtly.

"Dorothy's friend said you left in Lady Elizabeth Comerford's company." Oswald's moist lips pursed in a disapproving manner. " 'Tis unwise to be so indiscreet, William." He sneezed violently, wiped his nose with an embroidered hanky, then added ruminatively, "She's a beauty, I'll grant you that, but too unpredictable for my tastes. 'Tis rumored her heart belongs to another."

"The Marquis of Montague," William said obligingly.

"Eh? Lord Montague?" Oswald's brow wrinkled thoughtfully. "Ah, of course, young Ravensley. I forgot he'd inherited his uncle's estate some months ago. I heard he was at Caroline's last night, too. Did you see him?"

William shook his head, growing bored with the older man's prattle.

"Have you ever met the Marquis before? I know Glasgow's somewhat removed from his Highland hills, but I hear the mills are headquartered there in your city."

"No, I've never met him," William said as patiently as he could.

Oswald took another delicate pinch of snuff, from his golden box. "Charles Brentwaithe, a former associate of mine, handles the MacAilis-Villiers London branch now, and 'tis quite a formidable business, I'm told. Seems they've built up impressively since the '45. No small task for a Scotsman."

"Edward Villiers was partly responsible for that success," William reminded his uncle, sighing inwardly when he saw that Oswald did not feel the least bit inclined to let the subject drop.

"That one!" Oswald snorted derisively. "A worthless blackguard with an eye for money and pretty faces.

Popular consent is that his nephew's just like him, but I'm inclined to think he's worse."

"Do you know the Marquis?" William asked in surprise, leaning forward to refill his brandy glass a third time.

"Hell, everyone in town knows Montague! He couldn't have been older than nineteen or twenty when he first made a reputation for himself. Supposedly took Sir Richard Stanton's wife to bed, and the jealous husband, too ashamed to admit he'd been cuckolded by a lad in pantaloons, hired two assassins to do him in. Young Villiers was at his Surrey estate at the time, and the story goes that the two cutthroats spent less than ten minutes in his house trying to attack him in his sleep before they came runnin' out, one of 'em with a slashed face, the other with a severed finger. I'd not care to cross swords with him!"

"I've heard he's a supreme fencer," William agreed, lazily sipping his drink while wondering irritably how Elizabeth could possibly fancy herself in love with such an arrogant scoundrel. "After that I imagine 'twas one affair after another for the Marquis," he added.

Oswald shook his bull head back and forth. "No, indeed. He was quite fed up with the entire affair and took himself off to sea."

"To sea?" William echoed, startled.

"Aye. His father, the late earl, owned a small fleet of ships that plied trade in the Caribbean and the colonies, and Villers up and sailed away on one of 'em. Fast little brig she was, and worthy of any seafaring man, but he sold her before the war, her and other two, and they were armed and commissioned against France."

"Villiers had no desire to taste the privateering life?" William asked sarcastically. "From what you tell me he's a pirate at heart."

Oswald shrugged his pudgy shoulders. "I gather he wasn't interested in his country's power plays. He was gone three or four years that first time he went to sea. Sailed around Cape Horn, I believe 'twas said, and to Tobango and Tahiti, places like that. Wherever it was he came back with his coffers spilling over with gold and spices and the like. His character wasn't changed, though, and I'm inclined to believe his seafaring adventures only made him worse. Always had a black temper, he did, but it was shorter when he came back, and he'd gotten dangerous, too. Somebody out there taught him to shoot dead center and fence like a master. Not a man I'd care to cross at all."

"And since his return he's led the life of a retiring London gentleman," William finished, his interest in the topic of Lord Montague waning.

Oswald's massive stomach shook as he laughed and William's eyes were drawn to the tight waistline of his breeches, certain that the fastenings would pop at any moment. "Retiring? You must be daft, Will! Arrogant and cruel, he is, but with an eye for frilly lace and somehow the ladies find him appealing though I'll be damned if I know why. I warrant he's been in and out of a dozen romances since his return from the Far East and fought twice that many duels as well. His leaving for Scotland set the town on its ear, I can tell you that. Never seen so many teary-eyed woman in my life!"

"Then why did he leave if he had it all here?" William asked curiously.

"Must have been the excitement he was after. An estate in Surrey that practically runs itself and an endless round of balls and soirées are certainly not the things Ian Villiers thirsts for. Doubtless he was eager to match wits with that MacAilis fellow. Brentwaithe told me once he was a ruthless chap." Oswald belched thoughtfully. "Heard there's a daughter in the family, too, a breathtaking beauty though 'tis said she's as wild as the land."

"You know a deuced lot about the MacAilises," William pointed out, but not really surprised, since he was certain that Oswald knew more about most of the inhabitants of the British Isles than God himself. "More than I have, and I don't live too far from the Cairnlach mills. 'Tis said the lass's brothers are more protective of their sister than she-wolves of their young."

"So they'd never consider you an eligible suitor, eh, Will?" Oswald asked unexpectedly, his face suffusing with color as he gave way to a bout of unbridled mirth. "Do you admit that you're not good enough for the MacAilis lass? Not with your grandfather a dirt-poor blacksmith?"

"He was your father, Oswald," William reminded him, the blood pounding in his ears so strongly that it made him feel dizzy. The same unreasoning fury that had swept through him in Nellie Arling's filthy garret threatened to overwhelm him again and he struggled to calm himself, afraid of losing control of himself that way again.

"Well, I imagine I'll be off," Oswald remarked nervously, aware that he had gone too far considering the younger man's fierce pride. With a grunt he rose to his feet. "I'll be seeing you more often, won't I, lad? Your wife hunting will doubtless take some time."

William nodded complacently, relieved now that he was getting rid of Oswald's obnoxious presence. Accompanying his uncle to the front door he remarked, "I'll stop by and see Aunt Dorothy soon."

" 'Twould be a pleasure for both of us," Oswald beamed. "Damned good to have you here in London, my boy. Hope you stay a while."

A vision of Elizabeth Comerford's alabaster body rose unbidden to William's mind and his thin lips curved into a contented smile. "I believe I shall."

CHAPTER EIGHT

"I want you to take this letter to Mr. Charles Brentwaithe," Merewyn instructed David, handing him a sealed envelope. "I've written the address on the front, but you'll have to ask directions when you get to town. I've no idea where it is."

David took the missive from her and stuffed it into the picket of his trews. "Lord Francis assigned some errands for me to run this afternoon and I'll do it then," he promised.

Merewyn eyed him suspiciously. "What did you call him?"

David's brown eyes twinkled. "Oh, 'tis everyone here in the house what calls him that. 'Tis true, miss," he added defensively. "You don't ever see how bad he is. I'm half afraid to lie in my bed at night for fear of wrinkling the sheets."

Merewyn's clear laugh rang out and her slanted eyes glowed with amusement. "Honestly, David, sometimes I don't know what to make of you."

He shrugged nonchalantly. "I've sailed with captains afore who couldna rest until every sail was set just so, but our Lord Francis could be crowned for his ways. I'll tell you summat, miss," he added, lowering his voice conspirationally and glancing furtively over one shoul-

der, "I'll be right glad when Lord Montague takes us to
Scotland with him. When will that be?"

Merewyn's smile faded and her indigo eyes grew sad.
"I don't know, David. Maybe not ever. We can only
hope that my brothers come soon to fetch us."

"Will I be staying with you until the wool ships are
ready to sail?" David asked, his freckled face filled with
hope and childlike trust.

Merewyn nodded warmly. "Aye, David, you'll be
staying with me."

"And the Marquis? He'll be there, too?"

Her reply was curt. "No. He'll be at Montague."

David's disappointment was obvious. "But—"

"That's enough," Merewyn said firmly. "Please take
that letter downtown and don't, for heaven's sake, tell
anyone you have it!"

"Aye, aye, cap'n," he responded, dashing off down
the corridor towards the kitchen. Merewyn watched him
with a small frown on her face, praying that he would
deliver it safely into Charles Brentwaithe's hands. She
had managed to ferret out the information she needed
from Betsy, for the little maid, always eager to be help-
ful, had petitioned a footman to learn where in London,
if at all, a branch office of Cairnlach Mills could be
found.

Betsy had returned triumphantly to Merewyn's rooms
several hours later with the news that a former banker
named Charles Brentwaithe was handling the business
out of a small office near Bond Street. Merewyn, greatly
elated, had hurried off to her room to explain her plight
to Mr. Brentwaithe in a letter and beg his help.

She had felt no hesitation or remorse in unburdening
herself to a total stranger, desperate to get away from
London and William Rawlings, and especially the more
disturbing presence of Ian Villiers. Since their heated
argument yesterday she had seen nothing at all of him
and was secretly glad of that. She hated the time they

spent together, their constantly fluctuating enmity wearying her tremendously. How could he be so kind to her at one moment, making her breathlessly aware of his charm, only to revert in the next to the blackhearted giant she hated who was determined to discipline her like some wayward child?

A faint sneer curled her soft lips as Merewyn wandered thoughtfully to the salon window, drawing back the lace curtains to peer into the sun-drenched garden. Part of her, she loathed to admit, yearned for Ian, ached for his touch and the fulfillment of the desire he had unleashed in her untutored body with his ardent kisses and gentle caresses. The fascination she had for this man whom she despised was a mystery to her, and a constant source of worry—never sure when it might erupt to overshadow her reason and cause her to throw away the restraints she had so carefully held in check until now.

All the more reason, Merewyn decided with a scowl, that David deliver that letter to Mr. Brentwaithe right away. She didn't know how much longer the Marquis intended to hold to his promise of not taking her by force, but she didn't care at all to wait and find out. Better that she return home to Cairnlach quickly, where she would never have to lay eyes on that hated monster again.

"A word with you, if you don't mind, ma'am."

Merewyn whirled about, her heart sinking, as the deep, resonant voice startled her from her reverie. She cringed inwardly when she saw the imposing figure in black towering above her, the finely chiseled features set with angry determination, the look in his eyes indicating clearly that he was in no mood to be trifled with.

"Aye, my lord?" Merewyn asked warily, steeling herself for battle.

"What do you know about this?" he asked unpleasantly, and she bit back a gasp as he held an envelope up for her inspection, the same envelope she had given David only minutes ago.

"How did you get that?" she whispered faintly.

"So you admit that 'tis yours?"

"Of course I do," she snapped, her indigo eyes flashing as she glared up into his handsome face. "You know damned well it is, so will you please stop this cat and mouse game?"

"I intercepted David on the way out," Ian informed her, his tone making her blood run cold, "and had the good fortune of noticing what appeared to be a piece of my best parchment sticking out of his pocket. Imagine my surprise when I ordered him to hand it over to find that it was a sealed envelope that, upon being opened, revealed a most informative letter."

Merewyn's hollow cheeks burned, remembering that she had spared little detail in painting the Marquis as a blackguard who had tormented her ruthlessly since their journey from Boston. The knowledge that her last route of escape had now been effectively sealed brought tears of despair to her tilted eyes, but she refused to wipe them away, determined not to let him see how upset she was.

"I've told you before," the Marquis continued in an ominously quiet tone, his gray eyes still resting intently on her upturned face, "that you yourself hold the key to your freedom."

"And I've told you often enough," Merewyn countered, "that I won't become that which you ask, or permit you to gain control of MacAilis mills. Your suggestions are abhorrent and I refuse to consider them again. I will, however, make a deal with you."

Lord Montague's smile was unpleasant. "I do not bargain with women."

"I propose," she went on calmly, her small chin bravely set, "that you take me back to Cairnlach tomorrow, without conditions, and in turn I promise not to interfere in any way with your dealings with Alexander as long as I live."

"God's blood, woman," he ejaculated, totally astonished, "do you honestly believe me so stupid? No sooner do you find yourself safely at home than you'll run to Alexander with tales of how callously I treated you."

"My word is the word of a MacAilis," Merewyn said stubbornly, "and you can trust me to keep it."

His full lips parted in a humorless smile. "No, my dear, that's where you're wrong. I don't trust you, not one bit. This," he waved the accusing letter before her slim nose, "proves how eager you are to plunge a dirk into my back. I reject your proposal for another reason, too, and that is because I've already decided how to end this tiresome warfare once and for all."

"What do you intend to do?" Merewyn asked in a small voice, unnerved by his supreme confidence.

"You'll have to wait and find out," Ian replied cruelly, the smile on his lips becoming insolent. "There's plenty of time before your brothers come for you. Aye, I know you believe they're on the way and I'm thinking perhaps they are, too, and you'll simply have to wait until I choose to make my move."

He tossed the crumpled envelope into the stone fireplace and, while Merewyn watched, struck the flint and ignited it, his sharp features grimly set. When there was nothing left of the accusing letter but ashes he rose to his great height and came towards her. She stood her ground although she was visibly shaken, her head tilted back as she stared up at him, her cobalt eyes alive with conflicting emotions.

"My poor, victimized Merewyn," he said mockingly. "What a pity that we are so much alike and no matter what our intentions are we cannot help but try to destroy each other."

"Is that what you believe?" Merewyn whispered despairingly, certain that he had conceived some evil plan to do her bodily harm.

" 'Twill always be that way. If only we could turn these impassioned feelings toward building something good—but 'twill never be, and so I must accept the fact that you are the cross I must eternally bear."

"I don't understand you!" Merewyn cried, moving away from him, hating it when he spoke in riddles. "What is it you intend to do?"

"I told you that will have to wait," Ian reminded her coolly. "In the meantime I'm afraid I'm going to have to enforce your house arrest. You will not be permitted to leave the grounds unless I am with you, and no servants will run errands or carry messages for you at the risk of instant dismissal. That includes David, who will be excused for his actions today seeing that he is quite young and naturally inclined to do anything you ask."

"I hate you!" Merewyn whispered, tears starting afresh in her eyes, her slender body in the flounced yellow muslin trembling uncontrollably.

The Marquis raised an eyebrow inquiringly. "You've told me that often enough, my dear. Am I to interpret this as something new or simply as a reaffirmation of your feelings?"

She made no reply, struggling to keep from crying.

"Very well," he said, his harsh tone suddenly weary. "You're confined to the house for today. Tomorrow evening we've been invited to a dinner party given by Sir Edward and Lady Palington, and I expect you to be on your best behavior. Edward is one of my oldest friends and he and his wife are being kind enough to hold this gathering on such short notice to celebrate our engagement."

"How can you carry this mockery so far?" Merewyn demanded, wondering despairingly where it would all end. "Don't you think 'tis time you told everyone the truth?"

"Oh, you'd be surprised at how far I sometimes carry things," he responded, unperturbed by her outburst.

"But never fear, ma'am, I discard most of my whims once they grow tiresome." Suddenly, he moved forward, half lifting her off the floor as he placed his strong hands about her small waist, bringing her face close to his so that he could stare directly into the wide, fearful eyes. "That includes you, Merewyn, and I charge you not to forget it."

He set her down roughly and left the room, leaving her standing shaken and forlorn by the fireplace, the faint breeze from the opened window stirring the ashes of the letter to Charles Brentwaithe that had been her last hope of freeing herself from him forever.

Lord Montague did not return to the house until the following evening when he came to collect Merewyn for the Palingtons' party. Leaving the coach waiting in the circular drive, he ascended the steps to the front door, whistling tunelessly to himself, pleased with the starry summer sky above and the warmth of the velvet evening. He was looking forward to seeing the Palingtons—Edward was an old childhood friend from Surrey—and wanted very much for them to meet Merewyn, of whom they'd already heard quite a bit, her beauty and spirit having been discussed in countless salons and drawing rooms recently.

A faint smile tinged with pride touched the sensual mouth, for Ian knew that if Merewyn remained in London much longer she'd soon become the toast of the town, and well she deserved to be. 'Twas a relief to him that no one knew what an impossibly arrogant strumpet she really was.

"Good evening, Francis," he greeted the majordomo who met him in the hall. "Where is Merewyn?"

Francis, he noticed, appeared unusually nervous. "She's not quite ready, m'lord."

The Marquis' brows drew together suspiciously. "Not ready yet?" he echoed darkly. "We're late as it is. Send someone up to fetch her."

"You don't understand, m'lord," Francis added hastily, while the Marquis strode towards the staircase as though intending to go up himself. "Betsy said Miss MacAilis won't be going tonight."

The broad back stiffened and Ian paused in midstride, causing Francis to shift nervously in response to the black look on his handsome face. "What do you mean she won't be going?"

Francis had to look away from the glowering gaze. "Just that, m'lord."

"Well, is she ill?"

"No, m'lord, at least I don't think so. Betsy went up over two hours ago to help her bathe and dress and came back down, saying Miss MacAilis had ordered her to go away."

A murderous gleam appeared in the gray eyes. "We'll see about that."

"Wait, m'lord!" Francis cried. "You can't go in unannounced!" The foolishness of his words didn't even seem to dawn on him.

"I'm wondering if perhaps the time has come to replace you, Francis," the Marquis said thoughtfully, pausing at the top of the stairs to look down at the faithful servant. "You're growing awfully soft in your old age."

Francis turned away without replying, his shoulders slumped, knowing that no one, not even the King's army, could keep the Marquis out of that bedroom if he'd made up his mind to go in. He had instructed Betsy to warn her mistress of the dire consequences she was courting in ignoring the Marquis's orders, but Merewyn had been undaunted by the possible danger, stating politely but firmly that she had no intention whatsoever of attending the Palingtons' ball.

Ian strode down the short corridor that led to Merewyn's room, his anger beginning to boil over, his patience with her obstinance nearing the breaking point.

With a heave that almost pulled the door from its hinges he flung it open and stepped inside, his smoldering eyes going instantly to the small figure huddled beneath the satin covers in the big four-poster bed, her indigo eyes luminous in her pale face as she stared up into his black expression. She was apparently prepared to retire, wearing an embroidered lawn night rail, her hair unpinned and lying in shining waves about her slender shoulders.

"What the devil are you trying to do, Merewyn?" Ian demanded, coming forward to stand at the edge of the bed, his anger so strong that she could feel the heat of it envelope her. "Are you trying to provoke me into kiHing you? Believe me, I'm angry enough to do it."

Her night rail was opened at the throat and he could see her tiny Adam's apple bob nervously when she swallowed, but her voice was cool as she replied, "I'm not going to that party, Ian. I refuse to be a part of this grotesque lie. You've let it get too far out of hand."

A wicked smile curved the full lips. "Have I? Apparently you think me a man of small limits, my dear. But no matter, you're going with me and I'm not going to argue with you about it. Get up and put on something decent."

The tilted blue eyes blazed with mutiny. "I won't!"

He reached down and seized her shoulders in his strong hands, shaking her coldly, his gray eyes boring into hers. "Oh, yes you will, my dear. Since you refuse to dress yourself I'll just have to do it for you."

He turned and strode to the clothespress, where Betsy had hung away the dozen gowns he had commissioned from Mrs. Ludley to last Merewyn until he took her back to Scotland. Those that Lady Comerford had loaned her were also there, and Ian decided with a scowl that he'd have to return them to her immediately, before Merewyn took it in her head to wear them again. For some reason he didn't like the thought of Merewyn prancing about in public with the clothes of his former mistress clinging to her slim back.

A lavender satin evening gown caught his eye and he remembered having taken a fancy to the material in the milliner's shop, certain that the color would compliment Merewyn's fair looks. He pulled it out savagely, tossing it onto the bed and pointing at it with one long finger.

"You're wearing that."

Merewyn shook her head, refusing to look at him. "I'm not going."

His temper snapped, and with an outraged oath he stalked to the bed and pulled the covers off of her. With one savage motion he seized the neckline of her shift and tore it from her body, throwing it unceremoniously to the floor. "By God, woman," he breathed, his jaw muscles working, "you goad me too far."

Merewyn tried to cover herself, and he laughed harshly as he observed her useless efforts. "Why so modest? 'Tisn't anything I haven't seen before."

"Get out!" she cried, frightened by the look on his face, aware that his eyes were lingering far too long on her bare breasts.

"Not until you're dressed and ready to go."

Her lower lip trembled dangerously. "I tell you I won't!"

Ian's hands shot out and grabbed her by the waist, pulling her onto her feet in one swift motion so that she was standing almost between his long legs, her naked body brushing against his elegant coat. Her hair hung to her hips in a fragrant golden cloud and as she gazed up at him, her tilted eyes bright with unshed tears, he felt his anger vanishing as swiftly as it had come.

How vulnerable she looked standing before him, valiantly striving to hold back her tears, disheveled golden curls framing her heart-shaped face, her lips parted and so utterly inviting that Ian suddenly found himself unable to resist them. With a groan he pulled her to him, the buttons of his coat pressing into her soft flesh, his large hands moving about her curving hips to draw her even close.

Merewyn had expected his lips to hurt her with their pressure, his kiss to be hard and demanding, his tongue searching and tasting, but there was nothing brutal about this warm touch as he covered her mouth with his own. Her senses began to swim as his kiss grew deeper, drawing from her a response she could not help but give, her heart beating wildly against his hard chest. She was standing on the tips of her small toes, her silky body pressed against the length of him and he placed one strong hand beneath her small rear, fitting her even better between his legs until they were standing so close that only his clothing separated them from each other.

Ian's pulses pounded, drinking in the sensation that surrounded him of the scent of lavender in her hair, the taste of her lips, the softness of her body beneath his hands. He wanted her more than he had ever desired any woman in his life and he found himself suddenly helpless with need and want. His manhood rose hard against her and he was reminded with an ache of despair of the time he had lain above her, poised to plunder the sweet mysteries her woman's body offered him, remembering, too, that he had not been able to claim her as his own, though it had cost him everything to let her go.

But now there was no Lieutenant Spencer to stop them, no interfering crewmen or tempest-tossed seas. He was in his own home, the master of his surroundings, and the girl who trembled in his arms was more his by right than any woman he could legally call his wife. He would have her now or be damned as a man.

Lifting her easily into his arms, Ian laid her gently on the bed, his lips caressing the hollow of her smooth throat. Drawing back slightly he looked deep into her eyes, his own darkened with passion, and as he saw the answering fire in the golden depths he knew with a heady feeling of triumph that her need matched his own.

"I must have you, Merewyn," he whispered hoarsely. "God, don't turn me away."

She slipped her arms about his neck, pulling him closer, the sweetness of her sudden smile making him feel unaccountably weak. "You should have realized long ago, m'lord," she purred contentedly, "'tis easier to woo me with kindness than with bullying."

Sweat broke out on Ian's brow as the sweetness of her smile gave way to a sauciness he could not credit for one so innocent, and he groaned again for the want of her and pulled her to him, cradling the back of her head with his hand, his kiss hungry this time, demanding a satisfaction that Merewyn did not intend to withhold.

"Is everything all right, my lord?"

Francis's worried voice seemed to thunder through the door, although he had spoken in an almost timid whisper, afraid what the tense stillness in the room might indicate. Had the Marquis murdered her already?

Merewyn could feel Ian's body stiffen above hers and she lay quite still, her arms still wrapped about his powerful neck as he lifted his lips from hers, his breathing ragged, desperation and utter frustration in the dark depths of his eyes. Wearily he let her go and rose to his feet, adjusting his clothing that was hopelessly rumpled and running a hand through his tousled hair.

"We'll be down shortly, Francis," he said tiredly.

"Very good, m'lord." Francis's relief was obvious. "I'll tell the coachman to wait."

Ian turned to look at Merewyn, who still lay naked upon the bed, keeping his gaze fastened to her small face, deliberately ignoring the irresistible appeal of her flawless body. "We must go," he said flatly. "I can't do anything as rotten to Edward and Alicia as not showing up for our own engagement party. Merewyn, please come with me."

She was visibly shaken by his humble request and rose obediently, brushing past him to the chair where Betsy had laid out her underthings earlier. Slipping into her petticoats and corset she turned appealingly to the Marquis, who had been standing by the bed where she had left him, his expression as hard as though turned to stone, the gray eyes falling restlessly upon every object in the room save the slender girl before him.

Ian stirred and came forward in response to her silent request and Merewyn trembled as she turned her slim back to him and felt his fingers touch her while he laced and fastened the stays. Wordlessly, he turned away, the task completed, and picked up the lavender gown that still lay upon the bed, helping her slip it on and patiently fastening the hooks and eyes and countless buttons.

"You'll have to do your hair," he told her quietly, and she moved to the dressing table to comply, unnerved by his moodiness, and feeling for the first time in her life unaccountably shy in his presence.

Brushing the shining strands and plaiting them deftly, Merewyn pretended not to see his large form reflected in the glass, his eyes seeming to glow as he watched her, his square chin grimly set. Her fingers trembled while she pinned her hair into place, and as she turned around and smiled at him expectantly, a muscle in one lean cheek twitched and his hands clenched into fists.

"Do I look presentable enough to meet your oldest friend?" Merewyn asked, pretending not to notice.

The Marquis came forward to stand directly above her, his index finger beneath her pointed little chin, tilting back her head so that she was looking directly into his dark eyes. "You'd be beautiful even in rags," he told her hoarsely and his lips twitched as he recalled that, indeed, he had a few times seen her that way.

The gown Mrs. Ludley had created for her was far less elegant than the azure ballgown, but he decided he liked this simple one even better, for it allowed Merewyn's beauty to shine through unenhanced. The dressmaker had cut the shimmering satin so that it clung to her willowy figure, her breasts firm and enticing above a neckline cut modestly low. The color was what appealed to the Marquis the most, however, and he liked it even better now than he had in the shop. Merewyn's enormous eyes with their infuriatingly irresistible slant were a dark violet, the gold depths seeming to shine with a light of their own, and he turned abruptly away, afraid of what might happen if he lost himself within them.

Francis, waiting nervously in the hallway below, could scarcely believe the sight that met his eyes when he looked up at the sound of the bedroom door slamming shut. The Marquis, handsome and domineering in his gray velvet evening clothes, was leading Merewyn down the stairs, her small hand resting lightly on his arm. They were speaking together in low tones, and although Francis could not hear what they were saying, there was no mistaking the lack of tension in the Marquis's muscular body and the tractable smile on Merewyn's little face.

And here he had been expecting cold rage and stubborn petulance! He shook his head. God save him from these two temperamental thoroughbreds. He'd never be able to keep up with their quicksilver moods.

There was an amiable silence in the coach as it rolled down the streets that Merewyn could not ignore. She had no idea why the Marquis had chosen to treat her so kindly after Francis's timely interruption, for he had reacted with savage anger the last time it had happened. 'Twould seem that fate was forever toying with them, offering them tantalizing glimpses of what might exist between them, then cruelly bringing circumstances into play that emphasized their differences and the antagonism they usually felt towards one another.

But tonight Merewyn was not about to question the Marquis's mood or look too deeply into herself, or to agonize over the swiftness with which she had given in to her feelings and the insistent pressure of his lips on hers. They were being kind to one another tonight, the very air ripe with contentment, and she wasn't about to change that, determined to savor every sweet moment regardless of what wretchedness tomorrow might bring.

"How long have you known Edward?" she asked, hoping to learn something of Ian's mysterious past now that his frame of mind seemed sufficiently pleasant for her to risk asking.

She heard him chuckle and turned to find him staring up at the upholstered ceiling, a reminiscent smile on his finely molded lips. "Many years, ma'am, more than I care to think back on, and I caution you not to ask him too many questions. He has an idle tongue."

"Are you afraid I may learn something bad about you?" Merewyn asked with a laugh. "Surely you have a pristine past, my lord!"

"You'll find monks who have committed more sins than I," Ian assured her, his white teeth flashing as he smiled back at her, "for I am above all suspicion."

"Now that I find hard to believe," Merewyn retorted, wagging a finger warningly. "Have a care that none of those tales reach your fiancée's ears, my lord. She has a vengeful nature."

"And slips easily into the role of nagging wife," he added roguishly, his boyish grin so charming that it could have melted the heart of the most unrelenting woman.

Merewyn, responding to it with a warmth that tingled throughout her body, cautioned herself to be careful. She was giddy with joy at the companionship they shared, but she must not lose sight of who she was and what she meant to this tall man seated so close beside her. She sobered, a shadow passing across her face of which Ian was instantly aware, though a casual observer might have missed it altogether, and he fell silent, chiding himself for having bantered with her like a schoolboy.

The house before which the coach drew to a halt was not as grand as the Humphries', but Merewyn liked the small garden through which they passed, the brick walk covered with moss, the scent of flowers heavy in the warm night air. Tall windows flanked the polished front doors, lights blazed within, and she could hear talk and laughter floating out to meet them. For a moment she hesitated, feeling nervous and out of place, but then she felt the Marquis's reassuring hand touch the small of her back as he guided her up the stairs and she relaxed.

Sir Edward and Lady Alicia were greeting their guests in the gold-lacquered foyer; they were an attractive couple, both dark-haired and tall. Sir Edward towered over everyone save the Marquis, who strode forward with Merewyn at his side and gripped the smiling man's hand warmly.

"Damn, Ian, you're looking as good as ever," Sir Edward exclaimed without a trace of envy. "I warrant you'll even make a handsome corpse when you finally kick over."

"Edward, please," Lady Alicia protested, her blue eyes filled with apology as she looked at Merewyn. "Please forgive him. His manners are deplorable."

"Merewyn has lived a sheltered life," the Marquis added with feigned gravity. "One more oath, Ned, and you'll bring on the vapors."

Edward's twinkling eyes met Merewyn's astonished ones and he shook his head disbelievingly. "I'm sorry, Ian, I refuse to believe that the woman you've chosen to marry is a retiring, mousy sort of creature."

"Indeed I am not," Merewyn said clearly, recovering from her surprise at Lord Montague's levity. She decided at once that she liked the Palingtons for their directness and the deep affection they seemed to share for one another. Obviously they had a good marriage, she thought a trifle wistfully. If only she and. . . . Dear God, what on earth was she thinking? That she actually wanted to be married to that arrogant, ill-tempered Marquis? Never! She should be thankful their engagement was only pretense!

Edward was laughing approvingly. "I can see from her look you've picked one with spirit, Ian. I only wonder which one of you will murder the other first?"

"Edward!" Alicia protested in exasperation, giving the Marquis an appealing glance. "Will you please make him stop, Ian? Miss MacAilis must be thinking we're odd creatures indeed."

"Believe me, Alicia, Merewyn's something of an oddity herself," the Marquis replied, bringing Alicia's hand to his lips. "You're looking well, my dear."

She blushed at the compliment and Edward said without rancor, "Still have the power to charm the ladies, eh?"

"I do my best," Ian assured him while drawing Merewyn close to his side, smiling down at her so kindly that she felt her heart skip a beat. "And of course you know this is Merewyn MacAilis of Cairnlach, who has consented to be my obedient bride."

"Obedient?" Merewyn asked with a gleam in her dark violet eyes. "Why, Ian, I never knew obedience was part of the bargain!"

"I do believe you've got your hands full," Sir Edward repeated with unmasked glee. " 'Bout time the shoe was on the other foot."

"Oh, she'll be obedient soon enough," Ian replied arrogantly. "I intend to beat her into submission."

Alicia shook her dark head despairingly as she turned to Merewyn. "How can you let him talk like that?"

Merewyn shrugged, a faint smile curving her soft lips. "He may talk all he wants, but let him so much as lift a finger against me. . ." Her slanted eyes met his and he laughed unexpectedly and pulled her close.

They were forced to move on into the crowded drawing room moments later when the Palingtons were claimed by new arrivals, and Merewyn found herself separated from the Marquis only to be instantly surrounded by acquaintances she had met at the Humphries' ball, almost all of them gentlemen who crowded forward to kiss her hand and inquire eagerly how she had been faring since they'd seen her last.

Merewyn caught one last glimpse of Ian's large frame, his eyes filled with amusement as he took in her entourage, before he vanished into the milling crowd. She felt momentarily lost without him but soon found little time for musing, her admirers demanding her undivided attention.

"Surely you must know just about everyone here," came Sir Edward's voice in her ear a short time later. "Is there anyone I need to introduce you to?"

"Quite a few, I'm afraid," Merewyn confessed. "Though I met some of them at the Humphries' ball, the rest are strangers to me."

"We move in different circles from the Humphries," Sir Edward explained, his hand at her elbow as he led her towards an intimidating group of matrons. "You won't find some of the more . . . er . . . rakish set here."

Did he mean to include Lady Elizabeth Comerford? Merewyn wondered hopefully. Though she had not voiced her fears, she had dreaded the thought of meeting with the jealous, green-eyed woman again. To her relief she soon discovered that the Marquis's former mistress was not in attendance and that the people Sir Edward introduced her to were all kind and gracious.

Not long afterwards dinner was announced, and Merewyn was led to the table by Sir Edward himself, the Marquis following with Alicia on his arm. Merewyn hadn't had the chance to speak to him at all since their arrival and was rather relieved that he was seated far enough away from her to make private conversation impossible. She had willingly gone along with his little game in the entrance hall, pretending for the Palingtons' sake that they were a happy couple, very much in love, because she hadn't wanted to cause uneasiness in the minds of his friends, to whom she herself had taken an instant liking.

But what was the use in that? Merewyn asked herself now. Ian had told Lady Humphries that blatant lie just to save Alex's name from scandal, but he hadn't exposed himself as a liar when he should have, and now it was already far too late. Everything had been blown out of proportion and she couldn't even count the number of people who had already congratulated her and asked when the wedding would be.

Merewyn's fine brow knitted into a frown. Whatever Lord Montague's game was, she intended to play it to the hilt this evening, determined to please the Palingtons, but she would have to insist as soon as they were alone that the foolishness ended.

"You've scarcely touched your oysters, Miss MacAilis."

It was the youthful Earl of Denmont who had spoken, the same stammering young man who had danced with her at the Humphries', his heart tacked to his sleeve, unable to hide his admiration for the indigo-eyed girl. He had been delighted to find her seated beside him this evening and had charged himself with the responsibility of seeing that she was not left wanting.

"In truth I've no great liking for them," Merewyn whispered to him, leaning closer to speak in his ear, the movement bringing an answering scowl to the Marquis's finely chiseled face as he watched from across the board.

The young Earl smiled understandingly. "I've no great fondness for them, either. Perhaps you'd care for salmon instead? I'm sure a Highlander like yourself wouldn't dare turn down such a delicacy."

"Naturally not," she agreed, and a shadow passed fleetingly over her delicate features as she thought of the salmon swimming in the Lieagh. A pang of homesickness overwhelmed her, bringing such intense longing for her brothers and Cairnlach that she looked quickly away from the Earl's expectant face, only to meet the glowering gray eyes of the Marquis, who was watching her intently.

Merewyn looked away quickly and addressed herself to the contents of her plate, mechanically eating the tender pink fillet set out before her, almost oblivious to its excellent taste. Her appetite rapidly improved, however, as the meal progressed and the liveried footmen returned time and again with yet more culinary delights. Pork, pheasant, delicately baked quail and venison accompanied by fresh vegetables and excellent sauces, were followed by still more fish, poultry and other game, a myriad of food that left Merewyn with the distinct feeling that she had gained a dozen pounds.

"Oh, I couldn't eat another bite," she protested as the Earl ladled a brimming spoonful of mincemeat onto her recently cleaned plate.

"Just a little," he wheedled.

"But I worked so hard to clear it and now you've piled it full again," she protested with a smile, indicating the china plate before her.

"There's still dessert to come," he reminded her. "And your wine glass is empty."

"I'm beginning to suspect you're trying to get me drunk," Merewyn accused as he signaled a hovering footman to refill her glass.

He blushed furiously beneath her arch gaze, but the wine had made him bold and loosened his normally halting tongue. " 'Twill add color to your cheeks," he told her impetuously, "which will serve to compliment the sparkle in your eyes."

Merewyn was greatly amused by the avid stare that accompanied his words, but she couldn't take offense, for he had been kind and attentive to her throughout the meal. And he had spared her from having to speak to the gentleman who sat on her right, a thoroughly lecherous chap who, everytime she turned his way to respond to a throatily uttered question, had fastened his eyes on her breasts as though trying to burn off her bodice with the intensity of his gaze.

Merewyn was glad when Alicia rose as a signal for the ladies to retire to the drawing room, leaving the men to their cigars and politics. She was afraid she'd burst if her table partner plied her with one more tidbit of food. Rising to her feet she swayed unsteadily and happened to catch the Marquis's eyes, his glowering look telling her that he had observed how freely she had imbibed.

She sniffed haughtily to herself. What did his disapproval matter? She wasn't his wife, thank the sweet Lord, and he didn't own her. She was free to do as she pleased, and that included drinking wine with a convivial young man who had been far kinder to her in the space of two days' acquaintance than Lord Montague in their entire uneasy relationship.

"Ian seems so happy," Alicia Palington remarked in Merewyn's ear as they entered the drawing room, pulling her aside for a private conversation. "I'm so glad he found you, Miss MacAilis. He's always been so restless and dissatisfied. I can't believe the change in him."

Merewyn blinked at the older woman in surprise. If Lady Alicia thought the Marquis changed, how terrible must he have been in the past? Even now she thought him the most ill-tempered, dissatisfied individual she had ever met.

"Please," she murmured, at loss for a suitable reply, "won't you call me Merewyn? I want very much for us to be friends."

Alicia's comely features glowed and she grasped Merewyn's hands impulsively. "Oh, I'd like that so much! When I heard Ian was to be married I was so worried he'd . . . well," she blushed furiously, realizing she had let her tongue rattle on unchecked. "The women he's known in the past have never appealed to me," she finished lamely.

"I've already had the misfortune of meeting one of them," Merewyn said tartly.

"And you can still tease about it!" Alicia marveled. "Oh, Merewyn, how wonderful it must feel to know that Ian loves you so! It makes me all goose-bumpy to see the way he looks at you all the time."

Merewyn made no reply. Naturally, Alicia would misread the emotions that burned in the intimidating eyes as something other than the selfish lust it really was. Aye, Lord Montague wanted her, mainly because he could not have her, and once the excitement of the chase was over and his passions were satisfied, he'd quickly discard her for someone else—doubtless the green-eyed Lady Comerford who had made no secret of her intention to win him back!

"When I first saw the two of you come in," Alicia went on, not having noticed Merewyn's strained silence, "and saw Ian towering over you, I thought to myself that it wouldn't be long before he broke you. You are such a dainty little thing, after all, and though I've known Ian for years, I must confess in all honesty, Merewyn, that he can terrify me with his black moods and fierce temper. Would you hate me very much if I told you I wouldn't dare be married to him?"

Merewyn's laugh rang through the drawing room, causing several footmen to turn their heads admiringly at the sweet, unaffected sound. "You should be commended for your courage in speaking the truth."

Alicia laughed also. "Oh, Merewyn, I know you're the right one to keep him happy and warm his heart!" She frowned in sudden annoyance. "But listen to me, will you? You probably think me as empty-headed as they come for rattling on like this, but I really want your marriage to be a success. I want so much for the four of us to be friends."

Merewyn smiled in response, although inwardly she was seething at the Marquis. How could he fool his kind friends this way, making them believe he was going to settle down at last, when in truth he was living a colossal lie? She was determined to see that he set the matter straight immediately, though she regretted that the Palingtons would not be spared from hurt or from the embarrassment of learning they had given a party in honor of a couple who were not only not engaged, but also sworn enemies.

When the gentlemen returned to the drawing room they were accompanied by musicians, who immediately struck up a festive tune. Merewyn found herself confronted by the Earl of Denmont and three other admirers, all glaring at one another askant, each determined to have the first dance with the lavender-clad beauty.

"Excuse me, gentlemen," came the Marquis's deep and faintly annoyed voice from behind them. They all hesitated, and then parted reluctantly to allow him into their midst. Taking Merewyn's small hand in his, he smiled down at them without warmth. "I believe the first dance belongs to the prospective bridegroom?"

Ian could tell by Merewyn's rigid body as he led her out onto the floor that something was amiss, and as he glanced down into her delicate features and saw the hardness of the violet eyes, he knew that she was no longer in the gay mood that had so charmed the Palingtons and astounded him in the entrance foyer earlier.

"Your look is quite lethal, ma'am," he remarked lazily as they came together in the prescribed steps of the dance. "What have I done now?"

Before she could reply, he added warningly, "Perhaps it should be the other way around. Perhaps I should be condemning you for your behaviour at the table earlier."

"What do you mean?" Merewyn asked frostily, although she knew quite well.

The Marquis's handsome face was filled with annoyance. "Damn it, Merewyn, I'm talking about how you coddled that young pup as though you intended to take him as a lover. Do fawning milksops appeal to you more than I?"

"Even the lowliest beggar appeals to me more than you," she informed him haughtily, the fine eyebrows arched, only to look away as she saw the anger beginning to smolder in his eyes, obvious for all to see. "Oh, please," she begged, "can't we keep our arguments confined to privacy? I don't want to upset the Palingtons by fighting, or they'll begin to suspect our relationship isn't as blissful as they think."

"Edward and Alicia would think something terribly wrong if we didn't argue," he countered with a mocking smile. " 'Tis exactly what they expect. The sparks are bound to fly when you and I are together."

"How can you deceive your friends so sorely?" Merewyn asked with tightened lips. "Alicia told me she was delighted you and I were going to be married."

Ian's warm chuckle surprised her. "Alicia said that? Then you've passed muster with flying colors, my dear. Apparently you've won her approval."

"As assuredly as would anyone daft enough to agree to become your wife," Merewyn retorted. "Are you certain it isn't pity that moves her to be kind to me?"

Ian's grip on her slender fingers tightened painfully. "You'd better hold your tongue," he warned. "I'm not above boxing my fiancée's ears right here on the dance floor."

Merewyn's violet eyes reflected her inner pain. Would they never stop flying at each other's throats? she wondered miserably. Would she never be free of this insolent, swaggering blackguard? They could have been twins in character, Ian and his odious uncle—one arrogant and cruel, the other a thieving knave. God's blood, how she hated the name Villiers!

"Your thoughts must be quite unfriendly," Ian remarked, his mocking tone bringing her from her reverie. "I've never seen you scowl so fiercely before. Is the thought of becoming the Marchioness of Montague so intolerable to you?"

"I'll never accept that half-baked title," Merewyn told him icily, the golden depths of her tilted eyes scorching him with her hatred. " 'Twas a blood bribe to your uncle after the King murdered my people!"

The dance was ending as she spoke, and Ian grabbed her wrist so tightly that she winced, leading her through the crowd and out onto the terrace where he turned her to face him, shaking her arm so cruelly that she thought it would break.

"That does it, Merewyn," he said in a tone so menacing that her blood ran cold, "I'm not going to take any more of your insults."

"What do you intend to do?" she demanded arrogantly, although it took considerable effort to keep her voice steady. "Snap my neck in two? I recall you've threatened to do that on a number of occasions."

He refused to be baited, his nostrils flaring with barely controlled rage. "That would end your agony far too soon, my dear. No, what I have in mind for you will be far more satisfying. You, Merewyn, are really going to become my wife."

She fell silent, her heart leaping into her throat, staring at him as though he had sprouted a second head.

He laughed cruelly at her shocked expression. "You see? Half my revenge has already been won merely by the pleasure I derive from seeing that look on your face."

"You can't be serious!" she choked.

Ian brushed an imaginary speck of dust from his velvet sleeve, for all appearances quite bored with their conversation, but his glittering gray eyes gave evidence to the fact that he was enjoying himself thoroughly. "You delude yourself, my dear, because I am deadly serious. The necessary paperwork should be completed any day now, as well as the arrangements for our simple but quite legal ceremony." His cruel words taunted her. "By the end of the week, Merewyn, you will be my wife, and nothing your brothers can do will change that fact."

"But the banns haven't been posted," Merewyn murmured stupidly, "and we haven't been cried at the kirk—"

Ian laughed harshly, ignoring the chance that the sound might drift into the crowded drawing room behind him. "Did you always fancy a grand Scottish wedding, Merewyn, with pipers and reels and a proud Alexander to give you away? Best put those foolish notions out of your pretty head."

"So you'll finally emerge the winner in our on-going rivalry," Merewyn said through clenched teeth, having found her voice at last. "I freely admit 'tis a stroke of genius and I couldn't have come up with a more barbaric way of getting even with me after all the trouble I've caused you. But have you considered the consequences, my lord?" Despite her efforts her voice wavered and grew thinner. "You and I will be married! An entire lifetime follows that ceremony, and you'll be saddled with me to the end of your days!"

The full lips curved into a malicious smile. "Oh, no, ma'am, 'twill be you who are saddled with me, for I'll see to it that your life with me is made quite miserable."

" 'Twill work both ways," Merewyn warned, wondering if he was truly mad enough to carry out this dastardly deed.

"Oh, I truly doubt that," the Marquis predicted confidently. "I'll just lock you in the dungeon when I've had enough of you."

"How can you do this?" Merewyn quavered, believing him serious at last.

He sauntered to the balustrade and stood with his strong hands propped against the cool stone, staring down into the darkened garden below, his lean profile turned towards her. "It came to me not long ago that, even if I did take you home, I'd never be free of you, that you'd always be scheming behind my back and that I'd never know another moment's peace. Well, if I have indeed been damned eternally I might as well take the upper hand and make you mine so that I can at least deal with you directly, in any manner I choose, without having to go through your brothers to do it. A terrible sacrifice for me, I admit, but one I am quite willing to make."

He turned and came towards her again, smiling a little as she retreated a step. "Having you as my wife will also bring me an added advantage: the right to enter your bed, a prospect I find most appealing. Be forewarned, my dear, that I intend to avail myself often of your connubial charms."

"You fiend!" Merewyn blazed at him, raising her hand to strike him full in the face, his smugness infuriating her. "I'll see you dead first!"

He seized her hand before she could deliver the blow she so ached to give, twisting her wrist so that she cried out in pain and went limp against him. "Careful," he warned grimly, "Edward and Alicia may observe our little altercation, and we wouldn't want to cause them grief, would we?"

"I hate you!" Merewyn whispered, the tears dangerously close. "God, how I hate you!"

She did not see the harsh tightening of his jaw as she spoke, her face still averted, but she could hear the grating anger in his voice as he said quietly, "I think we better go back inside before we arouse suspicions, ma'am. But I charge you not to behave as though something were amiss. You will play the part of my loving fiancée, Merewyn, or regret the consequences."

"I won't!" she cried belligerently, only to feel her

throbbing wrist being twisted a second time.

"You will," he swore. "By God, you will."

David Brown, polishing silverware in the kitchen, looked up and groaned when he saw his mistress sweeping down upon him the next morning with a determined look on her young face. He had received such a severe tongue lashing from the Marquis for his last transgression concerning the letter to Mr. Brentwaithe that he trembled merely at the thought of what Merewyn wanted from him this time. She never looked like that unless she had made up her mind to do something drastic, more often than not against Lord Montague's orders, too.

"I'm not going to ask you to break any rules, David," Merewyn told him, having seen by his pursed lips and rigid shoulders that his suspicions were aroused. "I just want you to lend me a little money. Surely that can't be wrong?"

"What are you going to do with it?" David asked, seemingly preoccupied with the huge collection of salvers, chafing dishes, and tea services before him. "You've got summat in mind, if you don't mind my saying so, miss. I've seen that look in your eyes before."

"Then you'll help me?" Merewyn demanded hopefully.

David shook his red head soberly. "I canna."

"I thought we were friends!" Merewyn chided, truly disappointed.

The brown eyes reflected his inner struggle. "Aye, miss, we are, but I always seem to end up in the kettle whenever I help you."

Merewyn chewed her lower lip, regarding him thoughtfully. "Aye, that you do," she conceded slowly, "and I'd hate for you to be punished by Lord Montague for something I've done."

"You'll not be getting into trouble with that one

again?" David asked hopelessly, setting down the teapot he had been buffing.

Merewyn laughed in genuine amusement at his dismayed expression. "No, dear, you've naught to fear. I'm through trying to fight our great master. The truth is I want to make a short excursion and I need money for a carriage since he's forbidden me the use of his coach."

David's face grew red with shame and he hung his head sadly. "Och, miss, I'd help you in that if I could, but Lord Francis hasna paid me my wages yet. I've scarce a farthing to my name."

Merewyn hid her disappointment behind a cheerful smile. "No grave matter, David, I'll find it elsewhere."

"I'm sorry," he added dejectedly.

"I said 'twould be all right," Merewyn assured him. "It's not such a pressing engagement anyway."

David appeared relieved to hear this and dared to add, "You ken you shouldna be going against his lordship's orders even to run an errand, miss. He said you weren't to go out for any reason."

"I assure you, David," Merewyn said with a sweet smile, although her dark eyes flashed dangerously, "I don't intend to cross Lord Montague ever again."

"Betsy says you're marrying him," David put in happily. "Is it true, miss?"

Merewyn's reply was a disinterested shrug that David took as an affirmative. "I'm so glad," he told her with a grin. "There ain't no man better than his lordship nor a nicer lady than yourself."

"Oh, go on," Merewyn retorted, giving him a good-natured poke, "you'll turn my head with such nonsense."

Her smile lingered as she left the kitchen, only to be replaced by a fierce scowl once she entered the study. No better man, indeed! She could come up with the names of at least a dozen notorious criminals who possessed more virtues than the Marquis of Montague!

Casting a glance down the corridor to reassure herself that no one had seen her enter the Marquis's forbidden lair, Merewyn closed the door softly behind her and hurried to the mahogany desk that stood beneath the tall window. Francis had gone to Grosvenor Street for the morning and she felt certain that no one else would dare disturb her here. She just had to find some money for a carriage! How else would she be able to get down to the harbor to search for HMS *Columbia*?

The idea had come to her during the sleepless hours after the Marquis had brought her home. She had decided to find Sir Robert Lindsey and beg him to take her back to Scotland. After all, Merewyn had reasoned, the kindly man had traveled all the way across the Atlantic to rescue her once before, surely he could be called upon to do so again! Her soft lips tightened grimly. And if Sir Robert refused to help her, she had decided that she would simply find someone else who would. She wasn't about to consent to marry Ian Villiers, to become his concubine and his plaything. She'd rather die!

Apparently, the Marquis had removed most of his personal documents to Scotland, Merewyn saw, for the drawers of his desk were almost empty. She made a thorough search, hoping to find at least a few forgotten coins tucked away somewhere, but when she came up empty-handed she shut the drawers with a bang and turned to the tobacco tins, china vases, and carved boxes that stood about on the shelves and occasional tables in the room. After a quarter of an hour she had to admit defeat and collapsed in the big leather chair behind the desk, pursing her lips and wondering how she was going to get to the harbor without proper fare.

"I'll just have to walk," she told herself determinedly. 'Twould be a long way, but she really didn't have much of a choice, did she?

Hurrying upstairs to her room, Merewyn changed into a pair of sturdy walking shoes and tied a bonnet beneath her chin to protect herself from the glaring sun. Cautiously, she returned to the entrance hall, peering over her shoulder to make sure no one was watching, then slipped out of the front door and ran down the drive towards the tree-lined street. Not until she had turned the corner and the elegant townhouse was out of sight did she breathe easier.

Park Lane was almost deserted and Merewyn encountered no one as she left Mayfair behind. The hubbub along Pall Mall quickly surrounded her, however, and she tried her best to scramble across the choked thoroughfares without being run down by coaches, carriages, and sedan chairs. Once or twice a young buck on a high stepping mount kicked dust in her face, grinning down at her as though expecting some word of praise for his equestrian skill, only to be rewarded by an icy stare and muttered curses.

Street hawkers dogged her footsteps relentlessly, trying to offer her useless wares Merewyn could not readily afford. She soon found that if she ignored them they quickly grew discouraged and left her alone. Eyes glued to the walk beneath her feet, she hurried down the crowded streets, unmindful of the pushing, jostling pedestrians around her.

A screaming horde of filthy children descended upon her near Fleet Street, and Merewyn felt pity stir her heart as she looked into their pinched little faces as they danced around her.

"Penny, miss, give us a penny!"

"Just one, miss, please!"

"I'm sorry," Merewyn told them apologetically, "I haven't any money at all."

One of the larger boys eyed her disbelievingly. "Not wi' that fine dress yer be wearin', miss?" he demanded.

"I'm afraid I'm as poor as you," Merewyn replied with a friendly smile. "My clothes are all charity items."

"Then yer be somebody's mistress!" the lad crowed

knowingly, digging his companion excitedly in the ribs. "Me mum says 'tis 'ow yer all comes to dress so fine!"

The other children looked up at her in awe, their mouths hanging open, never having met an actual mistress face to face before. Merewyn's cheeks burned, the child's voice having carried far—but to her relief she saw that no one was paying the least bit of attention to them, all of the passersby intent on their own destinations, their expressions shuttered and far away.

Thankfully the little group of beggars had already lost interest in her, and were at the moment charging headlong up the street to tap on the windows of an elegant coach that had been stopped in the snarled traffic, its driver hurling oaths and whipping the horses in his haste to get through. Merewyn shook her head, relieved that they were gone, and increased her stride, determined to reach the Thames before another similar mishap occurred.

Morning had waned into a hot afternoon, the sun beating relentlessly upon Merewyn's head, and she quickly grew tired and thirsty. Although she had come a long way there were still no signs that she was nearing the river, no wheeling gulls or tall masts soaring above the grimy rooftops, but she lowered her head and plodded on, determined not to turn back. She asked directions from an elderly gentleman she passed on the street who appeared quite shocked at finding such an elegantly attired young girl wandering about unchaperoned, but he obliged politely and she thanked him gravely before marching on.

When the long rows of warehouses finally came into view, Merewyn quickened her dragging footsteps, forgetting how tired she was. Lifting her skirts she stepped down onto the docks and walked quickly towards the first ship, a square-rigged brig with tightly furled sails, hoping someone on board could tell her the whereabouts of the *Columbia*.

"You shouldn't be here, miss," came a gruff voice from behind her, and she whirled about as her arm was taken in a gentle yet firm grip. " 'Tis dangerous for young ladies," her captor added and she saw that he was a burly sea captain with thick white whiskers and a well-powdered wig, the buttons of his blue frock coat polished to a high gleam.

Merewyn relaxed and could not help but return his kindly smile, thinking how harmless and jolly he looked. "I'm trying to find a friend of mine," she explained as he released her, tilting back her head so that she could gaze at him from beneath the brim of her bonnet.

"All alone?" he asked, shaking his head back and forth.

" 'Tis important," Merewyn assured him hastily. "I'm looking for HMS *Columbia*. Do you know her? She arrived from Boston about a week ago."

The weather-beaten face softened with a smile. "Aye, I know her well, miss. Captain Sir Robert Lindsey and I were marines together."

Merewyn breathed a deep sigh of relief. "Oh, I'm so glad to hear it! Can you tell me, please, where she's anchored?"

"I'm afraid she's sailed again," he said apologetically. "On yesterday morning's tide. Bound for Harwich, Sir Robert told me."

Merewyn's expectant face crumbled. "They're g-gone?" she asked disbelievingly. Tears welled in the slanted blue eyes and she bit her lips to keep them from trembling. What on earth should she do now? She was exhausted and couldn't bear the thought of walking the same stretch home again, particularly because the afternoon sun had already crossed its zenith some time ago and she was worried about finding herself alone on the streets at dusk. In addition her feet hurt abysmally, her head throbbed, and she desperately longed for a drink of water.

"Are you all right, miss?" the kindly captain asked, noticing the color draining from her delicate cheeks.

"I-I'm fine," Merewyn assured him with a tremulous smile. "I suppose I might as well go home."

"Surely you can rest a little first," he objected. "Will you have some lemonade with me? My ship's not too far."

Merewyn shook her head decisively, though his offer was tempting. "My coachman's waiting for me up the road," she lied, "but thank you all the same."

He watched her walk away, a slim and oddly defensive young girl in lemon yellow muslin, the wide brim of her hat flopping over her smooth brow, and wondered what sort of trouble could make such an obviously spirited lass so downtrodden.

Merewyn's heart was beating nervously as she skirted the barrels and crates standing about on the pier. Doubtless Francis had already discovered her absence and had informed the Marquis. How she dreaded facing his wrath when she returned, wishing she had the courage to drown herself here in the murky water of the Thames rather than endure his punishment!

"But I'm not afraid of him!" she whispered to herself, her small chin with the satin ribbons tied beneath it obstinately set. Drowning would be a coward's way out and MacAilises weren't cowards!

William Rawlings descended from his carriage onto the cobbled street that ran the length of the vast network of warehouses along the Thames. The berths below were choked with ships, a confused tangle of masts and rigging rising into the hazy sky, and the docks were crowded with jostling seamen and richly cloaked merchants who had come down to inspect the contents of the holds of the ships recently arrived from the colonies. The humid London air was filled with their shouts and oaths as they fought to ascertain what sections of the cargo areas were consigned to them.

William's expression was grim as he descended into their midst, losing himself in the hustle and bustle of a harbor that, to him, looked at least fivefold as busy as Glasgow's.

"I'm looking for the *Halifax*," he said, addressing a burly sailor with bulging forearms who carried a large seaman's bag over one shoulder.

"Yonder," came the curt reply, accompanied by a pointing finger.

William thanked him absently, ignoring the answering grunt, and strode across the jutting arm of the pier toward a small brigantine moored fast by thick hawsers not far from where he had just been standing. The yardarms and sails were being lowered by the crew, the muscular men straining at the capstan, the vessel apparently just run in. William ignored them, turning instead to the companionway that led to the aft cabin.

The captain's quarters were spacious and tidy and smelled faintly of pitch and tobacco smoke. Captain Harold Franklin, a bewhiskered gentleman of fifty-two years, sat hunched over his desk, his skeletal frame stooped by encroaching rheumatism. Meticulously he completed his paperwork, his slightly twisted fingers tightly grasping the quill. But for the generosity of Squire Rawlings, Franklin knew he would be ruined, for no one else would have entrusted the bent, weakening sea captain with a command of his own. The Squire had assured him when he'd first hired Captain Franklin on that he was welcome to make the Glasgow to London runs aboard the *Halifax* as long as he felt fit, and the captain had been eternally grateful to his philanthropic employer for this chance.

As the narrow cabin door opened he looked up with an impatient scowl, wondering which of his crewmen would dare burst in without knocking, but the annoyance changed to astonishment when he saw the thin young man appear before him.

"Master William!" He sprang up and hurried across the polished floor. "What in hell be ye doin' in London Town?"

William grinned and sauntered inside. "Taking in a change in scenery. I was bored with Glasgow."

Captain Franklin winked conspirationally. "From what I've heard ye've already sampled all the wares back home. 'Tis wise to hunt on new turf."

William tried to still the suddenly nervous pounding of his heart. "What do you mean?" he asked with feigned ignorance. Did the old bastard suspect anything of his involvement with Glasgow's whores? By thunder, he prayed not!

Captain Franklin chuckled as he stomped towards the cabinet that contained his impressive collection of liquor. "Now dinna be playin' the fool with me, laddie. Everyone kens yer father be wantin' ye to wed. London has the bonniest lasses, I'm told, but will ye no be takin' a Scottish wife, Master William?"

William relaxed visibly and accepted the offered brandy with a brief nod of thanks, sinking comfortably into a sea chair. "So, you think I'm wife hunting, do you?"

The captain laughed again, seating himself behind his desk, his crinkled eyes regarding William intently. He had no particular liking for the Squire's dissolute young son, well aware that William's affection for his father was largely feigned and that he was eagerly awaiting the day he'd come into his inheritance. Hopefully the Squire would live to be ninety, Captain Franklin thought to himself. The good Lord kens we need more men like him —wealthy, powerful and dedicated to helpin' Glasgow's desperately poor. For the Squire's sake alone, the aging captain was determined to remain on friendly terms with his son.

"Ye be twenty-seven, Master William," he said kindly, letting none of his feelings show on his craggy face. "Time to be thinkin' seriously of finding yourself a comely lassie."

"Perhaps," William agreed tentatively.

Captain Franklin refrained from adding that the poor fop before him was in for one hell of a disappointment if he hoped to gain the title here in London that had eluded him for so long in Glasgow, for only penniless young girls would turn their eyes his way. Nay, he'd find no titled, wealthy heiresses looking for a fawning milksop with a cruel streak to boot. But then, William was handsome enough and knew how to use his charm to his advantage. Aye, if there was a spinsterish duchess somewhere in the British Isles, Captain Franklin felt certain William would sniff her out.

He glanced down at the paperwork liberally strewn across his desk and was reminded of the work still to be done. "Did ye want to see me about anything in particular?" he asked abruptly.

William lowered his glass, the question catching him off guard, and began nervously stroking his mustache. "Oswald told me you were due in," he said lamely, "and I thought I'd pay a visit and see how my parents are."

"Been long since ye've seen 'em?" Captain Franklin asked, wondering at William's sudden surge of fillial affection.

"Long enough. Father was feeling poorly when I left."

Captain Franklin was disgusted by the anticipatory gleam in William's eyes. "Yer da be fine," he replied, inwardly pleased to impart this news. "He had the ague a few weeks back, but he was doin' fine when I saw him last."

"I'm glad to hear it," William murmured absently. Twirling the empty glass in his thin fingers he asked casually, "Any other news from home?"

"Other news?"

"Aye. No earth shattering events to report?"

"Been quiet as far as I ken." Captain Franklin eyed the younger man suspiciously. What was it William was hoping to learn? 'Twas no idle gossip he was after, to be sure. No doubt he'd gotten himself in trouble back home and had run off to London, hoping it would blow over, telling his da he was hunting a wife. 'Twould be just like William, a born troublemaker if ever there was one.

"Did ye hear Lord Montague died in February?" he asked, suddenly recalling the news item that had caused such an uproar in Glasgow last spring.

William nodded his head. "I heard about it just before I left. Fell from his horse, didn't he? Well, if you ask me, 'twas a fitting end for a man who lived the way he did."

Captain Franklin's bushy brows drew into a straight line as he searched his memory. "They say a nephew inherited—an Earl, he was, from Surrey. From what I'm told he's worse than his uncle." He paused abruptly, remembering something else, and leaned forward expectantly. "That's not the worst, Master Will. Seems Glasgow had a wee bit of a scandal several months back."

The color drained from William's bony face, leaving it ashen, his lips twitching nervously. "A scandal?" he asked faintly.

"Aye, involving the MacAilises of Glen Cairn." The aging captain, absorbed in his tale, hadn't noticed William's strong reaction to his words. "She was kidnapped and taken abroad a ship bound for the colonies."

William's jaw went slack, forgetting his initial shock at the captain's words concerning a scandal. "What! Are you daft, Franklin? Who'd be mad enough to do that, knowing how powerful and well known her brother is?"

Captain Franklin lifted his thin shoulders. "Nobody rightly kens. All I ken is that they arrested two men in

Glasgow who were responsible and a King's ship was sent after the lassie's, but I've na heard anything else about it. The authorities be closed mouthed about the details."

"I can imagine," William stated, secretly elated that the captain had no news at all concerning Nellie Arling's murder. If his luck held out they might never recover her body from the Clyde. "I imagine Alexander is doing all he can to find his sister."

"Aye, and there'll be hell to pay when he does."

"You're probably right," William agreed, losing interest in the story. He had never met any of the MacAilises although he'd heard quite a bit about them over the years, and his relief at learning his secret was still safe overshadowed Captain Franklin's startling news concerning them. He rose to his feet, suddenly impatient to be off, and thanked the captain for the brandy he had consumed.

Franklin rose also. "Will ye no dine with me tonight, lad?"

"I'm sorry, I've already agreed to an engagement at Oswald's," William replied, aware that the captain had asked him merely to be polite. "I'm off, then," he added. "Please give my father my regards when you see him."

William was whistling when he came up on deck and cheerfully greeted the crew before stepping down onto the wharf, a contented smile playing on his lips. He felt as though a great weight had been lifted from his shoulders. Now he could begin pursuing other pleasures in earnest, with no nightmares of the past to haunt him. Strolling down the long wooden wharf he breathed deeply of the humid air with its odors of pungent pitch, brackish water, and the scent of tobacco being unloaded in golden bales from a travel-worn barkentine nearby. A colorful town, William thought to himself, and he was suddenly glad to be here.

Behind an enormous warehouse standing near the

street a splash of color caught William's eye, bright in contrast to the dull clothing worn by the seamen, and he turned curiously to look. His interest quickened when he saw that it was the lemon-yellow color of a flounced muslin gown that had claimed his attention, worn by a young woman engaged in seemingly earnest conversation with a bewhiskered gentleman who was shaking his head to and fro in a negative reply to a hopefully uttered question.

She was extremely well dressed, William saw, her walking outfit of bright yellow full-skirted and worn with a matching bonnet. Shining gold curls were piled high on her small, proudly carried head, and even though her heart-shaped face wore a downcast look, he could see that it was very beautiful, the cheekbones high and delicately molded, enormous blue eyes sitting on either side of a slim, upturned nose.

His hungry gaze traveled from the firm breasts clearly outlined in the muslin bodice to the tiny waist that he felt certain he could span with his hands if he tried. Something stirred William's memory as he looked at her, something elusive, or was it merely that he was responding to her extraordinary loveliness? William moved closer, wanting to get a better look at her face, and when he came within earshot and overheard her say something to the elderly gentleman, his breath suddenly caught in his throat. Though the words were unintelligible there could be no mistaking the Highland dialect.

Who was this devastating beauty, William wondered avidly—Scots, no less, and certainly the epitome of his dreams? From the look of her she was highborn and well-bred, a lady of quality, and Elizabeth Comerford's dark beauty paled in comparison to this breathtaking golden vision. Even as he watched she began walking towards the street, the gentleman with whom she had been speaking staring after her reflectively a moment before turning away. William stirred and hurried after her, knowing he couldn't let her go without at least learning who she was.

By the time he caught up with her she had started up the narrow alleyway leading towards Fleet Street, and William's curiosity grew. Didn't she have a carriage waiting for her nearby? It seemed inconceivable that she had come on foot, for no unchaperoned female would dare expose herself to the dangers of the Thames waterfront without at least a burly footman to accompany her!

Following several steps behind, William was finally able to catch a glimpse of her profile beneath the straw bonnet and saw to his surprise that her soft lips were trembling and that tears glistened in the beautiful eyes. She was walking ever slower, and there was a dejected slump to her slender shoulders that indicated she was utterly exhausted. William's steps quickened as she started across the deserted street with bowed head, but before she even reached the center of the thoroughfare an elegant touring carriage, its matched pair of blacks goaded into a run by the sting of an irresponsible driver's whip, came careening around a nearby corner, bearing straight for the slender girl in yellow who was now plodding across the street as though she had no strength left at all.

"Look out!" William shouted, and she looked up in confusion, though it was clear to him that she was not aware of the danger of being run over. He sprang forward, grabbing her about the waist in the nick of time, and pushed her towards the curb where both of them landed in a sprawled heap on the stones while the coach rumbled harmlessly past.

William rose to his feet and was immediately surrounded by a great number of people convening from all directions to lend assistance.

"Yer saved 'er life, man!" someone cried, clapping

William heartily on the back, but he chose to ignore the speaker. Dusting off his hands, he pushed his way through the small crowd gathered around the crumpled figure in lemon yellow lying on the street.

"Gor, an' she's fainted plum away!"

"Did yer see 'im, did yer, drivin' like the devil was on 'is 'eels? Makes me ill, they do, them perishin' coachmen."

"Bleedin' rogues! Think they owns the world!"

" 'Ow about it, sir? Is the lady all right?"

William knelt down and peered anxiously into the pale little face. "I think so," he responded slowly. "I believe she's only fainted."

"I've a shop not far up the street," someone said, "with a bunk in the back room. We could lay 'er there til she comes around."

"Please don't trouble yourself," William said hastily. "My carriage isn't far away."

He looked up at a small group of young boys who hovered curiously beyond the circle of concerned adults. "A penny for the first one who sends it here," he called out. " 'Tis a black and gold one parked on the roadside close to the *Halifax*. She's moored closest to the warehouse."

All four of them charged off, each determined to earn the coveted coin, and William turned again to the unconscious girl he supported in his arms, loosening the top buttons of her yellow gown to permit freer breathing.

"Is she ill?" demanded a wheezing, red-faced street hawker, bending closer.

William shook his head. "The heat got to her, I'm thinking."

"Aye. Takes 'em out in this weather, it does. Tsk, the things women do wear! Enough to bring on the vapors even for me!"

"Pity her be ill," commented a grimy little man in

rags, eyeing Merewyn's pale face admiringly. "I'll bet her be beautiful when she ain't so sickly lookin'."

"Shut yer bleedin' trap!" the street hawker commanded. "Can't you see she be a lady?"

William ignored the voices around him, and when the carriage rumbled to the curb a short time later, he doled out the promised reward to a beaming, thankful boy while his friends looked on enviously. With the astonished coachman's help, Merewyn was lifted up and laid gently onto the padded seat. The shopkeeper came huffing up from his corner shop, and William dipped his handkerchief into the bowl of water he had brought with him, laying it gently across the smooth brow.

The onlookers, their curiosity satisfied, began to drift away, and the shopkeeper, after being assured by William that his services were no longer needed, returned to his store.

"Home, sir?" the coachman asked, hovering on the street below, appreciatively studying the inert form in yellow muslin that lay upon the upholstery.

"We'll wait a moment until she comes around," William replied, seating himself beside the silent girl.

"Aye, sir." The coachman vanished, briskly closing the door behind him, the sound bringing a low moan from Merewyn, who was slowly returning to her senses. She moved a little and could feel the welcoming coolness of a damp cloth on her head. Her lashes fluttered and when she opened her eyes she saw a face hovering fuzzily above her.

"Ian?" she whispered hopefully.

"Lie still," came a voice that was not the Marquis's and sounded suspiciously Scottish to her ringing ears.

Merewyn blinked and the face swam into focus, a bony but not unpleasant one with concerned brown eyes and a long, hooked nose set above a well-groomed mustache. Merewyn frowned. Where had she seen that face before? Somewhere, she felt certain, but at the moment she was too confused to remember.

"What happened?" she asked vaguely.

William found the sweet voice with its Highland lilt almost irresistible, finding it impossible, too, to tear his gaze away from the tilted eyes, larger than any he had ever seen, and so blue that they appeared almost black. Gold flamed in their darkened depths, giving them a radiance all their own.

"You were overcome by the heat," he explained. "I've put you in my carriage, which is far more comfortable than lying out in the street."

Merewyn's mind was clearer now and she looked at him again, the blue eyes filled with dawning recognition. Blinking, she tried to force away the impossibly obvious, but the hated face that floated above her did not alter its bony features, and she gasped, realizing with a rush of dismay who he was.

William smiled his most disarming smile, thinking it was the impropriety of his actions that had upset her. "I sincerely thought 'twould be in your best interest to move you out of the sun. Your safety alone was foremost in my mind."

Merewyn's small teeth came down hard on her lower lip. He did not know her! It was obvious in the words he spoke and in the manner he was staring at her that he had no idea she was the woman he had accosted in Glasgow, ultimately sending her on a trip through Hell. She must get away from him quickly, Merewyn told herself anxiously, before his memory was triggered by something she said or did. With sheer force of will she managed to regain control of herself, effectively hiding the revulsion she felt at his nearness behind a tremulous smile, and William thought nothing unusual of her drawn expression, believing her fainting spell responsible.

"If you'll give me your address," he said politely, "I'll have my driver take you home."

Merewyn's heart gave another fearful leap. Above all she didn't want him to know where she was staying! " 'Tis kind of you," she managed, "but I can walk."

"You'll do no such thing," William replied, fascinated by her sweet voice and the simple beauty that radiated from her dark, slanted eyes. "I've a feeling you're a long way from where you should be and I wouldn't dream of putting you back on the street."

Merewyn dropped her gaze and straightened from her reclining position, unwittingly giving William a tantalizing view of her heaving bosom. Moving as far away from him as possible without appearing conspicuous, she said earnestly, "I really don't want to put you to any trouble."

"Trouble?" William echoed. "I assure you 'twould be my greatest pleasure to take you home, and I'm sure your parents would understand and forgive this unchaperoned excursion." He laughed suddenly and Merewyn was surprised at the amount of charm he exuded, wondering how many people were aware of his true character. "How remiss of me! My name, if you'll forgive me for not supplying it sooner, is William Rawlings, of Glasgow. I take it you are Scots?"

Reluctantly, Merewyn nodded her head. He said nothing more, cocking his head at an inquisitive angle and Merewyn knew that she was expected to supply him with her name. What would she do? she wondered nervously. Lie to him? She had no desire at all of entangling herself any deeper, and decided not to tell him anything at all.

Feigning another dizzy spell, she put her hands to her head and groaned. William leaned closer, his breath hot on her cheek.

"You aren't well," he observed worriedly. "Let me take you home. What address shall I give my driver?"

Merewyn did not hesitate this time. "Oh, please, sir, would it be too much trouble if you let me out on Park

Lane, north of the Park?" She managed a convincing look of guilt. "You see, my father would simply flay me alive if he knew I'd come down here today. I'm not allowed out without an escort, but I simply had to know if the *Resolution* had arrived in port."

William's smile faded. "I take it there is someone on board you wanted to see whom your parents disapprove of?"

One small slippered foot began a nervous tap on the floor of the carriage, but she continued with a guilty nod, "Aye, sir. My brother, to be exact. There's been some family trouble and. . ." She broke off as if memories made it too painful for her to go on, and William felt compassion steal through him. Impulsively, he laid his hand over hers, not even noticing how she winced in response.

"I fully understand," he said huskily, "and you can count on me to keep your secret. I'm sorry I delved so deeply into your private affairs."

" 'Tis quite all right," Merewyn assured him, the huskiness in her voice, William believed, due to gratitude.

"We'll be there shortly," he promised and leaned out the window to call orders to the driver. Leaning back with a contented sigh, he allowed his brown eyes to longer admiringly on his companion's bent head. Sweet Lord in heaven, he thought to himself, she was beautiful!

For Merewyn the coach ride seemed endless, although it was far shorter than the long trek she had made on foot, and she scarcely responded at all to William's questions, but the bony-faced young man was not daunted by her uncommunicative nature. She'd had quite a hell of a shock today, he reasoned, and should be excused if her manners were found wanting.

"Here we are," he announced as the vehicle lurched to a halt near the curb. Opening the door he climbed out and turned around, extending his hands to help her down. Merewyn suffered his touch with firmly compressed lips, breaking free of him as soon as her feet came into contact with the cobblestones, though William would have liked his hold on the small waist to linger a moment longer.

"Thank you again," she managed through gritted teeth.

He wanted to bring her hand to his lips, but she had hidden both behind her back as though half expecting he would, which left him with only his charming smile as he bowed low in her direction. "I hope we'll see each other again."

"Perhaps we will," Merewyn replied, the cobalt eyes restlessly avoiding his.

He watched as she hastened across the grass and vanished in the park behind a stand of ancient beeches, admiring the graceful sway of her curving hips. Settling down against the cushions of his coach, he closed his eyes and sighed deeply. Now there was a wench ripe for the taking, her sweetly virginal body ready for the pleasures only an experienced man could give. By God, he wanted her, and he intended to see that he got her!

Abruptly his eyes flew open and an ill-tempered oath burst from him. God's teeth, he'd not even learned the wench's name! Well, no matter, he soothed himself, he'd find out soon enough. A wealthy beauty like that would doubtless frequent all the social whirls and he felt sure he'd meet up with her again. By God, he only hoped 'twould be soon!

CHAPTER NINE

Ian Villiers prowled restlessly about the pleasant salon, pausing every now and then to sweep back the lace curtains and gaze savagely into the driving rain that obscured his view of the drive below. The raging thunderstorm had been threatening the city since early afternoon, and thunder had rumbled ominously as the Marquis urged his mount at a mad pace through the crowded streets in response to Francis's message that Merewyn was missing. Great heaving clouds hovered low in the sky and the stallion snorted fearfully, sensing the coming of the storm.

Ian had leaned even lower in the saddle, speaking soothingly to the nervous barb while his eyes roved the thoroughfare before him, alert to any danger, well aware that the stallion's mad pace could prove exceedingly dangerous in the noonday crowds. Lightning plundered the treetops and thunder crashed overhead a second time as the Marquis drew rein at last before the carriage house doors.

Nick Holder hurried out to meet him, his white hair blowing in the wind. "I'll walk him, m'lord!" he shouted above the crackling firebolts that seared the leaden sky above. " 'Twill rain any moment!"

Lord Montague nodded wordlessly and strode across

the courtyard, his cloak billowing behind him. As he reached the servant's entrance, the first drops of rain pelted him mercilessly and he hurried inside, his dark curls disheveled and his clothing dripping water. Francis was there to meet him, silently taking the wet cloak and dogging his master's footsteps as the glowering Marquis stalked through the kitchen, ignoring the astonishment of the cook at seeing her employer in this remote corner of the house, especially with him looking so ferocious.

"Well, Francis," the Marquis asked quietly as he entered the parlor, turning to regard the majordomo, who cringed outwardly at the cold expression on the angular features.

"I've no idea where she is, m'lord. She must have slipped out while I was with you because she was gone when I got back."

"That was hours ago."

Francis's heart plummeted at the ominous tone. "Aye, m'lord. I sent David as soon as I could, but you know as well as I you weren't there to receive him."

"I've been busy," the Marquis replied curtly, turning away from the dejected figure before him. "We're leaving for Ravensley on Thursday, as you know."

"Aye, m'lord." Francis moved closer to the broad figure standing by the window and said sadly, "I'm tendering my resignation, m'lord. Your orders have always been clear, and I'm to blame that Miss MacAilis left the house."

"And who would hire a fussy old man like you?" the Marquis inquired, shaking his dark head, a faint smile on his full lips. "No, Francis, I'd advise you to stay where you're assured regular wages."

"But—"

"That's enough," Lord Montague interrupted severely. "If you must know the truth, I never really expected any of you to keep Merewyn inside. Even the Royal Guard couldn't have done so once she'd put her mind to leaving." His voice grew hard. "I only wonder why she was foolish enough to run away."

"But she didn't," Francis protested.

Ian wheeled to look down into the withered face, his emotions hidden beneath an expressionless mask. "But your note said—"

"That she was gone, yes, m'lord, but I don't believe she's run away. I checked her rooms and everything is still in its proper place. David told me she'd asked him earlier this morning for money to run a simple errand."

Thunder rumbled overhead and the Marquis was silent, waiting for the sound to die away. Then he asked sharply, "What sort of errand?"

Francis sighed helplessly. "She wouldn't say. David said she promised him she'd not be going against your word, but by the time I returned from Grosvenor Road she'd vanished, and no one has seen hide nor hair of her since."

Lord Montague's handsome countenance had grown weary as the majordomo spoke, and he moved to the window, where he stood gazing moodily at the rain falling steadily on the drive. "You've no idea where she's gone?"

"No, m'lord. Oh, I feel simply terrible about this. I should have—"

"Stop blaming yourself," the Marquis ordered curtly. " 'Twas altogether unavoidable. I should have kept her tied to the bedpost under constant surveillance. Let me know when she returns." It was an unmistakable dismissal.

"Yes, m'lord."

Francis withdrew with a small sigh of relief, closing the door softly behind him. The violent outburst he had dreaded had not arrived and hopefully by the time Merewyn returned Lord Montague's temper would be cooler, though Francis admitted to himself that he was rather unconvinced that would happen.

Ian returned to his restless vigil before the window. Where the devil was that plaguey wench? If she'd only gone to run a simple errand, as David had claimed, she should have been back long ago. His full lips tightened. What sort of errand could she possibly have in mind? He was tired of the merry chase she'd led him on since he'd known her and was determined to put a stop to it once and for all.

The smile grew noticeably grim. Aye, come Friday it would indeed all be over. As the Marchioness of Montague, Merewyn wouldn't dare risk scandal by running away from him again.

Movement on the drive below brought his attention back with a snap and his gray eyes narrowed as he saw Merewyn hurrying towards the front door. The hem of her muslin gown was streaked with mud and grass stains and she was soaking wet, her hair sodden beneath a wilted, dripping hat. Lord Montague strode out of the parlor and stepped down into the entrance hall just as the pale little face with its luminous blue eyes peered timidly through the opened door. She bit back a gasp as she saw him standing before her, overwhelmingly large and forbidding, and she groaned inwardly, dreading the scene she knew was to come.

"I see you've been informed of my disappearance," she said calmly as she stepped inside, though her heart was racing. Water dripped from her small form, and Lord Montague shook his dark head as he looked down at her.

"I cannot keep track of the times you've appeared before me like a half-drowned rat," he commented darkly. "Go upstairs and change."

"I'd rather discuss this here and now," Merewyn informed him, her small chin tilted, her indigo eyes staring boldly into his.

"Will you tell me where you were today?" he asked simply.

The sodden curls shook back and forth.

"Then there's nothing left to say to each other. Go upstairs. Francis can't tolerate that kind of mess on his floors."

Merewyn hurried past him, half expecting his big hand to clasp painfully about her arm, but he let her go without another word and she could feel his intense gaze upon her back as she scrambled up the stairs. What on earth was he planning now? she asked herself as she pulled off her wet clothing and dried herself with a towel. Was this some sort of new strategy, or was he planning to strike when he could best catch her off guard? No matter what his scheme, she felt convinced that she'd not heard the end of it. He was too much the ill-tempered lout to let her go unpunished.

Merewyn was wary and silent when she returned downstairs, her hair drying in a fluffy mass of ochre curls that she had tied back with a satin ribbon. Her skirts rustled, bringing the Marquis's attention round as she stepped into the breakfast room. Tea had been laid out on the table and her small nose sniffed longingly at the smell of hot chocolate and freshly baked pastries.

"I thought you might be hungry," Ian said, holding out a chair and beckoning her to be seated.

Merewyn lowered herself slowly, her dark eyes distrustfully following his tall frame as he moved around the table and settled himself across from her.

"You did miss luncheon, after all," he added, his steady gaze resting on her upturned face. He knew her moods well enough by now and saw something stir within the limpid indigo depths of her eyes that made his slowly simmering anger change to puzzlement. "What is it, Merewyn?" he asked softly.

She felt shaken by his tone; her defenses abruptly crumbled and she found herself wishing she could confide in him what was troubling her so. But then her soft lips tightened with sudden determination. Fool! She mustn't allow her fear for William Rawlings to do away with logic!

"I'm just tired," she confessed with what she hoped was a convincing smile.

"I take it your excursion is responsible." Ian's tone was so curt that Merewyn wondered if perhaps she had been mistaken in thinking he had felt a momentary softening towards her. "Was it successful?"

"What is it you're planning this time, my lord?" Merewyn demanded. "I came back here expecting threats and abusive language and instead I find you suspiciously amicable."

One eyebrow shot up in mock astonishment. "Are you saying you find me totally incapable of exhibiting kindness, ma'am?"

The indigo eyes grew hard. "Where I'm concerned, aye. Well, then, to avoid what I'm certain will become a disagreeable scene despite your earlier assurance that you'd let the matter drop, I may as well tell you where I've been." She took a deep breath and said, "I went down to the harbor today to meet with Sir Robert Lindsey. I was hoping he'd be kind enough to take me back to Scotland, but the *Columbia* had gone further north."

The lean jaw tightened ominously as Ian leaned forward to peer at her closely. "Damn it, Merewyn, don't tell me you went there alone?"

She nodded her head, her eyes wide.

"You plague-ridden little fool!" he burst out. "Aren't you aware of what type of people haunt the waterfront?" The smoldering gray eyes narrowed. "Did anyone give you trouble, Merewyn?"

"No," she whispered, not trusting her voice enough to speak more loudly.

Ian settled back in his chair, the tension draining away, and a self-satisfied smile curved the sensual lips. "Very good. I wouldn't want your purity spoiled so soon before our wedding."

Stung, Merewyn could not reply, and her dark eyes dropped from his mocking gaze.

"As for your desperate effort to free yourself of me—" He laughed and the sound sent shivers down her spine. "Come Friday I won't care at all what you do. As a married woman you'll hopefully come to realize that such headstrong, childish behavior is vastly unbecoming."

Merewyn pushed away the piece of iced cake she had been eating, her appetite suddenly gone. After everything she had endured today she couldn't bear listening to that drawling, insulting voice goading her into an argument she knew she couldn't win. Wordlessly, she rose to her feet and left the room, grateful that he made no move to stop her.

Ian watched the satin-clad figure with its stiffly set shoulders vanish through the doorway, and the cynical smile faded from his lips. Sighing heavily, he set aside his glass of wine, having lost his desire for it, and brooded silently about the enigma that was soon to become his wife. By God, he'd break her of that aloofness once she was his, he swore, and tear asunder that maddening vulnerability that protected her as completely as any iron wall, knowing no man with even half a conscience could get past those limpid blue eyes when she chose to use them as weapons—but he'd not rest until he had succeeded.

Oh, aye, he intended to win. No more intrusions or interruptions would keep him from taking that which he desired above all other things. The thought of possessing that enticingly soft body and the flaming will of the woman to whom it belonged was occupying his waking hours far more than he cared to admit. Soon, he promised himself, he would make her his, and change her defiance to willingness.

"Will you be wanting anything else, m'lord?"

Francis was hovering anxiously in the doorway and the Marquis rose abruptly to his feet. "No," he growled. "If you want me for anything I'll be at the Palingtons'."

"Very good, m'lord," the majordomo murmured, wondering what Miss MacAilis had said to the Marquis to make him look so murderous.

"Ah, good evening, my boy. Good of you to come."

"You were kind to invite me, Uncle Oswald."

William bowed dutifully to the corpulent figure in puce and gold that reclined in an oversized chair near the large hearth where, despite the warmth of the evening, a fire burned. Distastefully, he looked down into Oswald's face where the perspiration on his brow mingled with the powder he had applied too liberally to his wig. His fat lips were parted and his breath wheezed in and out of his lungs.

"Are you certain you're well enough to receive visitors?" William asked.

Oswald Trantham waved this aside with an impatient gesture. "Certainly, my boy! 'Tis just another attack of the gout and nothing serious enough to make such a ruckus over." He indicated the bandaged foot that was propped up on a velvet upholstered stool. "A few days like this and a good heating from the fire and I'll be as good as new."

"Unless you insist on eating so much," came a gently chiding voice from the doorway.

William turned as his aunt swept into the overheated parlor, her heady perfume adding to its overly stuffy air. Dorothy Trantham was exceedingly plain and her efforts to enhance her looks only emphasized her faults more woefully. Her narrow blue eyes appeared even more widely set apart when lined with kohl, and the rouge on her cheeks only served to make them look more fleshy than they actually were. Her large hands were covered with rings, and when she deposited a halfhearted kiss on her nephew's cheek William was almost suffocated by clouds of toilette water.

"How nice of you to visit with us," she said in a husky baritone that sounded quite masculine though she had spent years trying to master the sweet, high notes of a well-bred lady. "I'm certain there are a dozen more exciting places you could have gone to tonight."

"Family always comes first," William told her with a gallant smile, refraining from adding that invitations were not as plentiful as they had been when he'd first arrived in London. Perhaps his brief tryst with Lady Comerford had not been as discreet as he'd originally thought, and word had been passed around among the match-seeking mamas that William Rawlings was not of the proper ilk to be considered a suitable prospect for their daughters.

A frown passed across his bony features. Enjoyable as that night with Elizabeth had been, he'd not have considered it worth losing his position in society for, especially after he'd discovered that she had no interest in anyone but the Marquis of Montague. Foolish wench, didn't she realize that Montague himself would be married before the week was out?

"Now then, what's new, my boy?" Oswald asked, his question bringing William back to the present.

"I saw Captain Franklin aboard the *Halifax* earlier," William remarked promptly, seating himself on a striped damask armchair across from his uncle, forgetting how oppressively hot the stuffy parlour was. "He had the most interesting news to tell."

"From Glasgow?" Aunt Dorothy boomed, half-forgotten in a corner out of William's line of vision, her deep voice making him jump.

"Aye. 'Twould seem the MacAilis family is involved in a great misadventure."

Both Oswald and Dorothy leaned forward, eagerly expecting a scandal, and Williams wasted no time in obliging them. "Franklin told me the MacAilis lass was kidnapped not too long ago and taken aboard a colony ship as an indentured servant."

Oswald and his wife exchanged startled glances, never in their wildest dreams having expected those words to fall from their nephew's lips.

"Are you certain?" Oswald demanded, scowling irritably as an involuntary movement in his chair sent waves of pain through his bound foot.

William shrugged his thin shoulders. "I have it only on Franklin's word and I wouldn't call him the most reputable of tale bearers, but he assured me 'twas true. The men who kidnapped her have already been arrested. 'Twould seem they'd made a profitable business out of that sort of thing."

"I can't help but pity the poor MacAilises," Dorothy put in thoughtfully. "Oswald told me they inherited Ian Villiers as a business partner not too long ago, and he's certainly not the most tractable man to deal with. And now this kidnapping business!" She shook her elegantly coiffed head sorrowfully. "Those poor, poor people!"

"At least Villiers won't be bothering them during this crisis," Oswald added, turning to his nephew. "We heard yesterday he's going to marry some young woman here in London. Did you know about that?"

William nodded. "It was mentioned to me by an—er —acquaintance."

"Excuse me, madame." A footman was standing in the doorway, bowing low towards Dorothy. "Dinner is ready."

"So soon?" she asked, startled, then smiled at her husband. "Shall we go, Oswald? Do you feel well enough to walk to the dining room yourself? I'll have Simpson bring your cane."

"Damned fuss about nothing," Oswald complained, but as he tried to put weight on his bandaged foot he grimaced with pain and collapsed in his chair, his round face flushed. "Get me the stick," he commanded irritably to Dorothy, who had rushed forward to assist him.

"Let me help you, Uncle," William offered, extending his hand.

It was in Oswald's mind to refuse, but the tantalizing smell of mutton and mint jelly suddenly wafted to him through the opened door and he swallowed his pride sufficiently to accept his nephew's arm.

"Tell me something, Aunt Dorothy," William said when the three of them were seated about the large oak table, the board groaning with the weight of enough food to feed at least three times as many guests. "Do you know of another Scottish family in London?"

The kohl-lined eyes narrowed as his aunt searched her memory. "I don't think so, dear. You yourself are the only one I know of here this season. She paused, her wide, painted lips puckered, and then her face cleared. "Why, of course, there are the Lambs from Edinburgh!"

"The Lambs?" Oswald echoed. "I don't believe I've ever met them."

"Oh, there isn't much to say about them," Dorothy replied, dismissing the family with a disinterested wave of her large, bejeweled fingers. "They're kin to the Ashtons, a most unsociable bunch. You remember them, don't you, Oswald? They're forever being invited places, but they never think of entertaining on their own."

"Parasites," Oswald stated emphatically, truculently eyeing the meager portion of smoked goose liver paté a liveried servant had set before him.

"Now, Oswald, remember your condition," his wife warned, having caught sight of his mutinous expression. "Dr. Livessy says you eat far too much."

"Ivessy is a doddering jackass who studied medicine in Africa with the bush doctors."

William found himself growing unaccountably annoyed with his uncle's complaints. " 'Tis rather odd for the Lambs to be visiting London in the summer, don't you think, what with most of the people retired to their estates until fall? One wouldn't think there was much for them to do here."

"Heavens, I've no idea what goes on in their minds, but I can tell you that they're the most uninteresting people I've ever met." Dorothy scowled at the memories of her meetings with the Edinburgh family. "Mr. Lamb is as boorish as they come, and Mrs. Lamb can't open her mouth without singing the praises of her daughter. Lud, I've yet to meet an uglier creature than that child of hers!"

"They have a daughter?" William asked casually, his heart beginning to beat faster, ignoring his aunt's description of the girl, for Dorothy could be scathingly unfair in describing people she'd taken a strong dislike to.

His interest in the topic did not seem curious to his aunt, who rattled on irritably, "Indeed they do, and you'll never lay eyes on a more unpolished chit. She's barely fifteen, and yet her mother had the gall to bring her to a concert at Vauxhall last month. George Humphries had a private box reserved for all of us, and you can imagine how appalled we were when that overbearing strumpet arrived with her daughter in tow. Oswald," she added, poking her husband in the ribs with her elbow, "do you remember her décolletage? Heavens, her teats were all but hanging out and she didn't have more to them than a lad! Do you remember how blowsy her hair looked, too, after her mother took the curling tongs to them?" She shuddered, memories of the pitiful Lamb girl too painful to bear.

William lost interest, feeling certain that the unfortunate Miss Lamb was not the young woman he had rescued from beneath the wheels of the carriage that afternoon. Ignoring his aunt's continued tirade, he let his mind wander over the forbidden charms of the golden-haired beauty whose image he could readily summon into his thoughts. He felt as smitten as a lad in love for the first time, unable to forget the tantalizing tilt of those enormous cobalt eyes, the delicate rosy hue of her skin, and the gently rounding breasts. Aunt Dorothy couldn't possibly know every single person residing in the crowded city, William consoled himself. There had to be a Scottish family here she didn't know about. There had to be! And, by God, he'd find out who she was before he went mad with the mystery of her identity!

While William Rawlings suffered through the dull company of his overbearing uncle and simple-minded aunt, the object of his dreams was at the moment also occupied with memories of their encounter earlier that day. But where William yearned only to see her again, Merewyn was thinking desperately of a means of escaping London before he could find her.

After her silent withdrawal from the Marquis's unbearable company at tea time, she had spent a long and agonizing evening trying to cope with both the hurt he had instilled in her with his callous words and her fear that William would remember who she was before she could flee. Unable to bear the thought of what would happen if William chose to tell the Marquis that she had been imprisoned or, worse, tout it about every drawing room in London, Merewyn unbolted her bedroom door at last and tiptoed downstairs to seek out Francis's company, knowing she would find him in the kitchen this time of night.

"Is he gone?" Merewyn whispered to him through a crack in the heavy wooden door.

Francis turned at the sound of her voice to find her peering at him with wistful blue eyes. "Yes, miss. Several hours ago."

The steady gaze faltered. "I see. Did he say he would be coming back?"

"No, miss. He went to see Sir Edward Palington."

There was silence in response to this statement, and Francis asked kindly, "Would you care for a bite to eat, miss? 'Tis rather late and you didn't have any supper."

"I'm not really hungry, thank you," Merewyn informed him, but he opened the door wider so that she could see the roasting fowl turning on a spit over the fire.

"I was going to have this sent up to you anyway. I know how much you like chicken, and there's some soup left and fresh milk in the creamery that should go nicely with the berries David found at the market today."

"I suppose I could eat a little," Merewyn agreed half-heartedly to please him. Ten minutes later she was sitting at the big wooden table tackling the meat with ravenous energy, a satisfied Francis hovering in the background, Betsy sitting sleepily on the stone bench in the corner, waiting patiently for her mistress to finish eating so that she could clean up and go to bed.

"Are you going with us to Ravensley?" Merewyn asked, washing down the last of her supper with a healthy swallow of wine.

"No, indeed, miss," Francis replied much to her surprise, his expression one of utter distaste. "I've no wish to leave London for the wilds of the country."

Merewyn forced down a smile, wondering exactly how wild Surrey could be, what with the descriptions she had heard of sleepy hamlets and the fabulous country estates belonging to the socially prominent people who populated London during the season. "Is that why you didn't go with the Marquis to Scotland?" she guessed.

Francis nodded with tight-lipped contempt for those of the Villiers household who had volunteered to accompany their master there. He himself was quite content to remain in London and oversee both townhouses until Lord Montague arrived for occasional visits. As for that

knavish valet Davis—now there was a thoroughly impossible fellow who deserved to be packed off to the
Highlands and God grant that he would soon be eaten
by a wolf or stranded in a blizzard with naught but a
thin shirt on his back!

"Does that mean you won't be there for the—the
wedding?"

Francis's stern expression softened at Merewyn's hesi-
tant inquiry. "I'm afraid not, miss."

Despite her disappointment, Merewyn quickly reminded herself that there wasn't going to be a wedding.
She had no intention of marrying Lord Montague and
spending the rest of her life warming his bed whenever
he saw fit to have her, nor allow herself to become a
weapon in his warfare against her brothers. Where, oh
where was Alexander? she asked herself forlornly. By all
accounts he should have been here by now!

She glanced down and saw that Francis had set a bowl
of ripe berries before her topped with sugar and milk,
and she smiled up at him thankfully, bringing an embarrassed flush to the old man's cheeks that, to his relief,
had not been observed by little Betsy, who leaned groggily against the wall. He wouldn't want any of his staff
to think he was growing soft or that the sweet smile of
a pretty young girl could affect him so easily!

"Francis, you've spoiled me," Merewyn informed
him after a moment, setting the empty bowl aside and
stretching like a sleek, well-fed cat before rising gracefully to her feet. "I didn't realize I was so hungry!"

" 'Tis unwise to skip a meal," the majordomo remarked, motioning to Betsy that she was to carry the
dirty dishes to the basin. The little girl sighed, wishing
passionately that they could wait to be washed until
morning, but knowing full well that she wouldn't be excused until the kitchen was spotless. She couldn't find it
in her heart to blame her mistress for dawdling, however, sending a worshipful glance at Merewyn who

wished them both a good night and withdrew. After all, anyone who would soon be marrying the fierce, towering Marquis deserved all the sympathy she could get and, besides, Betsy was very fond of her mistress.

Upon quitting the kitchen Merewyn wandered restlessly to the study, where she stood for a moment staring down at the polished mahogany desk, a frown wrinkling her smooth brow. The entire room, decorated in an austerely masculine manner, seemed to breathe with the very presence of its intimidating owner. Would she ever be free of Ian Villiers? she asked herself wretchedly. 'Twas maddening to realize that in a city as overcrowded as London there was no one she could turn to for help.

"I will not become that which he expects me to be!" she stormed to herself, her hands balled into fists at her side as she glared down at the large leather chair behind the desk as though the Marquis himself were sitting there. "You won't win so easily, m'lord," she vowed, her voice shaking with agitation. "I swear on my father's grave I'll defeat you!"

But there was only mocking silence to answer her, a gentle reminder that she was helpless to fight him and that in two days' time she would be his wife. With Sir Robert Lindsey gone from London there was no one left who could help her, no one to whom she could turn. . . .

Suddenly Merewyn stood very still, her shallow breathing the only sound in the darkened room. No one? How could she think that when the obvious answer had been eluding her? Of course she had a friend here in London, someone she felt certain would not refuse to help her once her desperate situation was fully explained! A small, triumphant smile curved her soft lips and her blue eyes blazed with renewed determination. Tomorrow she would make arrangements to see this person and plan her escape. The risk involved was so slim, the suspicions she would arouse so slight that she cursed herself for not having thought of it sooner.

Lady Elizabeth Comerford paced the carpeted floor of the neat but sparsely furnished salon in William Rawlings's rented townhouse. Where the devil was he? she asked herself irritably. It was going on half past eleven and she was tired of waiting, tired of listening to the housekeeper's footsteps as the old woman passed constantly before the closed salon door, fairly bursting with curiosity at the uninvited presence of this fashionable yet ill-natured lady who had arrived several hours ago to see her employer.

"Mr. Rawlings isn't in," the housekeeper had said, her shock at finding a woman standing alone and unescorted in the doorway turning rapidly to malicious curiosity as she recognized Eliabeth Comerford.

"Do you know where he's gone?" Elizabeth demanded coldly, ignoring the knowing look in the old woman's eyes, and resisting with difficulty the impulse to give her a resounding box in the ears for her impertinence. She didn't care at all what sort of gossip she'd be arousing within William's household by appearing so late in the evening. So very much depended on this meeting that she was perfectly willing to risk becoming the object of all sorts of wild speculation.

"He has gone to Mr. Oswald Trantham's for dinner," the housekeeper replied, staring frostily down her long nose at the chestnut-haired woman wrapped in an elegant pelisse despite the warmth of the evening. Her narrowed eyes moved beyond her, down to the street, where she saw without any real surprise that it was empty. Doubtless, Lady Comerford had either ordered her coachman to park on a deserted street corner farther away or had already sent him back home.

"Then I shall wait for him here." Elizabeth pushed her way inside without waiting for an invitation and whirled about, staring with undisguised contempt at the housekeeper. "There is something I simply must discuss with Mr. Rawlings that cannot wait until morning. As soon as he returns will you tell him I'm here? Until then I do not wish to be disturbed."

"Very well," came the stiff reply, and Elizabeth was ushered into the salon where the door was closed behind her. Although her wish had been respected and she had seen nothing of the housekeeper, she was well aware that the insolent woman was haunting the corridor like a sniffing hound, hardly able to endure the wait until her employer returned. Doubtless she'd be pressing her ear to the door once both of them were inside, Elizabeth reflected with an annoyed scowl, but she intended to make sure that no one overheard what she had to say to William—no one!

Her green eyes burned with inner fire while she resumed her pacing, her satin skirts swirling about her as she glanced time and again the ormolu clock ticking on the mantel. When was William expected back? Damn him, there wasn't any time to lose! Only two days remained before Ian's wedding, and two days were precious short when one thought of what still remained to be done! God's blood, if she'd only known days ago what she had learned this morning, she could have gotten rid of Ian's honey-haired little tart long before this!

The housekeeper's excited chatter in the hall brought her head about, relief coursing through her when she overheard William's gruff reply. Then the door burst open and William strode in, his bony features flushed with wine, his wig askew, his stock loosened at the throat, the overall appearance of having imbibed too freely and eaten far too much. Elizabeth cursed beneath her breath. She needed William sober and with his wits about him. Ah, well, she thought, no matter. What she intended to say would sober him up fast enough.

"Well, Elizabeth?" William inquired lazily, his speech

surprisingly direct and not at all slurred as she had expected. "Did you wish to see me?"

She made no reply, fixing a baleful stare at the housekeeper who hovered expectantly in the doorway.

William's gaze followed hers. "That will be all, Mrs. Grey."

The housekeeper's eyes narrowed. "I thought mayhap you'd be carin' for some refreshments, you and the lady."

"We request nothing but privacy," William replied, smiling down at her although his eyes were cold. "And don't bother waiting up for me. I'll show the lady out myself when she goes."

Mrs. Grey's expression showed all too clearly that she didn't expect Lady Comerford to be leaving, remembering very well that she had made her stay a long, cozy one the last time.

"Thank you for your concern, Mrs. Grey," William added. "Good night." All but slamming the door in the old woman's round face, he turned again to regard Elizabeth with a curious expression, one eyebrow quizzically raised. "I realize you're not one to practice discretion, Elizabeth, but couldn't you have made your visit a wee bit less obvious?"

"Don't be ridiculous," Elizabeth snapped. "I've come to talk to you about something very important and it couldn't wait until morning. I wanted to come to you earlier, or send for you, but I am, though you refuse to acknowledge it, very discreet."

"So you waited until dark to see me." Willam sank into an armchair and propped his arms comfortably behind his head, regarding her with a smug smile on his thin lips. "Most wise of you, my dear. What is it you wanted to talk to me about? I gather 'tis of the utmost urgency since it couldn't wait until tomorrow."

Elizabeth was in no mood for bantering. With eyes

flashing she stared down at him boldly and demanded, "Why didn't you ever tell me you knew Merewyn MacAilis?"

Her question startled him with its unexpectedness and the smile that had been playing on his lips abruptly died. "I don't make it a habit of enumerating my acquaintances for everyone I meet," he told her with a frown, "and besides, I've never laid eyes on the girl before."

Elizabeth struggled to control her agitation. "Oh, come, William, there's no reason to pretend with me! We both know exactly what the other is about, and you knew damned well what my feelings for Ian Villiers were when we spent that night together, so you could have told me the truth about you and the bonnie Miss MacAilis."

William tugged irritably at his stock. "I haven't the foggiest notion what you're ranting about, my dear. Certainly I've heard of Miss MacAilis. Her family is very well known in Scotland, but I didn't think anyone here in London, especially you, had any idea who the MacAilises were."

Elizabeth was silent a moment, wondering why William was feigning total ignorance. Didn't he realize that both of them stood to gain with his disclosure of the truth? "Very well," she snapped, moving closer to his chair, her green eyes flashing as she stared down at him, "if you won't supply a confession I'll simply make it for you. With my own eyes I saw the two of you in a cozy tête-à-tête in your coach this afternoon, and I must say, William, I've yet to witness a less discreet assignation, since you seem so hell-bent on condemning me for my behavior! In broad daylight, it was, and neither of you taking any precautions about being recognized! Don't you realize Fleet Street is no place to go when you're trying to avoid people you know? Stop looking at me as though I've sprouted horns! I saw you with my own eyes!"

William's alcoholic haze was finally beginning to dissipate, but the mystery behind Elizabeth's comments was rapidly deepening. Standing before him with her cheeks flushed and nostrils flaring, she looked as though she had gone utterly mad. At the moment he could make no sense out of what she was saying, his chance meeting with the swooning girl on the docks of the Thames temporarily forgotten and in no way offering a link in his train of befuddled thoughts to Elizabeth's hysterical accusation.

"Let me get this straight," he said slowly. "You're saying that you saw Merewyn MacAilis in my coach this afternoon?"

Elizabeth could feel her impatience increasing. Dear God, how could he feign such a convincingly stupid expression when he knew damned well what she was talking about? What reason did he have to deny it any longer? "I am," she choked out, beside herself. "You let her off on an isolated stretch of Park Lane, doubtless to keep your meeting secret from probing eyes like mine. Miss Merewyn was wearing a bright yellow muslin gown with flounces. Now, William, will you stop this nonsense and admit 'twas you she was with!"

Realization dawned at last, and William shot to his feet, seizing Elizabeth's arms, his brown eyes glowing as he stared at her, and her anger began to ebb away, replaced by uncertainty and even a bit of fear.

"What are you saying?" he rasped, swaying unsteadily, his bloodshot eyes narrowing. "It was Merewyn MacAilis you saw with me?"

"Yes! Yes! Yes!" Elizabeth shouted. "Now, will you please stop behaving so oddly and admit to me you and Merewyn MacAilis have a secret tendresse for each other!"

William stared at her as though seeing her for the first time. "Elizabeth," he said slowly, "I swear to you that until you told me, I had no idea who the young lady in my coach was."

Now it was Lady Comerford's turn to look absolutely

dumbfounded, and William hurriedly explained the circumstances that had been involved in his meeting with the young Scottish girl earlier that day.

"She wouldn't tell me her name," William concluded, pouring himself a drink with an unsteady hand and downing it in one quick swallow. "If you hadn't seen us I'd still be ignorant as to her identity." He shook his head disbelievingly. "My God, Merewyn MacAilis herself!"

Elizabeth's clear laugh startled him, and he turned around to see her collapsed on the sofa, giving way to great gales of laughter, her green eyes brimming with tears of mirth. "Oh dear, this is rich! I simply don't know what to say! What a merry chase of cross purposes this has been!"

"I fail to see any humor in the situation," William said darkly.

She wiped her eyes and looked up at him gaily. "Don't you?"

"No."

Elizabeth sobered and leaned forward. "Are you saying, William, that you didn't know Merewyn MacAilis is Ian Villiers' fiancée?"

His shocked expression was answer enough and she waited for him to digest this news in silence, studying the rosy tips of her fingers until she saw him reach again for the brandy decanter.

"Put that away, will you?" she commanded crisply. "You've had more than enough."

"Gad, I'd need two more bottles to help me cope with the things you've told me," he said, although he grudgingly obeyed.

"How is it you didn't know?" Elizabeth asked curiously. "The subject has been bandied from one drawing room to another these past few days."

"I haven't been around much," William responded curtly. Dropping back down into his chair he studied her with heavy-lidded eyes. "So, my dear, if you came here tonight to shock me I must confess you've done an excellent job of it. I only wonder if you're telling me the truth because I heard on good authority today that Merewyn MacAilis was kidnapped from Glasgow earlier this summer and was taken to the colonies." The brown eyes narrowed suspiciously. "How can that be true if she's here in London betrothed to the Marquis of Montague?"

Elizabeth had grown very still at his words, her pale green eyes glittering. "So that's it!" she cried excitedly. "Ian told me when he first returned to London that he'd been to the colonies. At the time I couldn't understand what had prompted him to do so. He must have gone after her and brought her back here."

"Or," William said soberly, "he invented the kidnapping story himself." At Elizabeth's blank look he went on excitedly, "Don't you see? The Villiers and MacAilises are enemies of long standing. What better way for the Marquis to gain control over the entire business than to fabricate some wild tale to throw her brothers off the scent while he takes Merewyn down to London to coerce her into an unwanted marriage?" Abruptly his words faltered. "No, that couldn't be it. 'Tis far too mad a scheme to contemplate, even for a man like Villiers."

"Is it?" Elizabeth asked sharply.

William glanced at her from beneath his heavy brows. "What do you mean?"

"I happen to know there is little love lost between Lord Montague and his blushing bride-to-be. His feelings, I'm convinced, are lustful at best, and she is positively terrified of him."

Both of them looked at each other, each breathlessly aware of the dawning possibilities open to them in the face of these discoveries. Elizabeth was the first to speak.

" 'Tis quite simple, actually, now that we know the truth, and I'll be perfectly blunt, for there isn't much time to lose. I want Ian back and you, William, have made it plain to me that you're very interested in his little fiancée. I propose, then, that you take her away from London and the prospect of an unwanted marriage while I console the abandoned bridegroom." The pale green eyes glowed with anticipation. "I imagine the MacAilis brothers will be so grateful to you that they'll consider you the only suitable replacement for Merewyn's hand."

"And what do I do when Montague comes after me with murder in his heart? They say he's deadly with pistols and the sword." He shuddered involuntarily. "I'd hate to tangle with him."

Elizabeth dismissed his fears with an airy wave of one hand, confident that her new plan would work. She could scarcely believe her good fortune and was eager to pressure William into acting before he had a chance to think things through. How glad she was now that he was drunk, his senses befuddled!

"Ian will be too preoccupied to give his departed fiancée much thought," she told William glibly.

"Are you so certain of your hold over him?"

Elizabeth flushed angrily. "Of course I am!"

" 'Twas said your romance with Lord Montague was over even before he left for Scotland," William remarked candidly.

A sharp hiss informed him how well his words had hit their mark. "Jealous gossip, I assure you," Elizabeth said breezily, recovering herself. "Ian only fancies he wants to marry that little chit when in truth he's only interested in bedding her. But he won't, I tell you. He loves me, and you, William, will make sure this . . . this obstacle between us is permanently removed."

William settled down comfortable in his chair and thrust his hands deep into the pockets of his coat. "And how, pray tell, do you intend to accomplish that, my dear?"

"The first thing you must do is tell Merewyn that you know the truth about her unfortunate situation. You must send her a note in the morning asking for a private audience so that you can discuss it thoroughly without risking being overheard by anyone."

"And then?" William asked expectantly.

The rest of Elizabeth's words fell in a long tirade from her lips, and neither of them could realize that the truth was in no way the same one that Merewyn would be led to believe they had discovered. And in their ignorance, neither William nor Elizabeth could suspect the damage that their plotting would lead to.

Merewyn sighed deeply as she brushed her shining curls before the mirror and pinned them in a simple, yet very becoming fashion to her head. The reflection that stared back at her in the glass was pale, the expression glum, but she couldn't explain why she should be so unhappy now that she had stumbled upon the means of escaping London. After all, she had to get away before William Rawlings remembered who she was, and especially before she was forced into marriage with the Marquis. Wasn't that what she wanted to prevent above all other things?

Sighing again, so sorrowfully that she would have deeply touched the heart of anyone who might have heard it, Merewyn rose from the cushioned seat before the dressing table and picked up her gloves and bonnet. She had dressed with care that morning in a pale rose frock trimmed with sheer Bordeaux lace, the numerous petticoats beneath of shimmering gold, but as she turned to regard herself one final time in the glass she could find no satisfaction in her appearance.

Descending to the breakfast room she found another obstacle towards brightening her mood that presented itself in the intimidating form of the Marquis of Montague, who slouched indolently at the table sipping a cup of coffee.

His expressionless gray eyes narrowed when he saw her hesitate in the doorway and he remarked impatiently, "Come in, damn it, I'm not going to beat you."

Merewyn seated herself across from him, her small shoulders stiff and her slim nose pointed towards the ceiling, determined not to let him see how his unkind words hurt her.

"I see you're wearing another of Mrs. Ludley's creations," the Marquis observed lazily as the silence between them lengthened. " 'Tis very becoming."

Merewyn acknowledged this compliment with a cold stare. "Why are you here?" she asked at last.

"Can a man not enjoy breakfast in his own home?"

"Your home is on Grosvenor Road," she reminded him crossly.

"Parliament has yet to pass a law that says I cannot dine in any house I wish, provided I own it." The smile on his full lips was amused, but it did not reach the steel gray eyes. "As a matter of fact I came here to inform you that we'll be leaving for Ravensley at noon."

Merewyn fought to still her panic, the color draining from her cheeks as she looked across the board into his handsome, ruthless face. "Why so soon?" she asked in a whisper.

Ian shrugged his massive shoulders. "Let's just say I don't want to take any chances of losing you before the wedding. Your madcap outing yesterday made me realize that you're daft enough to risk just about anything. I want to make sure it doesn't happen again."

Merewyn's expression was mutinous, his arrogant words fanning within her a terrible desire to slap his smug face. "I'll try to be ready by then," she said reluctantly.

He chuckled. "I suggest you are, ma'am, for whatever isn't packed will simply be left behind."

Merewyn turned her slim back on him and began helping herself to the contents of the chafing dishes on the sideboard. Over one dainty shoulder she said cooly, still trying to appear nonchalant, "I have an engagement this morning that cannot be canceled."

There was a brief pause, then came the Marquis's casual inquiry: "Another excursion to the harbor, ma'am? Will you throw yourself at the mercy of any sea captain this time in your determination to be free of me?"

He could see her soft lips tremble, but her voice was firm as she replied, "Indeed not. I intend to make a call on Alicia Palington. She's expecting me. Since they haven't been invited to the wedding," she added stiffly, seating herself and beginning to eat, "I thought 'twas only proper to pay her one more call before I left."

Ian nodded approvingly. "Very thoughtful of you, ma'am. I've already given the coachman instructions to take you there."

Merewyn refused to acknowledge that his intimate knowledge of her affairs had come as a surprise. "How very kind of you," she said icily.

Ian's jaw tightened in response to her tone. "Naturally, I've also ordered him to bring you back immediately and threatened him with dismissal if he took you anywhere else."

"I promise to behave."

For a moment their eyes met across the table, hers wide and innocent, his probing and suspicious, and Merewyn could not help but feel something stir within her at the realization of how she was betraying him, but she forced herself to look away and the feeling was instantly gone.

Ten minutes later she came down into the courtyard to find the Marquis deep in conversation with the coachman, standing half a head taller than the gold- and crimson-liveried fellow whose tricorn covered a fastidiously tended wig. The high wheeled carriage was ready, the four stamping grays impatient to be off, and Merewyn prayed that she would reveal nothing of the nervous excitement surging within her as Ian turned to help her inside.

His strong hands slid intimately about her small waist and he all but lifted her inside, then closed the door and stood leaning against it while she settled herself against the squabs.

"You'll give my best to Alicia?" he asked, his boyish smile so beguilingly charming that she wondered what he was plotting.

"Certainly," she replied a trifle more warmly than she would have liked. God curse the swell-headed swine, why did he always affect her so easily with his charm?

"Don't scowl so fiercely," Ian warned her amiably. " 'Twill give you wrinkles prematurely."

"I plan to have at least a dozen of them before my next birthday," Merewyn promised, her blue eyes flashing, "so that you'll be saddled with an unspeakably ugly hag the rest of your days."

To her surprise and anger he laughed in a purely unaffected manner. "I wouldn't dream of permitting your beauty to go to waste, my dear. You'll be coddled and cozened like a pampered queen, that I swear to you."

"And what of your vow to extract revenge by making my life with you miserable?" she asked coldly. "You are filled, as always, with contradictions, my lord."

"And you cannot bait me today, ma'am, no matter how hard you try." The steely eyes were fastened on her soft red lips. "By tomorrow at this time you will be my wife."

Merewyn's expression froze, for there was no mistaking the desire in his dark eyes, and as she turned her head deliberately away from him she heard him curse softly beneath his breath, then hurl orders at John Bolling, the coachman, so that the carriage took off with an unexpected jerk that almost unseated her. Thank God she had resolved to ask Alicia for help, Merewyn fumed to herself as the carriage turned down the street and vanished from Lord Montague's sight. She couldn't wait to be free of him!

The drive to the Palingtons' townhouse was a short one, although it involved jockeying through a considerable amount of traffic. As the carriage lurched to countless halts only to roll forward again seconds later in the mainstream on the crowded thoroughfare, Merewyn began to grow glad that they were leaving London that day. Though she found it a fascinating city, unlike any other on earth, she longed for the country and the peace and solitude that were so integral a part of it.

Though she had never spoken of her homesickness to anyone, not even David, she had missed the solitary moors and the majestic mountains of Scotland far more than she dared admit even to herself. The parties and balls Ian had taken her to during her brief stay had been festive and exciting, but she would cheerfully have traded all of them for one long gallop across the barren moorland. And if Alicia could be persuaded to help her, Merewyn told herself happily, she might be enjoying that ride far sooner than she'd anticipated.

A worried frown marred the smoothness of her brow. Actually, she would be taking quite a risk in confessing the truth to Alicia Palington, whom she had met only once before, but she had sensed on that evening that Alicia was honest and trustworthy, and she hoped that Alicia's confessed awe of the Marquis of Montague would also serve to make her plight seem more horrible in the older woman's eyes.

The thought of going home lent Merewyn courage to go through with her scheme. Naturally, Ian would be furious that she had eluded him, but once she was safe behind the thick walls of Cairnlach she would never have to fear him again.

"Get a move on, you filthy whore's son!" she heard the coachman shout unexpectedly and leaned out the window to see what was causing the delay. An elegant touring carriage had rudely cut in front of them from a narrow sidestreet and was now dawdling up the twisting lane at a pace far too slow for John Bolling, who was already having more than enough difficulty in keeping his eager horses in check.

A group of small children standing on the corner caught sight of Merewyn's shining hair and elegant hat as she leaned out of the window, and descended upon her in a screaming horde, eager to take advantage of the vehicle's slow pace.

"Get away there!" the coachman roared down to them, his face suffused with color, angry at his helplessness.

"Oh, go on, guv!" a bedraggled ragamuffin called back at him, cheekily shaking his small fist in imitation of the coachman's gloved threat. "Penny, yer ladyship?" he asked in the same breath, staring up into Merewyn's face with a hopeful smile.

A chorus of demands accompanied his and Merewyn could only smile and shake her head at them, wishing she did have some money, for she would gladly have given it to the pitiful little beggars. There were quite a number of them trotting alongside the carriage now, and some of them grew bold enough to climb onto the running board, where they stood and waved their grimy hands through the window.

"Please, yer ladyship, just a penny!"

Merewyn, confronted by this mass of dirty, pleading faces and reaching hands, drew back into the protective confines of the vehicle. Never had she known the street beggars to be so bold! What had gotten into them?

"Get away or I'll thrash the lot of you!" the

coachman bellowed, having observed the melee from high up on his seat. At that moment the lumbering coach before him took another turn and drove off, leaving the street free before him, and he wasted no time in urging the grays to a smart trot. The children fell back, disappointed, and Merewyn could not help but pity them as she watched them vanish in the heavy traffic. Poor wee tykes, how she wished she could have helped them!

Leaning back with a small, unhappy sigh, she smoothed the folds of her gown, and as she did so she chanced to look down onto the floor of the carriage where she spied a crumbled piece of paper lying next to her slippered foot. Frowning, she picked it up, cursing the children for tossing garbage inside, but when she turned it over she discovered that it was sealed shut with wax and that apparently something was written inside.

Laying it down on the seat beside her, she smoothed it out with her gloved hand and read the words written there in small, neat lines:

> Miss MacAilis:
> I know everything about you, and as I would rather not cause a spectacle with my information or damage your good name, I would like to meet privately with you. Would you be so kind as to choose an appropriate time and place and sent word to me? Please believe that I want to help.
>   Your obd. servant,
>   William Rawlings

The meeting with Alicia did not go very well. No sooner had Merewyn stepped out of the carriage and was met in the entrance hall than Alicia exclaimed in concern, "My goodness, you look simply dreadful!"

The indigo eyes were expressionless. "Do I?" Merewyn asked vaguely, staring down at her gown, half

expecting to find it covered with mud. To her bewilderment she saw that the rose-colored skirts and flounced
petticoats were clean and meticulously pressed.

"No, no, I don't mean your outfit," Alicia explained,
taking Merewyn's hand in hers. "Do you feel faint,
dear? You look awfully pale."

"I-I'm not sure."

"Sarah!" Alicia called, and immediately a competent-
looking young maid with flaming red hair appeared in
the small entrance foyer.

"Yes, m'lady?"

"Take Miss MacAilis to the salon and bring her
something cold to drink." Alicia patted Merewyn's limp
hand, which still rested in her own. "I'll be with you in
a minute."

Gathering up her skirts the tall, dark haired woman
hurried down the steps to interview the Montague
coachman, who was planning to await his mistress's return in the Palington kitchen, where he hoped a cold
tankard of ale might be waiting. At Alicia's anxious
question he scowled and nodded vigorously.

"Aye, your ladyship, 'twouldn't surprise me one bit if
'twas something brought on comin' over. We were
mobbed right proper by those damned impudent little
beggars, if you'll pardon my words," he added hastily,
blushing furiously. "Climbin' all over the carriage, they
was. Enough to bring on the vapors even for a lady the
likes of Miss MacAilis."

"She doesn't look well at all," Alicia added worriedly.
"Will you take her home as soon as she's feeling a little
stronger?"

John Bolling squirmed at the fleeting image of the
Marquis's angry countenance, wondering if his employer would blame him for the scene that had taken
place out on the street. Deuced sensitive women, he
thought irritably. Didn't take the least little bit of excitement to bring about swooning! Even as the thought

passed through his mind he knew it to be unfair. Miss MacAilis was a young woman of admirable spirit and stamina. She couldn't be blamed if she'd been overwhelmed by a passel of hungry, smelly beggar brats! God grant he didn't see any of them on the way back or he'd lay his whip briskly to their skinny hides!

"As you wish, m'lady," he replied formally, letting none of his misgivings show in his face.

Alicia hurried back inside, where she found her guest reclining on the chaise lounge, a worried Sarah bending solicitously over her. Seeing her mistress appear in the doorway, Sarah crossed the room and spoke to her in low tones.

"Her color's back, m'lady, but I don't like the looks of it. She doesn't even seem to know I'm here. 'Tis like she's in shock or something."

Alicia chewed her lip. "Lord Montague's coachman says half a dozen street beggars tried to climb into the coach on the way here."

Sarah's pleasant countenance gave way to one of profound shock. "Tsk, they're getting bold! When the streets be'ent safe for carriages anymore, where are decent folk to turn to?"

Alicia had no answer for this.

"I think she better go home," Sarah added firmly.

Merewyn, having understood these words, slowly turned her head and looked up at Alicia as though suddenly aware of her for the first time. "Send me home?" she echoed. "Whatever for? I've only just arrived."

Alicia seated herself on the end of the settee and looked into the pale face with a frown. "Are you feeling better, dear?"

The shock was slowly beginning to wear off, and Merewyn tried hard to gather her wits about her, realizing she would have to deal with William Rawlings's message later. First she had to reassure Alicia, who already looked half frightened to death, that she was fine, but as for broaching the subject that had been her reason for coming, 'twould simply have to wait.

A tremulous smile curved the soft lips. "I'm sorry, Alicia, I didn't mean to give you such a fright. I-I don't know what came over me, but I'm much better now."

Alicia's worried expression gave way to one of utter fury. "Well, I don't blame you one bit! The nerve of those ruffians! Edward always insists I have an outrider along when I go into town and now I'm convinced he has good reason. None of them hurt you, did they?"

Merewyn, who was totally mystified by Alicia's outburst, could only shake her head blankly, but this seemed to satisfy her.

"Good! Honestly, I don't object to throwing them a few coins now and then, but when they try to climb inside, well, 'tis enough to make you wish they'd all be banished to Newgate!"

Merewyn was beginning to make some sort of sense out of Alicia's words and guessed that the coachman had told her of the small horde of aggressive beggars they had encountered on the drive over. She shivered involuntarily, feeling certain William Rawlings had paid them to make a ruckus and toss the note inside without anyone being aware of it. The thought of having been followed and spied upon made her feel ill.

"Are you feeling better?" Alicia asked again. "Perhaps you'd better go home."

"Oh, please, Alicia, don't worry so! I'm fine now, and I wanted so much to visit with you before we left for Surrey."

"Very well," Alicia said grudgingly, though inwardly she was pleased. Turning to Sarah, who hovered in the doorway she added, "Please bring some tea, Sarah."

"Yes, m'lady."

Though Alicia chatted engagingly, Merewyn could afterwards remember little of what had been said. Perhaps sensing that her guest was not as fully recovered as her unwavering smile would have her believe, Alicia made the visit short and sent Merewyn away far sooner than she would have liked. Watching from the front door as the carriage rolled off down the street, she made a mental note to speak to her husband that evening, for Edward had several influential friends in Parliament who might be pursuaded to do something to disperse the beggars who roved relentlessly through London's most elegant sections.

During the drive back to the Marquis's residence Merewyn had more of a chance to compose herself. Turning over the letter that she had hidden behind the seat during her brief visit with Alicia, she read it again and committed to memory the address written at the bottom. Then she crumpled it up and stuffed it into her reticule, determined to burn it later.

There was no way she could meet with William before their scheduled departure for Surrey. She would have to write and inform him of her trip to Ravensley and hope that he would make arrangements to come and see her there. What sort of demands would he make of her? she wondered forlornly. Surely he had no intention of helping her as his letter had stated! Doubtless he would blackmail her with his knowledge for money or, God knows, something else. She shivered and tried to push the nagging doubts from her mind.

Lord Montague was waiting for her at the end of the circular drive when the carriage returned, and as he helped her down he inquired worriedly, "Didn't you have a pleasant visit, Merewyn? You look pale."

"I'm rather tired," she confessed shakily, freeing herself from his grasp as soon as she was on the ground.

He surprised her by saying kindly, "Perhaps we should delay our departure until you've had a chance to rest."

"No!" Merewyn cried immediately, terrified of the thought of spending another day in London now that

William Rawlings had remembered her.

The steely gray eyes were filled with amazement at her outburst. "Am I led to believe you are eager to become my wife, ma'am?"

"You may believe whatever you wish," Merewyn snapped, not in the least bit desirous of trading words with him, "but since you have given orders to leave at noon that is when I intend to go."

Ian watched her brush past him, her petticoats rustling as she ascended the steps to the house, then turned with a thunderous expression to John Bolling, who was waiting nervously to explain why Miss MacAilis was so terribly out of sorts.

"You will load the luggage and see that Miss MacAilis's trunks are secured," the Marquis said in a forbidding tone. "We will be leaving in an hour."

"Yes, your lordship," the coachman quavered. Then he sighed in relief as the Marquis strode off after his fiancée without asking for an explanation. Thank God he'd not had to face his master's wrath!

During the flurry of activity that surrounded the leave-taking, Merewyn was able to slip into the kitchen while Francis was busy elsewhere, and waylaid David for a private conversation. She had penned a brief message to William Rawlings, one that had caused her an agony of indecision and fear, and prayed that when he learned she was already in Surrey his resolve to contact her would fade away.

"I want you to deliver this for me," she told David in a tone that brooked no argument, "but not until the Marquis and I are gone. If anyone, especially Francis, learns that you have it, I'll cut off your ears and serve them to the dogs."

David, who had never heard his mistress speak to him in this manner before, looked up at her speculatively, his brown eyes wide and his jaw hanging slack.

"Oh, aye, I mean every word I say," Merewyn assured him crisply.

"Aye, miss," he murmured.

"I know I can trust you, David," she relented.

Sensing that she wasn't as angry as she seemed, he asked sorrowfully, "When will you be coming back?"

A doubtful expression crossed the delicate features and the tilted blue eyes grew soft. "I'm not sure that I am, David." Seeing his startled look she added teasingly, "Dinna fash yersel', laddie, we'll be in Cairnlach afore ye ken."

He grinned and tucked her letter into the pocket of his trews. "I'll deliver this or die in the attempt."

Merewyn's smile was less amused than he would have liked. "You'll not have to go to such lengths, I'm sure."

The majordomo's appearance in the kitchen interrupted their conversation. "Please, miss," he begged, "can you see to your belongings? I believe we've packed everything but I want to be sure. His lordship is in quite a temper and I don't want to keep him waiting."

The soft lips tightened with weary determination. "Neither do I, Francis."

A few minutes later Merewyn bid farewell to David, Betsy, and Francis and permitted a manservant to help her up into the coach. A fresh team of snorting, high-spirited bays were standing in the traces, their gleaming coats already damp with sweat. Lord Montague abruptly appeared beside the vehicle, his black boots polished, carrying a bone-handled whip in one long-fingered hand.

Peering into the coach he said curtly to Merewyn, "I trust you will have a comfortable trip, ma'am."

She was unable to contain her surprise. "Aren't you driving with me?"

He gestured with the tip of the quirt to the stamping black stallion that Nick Holder was leading out of the stable. "I will be riding."

Merewyn didn't know whether to be relieved or disappointed, and for a moment there was silence as he stood gazing into the darkened confines of the vehicle where the shadows falling on her face made her features seem more sharply defined than they had ever been, giving her youthful countenance a beauty far beyond her years. Her golden hair was pinned beneath a small hat trimmed with netting, and Ian found himself wondering, not for the first time, how such a sheltered and rough-spirited young girl could possess such an air of delicate maturity and finish.

"Perhaps it is Mrs. Ludley's skill with the needle," he said, staring speculatively at her hat and the matching pelisse she wore to ward off the chill of the rain-threatened afternoon.

"My lord?" Merewyn asked curiously, and he realized he had spoken aloud.

"No matter," he responded curtly and withdrew. Merewyn watched as he swung effortlessly onto the stallion's broad back, his long legs sliding skilfully into the stirrups and the wind stirring his thick brown hair. With a creak of leather and wood the coach gained momentum, rolling down the drive, the broad-shouldered figure of the Marquis riding before it. Merewyn leaned back with a defeated sigh, thinking to herself that, come hell or high water, she doubted she had any more say about her future.

CHAPTER TEN

The chapel at Ravensley was annexed to the main building; an imposing structure built of herringbone-patterned brick that had softened to a rosy hue over the years. Ivy grew riotiously over the corniced turrets and mullioned windows and even the beautifully detailed stained glass window, a gift from the Archbishop of Canterbury to Ian Villiers's great-grandfather, was partially covered by the indestructible creepers.

The interior of the tiny chapel was meticulously cared for, however, and the slate floor gleamed with polish, and the pews with their intricate carvings were rubbed with beeswax. The alter was covered with an old and obviously very valuable embroidered velvet cloth depicting Biblical scenes, and the late afternoon sunlight fell through the multicolored glass behind it, illuminating the entire chapel with eerily beautiful dancing light while the gloom in the corners was dispelled with candles set into polished brass sconces.

The effect was striking, but Merewyn, standing with an ill-concealed trembling in the narthex, scarcely noticed her surroundings. She was peering anxiously towards the arched door beside the altar that was at present closed, knowing that at any moment the minister, to whom she had spoken for the first time several minutes ago, would emerge with the Marquis. It was Ian's appearance that was causing her so much anxiety, for she had seen nothing of him since he had abruptly vanished after their arrival late yesterday afternoon. She was terrified that he intended to humiliate her during the ceremony, suspecting strongly that he would either arrive agonizingly late or wearing the most outlandish of clothes, or perhaps even the mud-stained boots and wrinkled breeches he had donned for the ride from London.

"Don't be nervous, child. 'Twill be a beautiful wedding."

Feeling the gentle hand on her sleeve, Merewyn turned her head and tried to smile bravely at the small, gray-haired woman standing at her side. Martha Simpson had fussed over her all morning, a prattling, kindhearted creature who had calmed most of Merewyn's fears with her competent air and extremely humorous (though Merewyn suspected largely fictitious) tales of the Marquis's boyhood. Marty, as she was affectionately called by everyone at Ravensley, had all but raised him herself.

"Did I tell you, child, that you be the most beautiful bride I've ever laid eyes on?" Marty continued, seeing that Merewyn's soft lips were trembling despite her effort to smile in a reassuring manner. "Prettier even than the Lady Eleanor, the Marquis's mother, and she was an angel sent from heaven. Here, now, let me fix your veil. 'Tis almost time."

The wedding gown, a breathtakingly magnificent creation of billowing white brocade and beautiful lace, had been lying on the coverlet of Merewyn's bed when she awoke that morning. Already accustomed to Mrs. Ludley's uncanny skill with the needle, Merewyn had nonetheless been unable to contain her awe at the sight of the delicate embroidery that covered the bodice and the countless tiny pearl buttons sewn painstakingly to the sleeves and down the back. A veil of matching material lay beside the gown, the same veil that now covered her heart-shaped face so that only the glittering indigo eyes were visible.

Marty stepped back with a sigh of satisfaction to admire the vision of loveliness that would shortly be the new Marchioness of Montague. When she had first clapped eyes on the exhausted and hollow-eyed little girl that had stumbled out of the coach yesterday, she had had her doubts that Ian, whom she loved as her own, had made the right choice, but after spending the morning doing Merewyn's hair and chatting with her to calm the child's obviously rattled nerves, she had come to the conclusion that no one of her own choosing could have suited the Marquis better.

" 'Twill be a beautiful ceremony, you'll see," she added encouragingly, but this time Merewyn gave no indication that she had heard. Behind the translucent veil her small face had gone white and her tilted eyes widened with disbelief. Marty turned quickly to see that the Marquis had emerged from the vestibule.

"Go on, now," she whispered to Merewyn, and had to prod her twice before her orders were obeyed.

Merewyn doubted she had ever seen the Marquis look more handsome than he did at the moment arrayed in dark burgundy satin, the waistcoat shot through with gold threads. His knee breeches were also gold, and in his white stock he wore a glittering, blood-red ruby set in heavily hammered gold. His dark hair was unpowdered and tied in a queue and though it was an unconventional fashion for so formal an occasion, Merewyn could not help but feel that he looked far more distinguished than any of the dandies she had seen at the London assemblies. Her heart was fluttering so at the sight of him that she could almost believe she was anticipating the moment when she would become his wife, married to him for love and not because he was extracting vengeance from her.

There was a smile playing on his sensual lips as she came to stand beside him, and for a moment Merewyn almost believed that the look in his dark eyes was one of admiration and even tenderness, but as the minister began speaking in a sonorous voice his aristocratic countenance grew sober, and he turned away without comment to face forward.

Merewyn could remember little of the ceremony itself. Standing at the Marquis's side in the nearly empty chapel, the top of her veil-covered head barely on line with his chin, she felt as though she were dreaming, and that she would awaken at any moment. And yet she was reminded that it was all too real when she felt Ian's strong hand close about hers almost painfully and when she looked up, stricken, into his eyes, she realized that both he and the minister were expecting an answer to the question: Would she before God honor and obey her husband? For one wild, fanciful moment she contemplated refusing, but the pressure around her slim fingers tightened cruelly and she knew it would be foolish to do so.

"I d-do," she quavered, sending the Marquis a mutinous look, her indigo eyes flashing, only to receive a mocking smile in response. When he released her hand she stared down at it in confusion, surprised to find a delicate gold band about one tapering finger, and even as she contemplated this phenomenon she felt the veil being lifted from her face and the Marquis's arms about her as he pressed his lips against hers in a hard, compelling kiss that warned her he would brook no disobedience from her ever again.

Then they were standing outside and Merewyn felt Marty's warm embrace and stared down in bewilderment into the older woman's tear-filled eyes. "God grant you happiness, your ladyship," she murmured joyfully.

"Aye, 'twill have to come divinely," Merewyn commented dryly, "for I doubt I shall receive it here."

The Marquis glanced at her sharply, then left her to speak with the minister and the few servants who had served as witnesses and were milling nervously about, unsure what was expected of them next.

"Come upstairs and rest," Marty advised, seeing that Merewyn was very pale. " 'Twas too much excitement, I gather, to cope with all in one day!"

Merewyn allowed herself to be led back to the bridal suite where, in the salmon and gold apartment belonging to the lady of the manor, she sank down onto the window seat and stared with bemused disbelief at the gold band around her finger. So it had happened at last, she thought to herself, almost unaware of Marty removing her veil and folding it away before tiptoeing out. She was Ian's wife, but why should that realization make her feel so numb and drained of emotions? She should be furious, should have resisted more instead of acquiescing like some meek lamb led off to slaughter. Instead, she felt as though she were living in a dream and that the knowledge that she was now the Marchioness of Montague hadn't really sunk in.

Her slanted eyes wandered restlessly to the landscape beneath her window. The sun had begun its downward descent and rays of light streamed through the dissipating clouds to illuminate the wet ground with patches of radiant gold. A river wound its way lazily across the northernmost border of the property and Merewyn could see the arched stone bridge over which her coach had passed late yesterday afternoon.

Ravensley was a pleasant estate, she couldn't help thinking to herself. Smaller by half than Cairnlach, it nonetheless possessed a character of its own, the rooms high-ceilinged and spacious, and decorated in an invitingly comfortable blend of provincial furnishings. She might have enjoyed being here under other circumstances and perhaps even come to love it but for the rankling knowledge that it was the ancestral home of the Villiers, who had tried to ruin her family.

"But you're a Villiers now, too," Merewyn whispered to herself, and as the hated name fell from her soft lips the icy calm that had surrounded her since her arrival vanished suddenly to be replaced by helpless rage. Pulling the ring from her finger she dashed it with a furious oath against the wall and watched with grim satisfaction as it rolled into the cold stone hearth where it lay winking in the candlelight falling from the mantel above.

Turning heel, she stalked to the cupboard and pulled down her valise, tossing it onto the bed and ripping her belongings out of the drawers in which Marty had so painstakingly laid them only several hours ago. With firmly compressed lips she began stuffing underclothes and gloves, toilette water, whatever came into hand, inside.

"Do you always pack so neatly?"

Merewyn jumped and whirled about to find the Marquis leaning against the doorjamb, arms folded across his broad chest, a sardonic smile playing on his full lips, the dark eyes watching her intently.

"I'll never get used to your habit of sneaking up behind me," Merewyn snapped, resuming her task in a more frenzied fashion than before.

"You'll have a lifetime in which to change that," he reminded her, sauntering inside.

Merewyn froze at this, then replied tightly, "Ah, but you are quite mistaken, my lord. I'm leaving."

He stepped aside politely to allow her to brush past him to the dressing table where she swept off the articles in one motion and carried them back to the bed.

"May I help you?" he inquired as she struggled to close the fastenings on the bulging valise.

"Leave me alone!" Merewyn cried as he moved to stand beside her. Retreating, she found herself pressed against the bed so that she could go no further, looking up at him with wide eyes as he came closer, pausing directly before her to look soberly into her upturned face.

"Why are you leaving?"

His simple question confused her. "Because I cannot tolerate being a Villiers," she faltered lamely, but somehow that didn't seem to matter as much as it had several minutes ago.

"You can run wherever you please, Merewyn," the Marquis told her quietly, "but you cannot escape the truth. You made an oath before God today that binds you to me irrevocably."

"And I swore to honor and obey you," she added angrily, wishing he wouldn't stand so close, "and I have no intentions of holding to that vow, either!"

Ian reached out and caught her wrists as she lifted her arms to push him away, effectively cutting off her escape. But where she had expected the pressure to be painful, she found to her surprise that he was holding her lightly and that the look on his handsome face was not one of annoyance or rage but, bewilderingly, something akin to sadness.

"Will you always be at odds with me, Merewyn?"

She felt unaccountably shaken by his tone and though she tried to look away from the gray eyes gazing down into hers, she found she could not. Drawing upon some inner strength she said coldly, "May I remind you that you forced me into that position? You promised me you'd see my life a hell on earth. Why, then, should I treat you kindly?"

Ian shook his dark head despairingly. "I see that our past is going to haunt us forever."

"And why shouldn't it?" Despite her hard words, Merewyn's confusion was growing. Could it be possible that he was hinting at making peace between them, to begin anew now that they were man and wife? She wanted to believe that, desperately so, but how could she afford to trust him when he had hurt her so cruelly in the past? Was this merely another of his tricks to use her? Doubts plagued her and she was scarcely aware that Ian had released her and retreated to the window, where he stood gazing moodily out into the gathering twilight, his hands clasped behind his broad back.

"I see that you are still cynical and suspicious," he said, his back still turned to her. "Perhaps in time that will change."

Merewyn did not have time to reply, for a manservant appeared unexpectedly in the doorway to announce in a nervous tone of voice that dinner was being served before turning heel and withdrawing quickly, not caring at all for the tension in the air.

"Shall we go down?" the Marquis suggested, holding out his hand to her.

Merewyn hesitated, then allowed his strong fingers to close over hers. "Very well, my lord," she murmured.

The Marquis tucked her hand comfortably into his. "You must call me Ian, now," he told her. "I am your husband, after all."

"You needn't remind me. 'Tis something I shan't ever forget."

His full lips tightened but he asked pleasantly, "And you promise that you will try not to run away?"

Merewyn sighed, wishing she could trust her heart and believe that his kindness towards her was not feigned. "I promise, my lord."

"Ian."

"I promise, Ian."

"Wait a moment," he said, the glitter of gold in the fireplace having caught his eye. Stooping down he picked up the wedding ring and turned it over carefully to satisfy himself that it was not dented or scratched, then slipped it firmly back onto her slender finger.

"You ought to be more careful," he warned, smiling casually into her upturned face, "or you'll lose it again.

'Tis meant to stay with you for life. Now, shall we go?"

"Aye, my lord," Merewyn replied meekly, relieved that he had not chosen to chastise her.

"Ian," he prompted.

"Ian," she repeated crossly.

The great hall with its vaulted ceiling and numerous wall hangings was illuminated by softly shimmering candlelight. The dark oak refectory table was set at one end with fine bone china and highly polished silverware, and no sooner had Merewyn seated herself than two footmen hurried inside carrying a tureen of soup and a bottle of champagne set inside a chilled bucket.

"I'm afraid our wedding feast is reduced to a simple twosome," the Marquis apologized, his dark eyes gleaming brightly as he looked at her, "but we can make it festive nonetheless."

Merewyn's small nose wrinkled with distaste. "I'm afraid I'm not in a very festive mood."

"No?" He feigned astonishment. "What a pity! I thought weddings were supposed to be happy occasions."

"Not if the match was made in Hell."

The footman who was setting before Merewyn a plate filled with smoked salmon started visibly, but managed to keep his face an expressionless mask. Merewyn paid him not the slightest attention. Her indigo eyes were riveted on the Marquis, who was seated across from her, resplendent in his wedding attire. His behavior, so kind and solicitous, was making her suspicious and even a bit fearful. What nasty scheme had the brute concocted for her now with his sweet words and admiring looks?

As soon as the main course had been served Ian motioned the footmen out, and when they were alone in the hall he said coldly, "I expect you to stop making comments of that nature before the servants."

This was the Marquis Merewyn knew best and she slipped at once into the disdainful role that came so easily to her nowadays. "I shall say whatever I please to whomever I wish. After all, I am a Marchioness now."

"Then act like one. Damn it, Merewyn, do you think I want the servants believing I've married some youthful termagent?"

The sneer in the soft voice was painfully obvious. "You should have thought of that before you married me."

Ian's temper was clearly beginning to simmer, but he strove to remain reasonable. "Very well, behave as primitive as you wish. I'd like to ask one favor of you, however, and that is to be kind to Marty. She seems extremely fond of you already and I wouldn't want to cause her any unhappiness."

Merewyn blinked, finding it difficult to believe that he could display so much compassion towards another person. True, the little gray-haired woman seemed to be someone special, but she wouldn't have thought the Marquis capable of caring for anyone but himself. "You seem very fond of her," she remarked.

"I am." There was no trace of mockery in his deep voice. "She's been here since my mother married my father, and after my mother died she raised me herself."

The words were bluntly spoken, but Merewyn knew him well enough now to know that they had not been lightly uttered. Though she would have liked to ask him more about his family, realizing suddenly how little she did know about him, she was reluctant, certain that the newfound intimacy between them, for which Ian was obviously responsible, was a mere façade for the servants' benefit. No telling what he might say to her if she professed interest in the Villiers family!

Merewyn remained silent for the remainder of the meal, but the more her reticence grew, the more Lord Montague appeared to wax conversational. She listened with grudging interest while he explained the scenes depicted on the tapestries hanging on the walls about them, impressed with his knowledge of history although she would rather have bitten off her tongue than say so. The Villiers, she reluctantly discovered, had been a courageous tribe, staunchly following their kings into battle and even siding, to Merewyn's astonishment, with Charles II, the Stuart King, against the rebellious Roundheads led by Oliver Cromwell.

"So, you see, not all Villiers are anti-Jacobites," Ian concluded with a boyish grin, leaning forward to fill her glass with more champagne, his gray eyes twinkling. "Wait, don't speak," he added as Merewyn began to protest. "Politics and Jacobites are hotbed topics for you and I. Do you realize we've spent an entire meal together without arguing once? I'd like to keep it that way."

Merewyn was too proud to admit that she had enjoyed their dinner and hid her feelings behind a haughty scowl.

Ian, peering into her delicate heart-shaped face, could not help but laugh. "I warrant there's never been a lass with more stubborn pride than you, ma'am. Why can't you simply admit to me you've enjoyed my company this evening?"

"Because 'twould be a monstrous lie," Merewyn responded, rising rather unsteadily to her feet. She was infuriated to hear him chuckle, and rounded on him, her indigo eyes flashing. "Oh, how typical of you to find humor at my expense, m'lord!"

'Tis your own fault for consuming so much champagne," he chided.

"You're insufferable," Merewyn snapped and stalked out of the room, wavering as she did, but her slim back and shoulders were ramrod stiff and her little nose was pointed towards the rafters. Ian, watching the unconsciously seductive sway of her curving hips, found it difficult to be angry with her although he should have been. Thus far, every attempt he had made at a reconciliation between them had been met with cold indifference. Still, he could not find it in his heart to blame her. She had every right to be suspicious of his motives, nor could he bring himself to put his heart upon his sleeve and admit openly that he firmly intended to right matters between them now that they were married.

Aye, to forget the past and make the best of the present—so he would have liked to begin his life with Merewyn as his wife. Reluctant to leave matters as they were, Ian hurried up the winding staircase and entered Merewyn's bedroom to find her standing before the dressing table struggling futilely with the pearl buttons and fastenings of her wedding gown.

Pausing on the threshold he listened with an amused smile to the choice oaths she muttered beneath her breath, much as he had done before supper when he had watched her packing her belongings in her feverish haste; then sauntered inside and remarked, " 'Twould seem I am forever destined to play the role of your tiring woman."

Merewyn whirled about at the sound of his deep voice, a rosy flush creeping to her hollow cheeks. "Wh-what do you mean?"

"Surely you haven't forgotten that day in Boston when I entered your room to find you prancing about with your back undone?"

"You had no right to come into my room then," Merewyn countered, moving away from him, "and you certainly don't now."

Ian raised one eyebrow archly. "I don't? Surely you haven't already forgotten that I am your husband, ma'am, with the right to go wherever I please. Turn around."

The command was clipped and blunt and she surprised him by obediently turning her slim back towards him.

"I don't know why you can't send Marty up to do this

for me," Merewyn said, her voice trembling slightly. His strong fingers were brushing lightly against her skin and she could feel his warm breath at the nape of her neck.

"I sent Marty to bed hours ago. 'Tis extremely late, my dear, or didn't you realize that we sat up dining for quite some time?"

"I was wondering why the footmen were yawning so."

Ian laughed at this and took her by the shoulders, turning her around so that she was facing him. She tilted back her head to look up into his eyes, then wished she hadn't, for there was no mistaking the anticipatory gleam that had sprung into their steely depths. She began to tremble again, remembering that they were now legally married and that he could do with her as he pleased. The champagne still clouded her brain and she found herself wishing that she hadn't drunk so much, aware that she would need her wits about her.

"Thank you," she said with as much dignity as she could muster, considering that she was standing before him with her brocade gown unbuttoned to the waist in the back. "And good night."

"Am I to take that as a dismissal?" the Marquis asked lazily, and if her brain hadn't been so clouded with alcohol Merewyn might have heard the faint hardening of his tone.

"I'm tired," she said, trying to sound brave, but her gaze faltered beneath the burning intensity of his and the indigo eyes slid away. Ian was still holding her fast by the shoulders, but now one strong hand moved beneath her small chin, tilting it so that she had no choice but to look up at him.

"Merewyn," he said hoarsely, "you would send me away? Tonight of all nights?"

His question confused her, as had his odd behavior all evening. Twice in the past he had tried to take her, brutally, without consideration of her own feelings, his desire born of anger and the need to dominate her rebellious will. Dear God, how was she expected to resist him this time when he crumpled her defenses with his God-rotting charm? After all, he had married her against her will, was planning to seduce her with kindness, and would doubtless even laugh at her fawning response to his newly exhibited gentleness!

"Aye, I'd send you away tonight," she spat at him, "and with a dirk in your bloody cold heart if I had one!"

Ian, who had watched the uncertainty in the gold-flecked depths of her eyes change slowly to anger, was not startled by her outburst. Shaking his dark head he looked down at her with mock pity. "Even the acquisition of a title can't kill that piece of barbarian in you, can it?"

"Why, you boorish cad!" Merewyn shouted and flung herself at him, her hands balled into fists. But he warded her off easily, clasping her slim wrists in his big hands.

"Really, my dear," he drawled, "these scenes are becoming rather tiresome. Can't you think of a more inventive way of inflicting pain? Chest pummeling has grown rather dull." His casual tone was by no means reflected on his hawkish features that were grimly set, but Merewyn, her face averted, did not notice. Tears of pain and frustration welled in her eyes, aware that he was speaking the truth. All too often their meetings had ended this way, with bitter words and frayed tempers. Would the rest of their lives together consist of one battle after another?

"I can't bear it!" she moaned, afraid that this would be the case.

Instantly, the pressure around her wrists disappeared and Merewyn stared up at him, unwilling to believe that he had given in so easily. When Ian caught the glitter of tears in her eyes his lean jaw tightened.

"I'm sorry, Merewyn, I didn't mean to hurt you."

"Liar! 'Tis all you ever want to do! That or humiliate me, isn't that how you promised to treat me as your wife?" Her voice trembled dangerously and she looked away, not wanting to shed tears in front of him.

There was a long moment of silence and Merewyn, struggling with her own anger and hurt, was not aware that Ian had reached into the pocket of his coat and was holding something out to her until he said her name. When she looked up she saw an oblong wooden box in his hands.

"I forgot to give this to you at dinner."

"What is it?" She was more suspicious of his kind tone than the contents of the box.

The faint smile that tugged at his full lips made him seem far less intimidating. "Your wedding present."

Merewyn took it hesitantly and opened the brass clasp, then gasped when the contents were revealed to be beautiful jewels set in necklaces, rings, brooches, and ear bobs, all of them sapphires set with diamonds, a priceless collection that sparkled in the candlelight. "They're just like the ones you let me wear to the Palingtons' party," Merewyn breathed.

"They were my mother's jewels," Ian explained. "I want you to have them now."

Merewyn could not think of a suitable reply. She had never seen so much wealth amassed in one place before, nor jewelry so delicately crafted—a collection worthy, she felt certain, of the Queen herself.

"Actually, you should have worn them during the ceremony," Ian was saying, coming to stand before her, "but under the circumstances I wasn't sure if you'd have accepted them."

The upturned face was filled with disbelief. "What made you think I'd accept them now?"

"Because you are my wife, Merewyn, and I don't believe that any Villiers bride has ever refused them, regardless of how much they might have despised their husbands." His voice grew hoarse. "I offer them to you as a legacy, not only because it would have made my mother happy, but because I hope that someday you will give them to our son when he takes a bride of his own."

The indigo eyes were so wide that he could easily see the golden fire in their darkened depths. His own seemed unable to tear themselves away, but when they did, they roved hungrily over the other features of her delicate face, coming to rest at last on the rosy, slightly parted lips.

"Merewyn," he whispered huskily and pulled her to him, half afraid that she would grow rigid in his arms, her aversion to him obvious in every fiber of her being. To his utter astonishment she felt pliant to his touch so that he was able to press her even closer to him. Unable to credit her acquiescence, Ian bent his head until his mouth touched hers, gently at first, then with a growing confidence until he felt her lips part beneath his. A thrill shot through him as she responded, and for the first time he knew the heady joy of conquest tempered by shared passion, knowing that no one could keep him from taking his heart's delight at last.

The magnificent brocade wedding gown fell to the floor, the petticoats and corset quickly following. Gently, Ian unpinned the chignon at the nape of Merewyn's slender neck so that the golden hair spilled into his hands, its scent and softness exciting him even more. Burying his face in it he inhaled deeply, then hungrily sought her lips again, unwilling to let them go for even a moment.

Merewyn opened her eyes as Ian laid her gently onto the bed, enjoying despite herself the sight of his lean, muscular body hovering over her. His sun-browned arms rippled with muscles and she reached out wonderingly to touch them, mystified by the difference in his hard, masculine body and her soft, womanly one. Her large tilted eyes met his and he saw that there was no fear in them, only a banking passion, and he bent his head and allowed his lips to travel hungrily across her taut breasts. His strong hands roved her body, exploring her as he had twice before, and Merewyn found that she hungered for his touch, every sense aware of the pleasure he was arousing within her.

Her arms moved about his neck and she pressed her lips to his, her little tongue seeking and tasting, governed more by instinct than experience. Her response seemed to increase his own ardor and he placed his large hands about her small waist, pulling her beneath him, unable to wait any longer, his desire for her consuming him and driving him to the breaking point.

Despite his need Ian knew that he would hurt her if he gave way to utter abandon, and he forced himself to curb his mounting impatience. With passion-darkened eyes he looked down into Merewyn's heart-shaped face, framed by the golden curls he had always thought so beautiful. Her lips were still parted from his last kiss and the softness in her tilted, gold-flecked eyes brought a joy that was almost pain to his heart. With a groan he fell upon her, forgetting his intent to wait, but to his surprise she rose to meet him, quivering only slightly at the unexpected pain, but recovering quickly as he kissed and fondled her, murmuring endearments into her ear.

Then they were moving together, Merewyn unable to get enough of him, and as she pressed herself against the length of him, his burning need ignited deep within her a fire that had, until that moment, been only a small flame of her love for him. Then he was deep inside her, touching her in a way she had never dreamed possible, and an almost inaudible whimper of joy passed through her lips. Ian heard it nonetheless and caught her quivering body as close to his heart as he could so that they merged together in that final moment to forge an ecstasy neither could have equalled without the other.

Afterwards Merewyn lay still, starting slightly when she felt Ian's lips softly touch her cheek, and she opened her eyes to find his own so close that she could see the lingering fire still smoldering in their steely depths. His handsome visage was filled with a rare tenderness, the harshness that seemed such an integral part of his finely chiseled features no longer there, making her realize for the first time how gentle and unforbidding he could appear if he wished. Neither of them spoke, content merely to lie with their bodies touching, until Ian chuckled, a purely unaffected sound that warmed Merewyn's heart.

"What amuses you so?" she asked curiously.

One strong hand cupped her small chin so that he could kiss her hungrily. "If I had only given you those jewels weeks ago I could have spared myself quite a bit of trouble. Fie, ma'am, I didn't think MacAilises could be so easily bought."

Merewyn pressed her soft cheek against his lean one. "Oh, Ian, it wasn't the jewels! 'Twas what you said about—about a son."

He turned to look into her dark eyes and was delighted to see her blush. "Do you want children, Merewyn?"

"Aye," she responded shyly. "What you said made me realize for the first time that we were really and truly married and that we could start a family if we wished. I'd never given it any thought before, but suddenly I wanted very much to have sons." Again a rosy color spread across her smooth cheeks. "Your sons."

Ian laughed, but the sound was neither derisive nor mocking, and he took her delicate face in his hands and kissed her fondly, then more lingeringly. Merewyn moved closer so that they were lying against one another, then shifted so that he fit easily between her soft thighs. With a contented sigh she gave in to his insistent demands and let him love her once again.

"Well, your omnipotence, what are we going to do now?"

"Stop being so sarcastic, will you? You're giving me a headache."

Elizabeth Comerford massaged her aching temples with long, rosy-tipped fingers and gave William, who was staring down at her with annoyance, a withering look. "Just let me think a moment. I'll come up with something."

"Your plans aren't going to alter the facts." William gestured irritably at a piece of paper lying on the small table at which Elizabeth was sitting. "He's taken her to Ravensley two days early. For all we know they may even be married by now."

It was ten in the morning of a humid, overcast day, and William had burst into Elizabeth's sitting room without invitation, surprising her as she lounged on the chaise in nothing more than a lawn night rail and bed-jacket. Slamming the door shut in the face of her scandalized maid, he had overridden her own protests by tossing the letter at her accusingly.

"When did you receive this?" Elizabeth asked, reading it a second time.

"Not fifteen minutes ago. 'Twas delivered by some redheaded tyke who said Merewyn had given it to him with express orders that 'twas to be brought to me at once."

"But according to this they left yesterday," Elizabeth pointed out.

William scowled impatiently. "I know that! The lad said he'd not been able to slip away until now. Faugh, I hope the delay hasn't cost us everything!"

The pale green eyes began to glitter speculatively. "I seriously doubt it has."

The anger in William's bony countenance vanished as he looked down into the classically beautiful features of the chestnut-haired woman before him. "I take it you know what to do about this?"

"Certainly. For one thing, this letter proves our assumption was correct."

"And how does it prove that?"

Elizabeth sighed impatiently. "Honestly, William, sometimes your inability to grasp the obvious can be so tiresome! It simply means," she added quickly, seeing the darkened brow and the heavy-lidded eyes beginning to burn with anger, "that Ian is really planning to marry her against her wishes. If she had chosen to come to England of her own free will she would have dismissed your letter as nonsense and thought nothing more of it. But here she states that they are leaving for Surrey and that she wishes you to contact her as soon as possible. Doesn't that tell you she needs your help?"

William nodded slowly, then with growing conviction. "Aye, aye, it does!" Eagerly he added, "What do we do now?"

Elizabeth was silent for a moment, thinking, letting nothing distract her, especially William's unwinking stare that reminded her of the eyes of a hound begging a tidbit from his master. "You will go to Surrey immediately and spirit the young lady to safety," she said at last.

William snorted derisively. "Aye, and beg Lord Montague for a by-your-leave, or perhaps even for the use of one of his carriages."

Elizabeth's tone was cold. "Ian will not be there. He'll be here, in London."

Despite his skepticism, William was forced to marvel at his accomplice's ingenuity. Sitting there looking ethereally beautiful with her gleaming brown hair coiled in a thick braid over one shoulder, it was hard to believe she was plotting so dastardly a deed. Dastardly? Nay, far from it! He was risking the wrath of a dangerous and enigmatic man to rescue a young woman from a distressful situation. Dastardly? He'd call it noble!

"How do you propose to bring Montague back to

London?" he asked, suddenly feeling very bold and invincible.

"This letter," Elizabeth replied, picking it up and smiling in satisfaction, "will be our bait. I will have it delivered to Ravensley at once. If I know Ian well enough, and I believe I do, he will come here immediately to seek you out. You will have conveniently returned to Scotland, so the housekeeper will inform the irate Marquis when he arrives, whereas in truth you'll be waiting not far from Ravensley to take advantage of his absence."

"And then?" William prompted, not really liking the sound of things, wanting to avoid giving the Marquis knowledge of his existence if it was at all possible.

Elizabeth shrugged. "I can't predict either of their reactions. Quite a bit depends on how you handle yourself, but I imagine that Miss MacAilis will be so relieved to see you that she'll agree at once to go away with you before Ian returns."

William frowned doubtfully. "I'm not sure that will be the case."

The green eyes stared up at him contemptuously. "I never promised you 'twould be easy, especially when you're dealing with a man like the Marquis. If you want her badly enough you'll risk it."

"And what about you?" William asked after a brief pause.

Elizabeth gave a secret smile of satisfaction, for William's lack of courage had worried her all along. Now that she knew that she had him firmly hooked she could have crowed with delight. Soon, now, Ian would again be hers. "Naturally I'll be waiting for him when he gets to London, and when he learns that his dear little bride has left him at the altar he'll need quite a bit of comforting."

"For which you have considerable talent," William agreed, permitting his hand to caress her smooth cheek.

"Don't worry," he laughed when she moved involuntarily away, "I'm interested in only one particular blue-eyed witch."

"Then 'tis settled. I'll have the letter sent immediately, for there's little time to lose, and I'd advise you to be in Surrey by nightfall. There's a small village not far from the manor house called Farthingdale with a reputable inn, but be certain you don't give your real name."

"Believe me," William assured her, kissing her hand in farewell, "I wouldn't dream of making such a foolish mistake."

Watching him saunter out the door Elizabeth decided that she wasn't so sure.

"Here, let me help you with that."

Merewyn turned quickly when her small hand was taken by a large, deeply browned one, and allowed the pruning shears to be gently pried from her grasp. Ian was standing beside her, his lean cheek close to hers, and she found herself blushing when she recalled their love-making of the night before, how she had responded to his gentle touch and impassioned kisses time and again before drifting off to a deep, restful slumber.

He had been gone when she awoke the next morning, the door between their rooms firmly closed, but Merewyn had been content to spend a few minutes alone, stretching and yawning deliciously in the big bed before Marty arrived with her breakfast tray. Though it was a sultry morning with leaden clouds obscuring the sun, Merewyn had wandered restlessly outdoors after eating where the beautiful roses in the garden had caught her eye. She had been cutting the sweetly scented blossoms and laying them into a basket she carried beneath one arm when Ian had surprised her from behind.

Rather than releasing her now that he had the shears in his possession, he lifted her hand to his lips and pressed a kiss into her palm, his gray eyes holding hers.

"You could hurt yourself," he admonished. "I'll cut them for you."

"There are so many different colors," Merewyn observed, the gold-flecked depths of her eyes alive with emotions as she stared back at him, her soft lips so inviting that Ian could not resist stealing a kiss from them.

"Roses were my mother's favorites," he told her, snipping a long stem of a barely opened blood-red rose and tucking it in the front of her pale blue muslin frock after carefully removing the thorns.

"I like them very much," Merewyn said, smiling up at him shyly, still somewhat unaccustomed to this new-found love that had sprung up between them, "but they aren't my favorites."

"Then what are?" Ian asked, tucking her arm beneath his and strolling with her towards another bed of perfumed flowers. "Tell me and I shall have them planted by evening."

Merewyn laughed, her tilted eyes filled with love as she gazed up at him, unable to credit the change in him. He looked the same as ever to her, handsome and domineering in his nankeen breeches and small clothes, the breeze ruffling his dark hair, and yet the harshness in his hawkish features was somehow gone and she sensed with a deep feeling of contentment that she would never fear him again.

"I fear you will be unable to obtain the flowers I love best, my lord."

"Nonsense. There is naught on this earth impossible for me to obtain."

"These, aye. 'Tis the heather I love, and the bluebells and mountain gentian, the arnicas and broom."

"So what you are really trying to tell me," he said, turning her about to face him, "is that you are homesick for the things I can't give you here."

Merewyn nodded, dropping her eyes from the burning intensity of his, suddenly desperately afraid of the naked emotions she saw there, afraid that for him they were merely the lingering results of a physical need she had satisfied for him with her body.

"I believe we should wait a few more days," Ian said, wondering at the shadow that crossed fleetingly over the delicate features and wishing he had the means to keep it from appearing ever again. " 'Tis highly likely your brothers are on their way to London and I believe they'd be extremely angry if they came all this way only to discover we were already gone."

"Then you'll take me?" Merewyn breathed, scarcely daring to hope.

Ian found it difficult to tear his gaze away from the enormous pleading eyes, their golden depths seeming to hypnotize him. "Were you thinking I'd intended to make you a prisoner here?" he teased.

He heard her sharp intake of breath and cursed himself, aware that his past transgressions wouldn't be as quickly forgotten as he would like. But then she smiled at him so saucily that he felt his heart skip a beat.

"Surely you don't believe you could contain me, m'lord?"

"I have long ago learned 'tis useless to pit myself against you, my dear," he assured her with a grin. "Can you curb your impatience for another week?"

He felt two slender arms curl themselves about his neck and drank in the scent of her as she pressed her soft lips to his. "If you make my stay worthwhile," Merewyn replied, her face buried in the softness of his muslin shirt, "aye."

Arm in arm they strolled back indoors, Ian marveling at the change in Merewyn, his wife, who seemed to have forgotten in the course of an enchanted evening her animosity and fear, and had emerged as a teasing, delightful creature who could hold him captive with only one compelling look from her shining blue eyes.

"I've been a total fool," Merewyn confessed unexpectedly, her voice a whisper so that he had to bend down to catch her words.

"Crude, impolite, obstinate, and rebellious, aye, but never a fool," he assured her with a crooked smile.

Merewyn leaned with a sigh against his muscular arm. "Oh, Ian, I'm being serious! If only I'd admitted to myself sooner what I discovered last night I could have saved both of us a great deal of heartache."

"And what did you discover, my sweet, saucy wench?"

Shyness overwhelmed her a second time and she faltered, "That I didn't h-hate you as much as I thought I did."

Ian's clear laugh rang through the sultry air. "And a finer confession of love I've yet to hear. In that, my sweet, I believe we can both be found guilty. I fear you and I are too proud for our own good."

In the doorway leading from the terrace to the parlor he pulled her against him, covering her mouth with his, and Merewyn stood on the tips of her toes, her arms entwined about his neck, returning his kiss with an ardor that amazed and delighted him.

"Here, now, you'll be crushing them roses!" came Marty's chiding voice.

Both turned, Merewyn blushing furiously while Ian smiled arrogantly, his arms still about her.

"There is only one flower on earth I intend to treat gently, and she's far lovelier than any rose," he told the old woman sternly.

Marty's faded eyes danced as she took in the young couple before her, never in her fondest dreams having believed she would ever see the Marquis find so much contentment in life. Where others had come to view Lord Montague as a hard, callous man, Marty, who perhaps knew him better than anyone else, had always suspected that his restless loneliness and yearning for

peace had been the cause of his arrogant, unap-
proachable demeanor. 'Twas what had driven him to sea
years ago and had prompted him to forsake his home
and friends for the wilds of the Scottish Highlands, a
sojourn that had apparently netted him far more than an
inheritance.

"Let me put them in water," Marty suggested, bustling forward to take the basket out of the Marquis's
hand. "And you've got visitors, too," she added over
her shoulder. "I was just comin' to tell you."

"Who is it?" Ian asked, annoyed.

"Master Wyland and his daughters, come to congratulate you on your wedding, I'd imagine."

"Who are they?" Merewyn asked curiously as the
Marquis groaned.

"Neighbors. Mr. Wyland has been hoping for years
I'd marry one of his daughters."

"Why didn't you?" she asked insolently as he led her
towards the withdrawing room where Marty had seated
them.

"You'll find out soon enough." His hand closed over
hers. "I expect you to behave, ma'am."

"I shall be the model hostess," she promised, laughter
lurking in her tilted eyes when she looked up at him.
"Am I presentable enough to receive our first visitors?"

He tried to find a flaw in her appearance and could
not. The heart-shaped face that was turned up to look
into his was achingly beautiful, the golden hair framing
it like a halo. His gaze traveled insolently to her creamy
bosom and narrow waist and he felt desire stir within
him, but reminded himself that he should concentrate
on the matters at hand.

"You look ugly as always. Now, please, inside with
you."

The Wyland trio was seated on the striped damask
sofa, two incredibly tall, reed thin young girls flanking
their equally gaunt papa. Mr. Wyland was sweating pro-

fusely in his heavily powdered wig and leather waistcoat, while his daughters fanned themselves vigorously with tiny ivory fans held in huge, ungainly paws. Both of them stared with ill-concealed envy at Merewyn, who was solicitously seated by her husband in an armchair facing them, and neither of them missed the caressing hand he let lie for a moment on her bare shoulder before bowing to their father.

"Thomas, 'tis kind of you to come."

"I couldn't believe the news when I heard it, even though it came from Reverend Braynock himself." Thomas Wyland had a thin, rasping voice, not at all in keeping with a man of his size. His sunken eyes fixed themselves mournfully on Merewyn. "As soon as they heard the girls pestered me to come meet your new wife. I take it this is she?"

"Indeed," Ian replied, his white teeth flashing as he gave Merewyn a smile which told her all too plainly that he was thoroughly bored already playing the role of proud newlywed. "May I present Merewyn Villiers, formerly a MacAilis of Glen Cairn, and now Marchioness of Montague?"

Where she had expected to feel a shudder of aversion at being called a Villiers, Merewyn felt only a small glow of pride that warmed her heart. She belonged to Ian now, and somehow the fact that she had vowed never to do so didn't seem quite that important anymore.

The Wyland girls, introduced as Letty and Lucinda, though Merewyn had no idea which was which, twittered their congratulations all the while studying her with baleful stares. Both of them had powdered and arranged their hair in styles suited to much older women and the gowns they wore of stiff, heavy crinoline were several years behind the current fashion. In comparison Merewyn reminded one of a graceful flower blossoming among dowdy weeds, but there was nothing condescending in her manner as she chatted with both of them, striving to put them at ease.

Ian, reclining in another armchair with his long legs comfortably crossed before him, watched her covertly from beneath heavy-lidded eyes that missed nothing. He found it difficult to believe Merewyn had not been born and nurtured in the bosom of London society, so flawless were her affectations of highborn snobbery and hostessing flair. Knowing the performance was mainly for his benefit, he was hard put not to laugh, marveling at the change in this child-woman he had believed in the past was a cold-hearted, truculent brat.

More surprising was the change in himself, for he had seriously believed that once his aching desire for the comely wench was sated he would have no further interest in her. How, then, to justify the quickening beat of his heart as he gazed longingly into her perfect features, her soft red lips teasing him to taste of their sweetness? Once he had thought the feelings within him were unsatisfied passions, but now he wasn't sure.

"Eh?" he asked peevishly, aware that one of the horse-faced Wyland girls had directed a question at him.

Lucinda blushed furiously, finding herself the target of his scrutinous gaze, then repeated her question in a breathless squeak. "I asked whether you and Lady Montague intend to make Ravensley your permanent home."

Ian could sense Merewyn's hopeful anticipation of his answer without even looking at her, and graced Lucinda with a smile that brought even more color to her Slavic cheekbones. "I seriously doubt my wife will permit us to settle anywhere else than in the Highlands."

"But 'tis so cold and lonely there!" Letitia protested while Lucinda nodded vigorous agreement.

"I'm certain we'll find enough amusements to help us pass the time," the Marquis replied while Merewyn hid her giggles behind her hand. There followed an uncomfortable silence, neither of the Wyland girls quite knowing how to respond to this, and after a few self-conscious remarks from their father, they took their dejected leave.

"How could you be so cruel to them?" Merewyn demanded as soon as they were alone in the drawing room.

Ian looked down at her with a mocking smile. "Cruel? I thought myself extremely gallant."

"You know exactly what I mean! Both of them are head over ears in love with you and you baited them unmercifully. God's blood, my lord, you didn't have to stare at me as though you were undressing me with your eyes!"

He seized her by the waist and pulled her to him, kissing her hungrily. " 'Twas all I could keep my mind on, ma'am. I'm sorry if I ruined your little social."

Laughingly Merewyn fended him off, though she found it difficult, what with the tips of her toes barely touching the floor as he lifted her into his strong arms and caressed her possessively. "Let me go," she commanded at last. "I want to see to luncheon. I'm starving."

"If I would have known that you'd eat me out of house and home I would have married someone else," Ian growled.

The tip of one dainty finger traced his firm chin lovingly. "Ah, but there you're wrong, m'lord." The indigo eyes danced. "You told me once yourself that we belong together, and I fear you'll rue those words some day."

"I believe I already do."

Marty had overseen the laying of the table for them and beamed happily when Merewyn entered the cheerful breakfast room and complimented her on the lovely arrangement of roses that graced the sideboard. "They be the ones you and his lordship picked this mornin'," she said with a contented sigh.

"They're beautiful," Merewyn murmured, burying her slim nose in the softness of the scented petals. "I wonder if they'll grow at Castle Montague?"

Marty's thin shoulders went up in a helpless shrug. "Lud, I couldn't tell you, dear. You'll have to ask the Marquis."

"Will you be coming to Scotland with us?" Merewyn asked hopefully.

"And what would I be doin' there all day long?" Marty asked sternly, though she had no intention of being left behind. "Master Ian outgrew any need for me years ago and only keeps me on because of the kindness of his heart. I'd be lonely with no one to talk to."

"What nonsense," Merewyn replied with a ghost of a smile, thinking how Marty and Annie would get on famously, grousing like two old magpies over their tea and fighting over the care of the bairns that would doubtless begin populating the nursery before long. Her clear blue eyes began to sparkle with anticipation. Aye, bairns she'd have, and all strapping lads to make their father proud!

Her attention was brought back to the present by the imposing figure of the Marquis, who strode past the open door, and she hurried after him, eagerly calling his name. "Do come eat with me!"

Ian turned with an apologetic smile, his hand resting on the latch of the study door. "I can't. I've got too much work to do."

Merewyn's expectant face clouded with disappointment. "But 'tis almost one o'clock!"

He returned to the doorway where she stood leaning dejectedly against the jamb and drew her tenderly into his arms. "An estate does not manage itself, my dear, and I've been away a long time."

Her little chin was obstinately raised. "I don't care. You can delay your work for one more hour, can't you?"

Ian gave an exasperated sigh that was belied by the twinkle in his dark gray eyes. "Very well, but I don't want you to get the false impression that you can manipulate me merely by pouting so prettily. I'll give in, but only this once."

"Truly, my lord," Merewyn exclaimed with a saucy smile, "you're a mutton-headed fool if you believe that!"

This time the sigh was far more serious. "I believe I am."

" 'Tis your own fault," Merewyn reminded him cruelly. "You were the one who forced me into this unwanted marriage."

His hands tightened a second time about her small waist and he pulled her towards him possessively. "Is it an unwanted marriage, Merewyn?" he asked.

Her gold-flecked eyes lingered on his sensual mouth. "N-no," she whispered rather breathlessly.

Satisfied, he let her go without giving her the kiss she had been expecting, flashing her a crooked smile when he saw her disappointed frown. "I charge you to remember that I'm not quite as besotted with you as you may think, ma'am."

"A pox on you eternally, m'lord Sassenach," Merewyn countered, flouncing past him towards the table, her hips swaying alluringly in the pale blue gown and bringing a flicker of answering fire to the steely depths of the Marquis's eyes.

Merewyn chatted engagingly throughout the meal, thus keeping Ian with her far longer than he would have liked, considering the amount of work he knew awaited him in the study. By the time he became aware of the hour he was astonished to find it almost four o'clock, and admonished his wife not to disturb him once he had sequestered himself with his ledgers and documents. Merewyn wisely decided to heed his warning, recalling that her brother always issued the same orders whenever he vanished into his study. Men, she thought disdainfully as he left her, promising to meet her for dinner, what was it about them that made them so tiresome?

The thunderstorm that had been threatening all day with lead-gray skies and ominous rumblings had never materialized, and Merewyn, rising from the table, was pleased to see a few errant rays of sunlight break through the oppressive layer of clouds. Stepping out onto the terrace she breathed deeply of the sweetly scented roses, then wandered down the tended paths toward the herb and ornamental gardens. Songbirds twittered in the ancient trees overhead and a warm breeze fanned the soft tendrils of golden hair that framed her delicate face.

If Ian's suspicions were true, Merewyn thought, then her brothers should be arriving any day now. What would they think of Ravensley, she wondered, turning to look admiringly at the imposing brick walls that rose from the treetops behind her. 'Twas a grand structure and one she would doubtless grow fond of as the years went by. Aye, she would ask Ian to take her here often, she decided, to escape the harsh Highland winters and to visit with Alicia, but nothing would ever take the place of Cairnlach in her heart.

And yet she would be living at Montague now, Merewyn reminded herself, pausing to sniff the fragrant blossoms of the honeysuckle that grew wild along the garden walls. Instead of pain and trepidation, the thought of going there excited her. 'Twas odd, she mused, how quickly she had come to accept the fact that she was now a Villiers, and although she would never erase her hatred for Ian's uncle, she had nonetheless come to the realization that there were more important things in life than blind clan pride and feudal hatred for an enemy. Her love for Ian had somehow made all of the past unimportant and she was prepared for a future of peaceful coexistence between her old family and her new one, thinking with a rueful smile that this was what Alexander had tried to convince her to do months ago.

"I believe I'm growing up," Merewyn told herself

with a lighthearted chuckle, the gravity of her thoughts amusing her. Aye, and it had taken the love of a man named Villiers to show her that her hatred and fear had been misguided and ill-founded. How astonished her brothers would be to hear her tell them such things, but Merewyn was forced to admit that she had not learned her lessons without suffering.

"Psst, yer ladyship!"

She whirled about, startled by the unexpected whisper, and retreated a step when she saw a young man in rough homespun step out onto the garden path from the dense hedgerow behind her. He couldn't have been much older than herself, but his shoulders were already stooped from long years of work in the fields and his face was burned from the sun; his thick mop of unkempt hair was bleached a color similar to her own.

"Who are you? What do you want?" Merewyn demanded, striving to sound like the bold, affronted lady of the manor while hiding her concern, certain that this was not a servant in the Marquis's employ. What, then, was he doing on Ravensley grounds?

The young man halted at a reassuring distance and respectfully pulled at his forelock. "Beggin' yer pardon, be ye Lady Montague?"

"I am," Merewyn acknowledged hesitantly, and as she studied his shabby appearance she began to feel her fear dissipating. "Do you wish to speak to me or my husband?" she asked more kindly. "He—"

"No, no, m'lady!" The brown eyes widened with fear. "I was told not to let 'is lordship know I was 'ere!"

Fresh suspicions sprang into Merewyn's mind and she asked sharply, "Then why are you here?"

He fumbled into the front of his greasy vest and drew out a folded piece of paper that he extended with a dirty hand. "I was told to deliver this to ye an' no one else."

"Who is it from?" Merewyn asked, making no move to take it from him.

"Gentleman at the inn, yer ladyship. Wouldn't give me 'is name. Said I'd be paid double if I got this to ye without anyone seein'."

A certain dread was beginning to rise within her heart and she stepped closer to take the paper from him. Her large blue eyes met his. "Did he say you were to wait for a reply?"

The young lad swallowed, never having gazed into eyes of such a brilliant color, convinced that the Marchioness of Montague was more beautiful than any angel he'd ever seen in pictures. "No, yer ladyship, but 'e said if yer was wantin' to send word to 'im ye were to go through me as I knows where to find 'im. Name's Jackie Wilson, yer ladyship, an' my pa's the Farthingdale smith."

Merewyn could scarcely control her agitation, the paper in her small hand seeming to burn her fingers, for she knew without a shadow of a doubt who had written it. "Thank you, Jackie."

He pulled at his forelock again, bowed awkwardly, and then vanished through the shrubbery as silently as he had come. Merewyn waited until she was alone in the garden, then unfolded the missive with trembling fingers. The note was brief and hastily written, informing her that he had arrived and was eagerly awaiting an audience with her whenever she could make arrangements to see him.

Merewyn read the blunt note through several times, her cheeks deathly pale, a dreadful numbness creeping into her heart. 'Twould be all over between Ian and herself if he ever learned that she had been in gaol. 'Twould make him the laughingstock of all London, and to a man with the Marquis's pride that would be unforgiveable. He would despise her forever. Two days ago she wouldn't have hesitated to send William Rawlings packing, or threatened to use her new status as the Marchioness of Montague to press charges against him for his criminal accusations, but now she wanted only to save the man she loved from the scandal and to bury forever the shame of her dark secret.

Picking up a stick that the brisk winds had blown from a chestnut tree earlier that morning, Merewyn scratched in the damp earth near the brick wall until she had dug a sizeable hole. Carefully, she tore the letter into countless tiny scraps and buried them, placing a large rock over the small mound of dirt to hide the signs of fresh activity from the gardeners. Dusting off her hands she stared down at her handiwork with a worried frown on her comely features. What form of blackmail would William Rawlings demand of her? Money, social advancement?

A shudder ran through her slim body as she remembered the revolting feeling of his slobbering mouth coming down on hers. Suppose he demanded something else from her? Something she would rather die than give? There had been no mistaking his interest in her that day she had regained consciousness in his coach to find him gazing down at her with a lustful gleam in his heavy-lidded eyes.

If only she could settle the matter in the proper way, by making it known that she had been wrongly accused when she was thrown into gaol, and that William himself deserved to be imprisoned. But her innocence would matter little to gleeful gossip mongers who would bandy the tale about every fashionable drawing room in London. Merewyn felt sure that Ian had made enough enemies in his stormy youth who would greatly relish the opportunity of finding fault with the mightly Lord Montague, and she herself was not immune from the hatred of women like Elizabeth Comerford.

A low moan of anguish fell from her lips. No sense in tormenting herself this way, she reminded herself. First, she would have to arrange to see William to learn exactly what he wanted from her, and lay her plans then. Her small chin lifted in sudden determination. She wasn't about to let him destroy the newfound happiness between Ian and herself. She was a MacAilis, after all, and a Marchioness, and she would use all the power and wealth behind her name and title to defeat the wretched man who was so determined to ruin her.

"Merewyn, what the devil are you doing?"

She looked up quickly to find the Marquis striding towards her, his dark hair blowing in the wind that, to her surprise, had increased noticeably in the last few minutes.

"Marty told me you'd gone outside," Ian added, reaching her side. "She was worried you'd be caught in the rain. Don't you realize 'twill start any moment?"

Merewyn glanced up at the dark clouds scuttling across the sky, realizing for the first time that the very air was charged with the impending storm. "I'm sorry," she murmured, "I didn't notice."

One muscular arm slid about her slender shoulders, his hawkish features filled with concern as he leaned down to peer into her face. "Merewyn, what is it?"

She smiled up at him reassuringly. "Nothing. I guess I was so lost in thought I didn't see the storm coming."

"I never realized I'd married a wench too stupid to come in out of the rain," Ian said, relieved to see her smile. "Come on, or we'll both get wet." He broke off abruptly. "Devil take it, Merewyn, can't you take a simple walk through the garden without getting filthy?" He turned over one small hand that was grimy with dirt. "And look at your gown! 'Tis streaked with mud!"

Merewyn laughed weakly, her tilted blue eyes sliding away from his. "I am a mess, aren't I?"

Ian's full lips twitched as he took in her bedraggled appearance. "What a child you are," he told her fondly, then seized her hand as the first big raindrops pelted them, and pulled her back up the path and indoors just as a torrent began to fall. "Now go upstairs and change," he told her sternly, standing with his hands on his narrow hips, glowering down at her from his great height. "Better yet, take a bath. I don't want you soiling my furniture."

"What about dinner?" Merewyn asked doubtfully, relieved that he had noticed nothing amiss, determined to behave as normally as possible. Under the circumstances she found it rather difficult, but if he noticed the strain in her gold-flecked eyes or heard it in her voice he said nothing.

" 'Twill have to wait. Damn," he growled, "I can see that marriage is going to be a tiresome affair for me."

Suddenly overwhelmed with love for him, and desperately afraid to lose him, Merewyn slipped her arms about his powerful neck and pressed herself against him. "Oh, Ian, I promise never to cause you trouble or do anything to make you ashamed of me!"

Surprised by the throbbing passion in the little voice that came out muffled against his shirtfront, and filled with rare tenderness, he held her slim body close and whispered reassuringly, "I wasn't serious, my lass, my love. Don't tell me I've already broken that staunch MacAilis arrogance? I find that hard to believe."

Merewyn tilted back her head to look at him and Ian was startled to find tears glittering in her indigo eyes. Her pert tone, however, informed him that naught was amiss. "Swell-headed Sassenach, do you honestly think you can break me?"

He laughed, reassured, as she had hoped him to be, and drew her clinging arms away, then patted her firmly on the buttocks with the palm of one big hand. "Hurry, now, I'm fair starved. Marty will have the bath brought up right away and I expect you to be finished within an hour."

"Aye, aye, Lord Longshanks," she said over one dainty shoulder and hurried up the stairs. It was fortunate for the Marquis that he did not see the expression of hopelessness and despair in her young face.

The warm scented water in the brass hip bath did much to calm Merewyn's frazzled nerves. Soaking her body, she closed her eyes and could almost dismiss William Rawlings's presence in the nearby village as insignificant. Nothing mattered at the moment save for the soothing water lapping about her limbs and the melodic tapping of the rain on the windowpanes. Tomorrow she'd worry about William, Merewyn promised herself, for tonight she intended to devote all her time to pleasing Ian and making him happy.

Her eyes flew open at the thought of the Marquis and his warning that she had better appear downstairs for dinner within the hour. Rising quickly from the tub, she reached for the soft towel Marty had laid out for her, the water running in rivulets down her pink, freshly scrubbed skin. She dried herself hurriedly, and as she rubbed the moisture from her long, tapering legs, she heard the door behind her closing softly. Thinking it was Marty, she turned to assure the older woman that she was making haste, but the protest froze on her lips when she found herself gazing up at the Marquis's towering form.

Merewyn grew still, the towel in her hands, seemingly unashamed of her nakedness as her dark eyes boldly met his. A pleased smile curved Ian's full lips as he became aware that she no longer feared him, and he came towards her, unable to tear his eyes away from the beauty of her slender form.

"I came to find out what was keeping you, my dear," he murmured huskily, "and I must confess that I'm rather pleased that you dallied."

"I didn't mean to keep you waiting," Merewyn said apologetically, though her voice sounded vague, as though she were paying her words little mind. Ian's eyes roved hungrily over the features of her upturned face as he moved closer so that his strong brown hands slid unexpectedly about her hips, caressing her smooth flesh with obvious longing.

" 'Twas well worth it," he told her meaningfully.

Merewyn slapped his hands away, smiling up at him coquettishly. "Really, m'lord, I'm beginning to believe you have only one thing on your mind."

His lips nibbled playfully at her neck. "At least I admit it freely."

"But dinner's waiting," Merewyn protested rather breathlessly.

"We answer to no one, Merewyn," Ian reminded her roughly before covering her mouth with his, parting her lips and kissing her deeply, causing a small flame to leap within her. Effortlessly he lifted her nude body into his powerful arms and laid her gently on the bed, and she sighed in contentment when he laid down at her side, the heat from his body making her shiver with delicious anticipation.

"Tell me that you'd rather have me love you than dine on leg of lamb," he commanded between kisses, his strong hands roving her confidently.

"You know I do," Merewyn murmured against his chest, her body growing ever pliant beneath his experienced touch.

A deep, triumphant laugh rumbled in his chest and he pulled her closer to him so that their hearts were beating against each other. For a moment both of them lay quite still, content to savor the intimacy that had sprung up between them; then Ian slid his arm beneath her and pulled her against him.

"My passionate little Merewyn," he whispered fondly, although there was a note of wonder in his voice.

Merewyn looked up at him curiously to find the gray eyes close, the expression on his handsome features one of tenderness and longing. Reaching up she caressed his lean cheek and he caught her slender hand in his big one and pressed a kiss into her palm.

"What is it?" Merewyn asked curiously. "What are you thinking of?"

"Of your avowed dislike for me, my love, and how hard it is for me to accept that those beautiful eyes of yours are looking at me without their usual blazing hatred."

"But you'll try to accept it, won't you, my lord?" Merewyn demanded archly, running her hand through the dark, wiry hair covering the rippling muscles of his wide chest.

Ian looked down into the delicate little face, delighted to see the glowing brilliance of those captivatingly tilted eyes. Merewyn's lips were parted, inviting him boldly to partake of their sweetness, and he pressed her body against the hard length of his, enjoying the warmth and softness of her skin and the feel of her small buttocks beneath his seeking hands.

"I'll try my best," Ian assured her hoarsely, and Merewyn felt herself growing weak with longing as he pressed his lips against hers, demanding a response she was only too willing to give. Her own desire made her bold and she ran her hands down his strong, muscular back, caressing him until he could scarcely think for the want of her, his kisses growing deeper, his breathing harsh and irregular.

Rolling her onto her back, Ian's big hands lingered about Merewyn's small waist, his dark head bent over her as his lips tasted her taut nipples. Merewyn sighed with pleasure as his hands slid up to caress their rounded fullness, his tongue both teasing and demanding. His sure, experienced touch was rough and yet gentle at the same time, luring her towards an end she no longer feared but awaited eagerly, sensing deep within her heart that Ian Villiers alone of all men could take her there.

Wanting to please him as he pleased her, eager to share with him her own mounting passion, Merewyn slid her hand across his hard, flat belly to caress him intimately, and Ian fell back with a groan, unable to credit the ardent response he had ignited within her. His loins on fire, he seized her hips and pulled her to him, fitting her slender form between his legs and Merewyn arched herself against him, enjoying the feel of his burning hardness against her soft flesh.

Then Ian was lying above her, poised to plunder the inviting sweetness of her woman's body, but he forced himself to wait, wanting to savor this moment of unparalleled intimacy. Staring down into the indigo eyes that had grown dark with a sultry passion he had never seen, Ian saw also her dawning realization of her own sexual awareness, a growing confidence of her ability to please him and her ability to contribute shamelessly of herself towards the ultimate consummation of their love.

Merewyn looked up and, meeting Ian's smoldering gaze, smiled at him softly, her slender thighs spreading beneath his, beckoning him to take everything she was capable of offering. Ian bent his head and felt her lips meet his in a stirring kiss, their tongues touching and tasting, and suddenly he was unable to resist any longer her impassioned invitation.

There was no pain at all for Merewyn as Ian thrust deep inside her, only a timeless moment of joy and the thrill of knowing how much he wanted her and that he wanted her only. He groaned as he felt her rise to meet him. Her slender arms entwined themselves around his powerful neck and her soft lips yielded further so that Ian was able to drink to the fullest of their incredible sweetness. He felt heady with the need to possess her, wanting to touch her even more intimately, to make her a part of him, and he drove deeper, his mind on fire, clutching her to him, his heart pounding.

Merewyn responded measure for measure to his heightened passion until she felt certain that the burning heat of their flesh wherever they touched would ul-

ELLEN TANNER MARSH

timately consume them. She moved against him, driven half wild by his touch, convinced that nothing in her wildest dreams could rival her love for this man.

"Oh, God, Ian," she whispered, feeling a terrible need to express the tumultuous emotions beginning to build within her, but Ian allowed her to say nothing more, catching her even closer to him, his powerful arms about her, his mouth crushing hers, until suddenly they were riding together on the crest of a wave of pure sensation, hurled to unbelievable, dizzying heights where ultimately Ian's final possession of her planted deep within Merewyn's body the promise of new life forged uniquely from their deep and everlasting love.

CHAPTER ELEVEN

"M'lady! M'lady, please wake up!"

The urgent plea penetrated instantly into Merewyn's deep sleep, bringing her abruptly to her senses. "What is it?" she asked, her voice groggy. Opening her eyes she could make out the small form of Martha Simpson standing at the foot of her bed, her gnarled hands twisted nervously together, a look of utter despair on her kindly, wrinkled face.

"What is it, Marty?" Merewyn repeated, sitting up.

" 'Tis his lordship!" Marty cried woefully.

Cold panic gripped Merewyn's heart. "Has he been hurt?"

"No, no, m'lady! He's gone off to London!"

The large blue eyes widened with disbelief. "To London? Now?" Merewyn glanced at the clock ticking on the mantel and saw that it was barely six. Pale silver light fell through a slit in the heavy drapes, heralding the dawn, and awakening pigeons cooed complacently in the eaves.

"Did he tell you why? Marty, whatever is the matter with you?"

"Oh, m'lady, I just don't know!" The faded brown eyes filled with sudden tears. "I've never seen him so angry!"

Merewyn slipped out of bed and impulsively put her arms about the older woman. "Why, Marty, 'tis nothing!" she comforted. "Sit down here and tell me what's upset you."

Pushing Marty gently into a chair nearby, Merewyn returned to her bed and seated herself on the satin coverlet, hugging her knees and pushing the golden curls out of her eyes. In her short stay at Ravensley she had never known Marty to be anything other than a competent, cheerful administrator, and she was greatly distressed to see how agitated she appeared now.

"You say Ian's not hurt?" she asked again, a worried frown wrinkling her smooth brow.

Marty's graying head bobbed a vigorous affirmative. "Oh, he's not hurt, m'lady. 'Tis his mood what worries me. I just know 'tis that letter what arrived for him this morning!"

"A letter? At this hour? Who was it from?"

Marty threw up her hands in defeat. "Dear Lord, I wish I knew! I opened the door myself—you know I'm always up at first light—and 'twas a private messenger said he'd come from London with a letter for the Marquis. I told him his lordship was still sleeping but there he appears behind me saying, 'I'm here, Marty, and I'll takes care of it,' so I left the two of 'em be." Her hands resumed their nervous twisting in her lap. "Not two minutes later he comes stormin' into the parlor where I'm doing some darning and tells me he's off for London. In all the years I've known him I've never seen him so out of sorts! Frightened me proper, it did."

Merewyn's misgivings increased. "Do you have any idea what that letter said? Did he tell you why he was going?"

"No, m'lady," Marty replied mournfully. "He had it in his hand and he wouldn't let me see it or tell me what 'twas about. When I asked he almost snapped my head off. Said I was a n-nosy old woman and he'd d-dismiss me if I said another word to him." She buried her face in her hands and her stooped shoulders shook. "Oh, m'lady, I ain't never heard him speak that way to me. Not ever!"

Merewyn felt compassion stir her heart. "Something awful must have upset him, Marty, and I'm sure he didn't mean to take it out on you." The indigo eyes clouded with worry. "I hope nothing terrible has happened. Ohh!" She gasped as a thought struck her, the color draining from her holoow cheeks.

"What is it, dear?" Marty asked, forgetting her own misery and hurrying to the big bed where she took Merewyn's cold hands consolingly in hers.

Merewyn's soft voice quavered. "Y-you don't think something has happened to my brothers? They're due in London any day now."

Marty's competent air returned now that she was able to channel her thoughts and energies towards the care of another human being. "Oh, what nonsense, your ladyship! 'Twouldn't have made the Marquis angry, which he most certainly was, and besides, he would have told you if that was the case!"

"Aye, I suppose you're right," Merewyn agreed, relieved. "But what could possibly have made him so angry? Don't you have any idea where that messenger came from?"

Marty shook her head sorrowfully. "He had on a uniform, but the good Lord knows, there be countless liveries for every household in London and I don't know half of them!"

Merewyn sighed deeply and began plaiting her long strands of hair with deft yet slightly trembling fingers. "I imagine the only thing we can do is wait until he comes back." Her heart went out to Ian, wishing that he had confided in her so that she might have shared this apparent crisis with him. "Will you get my habit please, Marty? Since I've been abandoned for an unknown length of time I might as well amuse myself with a ride."

Marty nodded, noticing that her young mistress's smile was extremely hollow, and her heart filled with pity and renewed dread. 'Twas true, she'd never seen the Marquis so enraged before, and heaven help the poor lass if his temper had something to do with her!

An hour later, with the sun shining down from a cloudless sky, Merewyn turned her mount across the arched bridge and down the road that led towards the village of Farthingdale. Her mood was bleak and she found her thoughts preoccupied more with Ian's abrupt departure than the visit to William Rawlings that awaited her, an opportunity she felt she must take now that the Marquis was conveniently absent.

Marty had informed her that the Marquis had given orders that she was not to ride out without proper escort, but Merewyn had overruled his demands, her arrogantly flashing blue eyes and haughty beauty turning the groom's determination to accompany her into stammering acquiescence. No one must know of her destination, least of all a servant who might feel it his duty to report to his employer that Lady Montague was making clandestine calls while he was away in London.

Merewyn's spirits rose for the first time since Marty had awakened her with her startling news. Perhaps Ian's absence was a blessing in disguise. If she could conclude her business with William Rawlings in this one meeting, the chances were good that Ian would never learn about her sordid past. With renewed optimism she urged her briskly trotting mare into a canter, covering the distance between Ravensley and Farthingdale in less than half an hour.

The smithy was located at the far end of the village square, a small cluster of buildings standing beneath towering shade trees. As Merewyn dismounted she was greeted by the crisp smell of smoke and the dull clanging of metal on metal, accompanied by the fearful snorting of a nervous horse and the muffled oaths of someone trying to subdue him. She peered through the entrance of the building but could see nothing at all in the dark interior, for she was blinded by the bright sunshine outside.

"Hello!" she called at last, and a moment later Jackie Wilson emerged from the gloom, bared to the waist, his breeches stained with soot. Merewyn's appearance startled him and his eyes grew round as he took in her trim figure encased in the biscuit-brown habit, the small jacket fitting snugly over her hips, a tiny hat sitting at a jaunty angle on top of her golden curls.

"Lady Montague!" he breathed, growing red-faced with shame at his own untidy, half-naked appearance.

"Hello, Jackie," Merewyn said with a smile, greeting him as though nothing was at all improper about their meeting. "I hope I'm not disturbing you."

He case an irritable glance into the darkness of the smithy behind him where the sounds of struggle between man and beast continued. "No, yer ladyship. Pa's busy with one o' Mr. Wyland's studs and he be a right stupid beastie to be sure."

. Merewyn assumed that Jackie was referring to the horse and not to his father, and nodded her head understandingly. "Oh, I've met Mr. Wyland, and I seriously doubt he has the proper disposition for handling a stallion."

The thin face lit with happiness, delighted to learn that the new Marchioness clearly understood something about the schooling of horses. "Aye, m'lady, that be what pa says." He cast another glance over his shoulder. "My brother's with 'im now and they can finish without me. I'll run a message over to the inn for ye." His color heightened considerably and he added humbly, "If that be why ye came, m'lady."

"Actually, I want you to take me to him, Jackie." The young man's jaw went slack and he blushed so

fiercely that it overshadowed the redness of his sun-
burned skin. "To the inn to see 'im, m'lady?"

Merewyn decided she would have to take a firm
stand. Raising her small chin she nodded determinedly.
"Aye, Jackie. We have something important to discuss."

Jackie scratched his head, trying hard to come up with
a suitable alternative. Didn't matter how early 'twas,
there'd be enough people up to see the Marchioness
going into the inn, and he wasn't about to expose such
a sweet and beautiful lady to any gossip, especially from
the proprietess Mrs. Tankersley, the old busybody.

"Will ye come with me, m'lady?" he asked hopefully,
his face clearing. "Ye can wait in the churchyard and I'll
fetch 'im to ye. Ain't nobody there today except the sex-
ton and 'e keeps to 'isself."

Merewyn accepted his proposal and he took the
mare's reins and walked with her the short distance to
the church, which stood upon a small knoll not too far
from the smithy. It was a pleasant structure of wood and
stone surrounded on all sides by trees and hedges. The
mare was tied to the post outside and Jackie made a
grand show of opening the small iron gate to permit
Merewyn entry into the cemetery.

"I'll be back quick as can be," he promised, and disappeared through the shrubs in the back of the grave-
yard. Merewyn, who was beginning to grow nervous
now that she was actually going to meet William Rawlings face to face, wandered restlessly about, peering
down at the tombstones and reading the names and
dates inscribed there without really seeing them at all.
The names meant nothing to her, and although she
spent several minutes trying to find the Villiers vault she
could not and decided that the family site must be located somewhere near the tiny Norman chapel at
Ravensley.

The sun was rising higher into the sky and she was
growing hot and fatigued. Seating herself on a marble
bench under the cooling shade of a spreading oak,

Merewyn fanned herself with her gloves and closed her eyes, wishing the interview she dreaded was already behind her. The sound of voices disturbed her reverie a few minutes later and she opened her eyes to see Jackie and another man approaching the entrance to the churchyard. There was no mistaking William Rawlings's reed-thin form nor the bony features and groomed mustache. He was impeccably dressed in a scarlet coat and buckskin breeches, his black boots highly polished, a tricorn sitting on top of his carefully tended periwig.

Merewyn's heart began to hammer at the sight of him and she rose quickly to her feet, nervously wetting her lips and trying her utmost to compose herself. Catching sight of her beneath the trees, William spoke a few brief words with Jackie, who slipped away in the direction of the smithy, then reached down to open the gate and came towards her with a pleasant smile on his thin lips.

"My dear Miss MacAilis," he said, coming to a halt before her and lifting her limp hand to his lips. "I must confess I was astonished to find Jackie at my door so early in the morning."

Merewyn hid her revulsion behind a tremulous smile, withdrawing her hand from his as discreetly as she could. "I am Lady Montague, now," she informed William coolly.

His brown eyes held hers. "Aye, I thought as much. Jackie called you 'her ladyship' when referring to you and I assumed naturally that the worst had already happened."

He gave her what he thought was his most disarming smile while his eyes hungrily roved the perfection of her heart-shaped face and the slimness of her figure in the becoming habit she wore. Inwardly he was rather shaken by her disclosure of marriage, but was nonetheless determined to overcome that hurdle. After all, she had turned to him for help, hadn't she, and marriages could still be annulled in this day and age despite the public furor it might cause.

"Shall we sit down?" he invited, indicating the bench Merewyn had just vacated.

"I'd rather stand," she said firmly, deciding that she must take the upper hand or else all would be lost. "There isn't too much we have to say to one another, sir, and I'm hoping we can conclude this business quickly."

William hid his surprise beneath a calm demeanor. "Of course. I can understand that this entire affair is abhorrent to you. My dear lady, what anguish it must have cost you to find yourself married to the Marquis!"

"My feelings will be left out of this discussion," Merewyn said tartly, "if you please." Her tilted indigo eyes met and held his steadily and he was stirred despite himself by the beauty in their golden depths. "What is it you want from me, sir?"

William frowned, not caring too much for her attitude. He had expected gratitude, not hostility and arrogance! 'Twould be up to him to regain control of the situation. After all, he had come here to do the rescuing, hadn't he? "I told you in my letter that I wanted to help."

Merewyn tossed her head angrily. "By threatening to go public with your information if I refused to see you?"

He spread his hands appealingly. "Please, Miss Mac —your ladyship, you must realize that I'd rather cut out my heart than cause you a moment's uneasiness, but I wanted to make absolutely sure that you would take up my offer." His voice grew husky. "I didn't have any idea who you were that day you fainted on the street, and you can imagine my surprise when I did learn! If only you had told me then, dear lady, I could have spared you the suffering surrounding this marriage."

"Aye, that you could have," Merewyn agreed grimly. "If you had made my past known you would have disgraced me so badly that I wouldn't have been fit for a chimney sweep to wed!"

William impulsively seized her hands. "Please calm yourself, dear lady! Naturally, everyone would have realized that you were a victim of unhappy circumstance and that the Marquis was to blame for your pitiful state. But that doesn't really matter, for you must believe that I have no intention of telling anyone what I know."

Merewyn was so startled to hear this that she allowed her hands to remain clasped in his, unaware of the hungry gleam in his eyes as he stared avidly into her upturned face. "Then what is it you want?" she quavered in confusion.

William drew her hands against his chest, stepping closer so that her skirts brushed against his booted legs, her nearness making his heart hammer. "I cannot hide my feelings," he murmured, impassioned by the tantalizing cupid's bow lips that were parted only inches from his own. "Pray, forgive me for being blunt, my dear, but 'tis you I want and naught else."

The indigo eyes widened with shock and the rosy color drained from her delicate cheekbones. "No!" she cried in horror, wrenching free of him and retreating behind the bench. "You're daft!"

"You misunderstand me," William hurriedly explained, seeing that he had frightened her and cursing himself inwardly for his lack of control. "I intend to rescue you from having to spend the rest of your life with that swine who forced you into this unwanted marriage!"

Merewyn made no reply, her breast heaving and falling while she gasped for air, her tilted eyes luminous in her deathly pale face.

"Please listen to me," William pleaded, pausing at the foot of the bench which separated them. "I know Lord Montague brought you here against your wishes and married you without your brother's consent. All I ask is that you let me take you home where he can never bother you again."

"I'll gladly give you money," Merewyn whispered, retreating another step as he made a movement towards her. "How much do you want?"

William came to an abrupt half, eyeing her quizzically. "Money? What in blazes do I need money for?"

The blue eyes began flashing with fire. "Surely you don't believe I'd agree to any other blackmail payment! You must be mad to demand my favors in return for keeping my past a secret!"

William was dumbfounded by her impassioned words. "Why on earth would I want to blackmail you?" he asked after a brief moment of silence. "I told you I wanted to help you!"

Merewyn's panic was growing steadily. Was this man out of his mind? How could he possibly harbor the notion that she would go away with him after all that he had done to her?

"Merewyn," William said pleadingly when the silence between them lengthened, "I realize this has come as a shock to you and I'm sorry to have to throw it all at you at once. But won't you please agree to let me take you back to Cairnlach? I swear I will conduct myself in the most gentlemanly way imaginable."

"You?" Merewyn demanded derisively. "After the way you treated me the first time we met?"

William was unnerved by the hatred gleaming in the indigo eyes and the contempt that curled her soft lips into a sneer. "If you mean my behavior in the coach—" he began but she gave a rude laugh.

"The coach? Sweet Christ, I'm talking about Glasgow, you idiot, and how you cornered me against the wall and then told that constable I'd tried to steal your rings! You are beneath contempt, sir, and where I had once resolved to spare my husband the truth about my having been imprisoned by paying the sum I felt sure you'd come to Farthingdale to name, I now intend to have no more dealings with you on any level! Remember that I am now the Marchioness of Montague and the wife of a powerful man. Should one whisper of this affair ever come to light in this country or in Scotland and I catch wind of it, I shall see you hanged for the scoundrel that you are!"

Her voice throbbed with emotion, the cold hatred within it bringing a flush to William's paling face. "You came here to blackmail me, sir, but I charge you now that I, too, will extract my pound of flesh if you do not hold your silence. The MacAilises and Villiers will be able to survive the scandal your disclosure may cause, but you, I doubt, will be able to withstand the long years of imprisonment you'll get when 'tis learned you attacked me and accused me falsely of prostitution and thievery!"

Her breathing short and laborious, Merewyn wheeled and dashed to the front of the church where her mare was contentedly nipping blades of grass. Slipping her small booted foot into the stirrup, she boosted herself into the saddle and jerked at the reins so savagely that the sensitive mare reared before taking off at a gallop. William Rawlings, standing as though turned to stone before the marble bench, watched the bobbing figure vanish from sight behind a grassy rise, then collapsed, shaken and stunned, onto the seat.

Sweet Jesus, he'd have to think this through! Pulling his handkerchief from his pocket he mopped his brow, annoyed to see that his hands were shaking. He kicked savagely at a pebble lying before him, a string of shocking oaths falling from his thin lips. As soon as Merewyn had mentioned Glasgow, William had realized right away that she was the girl he had kissed that long ago morning, helplessly aroused by her beauty and seeming innocence. Dear God, he'd forgotten completely about that incident, dismissing her as a whore who deserved a night or two in gaol for speaking so rudely to a gentleman. How in God's name was he to have known the strumpet was a lady; Merewyn MacAilis, of all people?

The threats Merewyn had made about seeing him imprisoned caused him to tremble all over again. If charges were pressed and investigations were made, doubtless they would also be able to link him to Nellie Arling's murder. Accosting a lady of prominent standing and falsely accusing her of thievery were crimes of serious nature, but none, William felt certain, that his father's money and influence couldn't work against despite the involvement of the MacAilis and Villiers name. But murder—God's blood, he'd swing from the gallows for that!

Easy, now, William, he cautioned himself, aware that he was shivering as though with the ague, his eyes glassy and his mouth dry. If he was to get himself out of this one he'd have to keep his wits about him, and he'd have to act now, before Lord Montague returned from London. Elizabeth had assured him the letter would arrive in Surrey shortly after he himself had, and his innocently stupid spy Jackie Wilson had told him that Lord Montague had left Ravensley early that morning. He licked his dry lips reflectively. That gave him at least two days in which to act, but what was it exactly he was going to do?

He didn't believe for a moment that Merewyn Villiers would keep to her word and remain silent. William shook his head disbelievingly. And here he had thought all this time that she was meeting him because he had offered to help her escape from an unwanted marriage, whereas she had believed he wanted to blackmail her with information concerning her past. By thunder, the whole rotting affair was so insane one could grow mad just thinking about it! Aye, and it no longer mattered that Merewyn despised her husband or had been kid-

napped by him, for William was convinced that she and
the Marquis would join forces to get rid of
him . . . unless he got rid of her first.

Beads of sweat glistened on William's brow as he sat
deep in thought in the silent churchyard, his head
bowed. Was he actually contemplating doing away with
the Marchioness of Montague? God's blood, perhaps it
wasn't the best possible answer, but he could think of no
other way to spare his own miserable hide!

The clink of silverware against china reassured an
eavesdropping Marty that Lady Montague was at least
making a halfhearted attempt at eating. The door to the
small salon into which she had carried her supper tray
was now firmly closed and Marty had no desire to disturb the despondent person within. Helplessly, she
turned away, wondering what had been plaguing Lady
Montague ever since her return from riding that morning. And here she had thought everything was working
out so well since the wedding, Lord Ian acting happier
than she had ever seen him, apparently very much in
love with his new wife.

Could there be a link between the Marquis's ill-tempered departure and Lady Montague's odd behavior?
Marty didn't like to think so, but some nagging doubt in
the back of her mind made her think that her suspicions
were not unfounded. Sorrowfully she shook her graying
head. Though she wanted to help she knew it was not
her place to ask questions.

Returning to the parlor a half-hour later she found
Merewyn still sitting at the small table, her chin propped
in her hand as she toyed with her food while staring off
into space.

"Is that all you be eating?" Marty asked, casting a
disapproving eye on the contents of the china plate.
"You've scarcely touched a thing!"

Merewyn roused herself with visible effort and gave

the old woman a wan smile. "I'm not hungry, Marty. What time is it?"

"After nine, m'lady."

"I think I'll go to bed."

At the door Merewyn turned, her heart-shaped face filled with uncertainty. "Do you think the Marquis will return tonight?"

Marty sighed apologetically. "I just don't know, your ladyship." Seeing Merewyn's disappointed expression she added encouragingly. "Mayhap he'll be back tomorrow."

"I hope so," Merewyn said softly and bid the former nanny a distracted good night. Slowly ascending the main staircase her thoughts returned to the scene with William Rawlings in the churchyard, where they had been dwelling all day long. She could not understand, even after long hours of reflection, why William had kept insisting that he merely wanted to rescue her from what he had termed an unwanted marriage. Though she felt confident that her threats to press charges would keep him silent, she could not help but puzzle over his odd behavior. Surely he must have realized that she would hate him forever for what he had done to her. Why, then, had he kept begging her to come away with him?

Merewyn shuddered with revulsion. Doubtless the man was daft and she should be relieved that he no longer posed a threat to her happiness with Ian. Why, then, she wondered as she slipped silently into her bedroom, didn't she feel elated? How could she explain the misgivings lingering within her? Perhaps 'twas merely her added worry about Ian's strange departure that morning. Once he came home she'd soon forget all about William Rawlings and their strange, unpleasant meeting.

Quiet descended upon the manor house of Ravensley with the coming of the night. Bullfrogs croaked lazily from the pond in the garden and crickets shrilled in the tall grass. One by one the lights both in the main wing and the servants' quarters were extinguished until only the rising moon, casting its pale glow on the rosy colored bricks, provided the only relief from the inky darkness.

A solitary footman, having snuffed out the last of the candles in the great hall, yawned widely and started up the stairs when the turning of a key in the portal brought his head around. He gave a start of surprise as the heavy door swung wide, the single candle in his hand dimly illuminating the figure before him, but he would have been able to recognize Lord Montague even in the utter blackness because of his immense size.

"My lord!" he murmured, taken aback, and hurried down the stairs towards his master. "We didn't expect you back until tomorrow." Raising his candle to look up into the Marquis's face he suddenly retreated a step, awed by the wild expression on the aristocratic features.

Lord Montague's dark hair was disheveled, for he had ridden in great haste, and there was mud spattered on his cape and boots as a result of galloping through the London streets during a late afternoon thunderstorm. But it was his eyes that unnerved the young manservant the most, for they were glittering almost inhumanly and his lips were pulled back into what looked decidedly like a snarl.

"Is my wife abed?" Lord Montague growled, his deep voice making the servant's heart jump uncomfortably.

"Aye, m'lord. That is, I believe she has retired."

The shadowy from moved restlessly back into the darkness. "I'll be in my study. Fetch me a bottle of brandy."

"Very good, m'lord," the footman said quietly and withdrew, thinking he'd be lucky if hc emerged from that forbidden lair alive. What the devil was wrong with the Marquis? He grimaced ruefully. 'Twas ill luck to use a word like 'devil,' for surely Lord Montague could easi-

ly be mistaken for Satan when he looked the way he did
now.

Merewyn, sleeping soundly in her bed, had not heard
the Marquis's arrival although the stables were located
directly beneath her room and her windows had been
opened to take advantage of the cool night breezes. Despite her many worries she had drifted off into an exhausted sleep, free for a time from the doubts and fears
that had plagued her throughout the day. It wasn't until
the bedroom door crashed open that she was startled
into wakefulness some time later and she sat up, blinking sleepily and trying to peer through the dim moonlight at the massive form approaching her bed.

"Ian?" she whispered, certain that it could be no one
else.

There was no reply save for a leaping flame as the
tinder was struck, then an eerie glow from the candle
standing on the dressing table as he bent down to light
it. Merewyn slipped out of bed and padded barefoot
across the room, her gauze nightshift trailing behind
her, a long golden rope of hair hanging to her waist. The
Marquis was standing with his broad back towards her,
looking out of the window into the misty darkness, and
she paused several feet away, sensing that something
was wrong.

"Ian?" she repeated, then jumped involuntarily as he
rounded on her unexpectedly, gasping as she caught
sight of his set expression, for the finely chiseled features
were twisted into a mask of slow burning anger. "What
is it?" she asked, coming closer, instinctively seeking to
comfort him if, as appearances might indicate, something dreadful had happened in London.

The faint scent of brandy made her pause uncertainly,
searching his hawkish features with her eyes. Was he
drunk? And why was he acting so strangely? She made
a movement to go to him, but he held out a warning
hand to stop her.

"Stay where you are."

The words were clear and unslurred and the ringing command was unmistakable. Merewyn obeyed instantly.

"Y-you left so suddenly this morning," she began, her eyes resting intently on his ruthless profile. "I was worried that something had happened."

"What does this mean to you?" the Marquis demanded harshly, ignoring her words, and thrust a piece of paper under her nose from seemingly nowhere.

Merewyn took it with stiff fingers and moved back to the dressing table to peruse it in the light. A quick glance was enough to tell her that it was the same letter she had given David to deliver to William Rawlings and she went cold inside, the paper falling unnoticed to the floor.

"I see you recognize it." His tone was ominously still.

" 'Tis because I w-wrote it."

"For some reason it arrived here this morning and I rode to London straight away to confront this Rawlings fellow. You see, Merewyn, his name is not altogether unfamiliar to me. Do you remember that evening at Caroline Humphries when you claimed to have seen a man who reminded you of your brother's former auditor?" He plowed ruthlessly through her bewildered protests. "I wasn't satisfied with your explanation and asked Caroline for a guest list. Naturally, it told me nothing until this letter arrived and I remembered having seen the name on that list, I'd been wondering for quite some time now what you were hiding from me that night and now I know."

Merewyn's upturned face was filled with dismay. "Why didn't you ask me for an explanation this morning? Why did you have to go to London to see him?"

A muffled oath fell from his lips and Merewyn could see his jaw muscles twitching as he continued to stare out into the darkness. "I was going to run the swine through. Did you honestly believe I'd react any different after learning I'd been cuckolded?''

"Oh, no, Ian, no! 'Tis all a great misunderstanding! I can explain!'' Distraught, she hurried towards him, her eyes filled with pain, but his harsh words stopped her in midstride.

"Back from me, woman! I warn you, if you touch me I shall break your neck.''

Merewyn had never heard the vibrating hatred in his tone before and she felt ill, clutching dizzily for support at a nearby chair. "You don't understand,'' she whispered, wretchedly aware that it would be difficult to reason with him when he was in such a dangerous mood, especially when he had been drinking. "William Rawlings is—''

Ian groaned as the name fell from her lips and whirled about to face her, frightening her with his wild expression. "His housekeeper informed me he'd departed quite suddenly for Scotland, but somehow I found that hard to believe. 'Tis why I returned so quickly. Was that letter sent to lure me away, madame, leaving you free to enjoy his attentions?''

"Of course not!'' Merewyn cried although she sounded unconvincing, suddenly realizing herself that the letter had probably been delivered to Ravensley expressly for that purpose.

Ian was quick to sense her doubt and strode towards her, seizing her in his powerful hands and lifting her off the floor so that her face was only inches from his, her blue eyes wide with shock and a great deal of fear. "What a fool you've made of me, madame! I must admit you've planned your revenge far, far better than any of my best laid intentions! Hiding your outings with your lover behind cleverly couched tales of attempted escapes from London was a stroke of genius. I assume your little journey down to the harbor the other day was in truth a lurid afternoon spent in the arms of Master Rawlings himself?"

He shook her cruelly, his steely gray eyes seeming to glow with rage. "And then feigning affection for me after we were married, watching me bare my heart to you like an idiot while you were laughing up your sleeve, delighted with how you were deceiving me. God, how richly you planned this!"

Despite her panic and the pain he was inflicting with his bruising grip on her arms, Merewyn knew that she would somehow have to convince him of the truth before he throttled her or broke her in two with his vicious shaking. She had never seen him so angry in her life and deep within her a numb pain was growing, a pain brought about by his readiness to doubt her, to dismiss her love for him as pretense.

"Please listen to me, Ian," she begged breathlessly, his crushing hold forcing the air out of her lungs. "There has never been anyone but you, never! The man you believe my lover is actually a criminal who tried to blackmail me!"

Ian let her go so abruptly that she plummeted to the floor at his feet, her head ringing, hearing his harsh laugh from far above. "I'll grant you're a clever, scheming bitch, and I should have been forewarned. Since the day we met you've been intent on destroying me in one way or another. Well, madame," suddenly his voice grew hoarse and weary, "congratulate yourself. You have succeeded."

The tip of his boot nudged her painfully as he stepped over her, and then the door leading to his bedchamber slammed shut, the rush of air generated blowing out the candle on the dressing table and plunging her room into darkness. Merewyn lay for a moment fighting to hold back her tears, hopelessness, and frustration warring with mounting anger. Her fiery nature finally won out and she scrambled to her feet, cursing beneath her breath, determined to make him listen. Drunken, boorish dunderhead, she'd force him to hear her out if she had to tie him up to make him hold still!

"Ian Villiers, I demand that you listen to me!" she shouted, storming through the door only to find herself in an empty room. Confused, she looked about her at the austere furnishings—no trace of the Marquis or his belongings in sight. She chewed her lips in utter vexation. Where in God's name was he? Down in the study, perhaps, drowning his sorrows in more brandy? God's teeth, he'd not get away with this!

Not caring if she roused the entire household, Merewyn pounded down the great flight of stairs in the darkness, her golden hair flying wildly behind her, the gauzy material of her nightshift billowing about her bare feet. She found him in the study as she had predicted, draining the last bit of brandy from the bottle, but her resolve vanished when he looked up and she saw the deadly menace in his eyes. Abruptly, her steps faltered in the doorway.

"Ian, we have to talk," she said with far less bravado than she would have liked.

"There's nothing more to say," he told her, swallowing the contents of his glass, the anger in his voice having been replaced with an icy calm she found far more frightening. "I'm leaving for London."

"Now?" she demanded in amazement.

The steel gray eyes looked at her with utter contempt. "You have taken a lover, madame, and I don't intend to deny myself the same pleasure. I will be at Lady Comerford's if anyone wishes to see me."

His words sent searing pain through Merewyn's heart and she could only stand there numbly, staring up at him with wide, tragic eyes. He cursed violently when he met their anguished stare, then threw the glass he still held in his hand into the fireplace where it exploded into a shower of glittering fragments. Brushing past her he felt her small hand clutch at his sleeve but he shook her off savagely and strode outside, ignoring the muffled sobs that followed him although the sounds tore at his heart.

The stables were dark and silent as Ian entered. His stallion had been cooled and watered and stood munching the last bits of hay from the rack in his stall, turning his muscular neck to whicker a greeting as his master strode inside. The groom the Marquis had roused upon his arrival had apparently retired again and Ian had no wish to wake him a second time. In his anger he wanted to see no one, speak to no one, and he threw open the tack room door himself and lifted a saddle into his strong arms.

The stallion would be too tired to make yet another trip to London, so he chose a particularly heavily muscled gelding known for its speed and endurance. The gelding showed no surprise at being disturbed, complacently taking the bit and allowing himself to be led into the wide aisle where the saddle was dumped hastily onto his back and fastened beneath his belly.

"Ian, wait!"

The Marquis cursed savagely as he heard the small, choked voice coming from the darkness behind him. He already had one foot in the stirrup and quickly swung himself onto the gelding's broad back, moving out into the darkness beyond the stableyard in time to see Merewyn's disheveled golden hair and distraught little face appear before him. Tears were running down her hollow cheeks and her wide blue eyes were dark with suffering.

"Please don't go to her," she begged, reaching up and catching the gelding's reins with trembling fingers, the big horse snorting nervously at this strange apparition whose white nightclothes floated eerily about her in the breeze.

" 'Tis too late, madame," Ian told her in a voice that sounded hopelessly final. "You should have considered the consequences before you took William Rawlings to your bed."

He leaned over in the saddle and seized her wrist in his strong fingers, his rage-contorted features only inches from hers. "Did he please you better than I? Make you cry out with longing?" His tone made her blood run cold. "Well, I intend to do the same for Elizabeth, and you may rest assured, my dear, that my performance will lack none of the elements I gave to you."

"What are you saying?" Merewyn whispered. "That you never really c-cared for me?"

"Cared for you?" His laugh grated through clenched teeth. "My intent has always been just to bed you, madame, and use my skill at lovemaking to make you fall in love with me. Now that you have, I have achieved my primary objective: to gain enough control over you so that I can make the mills mine."

Merewyn could not move, for his tight hold on her wrist was pressing her against the stamping horse's side, forcing her to look up into the gray eyes that had only recently looked at her with love but were now filled with loathing and contempt. She felt as though she couldn't bear the pain another moment.

"It was the m-mills that you w-wanted?" she whispered.

"They have always been foremost in my mind," Ian replied cruelly. "Every word I've ever said to you, anything I might have done was all calculated towards achieving that end." He smiled, but it was more of a grimace in his harshly set face. "How much easier my task will be now that you are in love with me, madame."

Something in her silence and the ragged breathing that came from her parted lips made him curse again and he released her abruptly. Without another word he dug his heels into the gelding's sides, almost running

Merewyn over in the big beast's sprint forward. Ian had one last glimpse of her small form standing in the moonlight, her head drooping dejectedly, before the darkness swallowed her up and he was racing madly down the stone drive, white hot rage coursing through him.

The muscular gelding, his lungs and heart strong from years of training, made the long run with only slightly more rests than the stallion and was still going strong when the Marquis urged him through Kingston and Richmond. None of the houses he passed showed signs of life and only an occasional dog barked a warning to herald the rider's whirlwind approach. Ian leaned low in the saddle, giving scarcely a glance to the farms and estate houses he passed, his mind preoccupied with so many conflicting emotions that he thought he might be going mad with the nature of his musings.

During the long ride his anger began to wane, the simmering blood in his veins growing cooler, his rage becoming replaced with more and more despair whenever the vision of Merewyn's pain-filled young face floated before him, her indigo eyes enormous with grief. Though he tried to remind himself over and over again that she had betrayed him, had lain in the arms of another, he could not rekindle the deadly rage that had originally helped him cope with his discovery.

Even greater was the lessening of his desire to seek out Elizabeth Comerford's company. Upon leaving Ravensley he had been determined to assuage his feelings in Elizabeth's arms, but now the thought only brought revulsion and the realization that he hungered for one woman only, whose innocence had offered him a taste of paradise and who had demanded nothing of him in turn. But Merewyn hadn't been satisfied to have him alone, Ian reminded himself, his long fingers tightening savagely on the reins. Merewyn had given herself to another, permitted another's hands to rove her perfect body and kiss the softly yielding lips.

Had her passion-darkened indigo eyes looked up into William Rawlings with the same maddening glow? Had she smiled at him as saucily, making him feel weak with longing and a craving to possess her? Ian's lips parted into a fierce snarl and he brought down the whip he carried unmercifully onto his valiantly racing mount's hindquarters. He was a fool to have left her, to all but give that Rawlings swine a by-your-leave to possess his wife again. Suddenly he knew that he must go back, to run the fellow through, carve out his heart as he should have done instead of running away like a whipped cur with his tail between his legs to be comforted by a woman he no longer loved—nay, whom he had never loved—for Ian saw plainly now how greatly he had mistaken lust for that elusive yet deeply satisfying emotion.

Knowing that his horse would never endure the same mad pace all the way back to Ravensley, Lord Montague turned him decisively towards greater London and the carriage house that belonged to him and was stocked at the moment with half a dozen well-rested, suitable mounts. With luck he should be back in Surrey some time after dawn, and God grant that he would soon be able to feel a certain man's blood on his hands.

The London streets were silent and eerily deserted. Even the tavern lights were doused, the only signs of life being the drunkards who snored peacefully on the doorsteps and the dogs that foraged and fought amid the debris floating in the gutters. The festive routs that had taken place that evening were over with, the crowds dispersed and safely at home, and all the elegant houses standing along the wide, tree-lined streets were tightly closed up for the night.

Ian found the silence and the feeling of isolation oppressive, the doubts that had been plaguing him for some time now only magnified as his mount trotted slowly down the cobblestones, his muffled hoofbeats ringing in the dark night. A cool breeze, bringing with it the promise of autumn, ruffled Ian's hair, for he wore no hat, and sent flecks of foam from the gelding's thickly veined neck floating into the sky. Both man and beast appeared relieved to finally turn up the drive leading to the Marquis's home, and Ian gave the gelding an affectionate pat before dismounting in the stableyard.

The other horses, having heard their arrival, moved restlessly in their stalls, their stamping and whickering awakening Nick Holder, who slept in a tiny apartment above. The gray-haired, portly little man came hurrying down the ladder several minutes later with his shirt tails hanging out of his breeches and his eyes red with lack of sleep. It was with an utterly astonished expression that he took in the towering form of the Marquis before him, patiently walking the blowing gelding who, much to Nick's disapproval, showed signs of being run far too hard.

"What on earth, yer lordship," he began, tucking in his shirt and running a hand through his unkempt hair as he hurried forward. "Ye've come back again? Is something amiss at Ravensley, then?"

"Tack up another horse, Nick. Immediately. I'm returning to Surrey as soon as you're ready."

The head groom's sleep-flushed face filled with disbelief. Never in his life had he known the Marquis to exhibit such odd behavior and here he'd been with him for many, many years. How many trips to Surrey would this make in the course of two days' time? Three? Four? Holy Christ and from the look of it there was murder in Lord Montague's heart, for Nick had seen that expression in the cold, classic features only several times before, and that was when the Marquis had been preparing to fight a duel. He shivered involuntarily and took the reins from the Marquis's hand. Aye, 'twas blood lust he saw in the steel gray eyes, a look he knew wouldn't go away until blood had been spilled.

Better not ask no more questions, Nick advised him-

self, if he valued his own skin. Watching the Marquis
stride across the yard towards the house he pursed his
lips and urged the gelding into the barn. Better rouse
one of the lads to cool this big fellow so that he could
tack up Royal before the Marquis returned. Aye,
'twould be Royal, who hadn't been put through his
paces for three days now. He'd be fresh and eager to
run, and, by God, Nick'd have him ready in time or, as
he well knew, his job would be on the line.

Nick Holder was not the only one who sensed the terrible intent in Lord Montague's heart. Francis, having
been awakened by the unruliness of the horses in the
stables, had hurriedly dressed and came downstairs in
time to meet the Marquis in the corridor leading from
the rear entrance of the house. Even in the flickering
light of the candle he was holding, the majordomo could
easily see the grim expression on the handsome features
and the restless hunger in the gray eyes. Wisely, he asked
no questions.

"Good evening, m'lord—I beg your pardon, I mean
good morning." Despite the gravity of the situation and
his surprise at his master's unexpected appearance,
Francis refused to forsake his manners. "Would you be
caring for something to eat or drink?"

"Brandy, Francis, and quickly," the Marquis commanded, striding off towards his study. "I'm leaving for
Ravensley in a few minutes."

"Very good, m'lord." Francis's thoughts were teeming with unuttered questions, perfectly aware that he
would never in a hundred years be able to come up with
a logical reason for Lord Montague's appearance yesterday, when he had arrived in one of the foulest tempers
Francis had ever seen. Then there had been his abrupt
departure followed by this ill-boding arrival, and now
another consequent return to Ravensley. What in blazes
did all of it mean?

Placing the bottle that he had retrieved from the wine

cellar onto a lacquered tray along with a cut-crystal glass, the musing majordomo hurried back down the corridor and into the study where he found Lord Montague sitting at his desk, intently priming his dueling pistols. At the sight of the deadly weapons and the unsettling gleam in the cold gray eyes, Francis's heart leaped into his throat and he swallowed nervously. Setting the bottle and glass on the desk he became aware that his fingers were trembling.

"Are you nervous, Francis?" the Marquis asked unpleasantly.

The majordomo struggled to regain his composure but found himself growing even more shaken when he met the unnerving stare of the brooding man seated before him. "Those pistols make me nervous, m'lord," he confessed, retreating to a safe distance around the massive desk.

The Marquis smiled, but the gesture was unsettling, for there was no trace of warmth at all in his grimly set features. "Naturally it would. You have always objected to my duels in the past."

Francis's heart sank but he could not bring himself to ask the dreaded question. Instead, he pointed out that a duel fought by an exhausted, half-drunk man (this in response to the huge swallow of brandy the Marquis abruptly took) could very easily be lost. His cautions were not well received and as a muscle began to twitch in the Marquis's lean cheek, he realized he had said the very worst possible thing.

"I swear to you, Francis, this is one duel I will not lose."

The words sent a shiver down the majordomo's spine. "Perhaps 'twould be wisest if you rested first, your lordship, and left in the morning."

The long fingers tightened about the carved ivory handle of one of the pistols. "No, Francis. By then 'twould be too late. I was a fool to come here, a bloody, muck-eating fool, and my pride may have cost me everything. I must get back!" Ian rose to his feet, towering over the smaller man before him, his expression black with renewed rage. "Have Nick fetch my saddle holsters. I'll be down shortly and if my horse isn't ready tell him I'll put a bullet through his heart."

Francis needed no further orders, scuttling out of the door faster than he had moved in years, leaving the Marquis alone with his awesome pistols and terrible thoughts. Ian drained a second glass of brandy and smiled in grim satisfaction. The pistols were carefully cleaned, oiled, and primed for firing. He had no intention of waiting until he got back to Ravensley to ready them, convinced that he would need them as soon as he walked through the door. Fool, stupid, bloody fool, he told himself with bleak self-loathing. How could he have abandoned Merewyn like that? How could he have possibly convinced himself that he wanted the comfort of a woman like Elizabeth Comerford? No, he should have stayed and fought for her, refused to give in though his pride had been dealt a deadly blow. God's teeth, he hoped he wouldn't be too late!

Lost in thought, his handsome face set with the fury that was again burning in his heart, he became aware only gradually of the heavy pounding on the front door. Cocking his dark head he listened intently, then threw open the study door and strode down the corridor towards the entrance hall. Who in hell was mindless enough to disturb the household at this time of night?

"What in God's name do you want?" he roared, pulling the heavy door almost off its hinges and staring furiously down at the unwanted caller. His expression changed to astonishment as he saw the cloaked figure standing before him, the rugged features filled with an odd mixture of urgency and relief, and his harsh voice relented.

"Come in," Ian said gruffly, opening the door wide.

"Thank you."

The untimely visitor stepped past his host and turned around to face him, drawing off his tricorn and peering at him fiercely. "For the love of God, where is Merewyn?" Alexander demanded.

CHAPTER TWELVE

To Marty Simpson the dark corridors and empty rooms of a sleeping Ravensley had never frightened her before. She had spent enough nights during her long years of residence wandering sleepless through the silent rooms with only a flickering candle to light her way. She was a woman who had never required much sleep, always the last to retire, always the first to rise, and during the young Earl's stormy youth she had found many reasons to wander restlessly through the empty house, worrying fruitlessly about her impetuous charge.

Tonight, however, Marty found herself casting nervous glances over her stooped shoulders as she hurried from her apartment towards the bridal suite in the other wing. Odd comings and goings, voices and strange noises had disturbed her sleep for some time now and she had finally worked up enough nerve to peep in on the Marchioness to reassure herself that Merewyn was all right. As an added precaution she had awakened Collins, a particularly brawny footman, who was at the moment inspecting the downstairs rooms for signs of an intruder.

To her surprise Marty saw a beam of light shining from beneath Lady Montague's bedroom door, and as she approached she could hear the sounds of frantic activity going on within. She hesitated a moment, wondering if perhaps Lord Montague had returned, but when she heard what sounded suspiciously like a choked sob, she knocked boldly.

Instantly, there was charged silence on the other side, then a timid whisper came through the thick wood. "Who is it?"

"Marty, your ladyship. May I come in?"

The bolt slid back and Merewyn's little face appeared as the door swung wide. Marty was shocked by her mistress's appearance, for Merewyn was fully dressed, the trim skirts of her riding habit swirling about her slender ankles, her golden hair braided and pinned neatly to her head, covered by a small veiled hat. But it was Merewyn's expression that caused Marty the most concern, for her hollow cheeks were wet with tears and the beautiful blue eyes were swollen and red, the golden depths filled with almost unbearable grief.

"What is it, Marty?"

The old woman was unprepared for the flatness of her young mistress's tone and could only stammer. "I-I heard things, your ladyship, and I was worried about you."

"Lord Montague was here. Doubtless you heard him," Merewyn informed her with the same flat voice, turning around and vanishing into the room.

Marty quickly followed her inside, where she watched with growing apprehension as Merewyn stuffed the last of a carefully selected group of belongings into a bulging valise. "His lordship be here?" she asked incredulously.

"He's gone again," Merewyn told her shortly, struggling with the clasps. "He stayed long enough to tell me, in no uncertain terms, that he has married me for my fortune and wants nothing more to do with me." For a brief moment the soft lips trembled, but the voice was as calm and unemotional as before. "He has gone back to London to see Lady Comerford, and I am going home."

Marty Simpson had been dealt countless shocks and had lived through a great number of crises during her long years in the Villiers's employ, but she found herself unable to comprehend what had happened between Lord Montague and his strangely detached young wife. Therefore, she could say nothing and stood watching helplessly, the candle wavering in her shaky fingers and dripping hot wax on the carpet, as Merewyn finished closing the valise and lifted it from the bed.

For a brief moment the grief-stricken indigo eyes met the faded, deeply set ones of the faithful old woman. Then Merewyn shrugged and gave her a wan smile. "I'm going home, Marty. Good-bye."

"Wait, your ladyship!" Movement returned to Marty's frozen limbs and she hastened after the retreating figure in the brown velvet habit. "How are you going to get there? You can't leave this time of night!"

Merewyn gently shook off the restraining hand that had settled on her arm and lifted her chin imperiously. "Oh, aye, I can. I'm going to ride to Dorking. There's bound to be a stagecoach leaving in the morning."

"Oh, no, please, your ladyship!" Marty begged, tears springing into her eyes, thinking of the dangers that could befall her young mistress on the dark, deserted roads. "Whatever be wrong between you and Lord Ian can be changed! Nothing be too terrible what love can't handle!"

"He doesn't love me," Merewyn replied thickly, "and I never want to see him again. Do you hear me, Marty? Never!"

With stiff shoulders she marched across the landing and down the winding staircase, forcing open the front door and stepping outside. The night was cool and windy and the moon, nearing its fullest phase, cast its pale light upon the ground. The stables were deserted and Merewyn encountered no one as she coaxed her horse out of the stall, quickly slipping the bit between the mare's teeth. Alexander had taught her at an early age to tack her own horse and she buckled the bridle straps and girth with surprising deftness, considering that her fingers were trembling uncontrollably. In fact, her entire body was shaking, the tears so dangerously close that Merewyn had to bite her lips to keep from spilling them.

Resolutely, she forced her concentration to the task at hand, aware that she would burst into a fit of stormy weeping if she so much as dared think back an instant to the violent encounter with Ian and the hatred in his eyes as he had stared down at her from the back of his stamping horse.

She had no idea how long the journey would take, but suspected that it would be a long and tiring one. No matter. With every turn of the big wheels she'd be traveling farther away from the hateful ogre who had hurt her so badly, away from Ravensley and its awful memories and especially away from London where soon the rising sun would shine into the bedroom of a certain townhouse and awaken the Marquis and Elizabeth Comerford as they lay entwined together after a long night of loving.

A low moan escaped from the tightly compressed lips and hot tears sprang to Merewyn's eyes. Dashing them away with the back of her hand, she led the now-ready mare to the block and slid into the saddle, the valise tied to one of the saddle rings before her. Turning her head she saw that lights had sprung on in the house and guessed that Marty had awakened the other servants who would doubtless be sent in pursuit. Heart hammering, Merewyn brought the quirt down on the mare's flank and the startled beast took off at a gallop towards the arched bridge and freedom.

Though the moon was not yet full, its silvery light sufficiently lit her way, and the surefooted mare was able to keep up her pace once her rider had turned her down the westerly road toward Dorking. The wind moaned in the trees overhead and nightbirds flitted from place to place in their hunt for prey. Their shrill cries and the chirping of the insects in the fields along the roadside blended in a cacaphonous din that effectively cloaked the steady pounding of the horse's hooves as the silent girl and her long-legged mare sped by.

Merewyn had never been to the village of Dorking and had no idea how long she would have to travel, unwilling to spend her mare prematurely. She could not help but urge her mare faster and faster, however, afraid that one of the footmen from Ravensley might overtake her and force her to return. For the first few miles she threw numerous glances over one shoulder to reassure herself that she was was not being followed, and her precaution was rewarded when her mare ascended a small rise in the road and Merewyn could make out the shadowy figure of another rider coming up from below, hot in pursuit.

"Damn that Marty!" she cursed beneath her breath. "The woman has no right to interfere!"

What was she to do now? Should she try to outdistance her follower or should she draw rein until he had caught up with her and simply order him back to Ravensley? She was Lady Montague, after all, and all of the servants were legally in her employ despite the fact that her marriage was a sham. Still, she wouldn't put it past the pursuing footman to drag her back to Ravensley despite her protests, terrified of facing the Marquis's wrath.

Gritting her teeth, Merewyn leaned low over the mare's glossy neck, deciding 'twould be wisest to escape him if she could. She was going to go home and no mealy-mouthed servant of Ian Villiers was going to prevent her from doing so!

For a time the two horses maintained similar speeds, the distance between them remaining the same, but the pursuing horse was larger and stronger and, driven by his relentless rider, slowly began to close the gap between them. Merewyn, hearing hoofbeats pounding behind her, cast a worried glance over her shoulder to see that he was gaining on her. The moon had been rising steadily higher as the chase progressed and the entire landscape was now bathed in an eerie white light so that she could easily make him out. He was hatless, a black cloak billowing out behind him, and he was leaning forward while urging his horse faster by whipping him ruthlessly about the hindquarters.

Merewyn felt cold anger steal through her. No one in the Marquis's employ would dare treat one of his prize horses so brutally! Apparently this manservant was hell bent on catching her, and his obvious determination made her all the more resolved to escape him. She faced forward again, speaking encouragingly into the mare's ear, and the lathering little creature seemed to respond, drawing almost imperceptibly away from the horse pounding headlong behind.

Merewyn cast a triumphant glance over her shoulder, only to bite back a cry of dismay when she saw that the progress she had made had only been temporary. Stung again and again by his rider's whip, the long-legged mount had been spurred into a frenzy, increasing his stride so that the gap between them was closing at an alarming rate. Having lost sight of the mare during the brief moment in which she had pulled away, the rider had lifted his head to peer into the strangely lit gloom ahead of him, and Merewyn was able to look fully into his face for the first time.

She bit back a cry of horror, her heart thumping against her ribs, and turned to look again, desperately hoping that she had been mistaken. In the moonlight his face looked pale and hauntingly unreal, wrapped up in the black cloak so that it seemed to be floating disembodied above the horse's undulating form. But there was no mistaking the mustache and gaunt, prominent cheekbones, and as he neared Merewyn could clearly see the glinting metal of the pistol he carried in one hand.

William Rawlings cursed to himself as he saw the little mare move away from him a second time, knowing that if he laid the whip to his horse again he would goad him into an uncontrollably mad gallop. Instead, he loosened his hold on the reins even more and leaned low against the foam-flecked neck. The wind roared in his ears and he could feel the blood throbbing in his veins. He had to catch that slanted-eyed wench, he had to!

He had been haunting the gardens of Ravensley like a specter, trying to figure how best to slip into the house without rousing attention, when the pounding hoofbeats of an approaching horse had sent him scurrying back into the bushes where he had hidden his mount. The moon had not yet risen back then and he had had trouble identifying the rider who had stormed at a harrowing pace past his hiding place, showering him with pebbles and making his horse balk nervously.

William had listened with bated breath to the sounds of obscene shouts that were emitted from the stables seconds later and had cursed himself with utter frustration when he recognised the deep voice of Lord Montague. What in blazes had brought that devil's spawn back to Ravensley so soon? His fingers closed convulsively about the pistol he'd first drawn when he'd heard the approaching hoofbeats, but he knew that he would not be using it now, for his own chances would be slim indeed if he were forced to face the Marquis himself.

He stood for a moment mopping the sweat from his brow. What in God's name was he to do now, he asked himself, his hands shaking as he returned the pistol to its holster. Lady Montague could very well be telling her husband everything at this very moment and William shuddered as he thought of the consequences. Could he do away with both of them? God's blood, he was daft to even entertain the idea! Murder a peer, and one as ruthless as the Marquis of Montague?

Leaving his horse tied among the trees behind him, William waited until the lights in the stables were extinguished, then quickly crossed the open expanse between the garden and the house itself, glad that the moon was not yet bright enough to throw shadows. Pressing himself against the cool stone wall, he moved carefully, so as not to rustle the branches of the shrubbery planted beneath the windows, until he was crouching beneath one of them in which a solitary light was burning. Hoisting himself up onto the sill he tried to peer inside, but the drapes were tightly drawn and he could see nothing.

Disappointed, he dropped back down to the earth, straining to understand the subdued murmuring going on within, unable even to recognize if the voices were male or female. Shortly thereafter the light went out, leaving only the moonlight to illuminate the still figure cowering among the shrubs. What in hell was going on in there? William asked himself impatiently. Whatever it was, he'd be wise to leave the grounds now that the Marquis had returned, for he couldn't simply enter the house as he had originally intended now that Lord Montague was there. Damn Elizabeth, he cursed silently, why hadn't she been able to keep him with her? There was no way on earth he could possibly hope to win in a confrontation against that arrogant behemoth!

Rising slowly to his feet and dusting the dirt from his breeches, William crossed the lawn, speaking soothingly to his horse who waited with pricked ears in the garden. At the sound of his master's reassuring voice, the big animal lowered his head and resumed cropping grass, and William had to tug several times on the reins before he reluctantly allowed himself to be led away.

He had one foot in the stirrups and was preparing to mount when he heard a feminine voice, obviously greatly distressed, come from the direction of the stables.

"Ian, wait!"

William's breath caught in his throat and he froze, straining his eyes to peer through the gloom. What the devil was this? Then he saw Merewyn, her golden hair streaming behind her, running across the courtyard to intercept a horse that had just emerged from the dark interior of the barn. His own horse snorted, and William quickly placed a quieting hand on his muzzle.

"Steady, lad," he whispered, and then stood very still, listening. The wind was blowing in his direction and he was able to hear every word spoken between Merewyn and Lord Montague, including the Marquis's accusations concerning Merewyn and himself and how they had been deceiving him. A gleeful cackle fell from William's thin lips and he quickly covered his mouth with his hand. Oh, but this was rich! Lord Montague had managed to solve everything for him!

He watched, tears of joy welling in his eyes, as Merewyn clung desperately to her husband, only to be pushed away when the Marquis urged his mount to a mad gallop. She nearly fell but managed to catch herself in time, and William quickly pressed himself close against his horse's side when Lord Montague's mount came flashing past him. As the hoofbeats receded he turned to look for Merewyn, but she had vanished into the house, her choked sobs floating back to him on the night air.

William waited, shivering with impatience in the bushes, until he felt certain that Merewyn had again retired to her room. Only then did he dare chance leaving his hiding place, but he was driven back almost immediately by sounds coming from the stables. Peering between the branches, he cursed this stroke of bad luck, then blinked disbelievingly as he saw Merewyn Villiers leading a horse into the moonlit courtyard, a valise strapped to the pommel of the saddle. It was obvious to him immediately that she was either running away or preparing to follow her husband back to London. Either way, William thought with a complacent smile, settling himself comfortably in the saddle, Merewyn would never reach her destination alive.

The door to the study opened and a worried Francis thrust his head inside only to stop short on the threshold, staring about him in confusion at the empty room. Deep voices in the hallway brought his attention round, and he hurried down the corridor, wondering who could possibly be mad enough to arrive at this time of the morning, he shook his head resignedly, thinking he was much too old to endure this sort of excitement much longer.

Francis's eyes widened in shock when he saw the two men coming toward him from the entrance hall, for never in his life had he ever met anyone who could stand beside the Marquis and not be dwarfed by his enormous size. The strange man walking beside him was casually attired in buckskin breeches and a leather vest, a neatly folded but slightly stained stock about his neck, and a wrinkled cloak falling from his broad shoulders. Though he was almost of the same height as the Marquis and dark headed, his appearance was totally dissimilar, for where the Marquis was large and solidly built, this man was lean and long-limbed. Unlike the Marquis, whose features were sharply chiseled and aristocratic, his were rugged, as though carved from granite.

But it was not his height or his build that had startled Francis so. It was the resemblance he bore—faint but undisputable—to Merewyn, the Marquis's wife. Though their coloring was vastly different there could be no mistaking the firm chin and sharp jaw of a MacAilis. Nor, Francis decided with something of an inward groan, could one mistake the proud carriage of the head or the arrogant gleam in the eyes, which, although they weren't blue, were nonetheless slightly tilted, a characteristic that gave this man an arrestingly handsome countenance.

"Francis, have Nick saddle a fresh horse," the Marquis commanded, catching sight of the majordomo coming down the hallway toward him. "We're leaving for Ravensley immediately."

"Very good, my lord," Francis replied calmly and hurried off.

Alexander's eyes narrowed as he followed the Marquis into the study. "I repeat my question, Ian, is Merewyn here?"

"No." The Marquis's tone was curt. "She's at Ravensley, my estate in Surrey."

"What in hell is she doing there?"

The two men eyed one another as protagonists, neither one faltering beneath the bold gaze of the other. The tension in the small study was palpable, the sort of tension that could easily lead to bloodshed. Ian was the first to break the silence.

"Merewyn and I are married. She is my wife, Alex, and you can't do anything to alter the fact."

The MacAilis chieftain's lips tightened ominously. "Why, you mange-eaten cur, if you've pushed her into this I'll slit your throat."

"Calm yourself, Alex," Ian advised mildly, although his eyes never left the other's face. Here, he knew, was an enemy to contend with, a man whose size and strength closely matched his own, a rationally thinking fighter and not a fool. Moreover, he was Merewyn's brother and Ian had no wish to harm him. "Merewyn consented to marry me. I did not force her."

Alexander studied the arrogant features before him with a quizzical expression. "By God, you'd better be telling the truth."

"We're leaving for Ravensley shortly," the Marquis reminded him. "You can ask her yourself." A vision of her tear-stained little face, her tilted eyes enormous with grief, rose unbidden to his mind until he thrust it away, reminding himself that she had betrayed him, had lain in the arms of another man who might even be loving her at this very moment. God's blood, why wasn't Nick hurrying with the horses!

Alexander was quick to notice the change of emotions in the Marquis's handsome face. "What is it?" he asked. "Is Merewyn hurt? Did you harm her in any way?"

The Marquis scowled, then shrugged his broad shoulders nonchalantly. "You may as well know the truth. We had a disagreement and that's why I'm here and Merewyn is in Surrey."

"Malcolm and I both had a feeling you had something to do with Merewyn's being taken to London, even though I firmly believed you'd gone after her as a gesture of friendship to my family." His tone grew low and dangerous. "Now I'm not so sure that your intentions were entirely selfless."

The gray eyes grew icy cold. "Are you saying that I kidnapped her?"

Even Alexander was affected by the deadly menace in the Marquis's tone. He feared no man, but would have been a fool to dismiss the formidable Lord Montague as anything other than a potentially lethal adversary. And this man was also Merewyn's husband, he reminded himself, the man she loved, if Ian's words were to be believed. Doubts plagued him and he felt helpless, wishing she was safe, that all the weeks of anguish and worry since her disappearance from Cairnlach were finally over.

"There is one thing I'm grateful for," Alexander remarked, thinking that until Merewyn could be questioned he would try his best not to make an enemy out of her husband. "At least she's safe at Ravensley."

The Marquis's broad shoulders stiffened almost imperceptibly, but Alexander noticed nonetheless and felt his suspicions returning. "And why shouldn't Merewyn be safe?" Ian asked, his tone as cold as ice. "Do you think I'd harm my own wife, Alex?"

"Not you," Alexander replied shortly. "I've been out of my mind with worry the entire journey down here because of that Rawlings fellow. 'Twas said he'd gone to London, and the chances were too great that it wasn't a coincidence. At least I can rule out—"

In only two short strides the Marquis had crossed the distance between them and had seized Alexander's vest in both his big hands, all of the pent-up rage within him exploding. "You know about William Rawlings?" he shouted, beside himself. "Don't tell me Merewyn has always been his mistress! Were you going to arrange a match between them, is that it, Alex?"

The MacAilis chieftain stared into the smoldering gray eyes and wondered if the Marquis had taken leave of his senses. Never had he seen a man quite so enraged and realized he would have to handle himself very carefully to avoid turning that lethal anger against himself.

The gravity of the situation could not be ignored, however, and he demanded bluntly, "Are you saying you've seen the man here?"

Ian released him abruptly and turned away, running an agitated hand through his dark curls, trying his utmost to bring his emotions under control. "No, I haven't, but Merewyn—"

"Has he seen her?" Alexander interrupted, his face paling. "Does he know she's here?"

"Damn you to Hell, MacAilis!" the Marquis shouted, his expression livid. "What in God's name is the purpose of this inquisition? If you must know, Merewyn arranged secretly for Rawlings to meet her at Ravensley by luring me away to London! For all I know they may very well be together this very moment?"

Ian had never seen the color drain as quickly from a man's face as it did from Alexander MacAilis's. The muscles in his jaw worked convulsively and his Adam's apple bobbed up and down. "My God," he groaned, his voice ragged.

Alex's strong reaction instantly cooled the Marquis's anger. "What is it, for Christ's sake?" he demanded.

"We've got to get to Ravensley as quickly as we can. Ian, William Rawlings is wanted in Glasgow for strangling a prostitute. He's the one responsible for sending Merewyn to gaol where she was illegally bonded."

"And you think he may have come here to harm her?" the Marquis asked, unconvinced, wondering if Alexander was lying to him.

The MacAilis chieftain's face had grown haggard. " 'Tis possible. She was wrongly accused and he probably knows that he could be imprisoned if she chose to press charges. Worse still, he may be afraid that her testimony will link him to Nellie Arling's murder." His voice grew rougher still. " 'Tis reason enough, I think, for a man of his calibre to try to do her harm."

For a moment Ian Villiers's ruthless face was completely stripped of emotions and Alexander clearly saw the naked soul reflected in his eyes. It was a look he would not forget for the rest of his life despite the fact that it vanished as quickly as it had come, leaving a terrible desperation in its place. Without a word the Marquis left the study, pausing long enough to pick up the pistols he had primed, and the harsh expression on his hawkish face told Alexander that he intended to use them.

"You can tell me the details on the way," the Marquis said as they hurried to the stables where their horses were waiting. "Merewyn never told me that she'd been in gaol."

"I imagine 'twas her pride," Alexander remarked hoarsely.

The gray eyes were bleak. "I warrant she was afraid to tell me, thinking I'd mock her for it." The full lips tightened into an ominous line. "I warn you, Alex, I intend to ride hard, and if you can't keep up I won't wait."

"No need to worry," the MacAilis chieftain responded grimly. "I'll be right beside you."

Ian thrust the awesome-looking pistols into the holster and then vaulted into the saddle, his expression so black that it sent a shiver down Nick Holder's spine. Like a ghost from the grave he looked, the groom decided, certain that there'd be blood spilled somewhere before the day was done.

"Let's go," came the Marquis's quiet words, and the two horses vanished down the drive as though the wind was at their heels, both riders leaning low in their saddles.

Merewyn sensed that her mare was reaching the point of exhaustion. It would be foolish to try to outrun William, whose horse continued to gain. She would have to outwit him somehow and escape in the darkness, but how was she to do it with the moon shining almost as brightly as the sun? Worse still, panic was overriding her ability to reason, making it impossible for her to come up with a means of escape. Her mare was blowing hard now and her pace had slowed from the valiant gallop to a canter that would at any moment, Merewyn knew, change to a trot and eventually a staggering walk. Her eyes searched the landscape before her, frantically hoping to find some sort of hiding place, and then a small cry of joy escaped her lips as she caught sight of the shadowy walls of a building looming not too far ahead.

It was a house of sorts, Merewyn saw, the windows dark with no signs of life, but a house nonetheless that would contain people who would help her. A meandering drive led off through the trees to her right and she saw it in the nick of time, tugging viciously at the reins and pressing with her heels to turn her mount so that the exhausted mare veered at the last possible moment. Merewyn didn't even bother to look behind her to check if William had seen her turn. Urging the mare with both voice and quirt she dashed headlong into the courtyard and slid from the saddle before the horse had even come to a halt.

Leaving the snorting animal behind, she raced toward the arched front door and began pounding on it with her fists, screaming for help at the top of her lungs. To her horror the door began to groan beneath her frantic attack and then collapsed inward, revealing to Merewyn that she was not standing on the threshold of a residence but at the ruins of a great abbey. The four walls that had appeared so welcomingly strong from the road were crumbling to the ground and moonlight danced eerily on the shiny surface of the broken stones.

Behind her came the sound of hoofbeats, faint at first but then increasingly louder in cadence, and Merewyn knew that she didn't have time to remount her horse and slip away. She was trapped. Lifting her skirts she stepped through the doorway and threaded her way quickly across the rubble-strewn ground. At the far end of the enormous structure stood a crumbling stairway leading to an upper floor that was still intact. Here the roof had partially fallen away and moonlight streamed down through the cracks to light her way.

Her breathing ragged, Merewyn climbed upwards, pressing herself close against the wall, afraid to slip and plummet onto the hard stones below. Her eyes were like a cat's, accustomed to the semidarkness, and she saw as she neared the top of the stairs that the upper floor ran the length of one entire wall and that it contained a great number of hiding places in the form of countless nooks and crannies. If her luck held she might be able to hide here until William either gave up or began searching elsewhere, allowing her enough time to steal back to her mare and ride off in another direction.

"Merewyn, there's no sense in this! Come out!"

The faint shout came from far below, but it startled her nonetheless, sending chills down her spine, and she dashed across the upper floor, her eyes darting everywhere for a suitable hiding place.

"Come on, lass, I won't hurt you!"

Merewyn scrambled towards a niche formed when one of the walls had partially collapsed, the corner concealed behind several large segments of chiseled granite. Getting down on her hands and knees she squeezed herself between them and found herself with just enough room to crouch down, her back pressed against the mossy wall and her knees drawn up to her chin.

"Merewyn, we have to talk! By God, I swear I'll not hurt you!"

There was annoyance in William's voice now and she could hear him moving about below, rocks and pieces of wood hurling into the air as he threw them aside in his mad search. Worriedly, her eyes scanned the sky that was visible through a hole above, and she saw that the stars were growing brighter now that the moon was beginning to set. Soon it would be gone completely and the dawn would come, bringing with it sufficient light to reveal to William her hiding place. Before then Merewyn knew she would have to make her break—or she didn't stand a chance.

"Damn you, you little bitch, where are you?"

William's voice was further away now and Merewyn's heart leaped with hope. Did she dare leave now? Suppose she could take his horse with her and cut off his means of pursuit, leaving him stranded here while she rode back to Ravensley for help? The thought was so tempting that she was prepared to leave her little nook when suddenly she heard the sound of pebbles striking together not far away, and she froze, her heart hammering.

William was coming up the staircase. She could hear

his boots grating on the rough surface of the stones and his muffled curses as he felt his way slowly through the ever-increasing darkness. Merewyn cowered down, trying desperately to still the sound of her ragged breathing, praying that he wouldn't be able to penetrate her hiding place with his searching gaze. She heard him stumble over something and curse violently; then there was utter silence and Merewyn knew that he had come to a halt on the top of the stairs not twenty feet from where she was hidden, and was standing there listening intently. Merewyn made no movement, her face pressed against her arms, which were hugging her knees, the blood pounding in her ears and making her feel sick with fear. Minutes ticked by and still there came no sound from the silent man standing so very close, a pistol held in his shaking hand.

After what seemed like an eternity, Merewyn heard his footfalls again. He was moving systematically along the long walk, searching in every niche by thrusting the barrel of his pistol inside and feeling about for her body. Every now and then she could hear the dull metallic clink as the barrel struck stone and she shivered uncontrollably, certain that at any moment she would feel its cold surface poke into her ribs. Though William was too large to squeeze himself between the stones into her hiding place as she had done, he could easily touch her if he chose to thrust his arm inside.

Nauseated with fear, Merewyn could do nothing but keep herself absolutely still. The night was deathly quiet, interrupted only by the harsh breathing and mutterings of the man searching behind her. Water droplets condensing on the walls were beginning to drip down Merewyn's back and she was shivering not only from fear but also with the cold, for the cool night wind was blowing through every tiny crack in the walls about her.

William was now so close to her hiding place that Merewyn could have looked directly into his eyes if she had lifted her head and peered out of the cracks in the stones behind which she crouched. His muted footsteps were closer now and she could hear the ragged breath wheezing in and out of his lungs, his insane mutterings louder and more frightening than ever. Then the footsteps paused directly before her and she could hear his joints creaking as he went down on his knees to peer between the two segments of crumbled wall that made up the narrow entrance of her hiding place. A scream of pure terror rose in her throat, but even as she held her breath and bit down painfully on her lips to keep from uttering it, Merewyn heard her mare snorting from the ground far below.

Instantly, William scrambled to his feet and dashed down the stairs, making no attempt at stealth. As soon as he was gone, Merewyn emerged from her hiding place and began running along the landing in the opposite direction. Her mare's timely interruption had given her a second chance and she was determined this time to make good her escape. There had to be another staircase leading down to the ground at the far end of the landing, she thought to herself. It was now pitch black and she was forced to run with her hands held out in front of her to avoid running into the walls.

A large pile of rubble lay directly in her path and Merewyn, unable to see, stepped squarely into it, tripping over her skirts and falling heavily to the ground. She cried out as pain coursed through her scraped knees and torn hands, then lay still, gasping, the dust mingling with tears of helplessness. Get up, she moaned to herself, certain that William had heard her cry, but her aching, exhausted body refused to obey. Reaching out her hand Merewyn searched feverishly for a handhold with which to pull herself up, but as she felt along the rough stone floor ahead of her, her fingers suddenly came into contact with empty air.

Panic-stricken, she pulled herself upright and tapped

along the ground with her booted foot until suddenly, not two feet from where she had fallen, the tips of her toes no longer had support underneath. Merewyn shrank back, gasping and whimpering, the realization that she had narrowly escaped a terrible fall making her feel dizzy. Apparently, the rest of the abbey's upper story had collapsed long ago, leaving only the narrow segment of covered walk upon which she stood.

But how was she to escape if there was only one flight of stairs? The obvious solution—to return the way she had come—terrified her. Suppose she met William on the way down? There was absolutely no doubt in Merewyn's mind that he intended to kill her. She had no idea why he should want to do so, but the fact remained clear that she was hopelessly trapped unless . . .

Merewyn's mind began to work rapidly, and as she came up with the first coherent plan she'd made since setting foot in the ruins she found herself growing more clearheaded, a strange calm washing over her that stilled the fearful pounding of her heart and her ragged, desperate breathing. She had been spared by providence along from a bad, perhaps even fatal, fall. Suppose William made the same mistake but found himself not so lucky? 'Twas a terrible chance to take but she had little enough choice.

"Merewyn, where are you?"

William's voice floated to her from the darkness behind her and Merewyn realized suddenly that he was coming back up the staircase. Doubtless he had heard her cry out when she fell and had abandoned his search below. Merewyn knew now that this would be her final chance. Drawing a shaky breath she cried out as bravely as she could, "You'll never catch me, you despicable blackguard! You're a dead man!"

As she finished speaking she stamped her booted feet hard on the stones, hoping to mimic the sound of running, then pressed herself as close against the wall as she

could. Behind her she could hear William exhale in a
long, low hiss of glee, certain that he had found her at
last; then the heavy pounding of his boots as he came in
pursuit.

"So you think you can escape me, my bonnie lass?"
she heard him rasp out. The night was still too dark for
Merewyn to see him, but she could faintly make out his
shadow looming towards her and felt the material of his
cloak brush against her as he ran by. Then came the
sound of rattling pebbles, a terrified scream, and a split
second of silence before a dull, sickening thud.

Merewyn felt her hair stand on end and for a moment
she stood paralyzed against the wall, the silence seeming
to roar in her ears. She could scarcely believe that her
plan had worked—that William had fallen into the
rubble-strewn room below. But how could she be certain
that he had injured himself sufficiently to incapacitate
him? Her slim body began to shiver uncontrollably.
Suppose he was dead? Suppose she had been responsible
for killing a man?

For what seemed an eternity she huddled motionless
against the damp stones of the upper abbey wall, straining her ears for some sound below, but she could hear
nothing save her own shallow breathing and the pounding of her heart against her ribs. Far below in the
darkness her mare snorted again, obviously relishing the
chance to indulge uninterrupted on the thick grass that
grew about the ruins, and the sound served to rouse
Merewyn from her stupor.

Turning her face upwards she stared curiously at the
strange gray light beginning to glow through the gaping
holes in the roof and she realized that dawn was coming.
Hesitantly, dreading what she would find, she inched
her way cautiously to the edge of the ledge upon which
she had been standing and looked down. Through the
rapidly increasing light she could clearly make out the
crumpled form of William Rawlings lying amid the

stones and fallen wood that had once been the main room of the abbey's chapter house. From her vantage point Merewyn had no idea if he was still alive, but the curious manner in which one of his arms lay twisted beneath him made her suspect that it had been broken in the fall. It was difficult to see his face, which was concealed by fallen rubble, but Merewyn was certain that his eyes were closed.

Lifting her torn skirts she stepped gingerly over the debris that had tripped her earlier, then ran as fast as her aching legs would carry her towards the staircase. She had lost her hat some time ago and her hair hung in disheveled strands before her eyes. Pushing them impatiently out of the way she thought to herself that while a hat was easily replaceable, she certainly wasn't.

Quickly, she scrambled down the steps and began to make her way towards the fallen door, which was visible now in the pale gray light of dawn. As she started across the uneven ground, a shot rang out unexpectedly behind her, the thick stone walls of the ruins echoing with the explosion, sending shock waves clear to the crumbling foundations. Merewyn never had time to realize that William had fired his gun, for something burned through her shoulder, wiping out everything but the unbearable pain, and as she cried out and clutched at her arm she felt the palm of her hand come away covered with a hot, sticky substance.

Behind her Merewyn could hear the sound of demonic laughter and she turned quickly, her tilted eyes enormous with fear and pain, to see William Rawlings's pale, gaunt face staring out at her from the folds of his cloak, the smoking pistol held in his twisted arm, which he had propped up with his good one. She screamed in mortal terror and staggered to her feet, still clutching her wounded shoulder with her hand, the velvet material stained a dull crimson.

William gave a bellow of outraged frustration when

he saw her reel through the doorway that led outside, but Merewyn did not pause in her stride. Gritting her teeth, her head whirling dizzily, she searched about frantically for her mare and found her grazing peacefully not too far away, William's mount nearby.

The mare snorted in fear when Merewyn approached, her nostrils dilating at the scent of blood, but Merewyn spoke soothingly and the animal quieted immediately. She found it nearly impossible to mount, agonizing waves of pain shooting throughout her body, but fear prodded her on. Her movements were clumsy, however —her skirts caught in the stirrup as she pulled herself up, and when she bent to free them the nervous mare balked and pranced sideways unexpectedly. Merewyn, clinging precariously to her back, was thrown off balance and landed with jarring pain in the dust. Waves of dizziness washed over her and her eyelids fluttered as she fought against unconsciousness, sick with the throbbing fire in her shoulder. . . but the blackness was persistent and finally won.

The great house of Ravensley was ablaze with lights when Lord Montague and the MacAilis chief cantered into the cobblestone courtyard. Torches burned in the walls beside the gate and nearly every downstairs window was framed with light from within.

"What in blazes is going on?" Ian demanded aloud. Slipping from the saddle he tossed the reins to a groom, who hurried out to meet him and strode quickly inside with Alexander following behind.

No sooner had he entered the great hall with its vaulted ceiling than he was fallen upon by a nearly hysterical Marty, who threw her thin arms about him and cried, "Oh, thank goodness you be here, your lordship!"

Gently detaching himself from her fierce grip, Ian lifted his head and saw that some of the other servants had gathered behind the housekeeper, their expressions grave. The foreboding that had plagued him since Alexander had related to him the truth about Merewyn's relationship with William Rawlings now escalated into full-blown fear. Staring down into Marty's wide eyes he shook her gently, trying to claim her attention.

"Marty, what is it? Where's Merewyn?"

Her fearful words confirmed his worst fears. "Gone, your lordship, gone these past few hours!"

Behind him Alexander made an involuntary movement, but Ian was aware only of the cold hand that seemed to settle with an icy grip about his heart. "Gone where?" he demanded, his voice grating in his ears.

Marty dabbed ineffectually at the tears streaming from her eyes. "She left b-because of you, m'lord. She said she was going h-home. I tried to stop her but I couldn't. She took the little mare you bought for her and left."

"Didn't any of you try to stop her?" Ian demanded, his ringing question bringing guilt and despair to the faces of the servants.

"Begging your pardon, m'lord," said Collins, the elected spokesman, a tall, fair headed young man in his late twenties. "We rode all the way to Dorking, which is where Lady Montague said she was headed, but she wasn't there."

The nightmarish feeling increased and Ian could feel the sweat beginning to break out on his brow. "Are you saying she never made it to Dorking, Mr. Collins?"

The footman quailed beneath the intense gaze. "Yes, m'lord, unless she changed her mind and went elsewhere."

"Was she alone when she left?" the Marquis asked quietly, addressing Marty who stood weeping before him.

"Aye, your lordship. Oh, I just knowed something

awful's happened to her!"

Alexander and Ian exchanged glances charged with unspoken fears.

"And you're absolutely certain she was headed for Dorking?"

The gray head bobbed vigorously.

"Collins, did you have the other roads checked? She might have had another town in mind and mentioned Dorking to throw us off."

The young man nodded, relieved that he had taken that precaution. "We tried all roads north, south, east, and west. I also sent two men down to Farthingdale to see if she'd gone there."

"And?"

"They haven't gotten back yet. Everything else came up null."

Ian turned away without a word, his handsome face deeply lined, making him look very old and unwell. There was silence from the small group in the raftered hall, waiting to hear what he would say, none of them paying any attention at all to the dark-haired stranger standing quietly in the shadows until his deep, accented voice startled all of them:

"Perhaps we should send someone to the village to find out if William Rawlings is even here, Ian. For all we know he may have returned to Scotland after all."

The broad shoulders slumped wearily. " 'Twould be a waste of time, Alex. I know he's here. But we can't spend all of our time chasing about the countryside like blindmen. We have to know exactly where to turn to. I—"

"Excuse me, your lordship."

Everyone turned to look inquiringly at the thin, middle-aged man in Ravensley livery who had entered the hall unnoticed from the back staircase, a red-faced, nervous young fellow standing at his side. An expectant hush fell and the manservant wasted no time in addressing his haunted-looking employer.

"This is Jackie Wilson, m'lord, and he has something to tell you."

Ten minutes later Alexander and Lord Montague, accompanied by a half-dozen servants, all of them heavily armed, rode off in the direction of Dorking. The sky was awash with pearly gray light and to the east a faint golden tinge to the heavens was heralding the coming dawn. Their destination was a Norman Abbey, destroyed by the Roundheads over a hundred years ago, the only building of sorts between Ravensley and Dorking itself. Here, the Marquis fervently prayed Merewyn would have hidden herself if she had, as they all suspected, been followed by William Rawlings. But as a precautionary measure the rest of the Ravensley servants had been sent out to scour the rest of the countryside and to rouse the farmers and villagers in a massive hunt for the missing Lady Montague.

Upon hearing Jackie Wilson's tale, Ian's worst fears had been confirmed, and the return of the second manservant dispatched by the resourceful Collins had only compounded them further. He had reported that a guest who fit William Rawlings's description had been lodged at the Farthingdale inn since last night, but had checked out abruptly several hours ago. There was little doubt in Ian's mind that William, under an assumed name, had come to Ravensley to do Merewyn harm.

Since John Collins and his men had found no trace of Merewyn in Dorking, it could safely be assumed that she had been detained en route there. Ian's first logical choice had been to search the abbey ruins, but as he urged his stallion onward at a killing pace there was a numb feeling of dread deep within his heart. Could Merewyn have been prevented from reaching Dorking because of some injury? Had William Rawlings managed to catch her before she could safely reach the inn there? He didn't dare admit that likelihood to himself.

Alexander, riding at the Marquis's side, could tell by
the grim expression on his face that their thoughts were
running a similar course. Never had he seen a man age
as rapidly as the Marquis seemed to, growing more haggard and hungry-looking by the minute. But the deadly
glint in his steely eyes never wavered, a lean look Alexander had seen several times in the glowing eyes of the
wolves he'd killed in the dead of winter when, half starving, they had ventured down in broad daylight to
Cairnlach from the mountains.

There had been little opportunity for conversation
during the mad ride from the sprawling city of London,
but Alexander had managed to tell the Marquis briefly
of Merewyn's arrest and her tenure in gaol, the details,
gleaned from the authorities' questioning of the two
men arrested in connection with Merewyn's disappearance: a certain Edmund Unsworth and a ferret-like
prison guard named Andy MacElthy. Ian had listened
with the same grim expression he had worn all night,
and had then given Alexander a terse account of what
had happened to Merewyn and himself since he had left
Glasgow aboard HMS *Columbia* last spring.

His explanation had raised many questions that Alexander did not have the time or desire to ask. His primary
concern now was to find his sister, and he prayed with
his entire soul that they would find her alive and safe.
Casting another furtive glance at the big man galloping
beside him, Alexander hoped fervently that he would be
able to get his hands on William Rawlings before the
Marquis did, for he doubted that there would be much
left over for him once Ian had finished with him.

CHAPTER THIRTEEN

Merewyn had no idea how long she lay on her back on the hard ground, the deep furrow the lead ball had plowed through her shoulder continuing to seep blood, though fortunately not at an alarming rate. She returned to consciousness only when she felt a booted foot kick her painfully in the ribs and she opened her eyes, gasping to find the early morning sun shining full in her face. She blinked and something else came into view, the shadow of a man bending over her, and she recoiled as she recognized the gaunt features and glowing eyes of William Rawlings.

"No," she moaned, turning her head to shut out the sight of him.

His breath came in ragged gasps. "You thought me dead, didn't you, my dear? I might as well be for all the use I'll ever have of this arm again." He held up his uselessly hanging right arm for her to see and his hated voice floated to her in a haze.

"Took me quite some time to drag myself out here, it did, but now I've made it, and I'm glad you're not dead as yet, so I'll have the pleasure of watching you die."

Merewyn's pain-darkened eyes stared up at him dully. "Why?" she whispered, "Why do you want to kill me? I s-swore I'd never tell."

His teeth were bared in a hideous snarl. "Did you expect me to believe that? No, you and your wee secret about me were too much of a threat. You see, Merewyn, I murdered a woman in Glasgow. 'Tis why I had to come to London, and I was afraid your charges against me, even though I've always been a paragon of Glasgow society, would enable them to trace that murder to me."

"You'll n-never get away with this," Merewyn said, her mind working dully as she stared vaguely into the hate-contorted features. William was standing above her, his booted legs spread, sweat trickling down his cheeks, his right arm hanging at a grotesque angle to his gaunt body.

"I won't?" The cold words made her tremble and she closed her eyes wearily, hoping to shut out the sight of him. His sibilant voice continued to plague her, taunting her with what he was saying. " 'Twould seem your esteemed husband believes me to be your lover." He threw back his head and laughed mockingly. "God, how pat for me, wouldn't you say, Merewyn, my dear? Naturally, they'll all think you've run away with me, for I intend to leave tonight for Italy, and no one will ever see either of us again. Convenient, eh?"

"You're insane!" Merewyn cried, her pale cheeks flushing with the exertion of speaking. Opening her eyes she saw that William seemed to have lost his pistol and was clutching a smooth rock in his good hand as he grinned down at her menacingly. Dear God, did he intend to kill her by cracking her skull? A shuddering sigh wracked her aching body and she found herself wishing that his badly aimed shot had killed her after all.

"Insane?" William asked disagreeably, his heavy-lidded eyes glinting. "Not a kind word for a fellow Scotsman, dear Lady Montague."

"You aren't f-fit to lick the boots of a l-lowly shepherd," Merewyn retorted with the last of her strength. From somewhere deep within her came a sudden and incredibly vivid vision of Cairnlach, the mention of Scotland having reminded her of home. She could see clearly the smooth stone walls and the mist-covered braes that flanked it on two sides, the sheep grazing contentedly in their stone wall enclosures, Alexander riding about his land on his beloved Greyfriar.

Was this the end of her life, then? Would she never see Alex or Malcolm again? From deep within her rose a despairing rage against dying when there was so much of life left to be lived, and with an incoherent cry that echoed from the dim times when the Vikings had first overrun Skye in the mist, Merewyn lashed out at William with her small booted foot, kicking him fiercely in the shins and knocking him off balance.

He fell with a screech of pain upon his broken arm, but Merewyn didn't wait to see how badly she had hurt him. Rolling over onto her uninjured side, she pushed herself upright and began running blindly. Behind her William was staggering to his feet, bellowing threats as he began loping after her in a strange, ungainly manner, one side of his body dipping grotesquely as though he were crippled.

Merewyn was screaming in terror, looking about for her mare and realizing that she was gone. On horseback she might be able to escape the drooling, cursing hunchback plodding along behind her, knowing that he couldn't possibly ride with his terribly mangled arm. But here on the ground, with her own arm badly injured, weak with the loss of blood, they were equals, and she screamed again as she cast a glance over her uninjured shoulder and saw that he was gaining on her.

"Merewyn!"

Her head snapped up and she froze, dazed, as her entire field of vision filled with men on horseback, the two muscular mounts in the lead each bearing a dark-headed rider of great stature whose features seemed to swim fuzzily before her. The man on the left, broader and more powerfully built, drew two awesome-looking pistols out of his holsters and fired them before the others had even reached for theirs. Merewyn whirled in time to see William's body jerk in response as the shots hit home, a look of surprise spreading across his gaunt features before he dropped silently to the ground.

"Merewyn, my God, are you all right?"

She turned, the sound of the beloved voice penetrating her numbness, and cried out joyously when she saw Alexander hurrying towards her, his arms outstretched, his rugged features filled with a terrible mixture of despair and relief at seeing her alive, but obviously injured.

"Alex, oh, Alex!"

Merewyn ran to him, oblivious to the imposing figure of the Marquis striding towards her at her brother's side, and collapsed into his arms.

Ian watched them silently, making no move to destroy this reunion between brother and sister, his disbelieving eyes roving every detail of Merewyn's appearance. She was bareheaded and her golden curls hung in wild disarray down her back, the palms of her hands were cut and her riding habit was hopelessly torn. But it was the blood staining the velvet sleeve that caused him the most anxiety and finally he came forward, rare tenderness and concern in his eyes, and he touched her lightly on the shoulder.

"Merewyn, you're badly hurt. Let me take you back to Ravensley."

She turned to look at him, still in the protective circle of Alexander's arms, and Ian winced as he stared down into her ravaged expression, her beautiful little face grimy and scratched. An overwhelming desire to hold her close overcame him, to feel her body against his, to assure himself that she was really safe and that she was back again with him. He took a step towards her but she shrank away, moving closer to Alexander as though seeking his protection.

Ian stopped short, regarding her quizzically, feeling uncertain for the first time in his life. "Merewyn, let me take you home," he repeated. "Your shoulder needs attention."

The golden head turned deliberately away from the handsome, anxious features, and she grasped at the lapels of her brother's vest. "Please, Alex, may I ride with you?"

"Of course, my sweet," Alexander replied, giving his brother-in-law a look of surprise.

Ian's full lips tightened and the weariness that had hovered about him seemed to weigh more heavily upon him than ever before. Glancing briefly at the resolutely hunched little shoulders he seemed to sense that the rift between them was irreparable, and although it cost him everything, he turned his back on the bloodstained and shivering little form of his wife and gave curt orders to the silently waiting men to retrieve William Rawlings's fallen body.

Alexander mounted his horse and sat waiting for Merewyn to be lifted up before him. Ian picked her up into his strong arms and their faces almost touched, the intensely longing gray eyes briefly meeting the pain-filled indigo ones. Merewyn stiffened perceptibly and looked away, quietly suffering his touch until she was safely in the saddle before her brother. Alexander wheeled the gelding and started down the road and Merewyn, her small chin drooping against her chest, gave no further thought to the tall man standing with his arms hanging at his sides as he stared after them, the steely eyes bereft of hope.

CHAPTER FOURTEEN

A fine curtain of mist obscured the mountain peaks and stole on silken threads through the glens, beads of moisture dripping off the leaves of the bracken ferns and spreading a gauzy layer upon the leaded-pane windows of Cairnlach Castle. The byre on the hillside above echoed with the barking of dogs and the baaing of sheep being herded into the pens for the night. The air was damp and chilly, rife with the promise of autumn that was already turning the needles of the towering larches to gold and painting the heather purple.

Merewyn was sitting in the cozy study awaiting Malcolm's return from the hills, holding a heavy book in her lap, a shawl of fine cheviot wool spread across her thin shoulders. For almost an hour she had been turning the pages, but the meaning of the words escaped her and she gave up at last and sighed, closing the embossed-leather cover and setting the book aside.

She and Alexander had returned to Cairnlach a week ago, after a fortnight's stay at Ravensley where Merewyn had been confined to her bed until her shoulder mended sufficiently for her to risk traveling. She had seen nothing of Ian during those two weeks, not even a brief glimpse of him. He had been busy with the inquest that had taken place because of William Rawlings's

476

death, and even Alexander had gone away for an afternoon to testify before the magistrate and tell the court what had happened to Merewyn in Glasgow.

Merewyn could remember little of her convalescence in her pleasant bedchamber at Ravensley save for Marty's incessant fussing and Alexander's frequent visits. She had not asked for Ian, nor had Alex made any mention of him, and Merewyn concluded that he had no desire at all to see her. She had hoped, secretly, that he would come to her now that he knew he had been mistaken about her relationship with William, but as the days rolled by and he did not come, she came to realize that his damnable pride was keeping them apart. Often at night Merewyn could hear him pacing restlessly about his room while a light burned for long hours beneath the adjoining door, but not once did he open it to look in on her.

Merewyn told herself that she didn't care, that she would never forgive him for hurting her as he had, for making a mockery of her love for him. After all, it was the mills he had wanted, and surely his refusal to see her must mean that he had meant what he had said to her that night. The pain in her shoulder went away eventually, but the ache within her heart did not.

When the doctor pronounced Merewyn fit to travel she felt certain that Ian would at least come to bed her farewell, but the hours went by and their departure neared and still he didn't come. The last piece of luggage was loaded on, a tearful Marty hugged her good-bye after tucking her comfortably into the corner of the coach, and there was still no sign of the glowering, dark-haired man she longed to see. Merewyn didn't even know whether or not he was home that day, for the inquest had dragged on interminably and Alexander had told her two days ago that Ian had gone to London to speak to the authorities there. Still, she couldn't help but search every window with hopeful eyes as the coach rumbled down the drive, only to find every one of them empty, and she had bitten back her tears, aware that Alexander was watching her inquiringly.

The journey had taken countless days and nights for they traveled slowly, Merewyn's shoulder aching after long hours in the rocking vehicle although she never complained. Alexander studied her pale face often, worried by the dark circles beneath the lifeless eyes, and though she responded with smiles to his attempts to coax her into a better humor, he could tell that the gestures were halfhearted at best.

And then they were home, the turrets and battlements of Cairnlach rising from above the rolling emerald hills and filling Merewyn's eyes with sudden tears. An overjoyed Malcolm was there to meet them, an older, more sober man than Merewyn remembered, whose responsibility for the company had kept him from accompanying Alexander to England, a responsibility Merewyn had never known him to exhibit before.

Merewyn sighed deeply as she glanced about the comfortable study, thinking about the changes she had observed in her brother since her return home. Was it possible that Malcolm had really grown more reserved and somber since her absence, or could it be that he was merely taking his cue from her? She had to admit that she had been extremely withdrawn since her return, but why she should feel this great gap within her she couldn't rightly explain. Even Annie treated her differently, the intimacy between them gone, and Merewyn had caught the old woman studying her anxiously many times since she'd come home, only to have her look away quickly when her sharp hazel eyes met the slanted indigo ones.

Merewyn sighed again and pushed the book from her lap, rising to her feet and wandering restlessly to the window. Mist swirled outside the panes and the fading daylight revealed that more threatening rainclouds had moved in from the north. It was typical Highland weather, a wet and turbulent season that had always affected Merewyn mysteriously, bringing an exuberance to her spirit and an eagerness to face the challenges of the coming winter. How she loved the Highlands, taking strength from the wild landscape, feeling a kinship with the stalwart mountains and towering larches that grew so sturdily in the hard ground.

But even the beauty of the blooming heather and the fiery colors of the larch trees did not stir her as they once had. Sadly, she shook her small head, pursing her soft lips, unable to explain this mystery. Even the news she had heard from Malcolm—that Alex had begun visiting his former fiancée Jeannie Sinclair, who was living again with her parents—did not cheer her as it should have.

"What in blazes is wrong with me?" she asked Remus, who lay sleeping before the fire, his rib cage rising and falling with his rhythmic breathing.

At the sound of his mistress's soft voice, the big hound cocked his head but the mournful eyes told her nothing. Despite herself she was forced to smile, and dropped down on her knees to lovingly scratch his ears.

"How's the shoulder?" came a cheerful voice from the doorway.

Merewyn smiled in response as Malcolm strode in, his hair damp with clinging droplets of water, the soles of his boots covered with mud. "You better take those off before Annie sees the mess you're making on her floors," she warned.

Malcolm grinned and complied, tossing them unceremoniously into the corner and collapsing behind the big desk, propping his arms comfortably behind his head. "Summer herds come down from the hills this week," he remarked, watching her bent head as she continued to stroke Remus's soft fur. She was dressed in a warm gown of dark blue velvet, the sleeves piped with white satin ribbon to brighten its somber appearance, and a stray tendril of golden hair brushed against one soft temple. The profile she presented him was defensively young and lovely, and Malcolm found himself still unable to grasp the fact that she was actually the Marchioness of Montague, Ian Villiers's wife.

Though Alex had told him everything that had transpired in London and Surrey, there were still many things Malcolm would have liked to ask about the past few months, for his sister had changed considerably during her lengthy absence. There was a hard, unrelenting core underlying the strength she had always had, and a quietness he would have admired in her character if he hadn't been so convinced that it had not only been born of the suffering she must have endured during her stay in gaol and the long months at sea, but also because of some sadness she harbored within her.

Alexander had known just a few details concerning the reported falling out she had had with her husband shortly before the affair with William Rawlings had reached its shocking climax, but Malcolm suspected that, given Merewyn's fiery nature and Lord Montague's awesome temper, the sparks had doubtless been flying. He was content, as was his brother, to let matters lie until Merewyn had completely recovered from her injury, her stiff shoulder obviously plaguing her at times though she never uttered a word of complaint. But the fact still remained that she was now the wife of Lord Montague, and things would have to be resolved soon, both legally in terms of the company holdings, and in the obvious fact that Merewyn couldn't spend the rest of her life here at Cairnlach while Lord Montague prowled about his estate across the river.

"I think I'll go to bed."

Merewyn's quietly spoken comment brought Malcolm's thoughts back to the present. "So soon?"

"I'm tired."

He noticed with a twinge of worry that she was very pale and that the expression in the tilted eyes was strained. Smiling kindly, he rose to his feet. "Aye, 'tis a good idea. I'll walk up with you."

Merewyn shook her head reassuringly. "I'm fine." At the door she hesitated, her dark eyes watching him intently. "Malcolm?"

"Aye?"

"Do you think—" The soft lips trembled slightly and then she shook her head, smiling at him ruefully. "Never mind. Good night."

"Good night," Malcolm growled, unable to hide his distress. Damn Ian Villiers, damn him to Hell, he thought as the door shut softly behind her.

A steady drizzle awakened Merewyn the next morning. She had slept deeply for the first time in weeks and felt surprisingly cheerful as she breakfasted on the oat cakes and bramble jelly Annie brought in on a tray. Though she did not like being treated like an invalid, she suffered Annie's ministrations with stoic silence, aware that the old woman was trying to please her. Besides, she told herself, sipping appreciatively from the cold, fresh milk delivered from the larder, she rather liked being pampered this way after all.

She dressed herself in a lawn-green satin morning gown, being careful not to jar her mending shoulder, then brushed her long hair with stiff strokes, her left hand that wielded the brush extremely clumsy. Unable to pin her hair she braided it and tied it back with a green velvet ribbon, allowing the thick coil to hang down to her waist, and then examined herself critically in the looking glass above her dressing table.

Odd that she should look the same on the outside when she felt so different within, Merewyn thought solemnly to herself. Odd, too, that she could look so unaffected by her near brush with death. She shivered, reminding herself that she never wanted to think of those

harrowing hours in the ruins again, but visions rose unbidden into her mind to haunt her. She could still feel
the terror that had coursed through her in those dark,
lonely hours when she had hidden behind the stone wall,
hearing William cursing and muttering above her and
the horror she had felt when she had stared down at his
twisted, fallen body.

Strange that she had not even spared him a single
thought after Ian had put those two bullets into him,
felling him only a short distance from where she had
been standing. She could still remember the joy and relief that had coursed through her at the sight of Alexander coming towards her, so tall and comforting, and
yet, if the truth must be told, not quite as longed for as
the big man who had become his brother-in-law, nor
nearly as handsome.

Merewyn sighed heavily, thinking of the steely eyes
that had met hers so often in the past, their expression
ranging from smoldering anger to darkened passion. If
only he would look at her that way just once again, the
tenderness and desire there making her feel weak with
longing. But all of that was over, she reminded herself
forlornly. Ian had bedded her to satisfy his own lust and
all of the love she had thought he had harbored for her
had been feigned, assumed, a dastardly lie.

"Oh, Miss Merewyn, ye maun come quickly!"

It was Morag, the little upstairs maid, panting breathlessly in the doorway, forgetting in her excitement that
her mistress was now Lady Montague. Merewyn, who
had been standing lost in thought before her dressing
table turned quickly, seizing the girl's thin arms and
shaking her in agitation.

"What is it, Morag? Has Alex been hurt? Is something
wrong with Malcolm?"

Morag's eyes danced. "Nay, mistress, nay! 'Tis himself, it be, Lord Montague, downstairs askin' for ye!"

"You're lying!" Merewyn cried, the color draining from her hollow cheeks.

Morag looked aghast, having been convinced that this news would bring back the sunny smile that had always seemed such an integral part of her mistress's nature. She hadn't expected anger, especially directed at her! Her lower lip trembled. "I be speakin' the truth! He be askin' for ye i' the hall!"

Merewyn struggled to compose herself. "Where is the laird?" she asked worriedly.

"Gone tae the braes, Miss Merewyn, and Master Colm wi' him."

"Then I'm here alone?"

"Aye, miss." Morag nodded vigorously. "I mean, we be here, Miss Annie, the servants and me, but—"

"Please tell Lord Montague that I won't see him."

"But miss!" Morag wailed.

" 'Tis 'my lady,' " a deep voice corrected her and Morag whirled with a frightened squeal as the towering form of the Marquis filled the doorway. He was dressed casually in buckskin, his stock simply folded, his boots and coat still wet from the rain that was falling outside. His dark curls were disheveled and he carried a pair of gloves and a hat in one hand, from which droplets of water dripped onto the carpet. Morag uttered another squeal, more frightened than the first, and hurried forward to take them from him.

"Oh, yer lordship, oh!" she cried. "Annie will hae me head if she kens I didna take these frae ye at the door!" She peered up into his face as she spoke and her jaw went slack when she saw that she barely came to the middle of his broad chest. Like a timid mouse she scurried out of the room, forgetting completely that she was abandoning her mistress.

"You'd better leave," Merewyn told the Marquis when he turned his attention back to her and took several steps into the room. Somehow she had forgotten how tall and handsome he was, his breeches clinging to his muscular thighs, his damp coat adhering to his broad shoulders. He looked older than she remembered and seemed to have lost weight, giving him a lean, hungry look, and there were deep lines etched about his sensual lips that hadn't been there before.

"We have to talk, Merewyn," he said softly, his gray eyes lingering on her upturned face, thinking she had never looked more beautiful or desirable. The dark green gown she wore transformed her eyes into emeralds, their maddening tilt only emphasized by the dark shadows that still lingered beneath them. The thick golden braid that hung to her curving hips swung provocatively as she arrogantly tossed her head.

"The way we talked the night you returned from London, Ian? Do you wish me to give you the same chance to explain that you gave me?"

A spasm of pain crossed the handsome, finely chiseled features. "Merewyn, please understand that the evidence seemed so overwhelming. I was convinced you had betrayed me."

"Was your love for me so callous that you dismissed it at the first sign of doubt?" she demanded bitterly. A hollow laugh rang from her parted lips. "Oh, aye, how foolish of me. I recall you told me that you never loved me at all. 'Twas the mills you wanted all along."

Ian groaned despairingly. "Oh, God, Merewyn, surely you don't believe I really meant that? I was hurt by your seeming betrayal and wanted to strike out at you, the only woman who has ever had the power to wound me."

Merewyn's expression was stony. "And you expect me to accept your explanation trustingly? Why should I show you more confidence and trust than you showed me? Ian, your damnable pride and thick-headedness almost cost me my l-life!"

All of his pent-up angruish was visible in his handsome face and he came towards her with outstretched arms, wanting only to fold her against him, aching to touch and comfort her, a longing that he had denied himself for so long now. But Merewyn backed away, terror and loathing mingling on her delicate countenance, and he came to an abrupt halt, letting his arms fall uselessly to his sides. In all their stormy encounters she had never looked at him quite so hatefully before and he began to suspect despairingly that he might have lost her forever.

"Ian, please go," she whispered, her back pressed against the windowsill, her hands clenched into fists behind her. She couldn't bear to see him look so hopeless, he who had always been so supremely confident and so haughty, this long-legged blackguard who had swaggered into her life and charmed her despite herself with his wicked smile and disarming good looks.

"Merewyn, you are still my wife," Ian reminded her, humbled for the first time in his life, aware that his great strength and skill at manipulation, even his charm, would not be able to right the wrongs he had done or change her opinion of him.

"I haven't forgotten that for a moment," Merewyn assured him, looking down at the ring on her slender finger with a mixture of contempt and sadness. The bluish-green eyes flashed suddenly with indignation. "You have what you want now, m'lord, the mills and a lever to prize at my brother with. Just leave me alone— I'm through trying to fight you." Her thin shoulders slumped despondently. "Please go," she whispered, turning away from him.

Worried by her pallor and the thinness of her voice, Ian hurried across the room and slipped his strong hands about her small waist, drawing her against his hard chest. For a moment he could feel her body melt against him, but then she grew rigid and struggled free, whirling about to face him, the tilted eyes filled with anger.

"I'll not succumb to your experienced touch anymore, m'lord! Now will you go or shall I call one of the footmen to throw you out?"

"Your entire staff couldn't move me," he retorted with something of the old glint in his eyes, but sobered instantly when he saw Merewyn's unyielding expression. Moving away from her, aware that his nearness disturbed her, he fought to conquer the longing to touch her again, finding it difficult with her standing before him, looking more beautiful than he had ever seen her.

"I came here, Merewyn," he said briskly, striving to return to the matters at hand, "because there's something important I have to say to you. I wanted to talk to you at Ravensley, while you were still so badly hurt, but I was afraid that the sight of me might upset you and affect your recovery. Your brother agreed with me and we both decided 'twould be better that he brought you back here first."

"Then Alex knows about our—our argument?"

The gray eyes held hers steadily. "To some extent, aye. After the doctor had seen you and the inquest was over, I sat down with him and told him everything. On the ride over from London I'd given him some of the facts, but that night at Ravensley I spared nothing."

Merewyn's cheeks flamed. "N-nothing?"

A faint smile tugged at the corners of Ian's mouth. "Naturally, there are a few things that will always be just between you and me, and he is your brother, after all. I didn't want to upset him." The smile grew and curved the sensual lips so that suddenly he looked carefree, handsome, and young, the way Merewyn had always wanted him to be.

"Your brother's not an idiot, Merewyn, and I'm certain he realizes the extent of the attraction that was always there between the two of us. As a matter of fact, he approves of our marriage."

"Small wonder he didn't mention your name at all, or ask me any questions. Malcolm, either!" The slanted eyes began to flash at this apparent betrayal. "They expect us to reconcile! As I remember, 'twas Alex whose praise of your character sent me to Glasgow to begin with." She gazed up at him, the golden depths of her eyes growing hard. "Well, my lord, 'tis far too late. I'm through trying to sacrifice my life and happiness for Cairnlach's sake. I've learned that there are more important things in the world than family honor and pride."

"Merewyn, please," Ian said quietly. "I didn't come here to ask you to forgive me. I know now that I hurt you far too badly. Even though I was lying when I said that I'd married you for the mills, I don't expect you to believe me." His broad shoulders slumped wearily. "No, I've lied to you too often and used you to achieve my own ends. In my blind love for you, when I was even too proud to admit that I cared for you, I wanted only to prove to myself that what I felt for you was merely desire and a thirst for revenge against the things you said and did to me in turn.

"I couldn't admit to myself that you were different from all the women I'd ever known and that your obstinence and courage affected me deeply. Instead, I wanted to strike out and hurt you because I was afraid for the first time in my life that I was losing the upper hand to a willful little chit not half my size."

Ian moved restlessly towards the window, turning his broad back to her as he stared out at the fog-enshrouded landscape, the water dripping from the eaves above and running in mournful rivulets down the leaded panes. "Even that first day at Montague, when you dealt me that blow to my manly pride that angered me no end, I couldn't help but feel a curious fascination for you."

Merewyn, watching him from her protective stance in the corner of the room, could see the tightly clenched jaw muscles relaxing and the gray eyes beginning to glow with amusement at the memory. "You were such a bedraggled little thing and yet you spit and clawed at me like a fearless lion cub. Your odd mixture of spirit and affronted beauty intrigued me no end. 'Tis in part why I accompanied the *Columbia* to sea. And when I did find you, you drove me half mad with your uppish airs and refusal to humble yourself before me, but I didn't realize until much later that it was because I was so attracted to you. There is something about you, Merewyn, that touches me deeply in here."

Ian touched his broad chest close to his heart. "It transcends even the love I have for you. I feel as though you and I were made for each other, that we were destined to be together from the very first. Perhaps 'tis why we have hurt each other so. I do know it frightened me on occasion, because I found it so hard to believe that a man like me, who has always been in command of every situation, could suddenly find himself unable to govern even the feelings within his own heart."

Ian turned to peer into her solemn blue eyes, but no sooner had their glances met than Merewyn's soft lips tightened stoically and she turned away.

Ian sighed heavily. "I'm sorry, Merewyn, I didn't come here to bare my heart or plead with you to come back to Montague. I knew you wouldn't forgive me so easily and I can't blame you for that. Dear God, when I think of how I left you in the hands of that swine who shot and almost killed you—"

His expression seemed to grow even more haggard, the gray eyes filling with self-loathing. "I'll never forget the sight of you running away from that madman, your gown torn and bloodied. 'Tis an image I'll carry with me to the grave and one that will haunt me forever. If you wanted revenge against me for what I've done, madame, you should be relieved to learn that this will plague me the rest of my days."

Merewyn could feel her heart beginning to swell with pain and a longing to comfort him, seeing from his terrible expression that he had suffered a great deal, perhaps even more than she, for remorse was a hard emotion to bear, especially for a man as proud as the Marquis. But she said nothing, afraid to be hurt again, afraid to dare believe that he loved her.

Shaking himself free of his thoughts, Ian reached into the pocket of his vest and drew out a sealed envelope that he extended to her. "I stopped in Glasgow for a few days to have this drawn up by Mr. Bancroft. 'Tis legal and binding, Merewyn."

She moved forward to take it from him, their fingers touching, and she jerked back, hating herself for the warmth that ran through her. "What is it?" she asked, making no move to open it.

"I've sold out my half of Cairnlach's partnership for the price of one shilling, which I won't bother to collect from you. I'm turning the mills over to you, Merewyn. Completely. You and your brothers now have control over everything: the offices in Glasgow, London, and Inverlochy, the rights to the Lieagh River, and all the grazing lands surrounding Montague."

Merewyn's heart-shaped face filled with disbelief. They were standing so close that he could see the golden flecks in the dark blue background of her tilted eyes when she looked up at him, and he gazed at her longingly, remembering the sweet taste of her soft red lips. Despair overwhelmed him and he turned away with a groan, knowing he'd never be able to control himself if he was forced to continue standing so close.

Merewyn's soft, puzzled voice addressed his broad back. "Why, Ian?"

"Because I could think of no other way to convince you that I really had no interest whatsoever in gaining the mills through you." His voice grew hoarse. "You were all I wanted or needed to make my life rich,

Merewyn, but I couldn't admit that to myself and now I've destroyed it all with my blindness and stupidity."

Ian could hear her satin skirts rustle as she approached, her nearness bringing with it the scented perfume of her hair, and he clenched his teeth, refusing to look at her, knowing it would be madness to do so.

There was a long, bittersweet pause. Then Merewyn said softly, "Oh, Ian, I—"

The door to the bedroom burst open, startling both of them, and Annie Fitzhugh raced inside accompanied by a small army of servants, her wrinkled face taking on the hardness of old leather, her hazel eyes flashing fire in the face of this threat to her beloved mistress.

"Morag told me she'd let ye come up here," she told Lord Montague, not the least bit daunted by the fact that she had to tilt her head backwards to peer up into his finely chiseled features despite the fact that she herself was so tall. "I maun insist ye leave! Neither the laird nor Master Colm be here and Miss Merewyn doesna need nae upsets during her convalescence."

Merewyn, standing close at Ian's side, looked up with wide eyes to find him staring down at her, his lips twitching in that old mocking smile, but there was only tenderness in his eyes as they met hers. "I wouldn't dream of causing Merewyn another moment of anguish," he assured a startled Annie, his charming smile flustering her completely.

"Will ye be leavin' then?" she demanded imperiously, trying hard to regain her former coolness, "or shall we throw ye oot?" She turned towards the other servants as she spoke, demanding their support, but the menacing crowd was beginning to show signs of uncertainty now that they were actually confronted by the towering giant they had never laid eyes on before today: the legendary nephew of Edward Villiers himself, and from the whispered gossip they'd heard, reportedly more of a dangerous tyrant than his uncle had been.

"Calm yourself, please," the Marquis told Annie with all of the graciousness at his command. "I was already on my way out." He turned to look one last time at Merewyn and the arrogance vanished as he caught sight of her beautiful little face, the longing and pain in his gray eyes there for all to see. Abruptly, his expression hardened. He bowed wordlessly and strode out of the room, the servants parting respectfully to let the towering man pass by.

"Are ye all richt, dearie?" Annie asked worriedly, peering into Merewyn's wide eyes.

"I-I'm fine," Merewyn assured her, but her words were faint and her breath came in short gasps as she clutched the still sealed envelope to her breast, its cool, crinkled surface seeming to burn her fingers.

Ian Villiers wearily dismounted from his horse and stood for a moment in the stableyard, flexing his stiff muscles. It was twilight and the sun, shining for the first time in his memory here in Glen Cairn, was setting behind the mountains, softening their rocky silhouettes to a velvety purple. The Lieagh, flowing passively before the castle's blackened stone walls, reflected the array of colors in brightly glittering fragments that twinkled on the surface of the swiftly moving water. Autumn was in the air and there was a crispness to the tangy peat scent in the wind that had not been present the day before. Below in the glen the late ripening rye and barley stood gold and tall in the fields, the bright patchwork giving the land a magnificence the somber observer in his mud-splattered boots and tousled hair hadn't noticed before.

Ian had been up since dawn riding with his herds, for although he had turned over his holdings to the MacAilises there was still a great deal to be done now that winter was on the way, and he had neglected much during his long months of absence. Walking slowly towards the rear entrance of the castle he breathed deeply of the clean, fresh air, surprised to discover how much the beauty of the sunset stirred him. Where once he had despised the penetrating dampness of the Highland air and the desolate bogs and unyielding mountains, he could now see only an aching loveliness in the barren landscape, a rugged vista that seemed to have captured his mind and his heart.

Aye, it was a savage land, harsh and unrelenting to the people who eked out their daily existence here, but he found himself eager to partake of that challenge. Could it be that this thirst for life and its rough but fulfilling existence had been responsible for giving Merewyn the strength and courage he'd admired ever since the day he'd first laid eyes on her? Perhaps this, too, was why he had come to feel a kinship for this ruggedly beautiful land, for it seemed to be the very extension of the woman he loved above all others.

Aye, Ian decided, deep in thought, the underlying strength that was so integral a part of the beautiful girl who had captured his heart was no different from the stalwart immobility of the mountains rising gracefully to the heavens before him. Nor was the deep blue color of the Lieagh in the sunshine any brighter than those tilted, gold-flecked eyes, and even the whaups that called mournfully to one another as they flew overhead reminded him of her soft and stirring voice. Aye, she was a part of this land, and Ian was only now beginning to understand why Merewyn had fought so desperately to save her home from his threatening existence. To take Merewyn away from all of this would be like uprooting a precious flower from its native soil and transferring it to another climate. Though it might survive with loving care and assiduous attention, it would never thrive nor bloom as colorfully as in the ground where its roots could grow deep.

A weary smile lit the tired features. He would have liked to tell Merewyn of this discovery he had made, and hear how she would laugh to have him describe something she had known all along. The smile died on Ian's lips and the tender look in the gray eyes grew hard. Merewyn was no longer his, he reminded himself savagely. Almost a week had passed since he had offered her his only means of making peace between them and he had heard nothing, nothing from the silent castle across the river. Damn all of the MacAilises to Hell!

His mouth pulled down in anger, Ian strode through the service door, ignoring Davis's horrified look at the sight of the great clods of mud his boots were leaving on the polished stone floor. The valet's expression, however, quickly changed to that of a man who has something very important to say, and he hurried after his master who was heading for the grand staircase, a determined look on his face.

"Wait a moment, my lord," he began.

"Leave me be, Davis," the Marquis growled without pausing in his stride, "or I'll wring your goddamned neck."

Davis stared after the tall, receding figure, his mouth slack. What in God's name had gotten into him? he asked himself irritably. Lud, if these verbal abuses and black looks kept up much longer he'd go back to London and suffer his old nemesis Francis's complaints rather than endure more of this! As for the news he had been intending to impart to the Marquis—well, let the ill-tempered gent find out for himself!

Ian, every muscle in his body crying out in protest at the hard workout it had endured all day, could think only of the pleasures of a hot bath, scowling ferociously as he tried to force Merewyn's image from his mind. He would get her back, he vowed to himself, for he was a man who went after what he wanted with a vengeance, and in this he would not be denied. But he'd think of that tomorrow. Right now he was too tired and in great need of rest.

Jock Gowerie, the tiny, skeletal old man who still refused staunchly to wear anything but the same faded kilt, came scuttling out of the parlor where he had been dusting the furnishings, having heard the Marquis's heavy footfall in the corridor. "Och, there 'ee be, yer lordship," he cackled, his aged face split into the first smile Ian had ever seen upon those sunken features. "I got summat tae tell 'ee."

" 'Twill have to wait, Jock," the Marquis informed him curtly, brushing past him.

To his annoyance the little man fell into step beside him, taking three running strides for every one of the Marquis's. "But it be important," Jock panted. " 'Ee dinna ken wha' it be."

"And I don't care, either." The Marquis came to an abrupt halt at the foot of the winding staircase and stood staring down at the wispy-haired little man impatiently. "Doubtless you want to tell me more tales of Montague's glorious past under MacAilis rule. I'll have no more mention of that family again, Jock, or I'll toss you out on your bony arse. Do you hear me?"

His tone quelled even Jock Gowerie's gay spirits and the little man cowered back. "Aye, yer lordship, aye," he said sadly.

"Very good. Now, I want to take a bath. Have it sent up immediately."

As the Marquis started towards the stairs Jock sprang from his protective cower against the wall and tugged energetically at his master's coat. "Wait, yer lordship, I've summat tae tell 'ee."

Ian sighed wearily, thinking he had never met a more

simpleminded fellow in his life. "Very well," he said resignedly, "what is it?"

Before Jock could answer, Ian's attention was drawn to the landing above, where the sound of running footsteps heralded someone's approach. He looked up and froze as he saw Merewyn leaning over the balustrade, her beautiful heart-shaped face filled with delight, the soft lips curled in a welcoming smile, the dark blue eyes shining.

"There you are at last!" she called down in a sweet voice that made his heart beat faster. "I didn't think you'd ever get in! Why didn't you ever tell me all the servants gave notice, Ian? It must have been that damnable pride of yours." She giggled and started down the stairs towards him, her petticoats rustling as she moved, one tiny slipper peeking out from beneath the embroidered hem. "I can't really blame them. They were always too terrified of Edward to dare quit on him. No matter, I'll round them up tomorrow. After all, if I'm to live here with you I refuse to do all of the cooking and cleaning myself. We'll have to send for Marty and David, too, of course."

Ian found that he could not move at all, and so he stood watching her until she came to a halt on one of the steps that left her indigo eyes level with his, and for the first time he saw that her smile was decidedly strained and that there was an uncertain look in the tilted blue eyes that made it obvious to him how much she dreaded his rejection. Still, he couldn't speak, his burning gaze fastened to her lovely young face.

"I had to come," Merewyn whispered at last. "That document you left—"

She hesitated and tried to look away from the blazing gray eyes and found that she could not. "Oh, Ian, I don't want the mills or Montague lands. 'Twas enough for me to know that you l-love me." She peered at him worriedly. "You look so tired. Are you all right?"

In two strides Ian had covered the space between them and had pulled her into his arms, holding her as close to his heart as he could, relief and joy coursing through him as he felt her body yield against the insistent pressure of his arms. Never had she felt so soft or desirable to him before and he realized suddenly how much she belonged there, with her head pressed against his chest, her slender arms reaching up to entwine themselves about his neck.

"Do you want me to stay?" she asked, the look in her dark blue eyes making his knees weak.

"Oh, God, Merewyn . . ."

Ian bent his head until his lips found hers, a thrill shooting through him as he found them warm and inviting, and a heady feeling of triumph enveloped him, a feeling that told him he had found at last what his heart had been searching a lifetime for.

"Welcome home, m'lord," Merewyn murmured breathlessly.

Ian laughed exultantly and kissed her again, more deeply this time, his lips parting hers and eliciting from her a response that was only a small measure of her deep and abiding love for him. "Merewyn," he repeated hoarsely. Unable to resist any longer the passion beginning to burn in the darkening depths of her indigo eyes, he lifted her into his strong arms and carried her up the stairs.

Hearing the heavy door being kicked shut on the floor above, Jock Gowerie turned away, his tiny eyes crinkling with delight. Whooping gleefully he leaped into the air, unable to control his happiness.

"What the devil are you doing, you doddard?" came Davis's outraged voice from behind, having hurried out of the kitchen at the sound of the warlike yell that had made his blood run cold, convinced that the Highland clans had amassed for a Sassenach massacre.

"The MacAilises be back where they belong!" Jock shouted happily, his high-pitched voice echoing from the ceiling. And he began to perform, before the valet's disbelieving eyes, a wild, abandoned fling to celebrate the event.